WEREWOLF LOVE
By: M.M. Anderson

This book is dedicated to Ian and Mia, who taught me there is such a thing as unconditional love.

Chapter 1

THE RETURN OF SHE

Seamus licked Claudia's muzzle.

The brunette beast opened her eyes to find that she was no longer engaged in a passionate kiss. Instead, she was on her side, paws pressed against fur, her view of the luminous pink moon obstructed by broad muscular withers, a large hairy head, pointed ears, and a cold black nose.   Seamus planted another warm wet one.

Claudia joked to herself in a passing thought. *He'd better not sniff my butt.*

Pretty funny. Seamus sprang to his feet and shook a clump of leaves from his fur.

Oh no! It was ghost talk without the option of a verbal reply, unless the spoken response was a howl. Claudia sat up and performed a quick psyche check. *Am I thinking anything embarrassing?* Even though the mental clean-sweep exercise didn't locate any thoughts to erase, Claudia still felt queasy about future telekinetic exposure.

Seamus offered a suggestion: *You can learn to block. In the mean time, just hum.*

Claudia imagined a few bars of "It's a Small World".

Please! Anything but that!

Sorry. It's the first song that came to mind. She changed her tune.

Better.

Claudia stood and stretched in down dog pose.

How do you feel?

Huge. Claudia sensed that she was more than twice her human size. She walked a few paces. Her large werewolf body moved as well, and felt as comfortable, as her petite human form. *I don't feel like I'm wearing an awkward costume.* Claudia was conversely reminded of the time she'd dressed like Pretty Pony Princess for her kindergarten Halloween parade. *Los padres* had spent weeks creating the cardboard and cloth costume, complete with a glittery yarn mane and braided twine tail. Claudia remembered how she felt when she finally put on the much-awaited outfit—completely disenchanted. The corners of bent cardboard dug into her skin and the restrictive shape made it impossible for her to prance. If that weren't bad enough for a five-year-old to deal with, her tail wouldn't *whoosh* and there was no button on her flank that played the "Happy Trotting" theme song. But worst of all, when Claudia looked in the mirror, her masked face was grotesquely elongated and deformed—nothing like the real Pretty Pony Princess.

You're definitely a pretty werewolf princess.

Claudia thought *smile* and her tail wagged. Despite Seamus's compliment, she was still curious to see herself in werewolf form. Claudia wished for a mirror.

You'll have to take my word for it. Werewolves don't cast reflections and they can't be photographed either.

Really?

I'll let you know if you have kill stuck in your fangs.

Seamus!

Seamus nuzzled Claudia's neck.

She returned the affection.

Seamus's heart drummed an amplified empathetic reply.

Claudia heard it loud and clear.

Senses will be keener while you're in werewolf form.

Claudia felt like a kindergartner on the first day of school—overwhelmed. *There's so much to learn about the new me.*

Seamus nodded his big black head. *It's been five years and I'm still figuring out how this werewolf thing works.*

There was a soft sound beyond. Claudia's ears perked. She heard the faint flutter of owl wings and the squeaking of mouse prey somewhere in distance. She tilted her head slightly. Nature's noise was supplanted by a small group of male and female voices floating on the wind from the other side of the park wall. Claudia could make out that the couples were discussing where to go for a late dinner. The men had a taste for steaks; the women were opting for Thai. *Remarkable.*

Your night vision and scenting abilities are amazing too. Seamus lifted his snout and took in the passing breeze.

Claudia sniffed the night air too. There was something familiar.

Smell that? Three werewolves heading east, one of them is carrying a bunch of flowers. Seamus motioned for Claudia to follow. They took off running towards their approaching pack.

Claudia spotted a trio of four-legged figures bounding through the meadow clearing. The moon cast a pink hue on the lead runner's white coat. The werewolf to his left carried the fragrant flowers in his jaws. Claudia perceived that it was a mixed spring bouquet of daffodils, tulips, and irises. Her favorites.

Dragon set the colorful bouquet at Claudia's feet. *One must often change in order to be constant in happiness and wisdom. Congratulations.*

Claudia placed her paw on the flower stems and prodded the soft scented petals with her freckled nose. *How sweet.*

Sevlow's idea. TJ sat and scratched. *I swear this park's infested with fleas.*

Sevlow lowered his robust head in greeting as he took a step towards Claudia. *Hope your maiden transformation was pleasant.* The white werewolf's steely blue eyes surveyed her new form.

Claudia wondered if there were any other she werewolves.

Sevlow replied to her thought. *To my knowledge, there is not other turned or commissioned female.*

Sounds like it's about time to finally ratify the Equal Rights Amendment. TJ stopped itching. *Lasses are a whole lot better to look at than you lads. No offense, Sir.*

Claudia may well be the first of her turned kind. Sevlow blocked his thoughts for a brief moment.

Claudia's expression of surprise was accompanied by an inadvertent personal observation. *Sevlow's spent hundreds of years without a woman. How sad.*

Seamus switched the subject with a swish of the tail. *Sir, I was hoping you could explain a few things tonight, before our hunt.*

That's right. TJ maneuvered beside his friend and prodded him with head butts. *This is Seamus's first full moon with the pack too.*

Claudia liked the idea of a group werewolfing lesson. She had always been an eager student.

Dragon pawed the ground. *To be fond of learning is the first step towards self-preservation.*

Well articulated, Dragon. Sevlow did an about-face. *Tonight is an ideal occasion for instruction.* The white werewolf took a leap-start and sprinted towards a dark patch of forest beyond the lighted clearing. The pack followed.

Sevlow stood upon a gray boulder, the pink shadowy forest his classroom backdrop. *To answer Claudia's question, it's a werewolf pack's emotional connection that gives them the ability to instinctually hear, sense, and channel thoughts, feelings, sounds, and words.*

Claudia was reminded that spirits communicated in a similar manner.

Picture channeling is not difficult to perfect, said Sevlow.

TJ transmitted a cartoon of human-form Sevlow holding a blackboard pointer and mouthing the sounds, *blah, blah, blah.*

Dragon returned a phony photograph of TJ wearing a dunce cap, sitting on a high stool in the back of an empty schoolroom.

The next picture that flashed into Claudia's head showed Dragon slipping on a banana peel while being pelted by white polka dots.

They're spitballs, corrected TJ. *You ever see someone throw a polka dot?*

Claudia wished she could reply with a humorous illustration. She drew a blank.

Begin with something simple, suggested Seamus. *How about a tree?*

Claudia concentrated. *Tree… tree… tree… There are so many different types of trees. A mighty redwood or an evergreen? Is it spring or fall?* Claudia loved aspens, especially when their leaves turned yellow. *But what if it was winter and the tree was bare?* The many changing likenesses tumbled through Claudia's head and collided like static-y socks in a hot dryer.

Is that melting broccoli on a popsicle stick? Seamus teased.

Claudia countered with an unhappy smiley. ☹

Excellent focus and clarity. The master instructor congratulated his newest student. *I predict you'll perfect the skill in no time.*

Claudia wondered how Sevlow always remained so encouraging and patient.

A picture of a jug bearing three X's appeared from TJ's mind. It was accompanied by Dragon singing the pirate ditty: *Yo, ho,ho, and a bottle of rum.*

Claudia was sure she heard Sevlow chuckle.

Sevlow stepped down from the rock. *Would either of you veterans care to explain Elemental Utilization to Seamus and Claudia?*

Dragon saw himself poised behind an orate lectern.

TJ created a huge curling wave that engulfed the stand.

Claudia suddenly had the impression that she was drenched. At the same time she experienced the sensation of being pulled out to sea by a strong undertow. She panicked and crouched, her muscles tense and steadying. The ebbing ceased. It had somehow been halted by a powerful gust of wind that was now about to knock her off her planted paws. Claudia looked around for a secure stationary object to grab. Before she could find something to latch onto, all went calm again.

We can channel weather?

Seamus's surprised words echoed Claudia's own bewilderment. *How is that possible?*

Werewolves have an inherent capability to utilize the forces of nature, said Sevlow. *Earth, air, fire, water, we may harness them all, or chose to specialize.*

Dragon prefers air because he's long winded, declared TJ. *And I go to water because of my "incident"... Let's say it's how I've overcome my drowning fears.*

Wind power kept the door shut and the beelzebubbles contained in the subway engineer booth, said Dragon. *Forces can also be combined. With wind and water TJ and I can create whitecaps and wave walls.*

Now that you two are here it's probably best to diversify. That leaves fire and earth up for grabs. TJ sat beside the Master. *Of course, he's an expert in all elements.*

Mighty Mouse used to be our fire starter. Dragon lifted his paw while recalling a vivid memory. *He could produce one mean hot foot.*

Claudia detected an affectionate bittersweet energy flowing from Dragon's remembrance. *He misses his little buddy.*

But we don't talk about sappy stuff, replied TJ. *Think ESPN, not Lifetime channel.*

I'll try to remember that, TJ. Claudia considered the elements. *Seamus has a hot Aries temper and I'm a grounded September born. What if I learn how to perfect earth and Seamus can use fire?*

Well matched, said Sevlow. *Earth defuses fire; fire revitalizes earth.*

Seamus once more asked the question forming in Claudia's mind. *I felt like my fur was wet after TJ's wave, but it was still dry. Is elemental energy all in the mind?*

Yes, in the mind of the purveyor as well as the recipient, replied Sevlow. *The mind is a powerful tool. As I have before noted, physical warfare and psychological prowess are equally important werewolf skills.*

Claudia felt a sense of relief. If brains were as important as brawn, she would not be at a disadvantage in a pack of buff guys.

Male wolves are called brutes or dogs, corrected Dragon.

Claudia successfully blocked her first retort thought. Her tail wagged.

Can I get a hall pass? TJ was scratching again, his right foot scuffing behind his pointed ear. *We aren't the only creatures here in nature school.*

I'm starved, Seamus's stomach growled. *Sarge said he'd bring donuts. Hope he also has a doggie bag from dinner.* Seamus envisioned prime rib covered in sugar.

TJ added chocolate frosting and a Maraschino cherry to the image.

The bizarre cuisine appealed to Claudia. She was famished too. Claudia wondered why if weird food was appetizing now that she was an undead werewolf, why wasn't the notion of a hunt? The fact that she now possessed the impulse to slaughter humans both horrified and revolted her.

Think of the kill as our way of stopping a terrible crime, replied Seamus. *If you could eliminate a violent crime before it happened, wouldn't you?*

I like to think of the kill as preventative medicine, added TJ. *One chomp eliminates any future virus outbreak.*

Only exposure to genuine evil triggers our hunting urge, assured Sevlow. *Werewolves do not eradicate humans for food or sport. However, an unchecked temper may trigger a turn and cause an impetuous kill.*

Seamus looked away.

Claudia breathed a sigh of relief.

Let's make a sport outa finding some chow. TJ howled. *Class dismissed!*

Three subsequent sentiments unanimously agreed.

Sevlow's thoughts and emotions, however, were blocked. His azure eyes fixed on a point in the indiscernible distance.

Claudia was sure Sevlow saw or heard something and was keeping it a secret. She wasn't the only one who noticed.

Sir? Seamus inquired. *Is everything OK?*

Sevlow returned from his private reverie. *I must attend to a matter.*

Seamus glanced at his pack mates. *Should we wait here for you here?*

The white werewolf canvassed the four eager faces looking upon him and once again shielded the details of his pending pursuit. *It's a personal concern*, said Sevlow. *If we do not reconnect before sunrise, let us reconvene at the den.* The Master disappeared into the thick forest darkness before anyone could reply.

Claudia expected a worry wave to ripple through the pack. When the brutes did not react to Sevlow's abrupt departure, Claudia's apprehension diminished and her thoughts once again returned to finding food.

Sergeant Gaffney stood beside the driver's door of his radio car cautiously dolling donuts to the ravenous pack. "Keeping the wolves at bay," Gaffney stammered as he reached into the sticky cardboard container for a custard-filled treat. "That saying just took on a new meaning."

Poor Sarge looks frightened, Claudia thought. *Wish he could hear our inner conversation. He might relax a bit.*

My turning totally freaks him out. Now Sarge has a whole pack of werewolves to deal with. Seamus flopped down and scratched his back on the cement walkway. *I think TJ's right about fleas.*

Gaffney tossed the donut he was holding in his hand like a fetch ball.

TJ and Dragon both sprung for it and met mid-air. THUD! They growled and snarled and roughhoused one another for the sweet prize. The furry frothing freight trains collided into the side of Sarge's police car during their tussle.

Claudia could feel the crashing impact reverberate beneath her feet. *Ouch!* The radio car's passenger door displayed a new werewolf-size ding.

Sarge hopped into his dented police vehicle and slammed the door. He leaned out the open window and hurled the remaining Krinkle Kreme container. It landed behind a park bench. "Listen, don't get mad. I only bought three dozen and that's my last box."

TJ and Dragon chased after the carton and toppled the metal bench that stood between them and the donuts. Their masticating muzzles were soon covered in sprinkles, powdered sugar, and raspberry jelly.

"Why don't maybe you four go amuse yourselves somewheres else?" the Sarge shouted as he rolled up his window.

Maybe we ought to go, Claudia said. *I think we're ruining his night.*

Yeah, Seamus agreed. *We should let Sarge get back to his napping.* Seamus loped over to his pack mates. *When you're done sucking up crumbs, trash the box and let's find someone who deserves harassing.*

The pack didn't have far to go. An evil energy permeated the far portion of the park. Eight ears perked and four attentions piqued.

Claudia felt her werewolf senses kicking into high gear. Her brain seemed to be losing its cognitive capacity—she was shifting into canine autopilot, and her inner captain was directing her to hunt and destroy.

There was a rustling sound beyond the clearing. The pack dispersed, staying downwind of their intended prey.

Divide and conquer. Claudia flanked the perimeter; she sensed a malevolent feminine presence. Her keen eyes spotted a cloaked female figure. Claudia sniffed the air. The woman was wearing French perfume and her hair had been recently washed. The pads of Claudia's paws detected the woman's size, shape, and movement. She was physically fit and taller than average height; she gave Claudia an impression of strength and superiority. The woman made her way with grace and confidence into the pink moonlit meadow.

She kills often. Seamus whispered into Claudia's mind.

Her hands have spilled only innocent blood, TJ added.

Before Claudia could ask how they knew she realized they were correct.

What do you sense? Seamus asked.

Her heart has been hardened, Claudia perceived and replied. *She doesn't have any remorse for hurting others. I actually feel as if she's taking part in her own hunt tonight, playing some sort of cruel cat and mouse game.*

Seamus marveled. *Women can read women way better than a man can.*

Remind me to bring you along if I ever have a date, TJ teased.

Dragon's voice chimed in. *Let Claudia take her down.*

Claudia was suddenly excited by the prospect of her first kill. The fur on her neck and upper back responded by bristling upright.

We'll surround her and you attack, Dragon said.

Claudia hid in the forest shadows as the woman approached through the clearing.

She was getting nearer.

Claudia's focus intensified—her heart raced, pupils dilated. The maiden werewolf crouched in the dimness and poised herself for a strike.

She was ten feet away, getting closer, closer still.

Claudia the werewolf launched, fangs bared. CRASH! Instead of landing upon the woman, Claudia's airborne body slammed hard against a massive wall of white, causing her to tumble backwards like a hapless pup into the deep dewy grass, her first full moon ambush unexpectedly thwarted.

She stood her ground, unharmed.

Claudia returned to her feet, confused and disoriented. Standing before her loomed a familiar paternal presence. *Sevlow?*

Leave her be, instructed the Master. *She is my wife.*

Chapter 2

HELLO, I MUST BE GOING

Wife? The pack's incredulous reply was unanimous.

I had no idea you were married, Sir, Dragon marveled, keeping a keen watch over the cloaked woman standing in front of them.

Seamus took a shielding step and placed himself between the woman and Claudia. He flicked a patch of grass from Claudia's coat while he nuzzled her neck. *You OK?*

Yes.

Sevlow's eyes met Claudia's. *Forgive me.*

Instead of the usual warmth and compassion, Claudia detected anguish in the Master's words. She felt guilt, followed by a sudden need to defend her hunting actions. *I had no idea she was your wife. I only responded to the evil I sensed, that we all sensed.* Claudia looked to her pack-mates for affirmation.

Three furry heads nodded in agreement.

Claudia's kill instincts were justified, the Master replied.

Claudia breathed a sigh of relief. She looked at her would-be prey, recalling Sevlow's claim that he had not met another female werewolf.

Why didn't you tell us your wife is a werewolf? Seamus asked.

Why hasn't she changed with the full moon? Claudia surveyed the woman. *How is it possible for her to stay in human form?*

The cloaked Mrs. remained quiet and motionless during the mind-banter, protected behind Sevlow's massive white flanks.

It is not possible for a werewolf to remain in human form during a full moon, Sevlow replied. *My wife is a mortal.*

But… Claudia didn't dare continue to reflect on her loathsome impressions of the Master's wife. She lowered her head and turned away.

It is a long story, Sevlow confessed. *My wife was not always as she is today. Margo once had…* His thought trailed into a somber silence.

Margo, Claudia repeated the name as she scrutinized the cloaked woman.

Why hide under a dark hood? Seamus wondered. *Where was she headed?*

My guess is Margo's not only bad to the bone and up to no good, but also she's also easy on the eyes, TJ surmised. *No disrespect, Sir.*

An unaccompanied mortal woman in a desolate park probably wouldn't feel safe this time of the night." Dragon pawed at the ground. *Evil or not.*

Especially if she saw Sergeant Gaffney asleep in his radio car, Seamus added.

Self-preservation is one of my wife's greatest enduring attributes. Sevlow eased his defensive stance. *I imagine it has served her more than well. I regret it has been over two centuries since we last saw one another.*

Two centuries? Seamus repeated shaking his hairy head. *But you said your wife wasn't a werewolf. How could a mortal survive?*

Sevlow's tail wagged. His pleasure seemed to return during a brief blocked memory. *A very long story…*

Claudia kept her eyes fixed on the cloaked femme fetal. Margo didn't appear to be able to hear any of the internal conversation, but her body language indicated that she planned to make use of Sevlow's position while scheming her next move. *Your wife knows you're still her protector.*

As if on cue, Margo placed a gloved right hand upon Sevlow's head. With her left hand she removed the cloak's hood. A nearby park lamp illuminated her face.

There was another unanimous pack reply—a gasp.

Claudia froze, speechless and stunned, forgetting for a moment that she should not judge a book by its cover. *Margo is absolutely gorgeous*, Claudia remarked, expressing the sentiments on everyone else's blocked mind.

A potent and passionate longing escaped Sevlow's thoughts. *More beautiful than I have allowed myself to recall...*

Margo's ample lips were painted the color of ripe raspberries. Her coiffed mane was a blend of champagne and honey, the front section skillfully twisted and braided and secured at her head's crown with a bejeweled clip. The structured style accentuated her fine flawless features. Margo's years were early-summer and her eyes the mingled hues of mid-autumn, where green and gold and russet become one. Her slow smile revealed the cool confidence of a regal lioness, accustomed to winning the chase, by any means.

"My dear, Sevlow. I did not expect cross paths with you this early morn. New City must be a smaller place than I remember." Margo touched her lips in pensive mode. "When is it we were last together?" she chuckled. "I wager you remember every detail of the moment. It's locked away in your mind with other useless images and notions." She began kneading Sevlow's snowy pelt with her gloved fingertips.

The hairs on her husband's neck and upper back stood erect.

"It appears you have auspiciously altered my fate once again." There was no indication of gratitude in the Mrs.'s condescending tone.

Claudia detected a hint of French Creole in Margo's sanguine voice. She also noticed an oval bulge beneath the second finger of her left glove. Claudia tried to envision what type of ring a man like Sevlow would see fit to give his beloved bride. Before Claudia could conjure an image Margo removed her hand-covers, revealing a magnificent blue stone in a most unusual setting: a dime-sized star sapphire with its six gleaming points situated between what appeared to be the exposed jaws of a platinum werewolf. Two brilliant white diamonds comprised the beast's deep-set eyes. The word "exquisite" and an urge to try the ring on her own finger sprang from Claudia's mind.

TJ nudged Seamus. *Remember that when it's time to pop the question.*

Margo flaunted her ring before Sevlow's captivated countenance.

The Master's eyes were transfixed upon the dazzling azure gem. Their icy blue tints were one and the same.

"I cannot help but think of you whenever I gaze upon my hand," Margo taunted. "Which is why I choose to wear these." She dangled the black gloves before him. "You are my past, Sevlow; however, you *will* continue to enable my future." Margo slid her hands back into their covers. "Is servitude not your godly code of honor, my dear husband? Step aside, noble hound, and command your rank minions to retreat." Margo's voice oozed with mocking distain. With a single swift motion she once more concealed her face beneath the hood of her sinister shroud. "I must be going." Margo swept past Sevlow and the pack without so much as a good-bye glance.

Claudia watched in dumbfounded disbelief.

Sevlow did not respond with word or action. He did not have to. His centuries old heartache was palpable.

Margo made her way across the meadow clearing and disappeared into shadows of pink darkness. Though she had departed, her iniquitous vibes lingered and provoked.

TJ's next thought began with a "b". He blocked before the rest of the word escaped his seething psyche.

Yeah, and it rhymes with itch, Seamus growled.

And not the kind of itch that comes from insects, TJ added.

If man meditates upon good thoughts, the better will be his world and the world at large, Dragon said. *Problem is, right now I can't think of any good thoughts.*

Claudia's undead heart raced and her jaws frothed and quivered. She had never before wanted to hurt a human being the way she wanted to do so now. *I don't know whether to howl or cry.*

Me neither, seconded, thirded, and fourthed the trio of brutes.

Sevlow let out an unearthly howl. Leaves fell, roosting birds scattered into the night sky, and the ground trembled beneath the werewolves' paws.

This whole scene is wrong, TJ said after the Master's cry had dissipated into the night air. *Like when you're on in another city on a mission and your favorite primetime TV show comes on at 8:00 instead of 9:00.*

Seamus transmitted the theme from "The Twilight Zone".

Even the Master chuckled.

Claudia could feel the pack's lightness returning. She closed her eyes for a brief moment and exhaled the remainder of her fury before asking Sevlow if he was all right. Claudia opened her eyes, but it was too late for concern or consolation. Sevlow was gone.

Claudia awoke naked beneath a rancid rumpled sheet, on a lumpy mattress, in a room decorated with faded superhero posters and torn comic book pages affixed to the wall with stickers, masking tape, and wads of petrified chewing gum. She peered at the Spiderman clock on the finger-painted nightstand beside the bed. It read 8:06 AM. Claudia remembered returning to the wolf den with Seamus, TJ, and Dragon just before sunrise. They had entered through a hidden underground passageway. However, events from that point to the present were a baffling blur. A knock at the door interrupted Claudia's incomplete recollection. "Who's there?" Claudia called. She pulled the sheet up to her chin.

"Me, Seamus."

"Wait a minute." She canvassed the room for something to wrap herself in besides dirty linens.

"I fetched your dress and left you my spare underwear," Seamus said through the closed door. "Don't worry, they're clean."

"But nothing else around here seems to be." Claudia noticed her pink gown, black boxers, and a gray tee hanging over the footboard of the bed. She reached down and grabbed the shirt and shorts. "Glad you're not a briefs guy." I didn't expect to wake up in my birthday suit." Claudia dressed beneath the musty covers. "Thanks for not telling me to leave a change of clothes at the wolf den," she teased.

"Sorry. Wardrobe notification wasn't on my werewolf to-do list."

Claudia stepped out of bed and adjusted her baggy borrowed outfit. She checked her look in the grubby armoire mirror. The ill-fitting shirt and shorts hung to her knees. She rolled the boxers' waistband and then gathered the tee at her hip and looped the excess fabric into a decorative knot. "Much better."

Seamus opened the door a crack. "Loan you a pair of socks if you invite me in."

"Deal," Claudia replied. "This carpet is sticky-gooey. Looks like you forgot to fetch my pumps."

"What's a pump?" Seamus entered and gave Claudia more than a fleeting once-over. "Wow." He grinned. "Is there anything you don't look good in?"

Claudia's eyes fixed on Seamus. He was wearing faded jeans, a white long-sleeved NCPD polo, and a generous splash of cologne. She appreciated the effort Seamus had been making to mask his human-form dog odor, while not mentioning hers. "Ditto," Claudia returned the smile and the compliment.

"The first few transformations back to human form are slow-going," Seamus explained. "You were still unconscious and werewolf when the rest of us woke up, so I put you in here. Figured you'd want some privacy once you lost your fur coat."

"Thanks. This is Mighty Mouse's old room?"

"What was your first clue?"

Claudia wondered if Benjamin and Simon would ever cross back over for a visit. She also wondered why *los padres* hadn't attended her first transformation. They had never before missed any of Claudia or Alex's momentous events.

"How you feeling?" Seamus asked.

"Fine, I suppose." Claudia stopped wondering about ghosts and started acknowledging the fact that her upper thighs and lower back were tight and tender. She felt as if she'd been climbing stairs for the last twelve hours, on all fours.

"My muscles were sore as heck after my first change," Seamus confessed. Claudia was relieved that mind-talk shut off when human form returned. She kept the aches and pains to herself. Instead she wanted to discuss the night's odd events. "Has Sevlow returned?"

"Not yet," Seamus replied, with forced reassurance. "But TJ and Dragon mentioned that he sometimes goes back to St. Guinefort's after a full moon."

"I remember Sevlow telling us he'd meet here at the wolf den."

"Don't worry, he's been doing this werewolf-changing thing for a long time."

"I'm not concerned about Sevlow's transformiguration."

"Me neither." Seamus wrapped his arms around Claudia and planted a kiss.

Claudia returned the affection before pushing Seamus away. "What I *am* worried about is Sevlow's emotional well-being."

"Me too." Seamus puckered again.

Claudia took a step back. "Seamus, be serious. Didn't you sense Sevlow's grief? His werewolf heart is broken—he obviously still loves that *beast*."

"I wouldn't exactly call Margo a *beast* ..."

Claudia shook her head in disbelief. "What did a wise and compassionate man like Sevlow ever see in her?"

Seamus opened his mouth to reply.

Claudia interrupted. "Besides the obvious."

"But looks alone wouldn't keep her alive for two centuries," Seamus said.

"Right," Claudia replied. "So, the more compelling question is —how can Margo still be alive if she isn't undead?"

There was a knock before the door flew open.

"You two lovebirds gonna hide out in here all day?" TJ gripped the doorframe, filling the entryway with his massive presence.

"Maybe," Seamus replied.

"In this case 'maybe' means no. And don't go getting emotional when I tell you why." He looked directly at Claudia. "I think we might have us a situation, after all."

Claudia placed a hand on her hip and raised an eyebrow. "Define 'emotional' and 'situation' for me, TJ."

TJ imitated Claudia's pose.

Dragon squeezed through the doorway past TJ. "TJ means we need to discuss Sevlow." He leapt onto the bed. The frame creaked and cracked and then collapsed onto the filthy floor with a THUD!

Claudia was the only one who flinched at the sound of destruction that seemed to be a regular occurrence around he wolf den. When the others didn't mention the broken furniture, neither did she.

"We've been signaling Sevlow for the last hour," Dragon continued. "Haven't gotten any sort of answer."

"Signaling?" Claudia repeated. "You mean 'calling' and he didn't pick-up?"

"S-i-g-n-l... however you spell it," TJ said. "That's what Dragon and I have been doing while you slept and Seamus stood watchdog watching you sleep."

Dragon explained. "As a rule, the undead don't socialize with mortals or communicate confidential information by letter, phone, text, fax, or computer—just the occasional two-way radio. Information exchange isn't 100% secure, even when we weren't living in a post-9/11 world."

"So, how do we communicate?" Claudia asked.

"I'll get to that in a minute." TJ walked into the middle of the room and with the wave of his hand commanded center stage. "But first here's what NEVER to do." He held his left fist to his ear like a phone. "Hello, Oprah," TJ said, impersonating a female voice. "I saw your post, for people who enjoy unusual vocations, and I wanted to call and say I just *love* being a werewolf, a shewolf…. Really… But I prefer to think of myself as an anti-terrorist, turning rotten humans to dust and living agelessly for centuries in a secret underground hideout… Come on your show? Sure, be right over." TJ set down the imaginary receiver. "If the truth were ever told, we'd spend the rest of our undead lives dodging silver bullets and picking Homeland Security agents outa our teeth."

"Oprah's already had werewolves and vampires on her show," Claudia replied.

"Well, goodie for her," TJ mocked. "I was making a point—we are—that includes you—we are a clandestine clan. *Comprende, chica lobo?*"

"*Sí*, but you don't have to get emotional about it. The pack is ESPN, not the Lifetime channel, remember?"

"She got you." Seamus poked TJ.

Dragon cleared his throat. "About our situation, when werewolves must send a message," he continued. "We communicate a couple of different ways." Dragon pulled a small shiny metal tube from his pocket. "First way—"

Claudia recognized the device immediately. "A dog whistle?"

"A werewolf whistle," TJ corrected. "*Much* higher pitch."

Dragon tossed it to Seamus. "We all should carry one."

Seamus examined the whistle. He pressed it to his lips, and before TJ or Dragon could object, he blew.

What would have sounded like a soft exhale to a mortal was an audible blast of reverberating fire blazing through Claudia's tympanic membrane. "Stop!" She clasped her hands over her ears.

"That's loud!" Seamus slid the whistle into his pocket. "Cool."

"I know," TJ agreed. "It has a ten-mile range but these walls are stone and steel." He rubbed his ear. "Keeps sound out and in."

"We had to hide the whistles from Mighty Mouse," Dragon recalled. "He was always sneaking up behind us. OK, I confess, we started the whistle game."

"My ears must have regenerated a thousand times," TJ said.

Claudia remembered a boy from her brief school days, a second-grader who'd put metal trash can over his head during recess and then let two other boys whack it with a ruler. The stunt won him a dollar and admiration from his pals, but it lost him his hearing for a week. It was a gender-defining moment for Claudia. "Males and females are *not* wired the same way."

"I would agree," came a hushed but familiar voice.

"Sevlow!" Claudia cried. "We were so worried about you!"

Sevlow stood in the aft shadow of the bedroom doorway.

"TJ and I went back to the park and tried contacting you, Sir."

"My apologies for not responding to your signals, Dragon."
Sevlow's words faltered. He held his torn shirt closed with his right
hand and grabbed onto the door handle with his left. His movements
were strained and deliberate.

"Sir—" Seamus advanced. "You OK?"

Sevlow took a labored step towards the pack and into the light of
the room. There was a large red stain on his left breast.

"No!" cried Claudia.

Seamus rushed forward and caught the Master before he
collapsed.

Chapter 3

STAYING ALIVE

Margo removed a blood-filled glass container from her pocket and placed it beside a tray of labeled vials in the hotel suite refrigerator. She slid off her gloves and cloak and hurried into the bathroom where she deposited the garments in the tub before turning on both faucets, full force. Red rivers flowed from the black fabric.

Margo stood in front of the vanity mirror and stared at her expressionless visage. She felt nothing again, as it should be, as it must be. Margo took a deep breath and unfastened the ornate clip from her hair. She watched as her long locks cascaded across her shoulders and mingled in the folds of her sage silk chemise. Sevlow had always preferred her hair down, free and wild, the sea breezes her stylist and couture. *Another lifetime.* Margo closed her eyes. She could still smell her husband's musky sent on her skin, where he'd touched her face, her neck, held her wrists until she surrendered to his strength and two centuries of supernatural longing. She had expected Sevlow to stalk her in the shadows until daylight. She planned it. However, his fierce sunrise embrace and unearthly kiss had taken her by complete surprise, nearly thawed her frozen soul as she struggled to collect her scheming sober wits.

Margo shoved his sanguine kiss from her mind, from her tingling senses, and shifted the goal of her menacing mission onto the forefront of consciousness. She was herself again, in time to be reunited with the mine she'd come so far to quarry.

The hair clip she clenched in her hand snapped in two.

"When did you return?" a male voice called from the other side of the door.

Margo was propelled from her brief reverie.

There was a knock. "Why is the tub running?"

She turned off the bath water and wrung the cloak until it no longer dripped pink.

"What's taking so long?" He banged with a fury. "The pain has returned!"

She dried her hands on a plush white towel.

"Open up!"

Margo placed her left index finger on the bathroom door latch and paused. The diamond and star sapphire wolf head wedding ring faced her, like a discerning sentinel. She twisted the setting around until the platinum band was the only section visible.

"Let me in, Mother!"

Seamus assisted Sevlow to the broken bed.

"Claudia," the Master murmured through strained breath. "You have my permission to claim Benjamin's room as your own. It's in dire need of redecorating."

"She's trading the penthouse for the doghouse," TJ quipped.

"Thank you, Sir," Claudia replied. "But let's not worry about wallpaper and carpets right now. If everyone would quit making jokes." She glared at TJ. "Until we have a look at this injury."

"Inappropriate humor is our way of dealing with stress," TJ explained. "Keeps us dysfunctional and sane."

Seamus handed Claudia a grey towel. "You did a good job bandaging Liberace."

"Has this been washed in the last century?" She examined the cloth.

"Not if it was found in this room." Dragon shook his head.

Seamus removed Sevlow's jacket and shirt. He was not prepared for the sight of the gaping hole that exposed the Master's hemorrhaging heart, a tiny pearl handle dagger still protruding from the throbbing muscle.

Claudia shielded her face with the filthy rag.

Seamus removed the blade. He took the towel from Claudia and stuffed it into Sevlow's open flesh. The Master did not flinch. TJ handed Seamus a torn strip of bed sheet. He wrapped it like a tourniquet around Sevlow's chest. "Did she do this to you?"

Dragon propped a pillow behind Sevlow's head.

"I should not have let down my guard," the Master replied. "Margo has the speed and agility of a leopard when she hunts."

Seamus detected both pride and sadness in his words.

"Can't let her get away with it, Sir." TJ clenched his fists. I could turn right now and hunt her down.

"If you seek revenge, first dig two graves," Dragon cautioned, not looking at TJ.

TJ spun around and scowled at his friend. "This is no time for your Vietnamese version of Confucius bipartisanship—"

"I do not seek vengeance." Sevlow cast his bloodshot eyes towards the heavens. "Staying alive is my quest."

"You can't die!" Claudia cried. "Werewolves are immortals. Your wound will heal, same as my injuries healed after the train hit me."

"True, flesh will mend soon enough, and the blood Margo suctioned from my heart will be replenished." Sevlow closed his eyes. "A selfish deed, and not a mortal wound, may beckon my earthly demise."

Seamus feared the worst. To lose Sevlow might mean losing Claudia, the pack, all that he desired. In a word: family.

"Sir." TJ knelt beside the busted bed. "I've been with you over two hundred years. That's a lot of time across a whole host of history, good and bad. Never once have I seen you act selfishly. Heck, putting up with me and the rest of the pack, if I didn't know you were a werewolf, like I said in the subway tunnel when we found Liberace, I'd swear you're an angel."

Dragon nodded in agreement. "If I look into a man's heart, and find nothing wrong there, what is there to worry about? What is there to fear?"

"Sir, you saved my life," Seamus added. "And take care of orphans."

"You don't get it." Claudia gave the brutes a perceptive glare. "The only thing Sevlow ever did wrong was fall in love with Margo." She placed a frayed Superman blanket atop the Master. "He married Margo and keeps her young and alive. Then for some reason she ran off and broke his heart—figuratively and now literally. She's an evil menace on the loose. If his wife doesn't change her ways, Sevlow senses that he will have to pay with his werewolf life for Margo's atrocious acts."

"You getting messages from ghosts again?" TJ asked. "Or are you making stuff up as you go along?"

The Master's situation and Claudia's logical hypothesis were making Seamus's blood tingle. He curbed his urge to turn with a shoulder roll and neck jerk.

Dragon nodded. "What Claudia says makes sense."

"She is correct," Sevlow declared. "Innocent people have suffered and perished. I am culpable. I gave Margo immortality, but did not maintain control."

"The one who loves the least, controls the relationship," Dragon replied. "Not that I have any first-hand experience with women."

"Nor did I, prior to Margo," Sevlow confessed. "She is my first and only love."

Seamus couldn't help but wonder who would have the control—he or Claudia? Could love ever be equal? Seamus reached across the bed and touched Claudia's hand.

TJ moaned. "Getting a little too Lifetime Channel around here again."

"At least I didn't compare Sevlow to an angel," Seamus reminded.

"True that." TJ forced a loud belch. "OK, dial's back to ESPN."

"How did you meet Margo?" Claudia asked. "I'm sure she was a different woman long ago, when you fell in love with her."

Seamus remembered his recall experience with TJ. "Could you show us, Sir?"

Claudia raised an eyebrow. "I don't think Sevlow has home videos of their courtship and wedding."

"No, but he has memories," Seamus replied.

"And a picture's worth a thousand words," Dragon reminded.

"I can deal with Confucius wisdoms, but you're killing me with these sappy sayings." TJ put Dragon into a headlock. Dragon elbowed TJ in the abdomen. They tumbled backwards into the open armoire, jarring its hodgepodge contents onto the floor.

"So glad we aren't in a hospital with Sevlow." Claudia shook her head. "You two are a health and safety hazard."

"If I am going to enlist your aid with my personal matters, I must share with you some of the events that led to today." Sevlow sat up on the bed and removed the blanket and makeshift bandage. The bleeding had stopped. His heart was shrouded beneath a thin layer of newly formed skin. "For the sake of time, I will employ Seamus' suggested *modus operandi.*

Claudia appeared confused. "Seamus suggested you show us your memories. How's that possible?"

"The eyes are a window to the soul," Dragon said, ducking his head to avoid a stuffed teddy bear swinging from TJ's grip.

"Look into Sevlow's eyes and see his past?" Claudia asked "Like a movie?"

"Exactly. It's a mental movie we can watch together." Seamus held Claudia's gaze. "Clear your mind and concentrate on the little round black screen in the center of Sevlow's eyes."

The werewolves each took a place at the foot of Sevlow's bed.

The Master focused on a point in the distance and launched them through the opening of his torrid tale. "A lycanthrope trial was held in 1792, in Livonia, an area east of the Baltic Sea. I was implicated for acts of idolatry, polytheism, lycanthropy, and superstitious beliefs. My punishment, to be set adrift without provisions on a skiff…"

Seamus pushed away his own thoughts and looked into Sevlow's pupils as the Master spoke. He could feel himself drifting inward, past the icy blue irises, into a tunneled darkness filled with muffled sounds and indiscernible voices. A light at the other end appeared and grew larger, brighter, so bright that Seamus had to shield his brow, like an outfielder, searching for a fly ball in the noonday sun. Gradually, a scene came into view. Seamus stood beside a shallow wooden boat adrift on a wintry sea. In the vessel sat Sevlow. Except for shoulder-length hair and crude rustic clothing, the Master resembled his present-day self.

"What took you so long?"

Seamus was startled by TJ's voice. He turned around and saw TJ and Dragon walking towards him across the lapping waves. They were dressed in pirate garb.

"Shiver me timbers. Bet it's freaking cold out here," TJ said. "Good thing we're impervious to memory elements. These whitecaps might ruin my faux buckskin boots."

"Why are you dressed up for Halloween on the Jolly Roger?" Seamus teased. "That ugly tricorne makes you seven feet tall. What's with the duck feather?"

The feather disappeared from TJ's hat. "It was an ostrich plum, dummy."

"Look!" Dragon pointed at a tall sailing vessel approaching from the east. A rowboat had been deployed. "The pirate ship is going to rescue Sevlow."

"How do you know it's a pirate ship?" Seamus asked.

"Because Sevlow knows it's a pirate ship." Claudia appeared behind TJ. "Thanks for ditching me back there." She shook her finger at Seamus.

"I didn't ditch you. I—"

"Kidding." Claudia smiled. "Lucky for me, I'm a fast learner. Dragon, how'd you change outfits? I'd rather not have an adventure while wearing Seamus's underwear."

Dragon closed his eyes. "If you can imagine the clothes, you can wear them."

Claudia followed suit. An instant later she was sporting a tiara, an up-do with cascading curls, and a 18th century corseted ball gown, chartreuse with ivory lace trim.

"You're much better at imagining clothes than thinking up trees," TJ remarked.

Seamus shook his head and grinned. "That bulge under your skirt will keep me three feet away from you at all times. It's a dress fence."

"It's a crinoline," Claudia corrected. "All the fashionable ladies wore them."

"She's right." TJ nodded. "In my day those things were made of whale bones."

Claudia shut her eyes again and popped into a white puffy blouse, fitted sienna suede pants, and a pair of sensible-heel lace-up boots. "This is more practical. Now it's your turn Seamus. No jeans and t-shirts."

Seamus imagined a scene from *Buccaneers of the Caribbean*.

"You look like Bootstrap Bill!" Claudia gushed.

"You look like Bootstrap Bill," TJ mimicked. "And that dude in the rowboat could pass for a Frosty the Scarecrow."

Seamus watched as a lone gaunt rower moored beside Sevlow's craft. His tattered clothes, knotty beard, and frazzled hair were speckled with bits of ice-covered filth.

"Aye, sure ye'd died a the cold," the pirate stammered. "If me captain ha'dunt spotted ye adrift in the fog."

"My utmost gratitude, to your captain, and to you." Sevlow stepped into the salvage boat and gently pried the oars from the man's gnarled frozen fingers.

"Look at the Master's right index finger," Claudia remarked. "He's wearing the ring we saw on Margo's hand."

"One and the same." Dragon leaned closer to get a better look.

"Only a matter of time before Margo steals it," TJ predicted. "She's a pirate."

"You don't know that for certain," Claudia replied. "Maybe Sevlow gives her the ring. He does marry her, remember?"

"Anyone know how long Sevlow was been drifting?" Seamus asked, watching the Master row with gusto.

"Since his wedding day," TJ mumbled.

"A fortnight," Claudia replied.

"A fortnight," Seamus repeated. "Who speaks like that?"

"Am I the only one paying attention to Sevlow's recollections?" Claudia let out an exasperated sign. "It's like being at the movies with Alex. He tunes into the car chases, lets his mind wander during discourse, and then he asks me what's happening."

"What's happening?" TJ asked.

Seamus snickered. "I'm sorry, Claudia, you set yourself up for that one."

Claudia put her finger to her lips. "We're talking over the dialog."

"The name of your vessel?" Sevlow inquired. "I may know of her."

"*Le Coq*," the pirate replied. "Me captain is *le coq du troupeau*."

"Now we have to learn French," TJ grumbled. "Where are subtitles when you need them?"

"I had a Parisian governess," Claudia replied. "She taught me some French. *Le Coq* means the rooster, and *le coq du troupeau* translated is: the cock of the flock."

"I can guess what your governess taught Alex?" TJ broke into a high stepping cancan. "Hum a little Jacques Offenbach for me. I know you know the tune."

"Sevlow christened his tavern in honor of Margo," Seamus noted. "I wondered about that weird name."

"Means Margo's a pirate captain," Claudia said. "Impressive."

"Ginger Rogers did everything Fred Astaire did, but she did it backwards and in high heels," Dragon remarked.

Claudia smiled. "Quite a feat, for both women."

"Let's not forget who we're dealing with," TJ reminded. "Mademoiselle rooster pirate oozes bad news."

"Hey, and castaway Sevlow rows like a one-man trireme." Seamus pointed towards *Le Coq*. "While we're standing around talking, they're boarding the ship."

Seamus focused on Sevlow and immediately found himself standing in a crowd on the ship's deck, watching the Master ascend a rope ladder. He scanned the weathered grimy faces of the deckhands. Margo was not among them. Seamus did notice, however, that the men were a mixed mass of races. Caucasian, African, Native American, and Asian were equally represented in *Le Coq's* crew. A battle-scarred tattooed warrior took Sevlow by the arm and lifted him like a rag doll onto the ship.

"Queequeg lives," TJ said. "Name the movie, or book, and ship, and you go to the head of the class."

Seamus's high school memory was prodded. "Moby Dick?"

"The Pequot!" Dragon shouted, like a game-show contestant. "Call me Ishmael."

"Ishmael brown nose." TJ grabbed Dragon by the headscarf and landed a solid noogie attack. Dragon countered with a forceful wedgie. "OW! Now you're gonna—" They tumbled into the cannons.

Claudia stepped past the battling brutes and stood beside Seamus. "This is amazing," she marveled. "I can't believe I am actually standing aboard an 18th century pirate ship." Claudia tugged on Seamus's leather sash. "With you."

"Standing on the memory of an 18th century pirate ship," Seamus corrected. "I'd have paid more attention in History class if it was taught this way."

"They seem to be treating him like a guest," Claudia observed.

Seamus watched as Sevlow was guided along a path that led through the hushed gawking crew. A uniformed guard met Sevlow at the entrance to the galley below. Armed men watched from the navigation perch above.

"*Sont vous portant une arme?*" The guard pushed Sevlow hard against the door and checked him for weapons. None were found.

Seamus winced. "So much for the welcoming committee."

"Frenchy obviously has no idea who he's dealing with," TJ replied. "Werewolves don't need guns or knives to kick pirate butt."

"*Venez avec moi,*" the guard instructed. "*Préparez-vous à rencontrer le capitaine.*"

"He wants Sevlow to follow him," Claudia translated. "To prepare for his meeting with the Captain."

The guard ushered Sevlow to a cabin at the end of a long dim hallway and motioned for him to enter. The escort held up his index finger. "*Une heure,*" he said before closing the door and locking it from the outside.

The berth was small but tidy, equipped with a few provisions. There was a cot against the wall with a shelf above it that displayed an assortment of books. A tray containing a dark loaf of bread and a cheese wedge had been placed atop the cot. Also in the room was a pedestal table that held a cloth, pitcher, and washbasin. A change of men's clothing hung over the seat-back of an ornate claw-foot chair. A chamber pot was beside the chair.

"I recognize the bed and washbasin from the tomb room beneath St. Guinefort's," Claudia cringed. "And that…That pot."

"The chair's now in Sevlow's office at the school too," Dragon noted. "These furnishings must be important to him if he's kept them for over two centuries."

Sevlow poured water from the pitcher into the basin and began to disrobe.

"Some things are best left unseen." Claudia looked away. "We have an hour before he meets Margo."

Seamus stepped through the wall. The others joined him in the passageway. "We should be able to investigate anything on the ship that Sevlow has seen and remembers."

"He didn't open the Cock of the Flock until 1797," Dragon reminded. "That means Sevlow could have up to five years of *Le Coq* memories."

"My guess is, where there are armed guards, there's treasure," Seamus said.

"Yeah, Pepé Le Pew and his posse are packing iron to protect something besides the queen of mean." TJ waved his hand in front of a staunch staring guard.

"Let's check out the hull," Seamus suggested. As if from his own recollection, he piloted the pack through the vessel. "There are two decks below this one. The treasure vault is beneath them. It's separated from the supply area by an open section and reinforced wall. There's but one access to the room and it's protected at all times by sentries sporting a small arsenal of weapons." Another image popped into his brain. "And a booby-trapped maze." He was surprised by his sudden vivid knowledge.

"Dance the Minuet!" Claudia shouted. She covered her lips, as if embarrassed by her sudden outburst.

"Thanks for asking, but I'm not wearing my boogie shoes," TJ replied.

"Don't know why I blurted that out." Claudia blushed. "How odd."

The pack descended the stairs into the supply hold. Just as Seamus had described, heavily armed pirates stood aft, protecting what appeared to be an empty chamber.

"Claudia, I understand what you meant!" Dragon exclaimed. "Margo does the Minuet, through there, into the treasure room. It's ingenious!"

"Oh, my gosh! You're right!" Claudia ran past the guards and the brutes into the open chamber. "There's a secret safe path—she dances her way to the door." Claudia inspected the floor and beams. "This is depraved, but incredible!"

Seamus nodded in agreement. "Look, twine's been placed along the flooring planks. It's attached to triggers that release killing devices embedded in the walls and ceiling." He ran his finger across the edge of a two-sided ax.

"One wrong move and WHACK." TJ held his neck. "Decapitation."

"She's got daggers, guns, axes, bows, arrows, and a bubbly bottled concoction that'll melt skin to the bone, all poised to obliterate an intruder," Claudia marveled. "Wonder who constructed this place?"

"Bet she made the engineer walk the plank when he was done," Dragon said. "I hope we get to see Margo do the Minuet across the room."

TJ nodded. "Yeah, and I'd trade half the treasure behind door number one for the honor of tripping her while she do-se-dos through the chamber of horrors."

"Margo's not evil yet," Claudia reminded. "She's just protecting her goods."

"Really? Goods she acquired how?" TJ raised an eyebrow. "Margo inherited the ship and won the lottery?"

"You never know, TJ." Claudia walked across the strings and through the oak panels that led to the treasure room. She screamed with delight.

Seamus sprinted into the wall and found himself knee deep in bursting burlap bags of gold and silver coins and other spoils the likes of which he had trouble believing were genuine. There were bejeweled statues, exotic icons, and open barrels filled with bolts of colorful silken fabrics and threads. There were chests laden with an array of glistening stones, ornately carved furniture, and bushels filled with pearls of varying shapes, sizes, and colors. There were books and paintings and musical instruments tagged with numbers and stacked neatly as if they'd been recently inventoried.

TJ rubbed a golden lamp. "Where's that big blue genie? I want my three wishes."

"No wonder Margo's turned this place into Ft. Knox with a firing squad." Seamus examined the spoils. "This plunder is worth a fortune."

"Forget what I said earlier. I clearly see why Sevlow fell for Margo—she is rich and beautiful." TJ grinned like the Cheshire Cat. "My kind of woman!"

"Please, TJ, make up your mind," Claudia chided. "One minute you're a fan of Margo's and the next you're a foe."

"A materialistic conversion has taken place in my soul." TJ held up a glistening diamond necklace. "I have seen the light!"

"I'd like to play with treasure all day too, but I think we'd better get back and check on Sevlow." Seamus closed his eyes. When he opened them again the pack was standing in Sevlow's cabin. The Master was washed and dressed, his hair tied in a neat ponytail with a leather cord. Seamus noted that the Master appeared as he always did, serene and focused, as he sat in his future office chair, leafing through a book of poetry.

There were footsteps in the hall.

Claudia put her finger to her lips. "Shhh, someone's coming."

"Chill, Secret Squirrel," TJ said. "You forgetting no one can see or hear us?"

There was a knock. Sevlow set the book down and stood. The door opened. A familiar armed guard entered.

"Frenchy's back." TJ stepped into his path. The guard walked through him.

"*Le capitaine est prêt à vous voir.*"

"Margo is ready to see him," Claudia whispered.

Sevlow followed the guard to the Captain's quarters. The pack entered the well-appointed room. Margo stood facing the porthole, her back to Sevlow and the guard. The collar and cuffs of her crème dress coat were trimmed with colorful petit feathers.

"She even dresses like a proud rooster," Claudia remarked.

"*Laissez-nous la paix,*" the Captain instructed.

The guard exited, leaving Margo and Sevlow alone.

"She wants to have a private meeting with Sevlow," Claudia said.

"You can turn off the subtitles," TJ replied. "This show isn't too difficult to figure out. Bird lady wants something from our guy."

"*Faites vous parlez le français?*" Margo asked, still gazing at the sea.

"*Oui,*" Sevlow replied. "But I prefer to converse in English."

The Captain shifted her attention and confronted her guest, eye-to-eye. "Very well, *Monsieur* Sevlow. English it will be." A congenial smile etched across her lips. It was as bright as the mother of pearl broach that adorned her neck.

Seamus felt his cheeks warm and flush. It was difficult not to ogle *le coq du troupeau's* commanding presence and stunning beauty. He hoped Claudia hadn't noticed.

"It is alleged that you are a werewolf, Monsieur Sevlow." Margo addressed her guest directly. "What do you say to that accusation?"

"She doesn't beat around the bush," TJ remarked.

The Master nodded the affirmative. "It is true. I am a commissioned hound of the gods, or as you simply put it, a werewolf."

"There was occasion when I would not have believed such blasphemy," Margo professed. "However, my travels and my sundry crew have exposed me to wonders most men, and women, will never fathom."

"Many lands and cultures are represented aboard *Le Coq*," Sevlow observed. "It appears you have chosen your men judiciously."

"Stray dogs make the most loyal companions." Margo opened a decanter and poured them each a snifter of brandy. "I know how you came to be set adrift." Margo handed Sevlow his drink. "News travels quickly across the high seas." She lifted her glass. "To squawking gulls."

"Perhaps the birds will also divulge how you came to be the captain of this intrepid vessel?" Sevlow raised his glass to meet his host's.

Margo touched her rim to Sevlow's. A tiny chime announced the meeting of crystal. Margo took the first sip.

The Master followed suit.

Margo pointed to a chair. "Make yourself comfortable."

Seamus grinned. "It's not about comfort—it's a power play."

"Ten bucks says our werewolf stands for the entire meeting," TJ said.

"In the presence of a lady, and a Captain, my comfort is inconsequential." Sevlow bowed.

"As you please." Margo smiled.

"Come to me Papa." TJ imagined a $10 bill and snatched it out of the air.

"I inherited *Le Coq* from my father, Jacques Pierre Heroux," Margo began. "He was a French merchant ship captain from the East Indies, and I his only child."

Claudia nudged TJ.

"In Martinique, my mother's family grew and exported sugar and tobacco for three generations," Margo continued. "My mother was British; she taught me to speak English. When I was eleven years old my mother died from the fever. Jacques Pierre Heroux was a doting father. He brought me with him aboard *Le Coq*." Margo seemed to recall a humorous aside. "Against my maternal grandmother's wishes. She vehemently preferred that I return to Seacliff Manor, the family home in Cornwall, and learn the mores of a lady." Margo paused to take a sip of brandy. "Soirees were not my forte. I sided with my father. This ship has been my *maison* ever since."

"What became of your mother's family and home?"

"The plantation was destroyed a few years after my mother's death, during the rebellion. *Le Coq* was in port at the time preparing to load goods for a passage to England. My father was able to salvage the crop with the help of loyal servants who then joined our crew. He was also able to reclaim some of my mother's personal belongings: art, furniture, her beloved books."

"See." Claudia poked TJ. "The ship is inherited and not all of the treasure we saw below is stolen."

"You called it." TJ handed Claudia the $10.

Margo took another sip from her glass before continuing her tale. "The tragedy of losing the plantation foreshadowed a doomed voyage: *Le Coq* was attacked by pirates near Saint-Domingue. Much of our bounty was pillaged. The crew fought valiantly and was able to fend off the assault before our ship could be commandeered, but tragically, not before my father died in the mayhem. I was seventeen."

Sevlow lowered his eyes. "I am sorry for your loss."

"I have lived." Margo removed a handkerchief from her sleeve. It bore the monogram JPH. She touched it to her cheek. "After reclaiming most of what was taken from me that fateful day, I decided to embark upon a less conventional seafaring *Modus Operandi* as the ship's captain, *le coq du troupeau*."

Sevlow walked over to the open port. He seemed to be digesting her words. The twilight cast an azure shadow on the Master, a shadow that matched his icy blue eyes. After a pensive pause he fixed an inscrutable gaze on Margo. "It was a great risk to alter your voyage, to embark upon reconnaissance before the plunder below could be safely concealed in your grandmother's Truro harbor."

Margo's expression changed from solemn to surprised. The glass in her hand dropped, shattering against the table corner and spilling shards of crystal and brandy onto the floor. She leapt backwards to avoid the sharp amber splash. The aft section of her knees encountered the cushion of a settee. Margo found herself unceremoniously seated.

Sevlow did not flinch.

"Nothing ruffles his feathers," TJ marveled. "The man should play poker."

Margo remained in place and composed herself. "I don't know what you mean," she replied with renewed poise. "*Le Coq* was returning to England, from Martinique. A storm blew us off course. I neither relinquished a secure port in Cornwall nor sailed out of my way to seek you."

A lone seagull called in the distance. Sevlow nodded, as if he understood the plumed crier. "Is it about the bounty?" the werewolf inquired.

The Captain blushed.

"Mademoiselle, if you require my assistance, speak the truth."

Margo seemed to be contemplating her quandary. She returned to a more regal standing position and remained silent for an extended moment. Her body relaxed. Her countenance softened; she appeared to resign herself to honesty. "The lofty reward for your head would have enticed me," she confessed. "If your unearthly abilities were not priceless." Margo removed a folded piece of parchment paper from her pocket "Sailing out of my way to locate you was not about the bounty." She handed the note to Sevlow. "It is about staying alive."

Chapter 4

BORN TO RUN

Lyman Newlin sat at his corner office desk chewing on an unlit cigar, sorting through his overflowing in-box, and listening to Bruce Springhorn's hometown anthem crackling across the transistor radio airwaves of 1020, WAGO, *New City's AM rockin' to the oldies music station. Going where you've been before!*

Another quiet Saturday at the *Chronicle*.

"Junk, junk, maybe junk, not junk," Lyman noted as he separated office memos, lunch menu fliers, fan letters, inter-office manila folders, and other correspondence into three piles. Junk Mountain was winning the elevation contest.

"What's this?" Lyman asked aloud, removing the last piece of mail, a large silvery flying saucer shaped envelope wedged into the bottom of the tray. His name was neatly printed in red ink on a tab beneath the paper spacecraft dome. There was no return address, no stamp, and no sender signature. Lyman lifted the dome and removed a second smaller envelope marked with a single word in the same red print, *ENJOY!* Lyman broke the seal, removed the contents, and for a moment was paralyzed by his fantastic fortune. The envelope contained two admission passes to ComicSci, which was coming to the New City Convention Center for the first time in a decade. Lyman pressed the laminated cards to his chest and grinned like a well-fed toad. Renewed notoriety had its rewards.

In the wonderful world of all things comic books and science fiction flicks there was no more spectacular gathering than ComicSci, where the ridiculous courted the sublime. Lyman was proud to inhabit its realm of fabricated reality that turned geeks into gods. *Raiders of the Lost Galaxy, Star Lords, Invasion of the Body Slashers*—Lyman had watched all of the theater and television classics, replayed countless scenes, and rehearsed deft dialogue. Every night since the onset of puberty, in that quasi time of wake and slumber, he watched himself on his mental movie screen, donning a flashy flight suit and kicking intergalactic asteroid. The scenarios changed, but the players were always the same. Lyman Newlin as Captain Milkyway, protector of the universe and debonair paramour of Princess Stardust, who against her will was betrothed at birth to the loathsome Baron Blackhole. He and his sidekick, Red Giant, the archenemies of Captain Milkyway and all things courageous and honorable. Lyman's re-plumbed heart skipped an irregular beat. Would he finally get to meet his *Space Avenger* heroes? They'd be octogenarians by now. Could the quartet remember the letters of a star-stuck youth who grew up to be a mild mannered reporter for a great metropolitan newspaper, who writes for truth, justice, and the American way? Lyman looked at the date on the tickets. There was enough time to properly prepare for the event.

He reached for his desk phone and dialed. On the third ring he extended the receiver away from his head.

"Save your dime and my time! I'm not buying what you're selling!"

Lyman placed the phone back against his ear. "Bella, it's me…. Yes, I'm coming over at noon for lunch…. Don't worry. Put my phone on voicemail this morning…. Promise, no last minute calls to make me late…. What's tripe? Never mind—quick question. Remember telling me that you were a teenage sweatshop seamstress? Still sew?

Margo opened the bathroom door. A tall grim ashen man confronted her beneath the transom. "Where is it?" he demanded. I know you did not return empty-handed."

"Jacques, exertion accelerates your condition," Margo cautioned. "Try to rest until I'm ready to administer the injection."

"Rest? Is that your prescription?" Jacques asked. "I expire while you gallivant and then bathe away your sins. So much for maternal concern."

"You are not dying—you're aging." She maneuvered past him. "I will gather supplies and meet you in the parlor."

"Aging *is* dying, Mother!" Jacques followed behind her like a petulant child. "But how can I expect a 'Peter Pan' to comprehend my corporeal plight when she cheats father time with such ease and grace?"

"Why must your mockery always be directed at me?" Margo sighed. She opened the hotel suite entry closet and removed a small black medicine bag from her valise. "Have I not done my utmost to preserve your prime?" She took a pre-packaged alcohol swab and syringe from the case.

"My prime, Mother? Really?" His contempt was palpable. "Your unwillingness to seek an alternative serum sooner has caused me to age more rapidly. I am forced to linger in my fourth decade. Soon to be a half century decayed, which would make me nearly as old as Vincent, a plight superior only to death."

"I do not know for certain if Sevlow's pure werewolf blood is more potent than turned blood mixed with—" her voice faltered.

"Oh, do not feign a conscience, Mother," Jacques sneered. "It is your duty to kill for my sake. You brought me into this grotesque world of yours, where capricious mortality and wanton werewolves are the norm."

Margo imagined Sevlow in his regal animal form guarding her from the pack. They had sensed her sins. Margo's demise would have been swift and fair. There was no dishonor in the hunt. "The beasts have moral code," she remarked.

"What is that supposed to mean, Mother? Should I feel guilty for aspiring to live a youthful life? He propelled a stack of magazines from the credenza. They scattered across the marble floor. "You ruin my existence, and criticize my principles!"

"You're upset. I understand." Margo would do anything to ease her son's despair, but at the moment empathy was all she could offer.

"What do you know of aging or death?" he scoffed. "When the elixir dissipates without warning, I am the one who must suffer and grow older, not you! My perfect young mother, who will never comprehend what it is like for her hairline and gums to recede, for her skin to wrinkle and sag and her muscles to grow lax and diminish." He caught his reflection in the glass. "She will never gaze into a mirror and see her blonde hair streaked with grotesque gray."

Margo grabbed his fist before it made contact with the reflection. "Jacques!"

He pulled away. "There was a time when we passed for fraternal twins, Mother. Now I masquerade as your father."

"You're a mirror image of my father," Margo replied in a calm and soothing tone that shielded her exasperation. "And you bare his name. He was a honorable man."

"My grandfather, Jacques Pierre Heroux, who loved his daughter so much he was willing to die for her," Jacques proclaimed. He mimicked a preacher at the podium. "Heroux the hero, thrust himself in front of a musket aimed at his dear Margo."

With grateful remorse, Margo thought of another who had given his life for her…

"Do you love me as much, Mother? Would you die for me?"

"Yes, but right now I exist for you, Jacques. Your wellbeing is my sole mission."

"A mission that produces nothing but dysfunction and misery."

"I prefer to describe our way of life as *unique*," Margo defended. "And we are fortunate to live in comfort—Seacliff manor in England, this suite at the Piazza Hotel, cars, boats, and extended holidays abroad. We wear fine clothes and eat gourmet meals. Is that what you consider misery? Furthermore, I have never asked you to sacrifice or toil in order to earn your keep."

"There you go! Taunting me with the fact that I do no work!" Jacques scowled. "Instead, precious pirate treasures have been sold and monies invested. So unlike you, Mother, to miss an opportunity to boast of your triumphs and sacrifices. Perhaps it's because your swashbuckling butler is not here to stroke your ego while you two revel and reminiscence about days on the high seas. The boot-licker."

"Be respectful." Margo's response was quick and stern. "Vincent cares for us."

"Of course, he fetches tea and allows you to gouge him full of holes for my sake. If Vincent wasn't such a foul old troll I'd accuse you of pandering."

Margo blushed, but did not protest. She was past weary. She had not slept in two days; the encounter with Sevlow had drained her energy reserve, now another wearisome confrontation with her son. Margo made her way to the kitchenette in silence.

"It's as if you hate me," Jacques called after her. "If you loved me you would find a way to change history and make me young and robust again."

"If," Margo repeated. "That two-letter weapon you employ against me." Margo removed Sevlow's blood and another crimson vial from the mini refrigerator. She closed her eyes and whispered, "Forgive me."

"Forgiveness has its price, my dear mother!" Jacques snatched the sealed bottles from Margo's grasp and tossed them onto the sofa.

"What are you doing?"

"Give me that ring!" he ordered, seizing his mother's left hand. "You claim no one except your husband can remove it." He bent Margo's wrist until she fell to her knees. "But perhaps you are wittingly mistaken."

"Stop!" she pleaded.

"I deserve youth and immortality too!" He tried in vain to yank the ring over her knuckle. "I could snap the bone in two!"

The skin around her finger turned as blue as the moonstone jewel. "Jacques, you are hurting me!" she cried. "Are you mad?"

He abrupt released his grip on her and began pacing the room like a cornered criminal contemplating an escape route. "Mother, tell me you are not angry."

She did not respond.

"Say you are not angry!" he bellowed. "It is your fault I almost caused you injury. I don't want to behave badly. Mother, I simply wish you could make me happy, the way I was in my youth." Jacques sat on the carpet beside her and began to rock back and forth. His rage melted into maudlin. "Grandmother's house was lovely then. The curtains were not always drawn and the gardens were not overrun with weeds and vines. We would sit on the cliffs and watch the ships pass. You told me tales of buccaneers. I wanted to be just like you, Mother—so gorgeous and courageous. You would hug and kiss me and coo that I was the perfect child, your beautiful baby boy. Remember?"

She nodded. Tears filled her autumn eyes.

"Our home bloomed with activity. Friends would visit, bringing sweets and gifts. There were lavish parties in the ballroom, and on the veranda. There was music. You played the piano for me every evening before bed. It was my favorite time of the day." Jacques began to shiver and perspire. "You smiled at me when we spoke. You were never gloomy or cross. We didn't hide indoors or move from the country to the city and back again whenever people noticed and commented on your aging—or lack of. Our way of life was conventional and stationary. That is what I desire once more, Mother." His voice quavered. "It is not fair. Why was I born to run?"

Margo rubbed her swollen finger and wept.

"Mother, are you listening? Do you consider my feelings? How can you ignore my pain? You made me exert myself. On the contrary you kneel there like a charlatan cleric in repose while I suffer the consequences." Sweat glistened on his forehead and rolled down to his jowls. Jacques clutched his chest. "Get up. Help me."

Margo assisted her son to the sofa. She kissed his wet brow and placed a throw across his trembling shoulders. "Unbutton your shirt." She gathered supplies. Margo wiped a sterile alcohol pad across his left breast and readied the syringe.

Jacques closed his eyes.

Margo thrust the razor-sharp needle at a 90° angle into his

beating muscle and compressed the plunger. The barrel contained a mixture of blood from the two vials, one from the heart of a pure werewolf, and the other from the heart of an innocent lamb, ambushed by a skillful lioness with a starving cub to feed.

Chapter 5

A WING AND A PRAYER

The ship tossed gently upon the waves, rocking the captain's cabin from side to side in a rhythmic amalgam of wind, water, and wood. Margo and Sevlow swayed with the ocean cadence. Their taut bodies moving in easy fluidity like conditioned dancers performing a familiar waltz.

Sevlow surveyed the document in hand.

Seamus watched with interest. He suspected that the Master's keen immortal canine senses had chronicled its scent, origin, and script.

"This paper has been torn from a larger parchment." Sevlow pointed to a faded torn glyph at the top corner of the note. "The inks are different." He passed the parchment back to Margo. "How did you come to be in possession of this note?"

"My butler, Vincent," the Captain replied, reviewing the message clues before slipping it back into her hip pocket. "*Le Coq* made port in Ponta Delgada eleven days ago. It was to be a brief call before continuing on to England, to grandmother's concealed inlet." Margo shook her head in disbelief. "As you somehow have been able to deduce."

Like the green flash at sundown, Seamus caught a glimpse of a fleeting grin dash across Sevlow lips.

"Most of my men were given a night of leave. I too dined at the tavern. It is there I heard an inebriated sailor's tale of a werewolf put on trial, judged to be guilty on all counts, and set adrift for his blasphemous sins." It was Margo's turn to smile. "The fool boasted that he would collect a king's ransom for the beast's head."

"What soberness conceals, drunkenness reveals," Dragon said.

"Vincent left the tavern early and headed back to the ship," Margo continued her tale. "Along the way he observed two shrouded men conversing near the harbor. They separated upon seeing Vincent approach. He thought nothing of the encounter until he noticed this correspondence on the ground where the pair had been speaking. Vincent sought to follow after the men, but they were lost to the night. He read the message out of curiosity, then of course brought it directly to my attention."

"The suspense is killing me," TJ moaned. "I gotta know what that note says."

"There's a surprise shore attack in the works," Claudia said. "Margo's hideaway in Truro has been compromised."

"Granny and the butler in the kitchen with the candle stick." TJ envisioned into his hand a small brown envelope labeled CLUE.

"Are you certain that Vincent can be trusted?" Sevlow asked. His measured expression revealed that he had already embarked upon a plan of action.

"With my life," Margo replied. "Vincent served my mother's family for many years at Seacliff Manor and on Martinique, prior to the natives' revolt. When the plantation was lost, he joined our *Le Coq* crew and attended to my father. Following father's death, and my succession as captain, Vincent became both family and confidante. I assure you his loyalty is above reproach." Margo fluffed her feathers like a rooster posturing before the farmer. "Vincent is as trustworthy as a hound of the gods."

"I am impressed," Seamus remarked. "Margo remembered the werewolf tag."

Sevlow lifted the corner of a tapestry drape that covered what appeared to be a bell-shaped birdcage. He peered into the enclosure without disturbing the slumbering occupant. "Who besides Vincent knows your ship's course was altered to search for an exiled werewolf?"

"No one," Margo assured. "The crew was told that while in port I learned of a cargo vessel in distress, one in the position to pay handsomely for our immediate assistance." She paused. "I know how it appears, but I assure you, *Le Coq* is not a pirate vessel. I am in the business of assistance, for a fee. Salvage is a profitable endeavor." Margo stroked her diamond broach. "Compensation comes in many shapes and sizes."

"Cushion cut, about twenty carats," Claudia appraised. "It's exquisite."

"Some people have a jewelry box," Seamus said. "Margo has a jewelry hull."

"A hull of a lot of jewelry." TJ slapped his knee. "Get it?"

"What is our location?" Sevlow inquired.

Margo removed a map from her roll top desk and spread it across the table. "We are presently off the coast of France. If the drunkard was not misinformed, you had been drifting a fortnight." She traced Sevlow's course with her finger. "The stalwart currents brought you from the Baltic into the North Sea and then south into the Celtic Sea. Right here is where you were recovered." Margo tapped the map location.

"Without your search and fortuitous find, I would still be adrift."

The Captain did not reply to her guest's statement. Although her hand-on-hip slight hair toss and sultry sideways glance spoke volumes.

Claudia marveled. "The Master has definitely caught her fancy."

"Power is the ultimate aphrodisiac," Dragon remarked.

"I predict Margo falls for Sevlow big time after he prevents the mutiny," added Seamus. "Just like Claudia lost her heart to me when she was hit by the train."

"In more ways than one." Claudia kissed Seamus on both cheeks. "Listening to these European accents is making me feel very Continental."

TJ made a coughing noise that sounded a lot like, "Gag me."

"There are traitors aboard *Le Coq*," Sevlow cautioned. "However, I suspect they will not take action until the ship reaches the shores of Seacliff Manor. There are too many men aboard who are loyal to *le coq du troupeau*. The conspirators will require land reinforcements in order to be victorious."

"How do you propose I proceed?" Margo's tone and demeanor suggested she was prepared to comply with the werewolf's plan of action.

"Convey to your crew that I was a member of the distressed cargo ship," instructed Sevlow, holding her gaze in a way that suggested authority as well as interest.

"The ship caught fire," Margo continued. "You were thrown overboard by an explosion on deck. A skiff was lowered for your benefit, but another series of blasts made retrieval impossible."

"I drifted further and further away from my vessel," Sevlow added.

Margo expanded the unfolding fabricated tale. "A storm arose. From a muted distance you were able to discern a merchant ship responding to the SOS. Alas, they did not see the skiff floating alone upon the frigid waves."

Sevlow provided the denouement. "Many days passed. After nearly losing hope, my prayers were answered when *Le Coq* came into view... *Merci*."

Dragon sighed. "Gratitude is a memory of the heart"

"Is anyone else hearing violins?" Seamus stroked an imaginary bow across imaginary strings.

"This is a very different side of Sevlow," Claudia observed. "I'm a little shocked."

"Yeah, like when you're a kid and find out where babies come from." TJ shuddered. "Means your parents aren't the prudes you thought."

"My parents were openly loving in front of Alex and me." Claudia took Seamus's hand. "Our children will see the same affection someday."

"Whoa, whoa, whoa!" TJ raised his hands in protest. "It's a little early for baby talk. You two have been together for what, a few weeks?"

"We've know each other for five years," Claudia replied. "If you include my werewolf dreams."

"In the version I heard, they were nightmares," TJ noted. "Just like the nightmare that awaits Sevlow two centuries from now when Captain Cut Throat stabs him in the heart with her pearl-handled dagger."

"Love is a battlefield," Dragon sang, strumming an air guitar.

"Not all relationships end in tragedy. My parents are dead and still together," reminded Claudia. "True love lives on for an eternity."

"Maybe you've got the mate-for-life anglerfish gene." TJ inspected the couple. "Nope, don't see any fins and gills on you or Seamus so the odds aren't in your fairytale favor. Get ready for a break-up."

Claudia bristled. "Seamus and I will be together forever. Even if we don't marry and have children, we're committed to our love, trust, and friendship."

"Oh yeah? Dragon's my friend and I trust him." TJ put Dragon into a headlock. "But I'm not going to say I love him. Not in public, anyway."

"It's a full-fledged bromance," Dragon choked, knocking TJ off his feet with a swift kick and leg sweep.

Claudia jumped out of the way of the falling brutes.

Seamus was relieved by the antics. For fear of sounding unconvincing, he preferred not to comment on the subject of marriage or love everlasting. They had no model in his psyche to review or imitate. Love was a deep dark hole filled with questions and uncertainty. He surely had strong feelings for Claudia, but how did they compare to true love? Claudia learned from her parents. Who were his parents? Did they care about one another? Did they ever love him? If so, how did he end up a destitute child in an orphanage run by a white werewolf? Seamus's childhood was filled with bouts of self-doubt and recklessness. Would he ever be emotionally equipped to have a wife and children? It was a scary proposition, one Seamus preferred to postpone indefinitely. He returned his focus to the events unfolding before them. "Hey, remember, we're in this memory to help Sevlow."

"Seamus is right." Claudia blushed. "Sorry for causing the detour."

"What's a detour amongst friends?" Dragon pulled TJ to his feet. "Friends are the gods' apology for rotten relatives."

Sevlow removed the cover from the birdcage. A tawny pigeon

roosted beneath a suspended olive branch. "Your homing bird has a long journey approaching, a flight I suspect it has made before."

Margo took the bird from its enclosure and cradled it upon her forearm like a precious parcel. "Avi knows her way home." Margo stroked the pigeon. Avi cooed. "Grandmother is always relieved when she returns. It means *Le Coq* is not far behind."

Sevlow removed a quill and portion of parchment from Margo's desk. "May I?"

"See that?" Seamus pointed. "The paper has an ink smudge and missing corner."

"You're right." Claudia stepping closer. "Bet that note in Margo's pocket would fit, a perfect puzzle piece."

"Bingo," TJ called. "Sevlow just did a double-take. He's come to the same conclusion—the message writer had access to Margo's cabin."

The Master tore a second smaller corner off the paper, penned a short statement, and handed it to Margo without mentioning his observation.

Margo read the paper before wrapping and securing it to Avi's leg. "On this journey, she will carry more than notification of our forthcoming arrival." The Captain kissed her bird and set it on the sill of the open porthole. "Godspeed, my pet."

Avi flapped her wings and disappeared into the night.

Jacques awoke shortly before sundown. A damask duvet swathed his snug body and a down pillow cradled his bed head. Jacques tossed the covers as he stood to greet the day for a second time, feeling more energetic than a toddler high on tutti-frutti soda pop. He had the urge to share his spanking zeal. "Mother! I'm up!" Jacques pulled the drape chord and bathed himself in crimson sunset light, which was fast fading into a bruised lavender westerly glow. "Hurry! You must see this radiant sky. Where are you, Mother?" Jacques searched the bedrooms, the baths, the hallway, and the foyer closet.

Margo was nowhere to be found and she hadn't left a note.

Jacques cheery humor was short lived. "Now look what you've done—you've doused my excitement!" he shouted to the empty room. There was no reply. Not even an echo. Jacques threw himself back onto the sofa and pouted until the unobserved sulking obliged him to strike a more dramatic pose. He crossed his arms and tossed his legs like two falling timbers upon the coffee table, catching his heel on the rim of a silvery serving tray. It flipped with a TING, BANG, CLING before sailing through the air. Jacques caught a passing glimpse of his image in the polished metal. *Who was that handsome man in the reflection?* Jacques turned on the lamp, crawled across the carpet, and crouched above the platter. A rapt scrutiny commenced. There was something very different about his face. Although Jacques didn't appear to be younger, he seemed to be vastly *improved.* His skin glowed, his eyes twinkled, and his hair had oodles more body and shine. Jacques unbuttoned his dress shirt. He had muscles where there had been flaccid flesh, and a manly layer of golden fuzz where unadorned sallow skin had recently resided. Jacques flexed his new pecs and howled for joy. Pure werewolf blood had buff benefits. He wondered if physical appearances were the only lycanthrope enhancement. Could he run faster? Jump higher? Lift heavy objects with ease? Like a boy with a new toy, Jacques lost no time testing the plentiful possibilities. He karate chopped chairs, commenced airborne acrobatics, bunny hopped onto tabletops, and Tarzaned across the tailored drapes. The hotel room soon resembled a trailer park after a category 4 hurricane.

Margo returned to the hotel room carrying a brown paper Jean & Poluka bag. The scent of hot bread, roasted garlic green beans, grilled chicken, and fresh strawberries permeated the surrounding air. "Jacques, are you awake? I brought us dinner. Thought you might be—" Her sentence came to an abrupt halt the moment she took a gander of the penthouse suite in shambles and of her son dashing from room to room, flapping his shirttails like a goose preparing for flight. Jacques sprinted into Margo's room, vaulted himself onto the king-size bed and began jumping up and down with dizzying delight.

"I can soar through the air!" The abject astonishment etched across his mother's face propelled Jacques to bounce even higher. "Your husband's blood was far superior to old Vincent's." His blouse billowed in the manmade breeze. "Look, Mother! I have a hairy chest, muscles, and wings!"

"Oh, heavens," Margo prayed under her breath. "What have I created, this time?

Chapter 6

YESTERDAY ONCE MORE

Sergeant Gaffney returned to his office from substitute Park Patrol duty looking drowsy and disheveled, like a new dad with colicky quintuplets, or an old cop with four werewolf kits to lose sleep over. Every bump in the nightshift had made the Sarge stir from his shallow snooze. He worried it was the roughhousing brutes come back for more moonlit mayhem and munchies.

Sarge gobbled a handful of antacids, brushed a clump of rainbow donut sprinkles off his pants, and yawned before collapsing into his tattered swivel chair. He needed a power nap if he had any hope of constructing a reasonable ruse to explain the dents on his radio car. The NCPD Vehicle Operations Department required an automobile accident report, submitted online in triplicate. It was due before Sarge's shift ended. So much for shut-eye. Days like this he wished his ulcer could tolerate a cup of Joe, one creamer, one Sweet & Simple.

Sarge turned on his vintage PC and waited, and waited, and waited for it to boot. He scanned his desk for a time diversion. The weekly prison release report, printed on pumpkin orange paper, sat at the top of his in-box. After nearly thirty years of putting away bad guys, the prison report was Sergeant Gaffney's favorite monthly memo. He grabbed the document with glee. It was sort of like a seasoned baseball scout checking rosters and reviewing the stats of active players, looking for guys who he'd once-upon-a-time evaluated and sent to the pros. Gaffney felt a burst of adrenaline surge through his veins. He sat up straight, forgot his nap, and scanned the alphabetically arranged names.

Arroyo, Carlos: Grand theft auto, six months. 4/08

Bello, Paul: Tax evasion and extortion, two years. 4/15

Dillon, Patrick: Assault with a deadly weapon, jay walking, three years. 4/09

FATAL EXCEPTION appeared in neon letters across the Sarge's monitor screen. He restarted his computer and resumed reading the list of freed felons. Bruce Egan, Max Feinberg, Gerald Grant, Dwayne Harrison, Niles Jones, Dong "Buddy" Kim, Al Lippo, Juan Martinez, Ali Nahim, none of the names rang familiar. That is, until he reached the R's. Below L'Shawern Robinson was Roosky, Oleg Roosky, the unsung villain of Sergeant Gaffney's rookiehood. New City Department of Corrections was releasing him from Trikers Island maximum-security penitentiary, after nearly thirty years of incarceration. Like the smell of ripe gym socks, the name triggered the Sarge's memory and took him back to a time where movie tickets were a buck, television broadcast six channels (three national, two local, one public), and werewolves were mythical creatures. Once upon that summertime, Oleg Roosky was NCPD's most wanted bad guy. Arson, assault, robbery, there wasn't an offense the ruthless Russian import hadn't mastered and flaunted. Add to the corruption a taunting signature trademark, Roosky left a single ruble at the scene of his crimes. If not for Scorpio's mass media spectacle, Roosky would have been hotter-than-July front-page news. Reminded the Sarge of that unfortunate Angel, dying on the same day as the King of Pop. Timing is everything.

Time also turns sour grapes into vintage wine. There was an everything-old-is-new-again Roosky story to be told. Sergeant Gaffney picked up the phone and dialed. A mechanical voice answered. "You have reached the office of Lyman Newlin. Please leave a message after the tone." BEEP.

"Mr. Newlin. This is Sergeant Gaffney. Thought you might like to know that Oleg Roosky is being released from prison." The Sarge looked at the date beside Roosky's name. " He gets out today."

BEEEEEP! "If you'd like to leave a message, please press '1' and start recording at the sound of the tone." BEEEEEP!

Gaffney followed the canned command and tried again to connect with the voicemail system. "Hello. Mr. Newlin, this is—"

BEEEEEP! "If you'd like to leave a message, please press '1' and start recording at the sound of the tone." BEEEEEP!

The Sarge gave it a third go. "Oleg Roosky has been—"

BEEEEEP! "If you'd like to leave a message, please press '1' and start recording at the sound of the tone." BEEEEEP! "Good bye."

Sarge was left with a dial tone. He hung up and yawned. A faraway fog swept across Sergeant Gaffney's brain and blanketed his phone frustrations with dreamy images of a summer past. Oleg Roosky WANTED signs on weathered street posts, walking the beat, transistor radios broadcasting Bomber play-by-play from open tenement windows, the smell of kosher frankfurters simmering in stale water, a full head of hair… He closed his blinking burning eyes. In Sarge's Slumberland it was yesterday once more.

The dusky dank corridor smelled of corroded cement and pine scented cleanser. Similar to a spotlight on a forgotten stage, a lone broken barred window sent a faint fuzzy ray of sunlight down the path that separated cellblock A from B. The beam formed an illuminated oval on the ground at the end of the line, just outside of Oleg Roosky's prison chamber. His sentence had reached its conclusion. The iron curtain would soon slide open for the last time. He would be set free,

free to start the next act of his liberated life.

Oleg sat at the foot of his cot. He took a deep breath and imagined his future. He'd pick up where he left off. However, this time Roosky would be a star, an internationally notorious celebrity known for his dastardly deeds. No more page-three blurbs and black & white WANTED fliers pasted to telephone poles. Oleg saw himself scowling on the front cover of every paper, popular periodical, and four-color laminated post office notice from Ft. Lauderdale to Forks. Oleg Roosky was prepared for the notoriety; the bouncing ball was already in play.

Oleg flecked a speck of white lint off his jacket lapel and returned a pair of bronze rubles to his pants pocket. After twenty-eight years of wearing zebra jumpsuits, he was pleased to be dressed in his own civilian attire. The same black turtleneck and grey mohair suit he wore to sentencing. They still fit. Oleg prided himself on that fact. In prison he'd aged but not deteriorated, stewed but not fermented, his mind too was as sharp as ever, perhaps more so. Roosky had had many moons to study while he toiled daily in the well-stocked penitentiary book stacks. Roosky's clip-on I.D. tag read Librarian Assistant, his jail job for the last twenty years. Magazines and law journals were popular with the inmates. However, like a polished piece of photochromic Alexandrite in a garden of drab stones, Oleg stood out from the convict crowd. He preferred to immerse himself in Russian literature. Among his favorite authors: Nikolai Gogol, Mikhail Saltykov-Shchedrin, Ivan Goncharov, and the two greatest—Leo Tolstoy and Fyodor Dostoyevsky. Oleg's dependable labors over the deux decades earned him an hour of personal pick post dinner music, played on the library stereo as he mended and re-shelved the day's tattered and scattered books. Not surprisingly, Russian composers were Oleg's serenade selection: Igor Stravinsky, Mily Balakirev, Pyotr Ilyich Tchaikovsky, and his favorite—Nikolai Rimsky-Korsakov. *Flight of the Bumblebee*, no other composition could trigger a bigger power surge through Roosky's veins. It was music at its frenzied finest.

Working in the library stimulated Oleg's mind and relaxed his body. In addition the position provided a veiled opportunity for the dark Russian to rouse his black soul. Oleg Roosky kept tabs on Lyman Newlin via *Chronicle* articles. That the Scorpio newspaper reporter had recently made a professional comeback caused Roosky's heart to hum and flutter, like a bumblebee with intent to sting.

The approaching echo of prison guard boots on concrete composed a celebratory anthem. Oleg stood at attention. "*Grom pobedy, razdavaysya,*" he recited in a singsong whisper. The footsteps drew nearer. "Let thunder of victory sound." A key in lock jingle and turning tumbler clatter marked the crescendo. The cell door slid open. Oleg Roosky stepped into the spotlight.

"Your car and driver are waiting outside," the officer said as he lead former prisoner AU812 down the hall. "Paid your dues. This time keep your nose clean."

****

Roosky silently soaked up the New City skyline from the northbound span of the Trikers Island Bridge, named after Pieter Triker, Dutch settler, inventor of the three-wheeled cycle, and one-time owner of Triker's Island. The wealthy Dutchman sold the 400-acre landmass to New City for use as a Civil War detention facility.

"Keep nose clean," Oleg laughed, catching a glimpse of his pointy proboscis in the tinted car window. "Not size of nose that matter, but what inside."

"Say something, Boss?" Wally asked, AKA Waldemar Kowalczyk. Steelburgh, Pennsylvania Polish-American transplant. He left one hand on the steering wheel and half torso turned towards the backseat passenger. "New City's changed, huh?"

"Eyes on road, idiot! I die first day of new life—I kill you!"

"Ha, ha, Boss," Wally replied, "Been so long I almost forgot— your Russian accent makes everything you say sound mean." He resumed driving with both hands and eyes in time to spot and swerve around a bouncing renegade hubcap.

The unexpected jolts propelled Oleg across the bench seat, and then back again. He THUNKED his head on the armrest. "Last thing I want do is find new sidekick," Roosky mumbled, rubbing his temple while putting on his seatbelt. "But it on list."

"Gee, this is great," Wally gushed. "Can't believe we are finally back together again. There is so much to fill you in on. But first, how do you like the car?"

Oleg glanced around the interior of his beloved Dodge Super Bee. It was still in mint condition. No different than the day he'd stolen her off the lot.

"Kept this baby garaged and on blocks. Parts are the real McCoy," Wally boasted. "Same 383-cubic-inch Magnum V8 with a single four barrel carb rated at 300 bhp, three speed floor shift, tape stripes, and original Bee decals. Even applied a fresh coat of wax this morning. Notice how the color pops? Borscht red, your favorite." Wally tapped the dashboard. "She's as good as brand spanking new."

"Pat self on back," Oleg replied with a sneer. "Where we going?"

"Home, " Wally said. "I inherited the butcher shop and a storage

unit full of used bread bags from my uncle, God rest his miser soul."
Wally blessed himself and then peered at Oleg in the rearview mirror.
"The shop's cellar hideout is as you left it. We're ready, set, and back in
business."

Roosky rolled his rubles. "You send invitation?"

"Signed, sealed, delivered." Wally turned the Motorola radio
dial to 1020, WAGO, *New City's AM rockin' to the oldies music station.*
Going where you've been before! "Saved all the newspapers too," Wally
shouted, over a radio advertisement for ginkgo biloba suppositories.
"Put the articles into a scrapbook, just like you asked. Your arresting
officer got splat in a traffic accident; the DA croaked while frog
hunting, and the ninety-eight year old judge who sent you up the river is
on life-support. Hard to believe Lyman Newlin is the only one left on
your MOST HATED list."

Oleg growled.

"Can you believe the guy got famous again?" Wally flicked on
his turning signal and veered into the right lane expressway merge,
headed towards the New City town of Greenport. "Such injustice."

Oleg disengaged his seatbelt. "Change plans." He leaned over
the front seat and yanked the wheel left. The Super Bee nearly
sideswiped a cement truck.

"What the—!" Wally shouted, regaining control of the vehicle.

"First, drive to downtown," Oleg instructed, leaning back and
refastening his seatbelt. "I need see *Chronicle* newspaper building."

"If you're feeling nostalgic, you could of said so!" Wally
pointed to his heart. "Kowalczyk men don't have the best tickers."

"So."

"You're funny boss," Wally replied. "You just said 'so', which could mean 'so' as in I asked you to say 'so' if you wanted me to drive to the city or 'so' could be a response to me telling you about my bad heart, which isn't likely, but seemed to—"

"Shut up," Oleg groaned.

"Sorry, I'm talking over the radio, right? Bet you didn't get much music in the slammer. "Nothing like a catchy tune to put your mind at ease."

The Super Bee exited onto Main Avenue. Traffic was light. Pedestrians were few. Oleg had a direct view to the *Chronicle* building, a 1920's flatiron structure that sat at the corner crossroads delineating uptown from downtown. As the Super Bee approached it's intended destination, Oleg could not believe his good fortune. A certain little fat man was hailing a cab. Roosky resisted the urge to roar with gleeful abhoration.

Lyman Newlin entered an open Checker cab.

"Follow that taxi!" Oleg instructed. "But not conspicuous."

Wally slipped the Super Bee behind a bus that was behind the cab carrying the reporter. "Oooo, listen! Here's a song that'll take us back in time." Wally cranked the radio volume dial. The Carpenter's *Yesterday Once More* floated across the airwaves. "Remember, I used to make up my own words?" The driver sang along. "When they get to the part where he's making a fart, it can really make me laugh, just like before. It's yesterday once more…"

A nocturnal garden is Mother Nature's *boudoirs*. Canopies of trees, beds of flowers, and covers of ivy come alive at night, every sound a sensual serenade, every flicker of celestial light an invitation to observe the rhythmic pulse of breeze-blown primroses and marigolds surrounded by rich sod and wild moss in mounds and dewy divots, their separate fragrances melding into a single perfume. Under the owl's watchful eye, fox, badger, and deer make an appearance. The beasts of darkness play and stalk and breed in a dominion of divine serenity.

Vincent Wells took pleasure in wandering after dark through the estate gardens, especially after a kill. Over the last twenty decades, starlit strolls and moonlit pursuits had become his only personal delights, the bliss of his sleepless existence. The untamed strength and secrecy of the landscape reminded Vincent of his daring days on the high seas and his brief tavern tenure in New City. It was the thrill of darkness concealment that made him pine for his past and all the promise the gift of undead once presented. Alas, duty took precedent.

Caring for his mistress nevertheless provided the butler with some faithful fulfillment. That is if Vincent suppressed memories and knowledge, *vis-à-vis* what Margo had become and whom she had begotten. Reflecting upon the son-mother malevolence posed a permanent peril. Familial evil could trigger the werewolf urge to hunt as easily as the unfamiliar. Vincent had offered life, and Margo accepted. The hound was culpable and remorseful. His lycanthrope blood flowed through Jacques's veins. As a predatory precaution, the eternally indentured werewolf spent full moons far away from the manor, in seedy towns where heinous human stalkers targeted the downtrodden. His kills were swift and *de rigueur*. Aptitude enabled Vincent to serve two masters—Margo and Sevlow. The latter, Vincent prayed, would one day forgive him.

A telephone in the distance rang thrice and stopped. Vincent's keen sense of hearing told him the sound came from the manor, a kilometer north of where he lingered in pensive solitude. If the caller were Margo, she would immediately ring again. It was their signal. He waited. Less than a minute later a second set of chimes summoned him home.

Vincent sprinted and vaulted like an Olympic athlete in his prime, along cobbled paths, over high hedges, and under dangling branches until he reached Seacliff Manor. He sprang through the unlocked door, raced into the parlor, and answered his mistress's call, not the least bit winded. "Hello, Madam."

"Vincent, I need your assistance, at once" Margo whispered. Muffled banging and clanging noises could be heard.

"Are you in jeopardy?" the werewolf asked, feeling the hairs on his neck begin to bristle with alarm. He checked the clock on the wall. "It is past midnight. I can be in London before morning. Tell me where you are staying."

"Jacques and I did not go to London for the festival." Margo cleared her throat. "We are in New City."

Vincent attempted to answer, but found himself momentarily speechless as his brain digested the fact he'd been deceived by Margo's red herring.

"There is no time to explain. Jacques is behaving strangely."
The butler held his tongue.

"More so than usual," Margo added.

"He should have taken a dose of my blood when the requirement first became apparent." Vincent felt responsible for not insisting. "Is he able to travel? I will secure you seats on the next flight home."

"That is the problem," Margo said. "Jacques refuses to return home."

"Without a shot of blood blend he will age once again," Vincent reminded. "Surely that can convince Jacques to return."

"Our situation has a part-two." Margo paused. Jacques's voice could be heard in the background yelling for his mother to open the bathroom door. Margo rushed her words. "I have given Jacques an injection of pure werewolf blood."

Vincent gasped.

"Taken from Sevlow's heart, without his consent, of course."

"Madam!" was all Vincent could muster. A thousand other words, scenarios, and emotions flooded his thoughts. On the forefront was sympathy for the werewolf. To be wounded for a second time by Margo... *It was not what the Master deserved.*

"He will not come after me," Margo assured. "Sevlow saved my life before I stabbed him. After all these years he still loves me." There was no warmth in her voice.

Vincent observed that his mistress's cunning tone had returned. She was the remote mother lioness again. Hunting for her cub was all that mattered.

"When our passports were forged, I had one made for you as well. It is in the vault." There was a succession of knocks. Margo's voice shifted direction. "I will be through in a minute, Jacques."

"I am going to the park, with or without you!" the man boy yelled. His threat reverberated over the transcontinental line.

"Tend to him, Madam," Vincent said. "I will fly to New City as soon as possible."

"We are staying at the Piazza, in the penthouse suite." The phone went dead.

Vincent hung up his receiver. He would ready the house and pack a few belongings before departing for the airport. Heathcliff International offered the most non-stops to New City. He checked the vault. Besides a stash of centuries old riches his counterfeit passport was there, as Margo stated. Affixed to the passport was a bulging envelope baring Vincent's name. He opened it. The butler found a substantial stack of currency inside—American dollars, British pounds, Euros. The mistress prided herself on preparedness.

"New City," Vincent said aloud as he began to gather and place his belongings in a Goyard valise. The thought of returning to the Golden Apple excited him. The werewolf wondered if he would see Sevlow, even if it were just a fleeting glimpse. Did the Cock of the Flock still exist? Had the Master expanded his pack? How many grand missions had Vincent missed? The past was the past and could not be changed. Nevertheless, the old werewolf wished that somehow, someway, he could be worthy of a second act, to live a yesterday, once more.

Chapter 7

FIRE AND RAIN

The poised pack stood beside Sevlow along the ship's starboard railing, gazing into a drizzly moonless night that concluded day ten of the master's *Le Coq* memories. Sevlow had made himself unobtrusive as he passed time scrutinizing the workings of ship and crew. However, he had not laid eyes on Margo since the night in her cabin. Discrete disassociation was part of their preemptive plan.

The wet air was motionless, waylaid by a pending dread. Seamus and the pack expected, because Sevlow expected, that a bloody battle was looming. Although the outcome had been decided many decades earlier, Seamus's chest swelled with rapt anticipation. He enjoyed a good fight.

"In modest wind *Le Coq* will not reach shore before midnight," Margo whispered, appearing aft. Her words and inconspicuous attire caught Seamus by surprise. The Master, on the other hand, seemed to anticipate her appearance and update.

"This current makes certain that I arrive at Seacliff Manor before *Le Coq*," Sevlow replied in a tranquil tone. He removed a rope from its cleat and slipped it alongside the vessel. "Rain coupled with a new moon provides suitable cover for my departure." He fastened a bowline knot to the railing hitch.

"Looks like Sevlow's about to get the repel out here." TJ peered overboard. "Guess we're about to jump ship too."

"Dark skies cannot mask the sound of a splash." Margo reached off-balance for the ship's railing. She slipped.

The Master caught her before she fell.

"Whose splash was she referring to?" Dragon asked.

"Her own," TJ replied. "Captain Mean would've taken a swan dive if not for our man, Sevlow."

"It was more than a puddle slide. Margo doesn't seem well." Claudia surveyed the Captain. "She's pale."

"I am weak with fear." In the damp shimmer of lantern light, Margo's formerly fair face appeared ashen and hollow. "What if my grandmother..." her voice faltered.

Sevlow's expression revealed an epiphany. "On the contrary, fear has trumped hunger and kept you alive."

Margo's slight somber gaze displayed bemusement. She released herself from Sevlow's supportive arms. "How so?"

In an instant, Seamus knew what Sevlow had deduced. The Master solved the mystery of the torn parchment.

"Room service pirate wrote the note," TJ deduced. "Only he and Vincent have access to Captain Rooster's cabin."

"And he's been trying to poison her too," Seamus added.

"Meals are placed in your cabin at scheduled times, whether you are present to receive them or not," Sevlow said. "You appear to have lost your appetite."

"Which has saved my life," Margo remarked, clutching her stomach. "I have not ingested the snake's venom."

"Return to your quarters and summon Vincent," Sevlow instructed. "Tell him there is bread and cheese in my cabin. It is safe for consumption."

"Thank you," the Captain replied.

Sevlow readied himself for departure.

"Wait," Margo declared, shaking her head as if to dislodge a trapped thought. "I nearly forgot to mention an important detail." She stepped between Sevlow and the ship's railing. Her lips moved precariously close to his mouth as she spoke.

Sevlow did not retreat.

"There is a cavern at the base of the cliff," she whispered with watchfulness. "It contains a passageway to the manor greenhouse. The cavern entrance is camouflaged beneath a—" Margo was silenced by the clatter of advancing boot steps.

Sevlow pried his transfixed eyes away from Margo and reset them in the direction of the approaching tread.

Seamus could have sworn that he'd glimpsed a flame ignite in the Master's pupils. The fleeting sight and notion were followed by a blood-curdling scream. *Sevlow is harnessing the elements.*

"Fire!" came the not-too-distant cry. "I am on fire!"

"My ship!" Margo gasped, her face wrought with fright. She attempted to bolt past the werewolf.

Sevlow prevented her flight, with an embrace. "An illusion only." He spoke via hushed tone, his mouth touching her golden hair. "I have created a diversion."

"Not a fire…" The Captain pressed her chest pressed against him as her delicate hands clutched his back. "You are certain?"

"*Le Coq* is safe," Sevlow soothed with words and caresses.

Margo exhaled. Her breath bathed his neck.

Sevlow's expression displayed a pleasured pain.

The pack was taken aback by the Master's uncharacteristic display of ardor.

Sevlow pried himself away from the Captain. Yet he was not completely free. As a magnet clings to steel, his icy blue eyes remained locked upon hers.

More urgent footsteps strode upon the deck. "Locate the fire!" someone called.

"Be quick to your cabin before our meeting is observed." Sevlow's critical directive broke the romantic spell.

Margo fled.

The Master grasped the line and lowered himself from the ship's railing into the languid lapping waves. In an instant, man became beast. The white wolf disappeared beneath the cold black silence, an owl on the prowl.

"Are you sure this is eatable?" Lyman grimaced as he used his knife to smear the tripe through a dollop of marinara sauce. "Sheep, cow, or crustacean?" he asked, holding up a textured strip of rubbery meat and inspecting it from a safe distance.

"Don't play with your food!" Bella sprinkled a blizzard of grated Pecorino Romano across both their plates. "Eat it. Tastes like bubblegum chicken."

"Smells like garlic and tomatoes but resembles alien skin," Lyman noted. "Dr. Sparkle would have had a field day dissecting this in his moon lab."

"Can we talk about something besides Martian movies, comic books, and little green spacemen?" Bella stuck a well-buttered wad of Italian bread into her mouth. "I already promised I'd sew your Captain Milkshake suit," she reminded her lunch guest, through a spray of crusty crumbs.

"It's Captain Milkyway, to your Princess Stardust." Lyman flashed his hostess a seductive smile. "Want to play rocket ship?"

Bella blushed.

"Here comes the rocket ship." Lyman closed his eyes and leaned forward.

Bella pursed her lips.

Lyman was just about to land a French kiss when…

Bella jumped out of her seat and scampered to the kitchen window. "That's the third time!" She drew the half-open café sheers and surveyed the street.

Lyman's passionate pucker wilted into wonder. "What?" he defended." Only the first time today I tried to kiss you."

Bella opened the window and stuck her head out. "Weird looking shiny red car driving slowly past my house, for the third time." She squinted. "Dodge. Can't make out the model or license plate."

Lyman squeezed beside her. "Where?"

Bella pointed. "On the corner."

Lyman caught a glimpse of the vintage vehicle. "White rear lights." His heart skipped a beat; his knees went rigid, but his conscious mind wasn't sure why. Something long ago and far away was registering deep inside Lyman's grey matter…

Bella yanked herself and Lyman back through the open window. "They're driving the wrong way." She closed the cafés and crouched below the windowsill. "Don't let them see us spying."

The borscht red Dodge Super Bee powered in reverse until it stopped in front of Mama Stella's domicile. The backseat passenger lowered his window and glared in the direction of Bella's billowing sheers.

Lyman began to tremble as recognition rained, poured, flooded his sodden psyche. "Oleg Roosky," he muttered in dreaded disbelief.

The Russian seemed to sense the fear behind the curtain. He formed his thumb and index finger into a sideways "L" gun and pointed it at Mama Stella's window.

Bella read the passenger's lips. "Bang."

Lyman fell backwards onto the kitchen floor with a THUD.

The white wolf emerged from the sea, onto the shadowless shore beneath the cliffs. Like a dance of centrifugal force, he twisted and shook from nose to tail until his drenched coat was roused, revived, and nearly dry.

"Next full moon I'm going swimming." TJ broke into a wet dog-inspired disco display. "I want to shake, shake, shake, shake, shake, shake, shake my booty, shake my booty, shake my booty!""

Dragon joined TJ's song and dance.

"Seacliff Manor is lit up like a beacon." Claudia sidestepped her prancing pack mates. "Even if Margo's grandmother does a lighthouse imitation for *Le Coq's* benefit, I doubt she's alone in the tower."

"Sevlow doesn't think so either." Seamus pointed at the white wolf making his vertical rocky way to the dwelling above. "He's not going to waste any time looking for the camouflaged cavern."

****

Seacliff Manor was ablaze with unseemly activity. A small army of reckless thieves tromped through the gardens, roughhoused in the halls, and pillaged the parlor. Looted liquor flowed whilst scared servants in sleep attire scurried from room to room doling out hastily prepared dishes to the raucous ranks.

Like a reconnaissance Marine on midnight surveillance across enemy lines, the white wolf slinked behind shaded cover and observed

Margo's foes. The occupying force appeared to outnumber *Le Coq's* crew. Although sizable, the band of drunkards, misfits, and opportunistic slackers did not comprise an imposing militia.

Seamus figured they'd been enticed by the promise of an easy heist—to pilfer goods from a pirate and share in the spoils. He marveled at the fact that the Master could watch the high jinks without action. *I have a lesson to learn about patience.*

Claudia gave the group a once-over. "The key players are missing."

TJ flipped up two counting fingers. "Granny and the ringleader."

"Sevlow's not spoiling the party until he knows where they are," Dragon said.

"He's more conspicuous in werewolf form," Claudia commented. "Why doesn't Sevlow undergo transformation and blend into the crowd?"

"Gotta find himself some britches first," TJ answered. "Lest you forget we change back in the buff."

"Which is why Sevlow gave you and Mighty Mouse a room of your own," reminded Dragon. "Women and children get first dibs on lifeboats and privacy."

Seamus felt a sudden sense of relief and vindication.

"And it has nothing to do with favoritism," Dragon remarked, as if he'd read Seamus's insecure expression. "All werewolves are created equal."

"What's your commissioned werewolf wisdom?" Claudia eyed the agile white wolf as he leapt from ground to shed roof to tree branch to second-story balcony without making a sound or causing a commotion. "We may have been created equal, but Sevlow is definitely cut from a different mold."

★★★★★★★★★★★★★★★★

A shadow with a destination, the white wolf entered a boudoir from the open balcony doors and slipped behind a panel of tapestry drapes. He peered into the room that was lighted by twin candelabras, magnified by a set of Baroque mirrors. The air was still, except for an intermittent pulse of a muffled groan coming from a rear-facing chair at the far corner of the chamber. Sevlow left his cover to investigate.

The chair's aged female occupant did not notice the white werewolf until his teeth touched a curtain cord that fastened her wrists and ankles to the arms and legs of the Chippendale. Her moan shifted into siren mode.

Before her astonished eyes, the werewolf became naked man.

Grandmother threw herself about like a hooked fish on a hot boat deck. Her throaty distress cries intensified.

Sevlow held the chair steady. "Madam. I am here to assist, not harm." Sevlow removed the ties that bound and gagged her. "It is Margo who sent me."

Grandmother averted her gaze and sat mutely motionless. "You nearly scared the life out of me," she remarked in a brusque manner, as soon as she was able to speak.

Sevlow placed an arm over the back of her chair, his physique and pose mirroring that of Farnese Hercules. "Were you not forewarned?"

"Yes," Grandmother rubbed her bruised wrists. "Avi delivered the message." She removed her shawl and relinquishing it over her shoulder to the bare liberator.

"Thank you." The werewolf coved his mid-section with the

makeshift sarong before assisting Grandmother to her feet.

Danger. Help sent. Grandmother repeated the words on the carrier pigeon's note. "Were you not aware that these hooligans would be here, ransacking my home?" she demanded. "Perhaps at very least I could have been informed that my knight in shining armor would be a naked werewolf."

"I apologize, Madam."

Seamus amused by old woman's plunk. "I wouldn't want to mess with Margo's grandmother. Bet the guy who tied her up has a few bumps and bruises to show for it."

"Pint-sized and cheeky," remarked Dragon.

"Yeah, she reminds me of a badger in a night dress," added TJ.

"She accepts that Sevlow is a werewolf." Claudia appeared perplexed. "Don't you find that weird?"

"No," TJ said. "Old ladies are wise to the mystical. My granny hunted and trapped fairies for wishes. She caught the King Fairy and held him in a jar until he performed magic that finally made my father agree to free my mama and us children."

Claudia wrinkled her brow. "Seriously, TJ…"

TJ pointed his finger at the naysayer. "Tell me you aren't a werewolf and you don't talk to ghosts."

Claudia cracked a smile.

TJ conjured a blackboard and pointed to a chalky affirmation. "Now repeat after me: *I do believe in fairies.*"

Grandmother shuffled across the room and opened an armoire. "Many moons ago I was a blushing bride with a robust husband who possessed your stature," she passed Sevlow a selection of men's clothing. "He is gone. I am in my twilight. Yet, the memories and the wardrobe remain."

"Once again, my gratitude." Sevlow slipped into the garments without removing the loin cover until last.

"My only grandchild has her choice of eligible noblemen in England, in King George III's entire empire, for that matter. Instead of a proper marriage and motherhood, my beautiful willful Margo prefers perilous adventures on the high seas." Grandmother breathed an exasperated sigh. "She's her father's daughter."

"The acorn didn't fall far from the maternal tree, either," Dragon observed. "Granny would have made a good pirate."

Seamus nudged Claudia. "Something about Margo reminds me of you."

"Yeah," TJ said. "Expensive tastes and a thing for werewolves."

"Your intruders will not depart without a clash." Sevlow returned the borrowed shawl. "Is there a safe place for you to hide?" He explored the paneling fascia.

"That scar-faced scoundrel who interrupted my dreams and fastened me to a chair will be returning, demanding the whereabouts of Margo's treasures."

"I hear footsteps," Claudia warned. "Someone is coming down the hall."

Grandmother heard it too. She scurried across the room and took hold of the wall sconce beside her poster bed. Her grip triggered a secret opening. She stepped into the clandestine room beyond the partition. "He will not find me twice, nor will he and his band of unsavory vandals locate Margo's riches." Grandmother pressed another lever inside the chamber. "Without delay," she ordered. "Use your werewolf powers to rid Seacliff Manor of these assailants." The concealed divider glided back into place. "When *Le Coq* arrives," her voice muffled by the divide. "Instruct Margo to see me at once."

The bedroom door swung open with gusto. A scar-faced man entered and went straight for the Chippendale chair. It was vacant.

"She is not here," Sevlow remarked.

The intruder pulled a knife from his waistband. "Reveal yourself." His brogue was thick but discernible. "Who speaks to me?" the Scotsman demanded.

"A guest of Mademoiselle Heroux," Sevlow neither retreated nor advanced. "Perhaps you know her as *le coq du troupeau.*"

The intruder struck a defensive stance and pointed the brandished blade in Sevlow's direction. "Let fall any weapons and drop to your knees," he ordered.

"Like that's going to happen," Seamus scoffed. "The Master *is* a weapon."

Resembling a sudden ray of light piercing the night, Sevlow flashed across the boudoir and disarmed the intruder—two knives and a musketoon—before the Scotsman knew he'd been fast frisked.

"Huh?" The scar-faced man examined himself. "Where are…?"

"These?" Sevlow stood by the open balcony doors holding the Scotsman's armaments. He twisted the confiscated knives into a tangle of metal and then cracked the musketoon in two. "Diplomacy turns out to be a more viable option."

"Who are you?" the intruder inquired for a second time, in this insistence contained less demand more bewilderment.

The Master did not reply.

The scar-faced man studied Sevlow for a moment. "You are the werewolf who sailors spoke of in Ponta Delgada."

"And you are the conspirator who passed a note in the lamplight," Sevlow replied.

"It appears we are acquainted in a roundabout way." The Scotsman had regained a portion of his haughty composure. "As diplomats we have a duty to state our intent." His words were tinged with mockery.

"He doesn't speak like a lowly pirate," Claudia observed.

"You think rich, educated thieves are a modern phenomenon?" TJ raised his brow. "There was *noblesse oblige* pilfering on the High Seas long before Washington TARP'd Wall Street."

"I seek a share of the Captain's spoils," the Scotsman confessed. "If she still lives, I am certain *le coq du troupeau* fancies the bounty that's been placed upon your head."

"Your servant failed in his mission to poison the captain," Sevlow replied.

"For shame." The Scotsman mocked with three clicks of the tongue. "I have divulged my objective," he continued. "Tell me, what does the werewolf seek?"

The Master did not respond.

"Ah, the devil's disciple has desires," the scar-faced man inferred with a cackle.

"Scotty has his teams confused." Seamus struck a defensive pose.

"Wealth? Power?" the intruder queried, stroking his red beard. "Perhaps the concealed *cache* of a certain wanton woman?"

"Wanton? How derogatory!" Claudia snapped. "The Captain's insulted because she commands a salvage ship? In my opinion, Margo is one heck of a businesswoman!"

"I once considered Mademoiselle Heroux for myself," the Scotsman declared. "As I told her, even a trollop becomes a Lady when she marries a Lord."

"I was right." TJ gloated. "Howdie-Doodie is an aristocrat."

"He's a jerk with the nerve to call Margo a trollop! I hope some *lady* gave him that scar." Claudia fumed. "Sevlow should beat the sexist pig a lesson."

"You mean *teach*?" Dragon corrected, from behind TJ's mass.

"Is that steam is coming out of Claudia's ears?" TJ traded places with Dragon. "Hide and watch her turn."

"He's not worth sprouting over." Seamus placed a comforting hold on Claudia's shoulder. "Sevlow definitely has feelings for Margo, so if he hasn't lost his temper, two hundred years ago, neither should we."

Claudia's body relaxed. "You're right."

TJ pointed to the vista beyond the balcony. "Look."

The Master's keen eye had moments before caught sight of *Le Coq* entering the secluded harbor below the cliffs. Her armed rowboats had already been launched. A convoy was flanking the manor. "There is yet opportunity to withdraw your men by road." He offered the intruders a *modus exodus*.

"Right before might." Dragon answered Seamus's quizzical expression. "There's still time for scar face to alter his fate. If he refuses, all bets are off."

"I am aware of the risks." The Scotsman lifted a bejeweled letter opener from Grandmother's desk and slid it into his waistband. "Gains require an initial investment, and the occasional loss."

"Spoken like a true gambler," Claudia remarked. "I wager he

loses all."

Seamus stepped onto the balcony with Sevlow to view the approaching vessels. The ruckus below rose to a crazed crescendo as the trespassers were stirred to action.

"Our next meeting will be our last." The Scotsman took advantage of the distance between himself and the werewolf and departed from whence he came.

"So be it." Sevlow edged down the edifice and entered the fray.

****

The white wolf in human form made his way unhindered through the intoxicated garden mob to his greenhouse destination, where two armed sentries stood guard at the dimly lit entryway. The Master approached the duo. Like a jazz pianist melding base and melody, Sevlow's swift hands orchestrated the demise of both men in unison. Two throats were crushed and two weapons destroyed before a cautionary word could be uttered or a caveat shot fired. He tossed the corpses aside. Their remains became instant dust, swept away by the night breezes. Sevlow unhooked a lone lantern that hung above the door and entered the glass building, unchallenged and unfazed.

"Damn!" TJ shook his head. His face bared equal parts amazement and disbelief. "Two hundred years, first time I've ever seen Sevlow kill while in human form."

Seamus was also awestruck. "Proves the Master can control his temper, but it didn't help those guys any."

"A dealer raking in the chips after the dice has rolled and the losing numbers called," Dragon said. "That's why I don't bet on anything except myself."

A stash of gold coins in clay containers had been placed along the wall inside greenhouse entryway. Sevlow examined the contents.

"Those two were guarding *Le Coq's* last bounty." Seamus inspected the Spanish doubloons. "If I'm not mistaken, treasures are transported from the ship, up the passage, to this greenhouse."

Sevlow uncovered a hidden trap in the center of the room. He pushed aside a camouflaging cluster of straw and made his way down a steep stairway that led through the excavated cliffs to the beach below.

The pack followed.

Sevlow used his lantern to light torches on either side of the rocky wall. The pathway became illuminated as far as the eye could see.

"Before meeting Sevlow, I thought secret rooms and concealed corridors only existed in the movies." Claudia examined the stone walls that lined their path. "It's amazing. St. Guinefort's and The Cock of the Flock appear to have been designed and constructed by the same craftsmen who built Seacliff Manor."

"Elves," TJ explained. "St. Guinefort's, the Cock of the Flock, the Egyptian pyramids, all built by craftsman elves, not to be confused with Irish gnomes, who prefer to work in taverns or ride race horses."

Claudia studied his expression. "You've got to be joking."

"Maybe I am and maybe I'm not." TJ's face was inscrutable.

"What about Beelzebubbles?" Seamus recalled his maiden mission. "I saw things with my own two eyes that I still can't believe."

"Hangout with Sevlow for a few centuries." TJ patted Seamus on the back. "Your reality will change in ways dreams and nightmares couldn't begin to invent."

"Centuries…" Claudia stopped in her tracks. "Is there an end to werewolf missions? Mighty Mouse moved on to an afterlife with Simon. What's our fate?"

"Sevlow never mentioned an end." Dragon shrugged. "Why ask?"

Seamus agreed. He didn't want to think about the possibility of an afterlife when there was so much undead life left to be lived. He was about to say as much when something else caught his attention. "Hear that?"

Muffled voices echoed from the base of the cavern. Whoever was speaking was also engaged in purposeful advancement. A harmony of rhythmic footsteps trekked in their direction.

The Master quickened his pace along the descending earthen path.

Seamus jogged ahead of the pack. He had a bird's eye view over Sevlow's shoulder when Margo nearly collided with the Master around the bend. She was carrying a lantern and pointing a pistol.

Sevlow grabbed the Captain's wrist, preventing her from firing before inquiring.

"It is you!" Margo cried. Her serious veneer gave way to cheer. However, the Captain was not alone. Vincent and two heavily armed guards were in tow. "Do not shoot!" *le coq du troupeau* commanded.

The Master relaxed his grip, but did not release.

"What relief you arrived unharmed." Margo's hair was windswept and wild, her clothes damp and clingy from a wade through the surf. "How is…"

"Your grandmother is uninjured and secure in her secret chamber." Sevlow held her gaze. "She wishes to see her granddaughter."

"My utmost gratitude," Margo replied.

There was gunfire in the distance.

"This matter is far from over." The Master released her, his focus returning to the mission. "Is it possible to reach the hidden quarters without crossing the intruders?"

"Yes. There is another secret entry." Margo seemed puzzled. "Why?"

"Go there. I will find you when this is over."

"No." Margo looked to her group for confirmation. "We will help rid Seacliff Manor of these bandits." Her men appeared eager, ready, and able. "My teams are making their way up the cliffs as we speak."

More shots rang out. Margo's men awaited her command. She hesitated.

"Margo realizes a werewolf doesn't need mortal help," Claudia said. "If Sevlow knows she's safe he can work without worrying about her safety."

Seamus smiled at Claudia. "Sound familiar?"

Margo acquiesced. "I will put Grandmother's mind at ease."

"Good." Sevlow turned his attention to Vincent and the guards. "Please accompany the Captain to the hidden quarters."

It was time for a change.

✳✳✳✳✳✳✳✳✳✳✳✳✳✳✳✳

The white werewolf retraced his route back to the recently ransacked greenhouse. It was unoccupied. Sevlow prowled unnoticed into the garden where an inebriated horde of treasure-hungry hoodlums was in fisticuffs over the gold doubloons. Like a bowling ball on a slick alley, the powerhouse white werewolf snowplowed through the setting, banging and toppling the headpin and nine others nearby, a perfect splasher. The lupus finished his turn with a graceful follow-through launch that propelled his bulk atop the marble tool shed. He howled. His canine call resonating like a strike in the pit. As if on reset, the tumbled ten returned to their feet and hooked through the gutter, into the lane, and escaped Seacliff Manor before a new game could begin.

"I figure there about for times as many men still on the grounds," Seamus noted. "Including the Scotsman."

Sevlow made his way unchallenged towards the house, his mere presence prompting terrified trespassers to abandoned their positions and retreat.

"Werewolf news from Ponta Delgada travels fast," Seamus remarked.

"Or their heads aren't in the game." TJ pretended to dribble and shoot.

"Well the playing field is about to change." Dragon pointed to an advancing crowd of *Le Coq's* finest. "Queequeg is leading the charge."

Claudia took a quick count. "There seems to be an equal number of men from each side."

"Not for long," Seamus replied. "The house party has moved outside."

Rowdy reinforcements spilled from the manor into the night, renewing the retreating intruders' convictions. Margo's men arrived on the scene, trading shots and blows with the trespassers. Punches were thrown, blades swung, and pistols fired. Although outnumbered, *Le Coq's* crew had a sober advantage.

Sevlow made fast ferocious work of any man foolish enough to cross his werewolf path. It appeared the battle would be short-lived until a single warning shot aimed at a plate glass window drew the combatants' attention to a CRASH on the balcony above.

"Werewolf!" the Scotsman yelled from his perch. "The contest has ended!" A hooded minion dragged *le coq du troupeau* unceremoniously from the boudoir and thrust her against the balcony rail. "This king has captured your Queen," the scar-faced buccaneer announced. Margo's hands were bound behind her back, blood dripped from her nose and mouth. The Scotsman clutched the captain from behind, removed the bejeweled letter opener from his waistband, and placed it against her throat. "Devil hound, call off your men or she takes her last breath!"

"I predict death for carrot-top," TJ growled, fists tightened.

"What I'd give to be here with Sevlow in the flesh." Seamus felt the hairs on his neck itching to sprout.

"Me too." Ire was etched across Claudia's brow.

No sooner had Seamus wondered *vis-à-vis* the whereabouts of Vincent and *Le Coq's* guards than they too appeared on the terrace, battered and bound, in the custody of three grinning thieves.

The Scotsman nodded to the two men on his right. At his command the throats of Margo's guards were slashed and their bodies tossed cranium-first from the second-story gallery. Both skulls split and splattered like giant tomatoes against the cobble walkway below. Margo's horrified cry echoed through the night.

The embattled opponents stood transfixed, watching the gruesome events unfold.

Sevlow advanced, eyes simmering, teeth bared, hackles raised.

"Halt!" the Scotsman commanded. He pressed his left hand against Margo's breast and the tip of his left-hand weapon into the flesh beneath her chin. A trickle of blood oozed from a fresh puncture wound.

As if the moves had been choreographed, the Captain propelled her head back against the Scotsman's nose at the same moment Sevlow commenced his airborne offensive from below.

The crushing blow stung the scar-faced man. He staggered to the side, releasing Margo, but not dropping the weapon.

The Captain attempted to flee.

The Scotsman yanked her backwards by the hair. She tumbled onto the tile. "Prepare to die, whore!" He raised his blade.

The guard holding Vincent scuttled out of Margo's fall zone, unbalanced enough for his captive to disengage and propel himself like a human shield between the dagger and the Captain. Vincent's carotid artery took the hit and erupted, a scarlet geyser.

The Scotsman withdrew the weapon from its unintended victim and aimed it at the Captain for a second time. Before metal could connect with Margo's flesh, a pair of razor-sharp incisors severed the hand that held the blade.

The white werewolf whipped his tail and knocked the advancing guards off their feet. Unhindered, he slammed the Scotsman against Grandmother's open boudoir door. The subsequent lupus attack was fast and ferocious. Sevlow showed no mercy as he dismembered his human prey. In an instant the kill was over. Bloody bits littered the balcony. The Master stood on his hindquarters above the remains. His muzzle and coat caked with carnage.

The Captain cut her bound wrists free with the recovered letter opener.

"He's not through," Seamus observed. Sevlow's eyes had changed color, from ice blue to tempest grey.

The werewolf howled at a moon that did not shine. A stormy

illusion swept across the combatants. Skies in their minds flashed violent lightning and rumbled with angry thunder while virtual showers and winds caused hides to prickle and bodies to shiver. Men ran for cover that could not be found.

Margo, however, seemed impervious to the elements as she wept and cradled a dying comrade in her arms. "You saved my life." She pressed a makeshift dressing against Vincent's gaping wound.

Sevlow trotted over to the Captain and sniffed the bloodied hero. He nudged Margo's arm with his snout, as if asking to inspect the injury.

"I cannot move the bandage." Margo's voice faltered. "He has already lost a perilous amount of blood." The Captain's teary eyes pleaded with the werewolf. "If you have the ability to restore life, I beg that you save him."

Sevlow seemed to be contemplating the situation. His canine ears were erect, his furry head tilted to one side.

"Please…" Margo sobbed. "Vincent does not deserve to die. His heart is pure."

Seamus knew she'd uttered the magic words.

The Master crouched before Vincent.

As if obeying an instruction that was not spoken, Margo relinquished her ally to Sevlow and turned away, shielding her eyes from the ensuing scene.

Before Vincent's expiring heart could pound its last beat, the white werewolf tore through flesh and bones and infused his palpitating muscle with serum of the undead.

"Long live the old butler!" TJ proclaimed.

Sevlow transported the unconscious transitioning Vincent into

Grandmother's room and placed him atop the bed.

"Vincent will soon be one of us." Claudia followed them into the *boudoirs*. "Is he still alive, in our time?"

Neither TJ nor Dragon knew or had ever heard of, before this day, the man who'd saved Margo's life.

The situation reminded Seamus of his own turning. "I was kept in the dark too."

"The Master does not tell his left hand what his right hand is doing," Dragon replied. "Secrecy is the element of all goodness."

Sevlow returned to the balcony in human form, wearing another borrowed outfit. "Vincent will awaken a werewolf. It was the only way."

"How do I repay you for saving my family?" Margo threw her arms around Sevlow. "Name your bounty."

"Meeting *le coq du troupeau* has been reward enough." The Master removed a handkerchief from his pocket and wiped a *mélange* of blood, sweat, and tears from Margo's relieved and weary face. "The seas will be calmer with Vincent as guard dog." Sevlow released himself from the Captain's embrace, his visage once again enigmatic. "I bid *adieu*." He bowed to her before making his exit.

"*Adieu*?" Margo was propelled into action. She chased the werewolf and took hold of his arm. "Stay with me!"

It was clear from Sevlow's expression that the Captain's emphatic request both pained and delighted him. He paused to observe her once more before responding. "You are safe," he said at last. "My mission has ended."

"No, you are wrong!" Margo blocked his path. "It has just begun." Without warning or invitation she pressed her lips against his and stole their first kiss. It was brief and expressive, like an exclamation point. She answered Sevlow's obvious astonishment with more defiance. "Never leave. I am in love with you."

A fairytale enchantment with an antidote, Margo's kiss and declaration released the werewolf from his prim and proper protocol. Sevlow returned the Captain's affections with a supernatural fervor that spread like wild fire until it reached the their core. "I bond for life," Sevlow warned amid kisses.

"Then stay, forever." Margo grasped his flaxen hair.

Sevlow moaned. "My love is eternal. No death do us part."

"So be it."

The Master bent down on one knee. "Margo Heroux, will you marry me?"

"Yes!" Margo cried without hesitation.

The werewolf stood and removed his ring. "These three stones represent life, death, and eternity. Let the trio also act as a stop clock. I beseech Father Time to bestow upon you the same concession I have been given, to remain young." Sevlow placed the jeweled werewolf head on Margo's wedding finger. "Through the gods' power invested in me, I now pronounce us husband and wife." Sevlow kissed his bride.

As if to sanctify and celebrate the blessed bond, the heavens exploded with celestial fireworks. Lightning flashed, thunder boomed, and the sudden shower of shooting stars and falling rain hallowed the union, like holy water on the brow of a babe.

"Who knew werewolves could perform their own marriage ceremonies?" Seamus followed his question with a thought. *But can they break the bond too?*

"These two love birds move even faster than Claudia and

Seamus," TJ remarked.

A round of cheers and applause, led by Margo's merry men, erupted in the garden below. The newly weds waved to the crowd as lightning stuck, igniting a tree beside the balcony. The spruce became a towering candelabra drenched in blazing flames. Mother Nature's celebratory gift. And with that, the moment and the memory were over.

Chapter 8

LET IT BE

After dialing 9-1-1, Bella scurried and sputtered around the kitchen like a wind-up mouse with a defective key. "Where's the darn First-Aid kit?" she cried aloud while rummaging through crammed cabinets and untidy utility drawers.

Lyman remained horizontal and unresponsive on the olive green linoleum beneath the shut, locked closed-curtain window.

Bella took a break from her senior life-saving search and pressed an ear against Lyman's chest. There was breathing and beating. She shook, slapped, and sprinkled him with water. "Wake up you old poop! You're scaring me!" The reporter did not rouse. She sat beside him cross-legged. "Open your eyes!" Bella stroked his bristly cheek and rocked herself back and forth. "Where is that ambulance?" She checked her watch. "What would nurse Cherry Ames do?"

Necessity is the Mama Stella of invention.

A sudden idea removed the worry from Bella's face and replaced it with resolve. She righted herself and gathered supplies from around the kitchen—refrigerator crisper, dining tabletop, under-sink cupboard. Bella wrapped a peeled clove of garlic in a torn napkin and dipped it into ammonia. She placed the soggy swathed bulb up Lyman's left nostril, far enough that only the frayed paper ends were nose exposed. "One Mississippi, two Mississippi, three Mississippi…"

A ready piece of pumpernickel in a pop-up toaster, the prone patient returned to consciousness in the upright position.

"You're back!" Clarabella Stella showered Lyman with celebratory kisses, set to the tune of an approaching ambulance siren.

Sergeant Gaffney removed his policeman's cap and knuckle-tapped twice on the open hospital room door before entering. He was carrying a manila envelope labeled *OR*.

"Thanks for getting here so quickly," Lyman said from his adjustable bed, flanked by an assortment of shiny blinking beeping equipment: heart monitor, oxygen tank, pulse oximeter, and O2 saturation monitor.

Bella let go of Lyman's hand and snatched the envelope from Sergeant Gaffney's grip. "OR? He doesn't need an OR." She removed a paper-clipped report from its cover. "The doctor said he had an acute bout of panic, not another heart attack." Mama Stella passed the documents to Lyman. "I can't read this tiny print without my glasses."

"OR stands for Oleg Roosky, not operating room." Lyman reviewed the pages. "After nearly thirty years, he was freed today?"

"Tried leaving you a message this morning when I read the release report. Sorry we didn't connect." The Sarge shook his head. "Spoke to the warden after Mrs. Stella called. Seems Roosky was a model inmate, worked in the prison library for most of his incarceration, never a problem."

"Oh, yeah, goodie-two-shoes my butt," Mama Stella growled like a bear protecting her cub. "Roosky pointed his gun fingers at Lyman and fired! He's a danger and a menace and I want him arrested. Immediately!"

Sergeant Gaffney did not reply. A statement that did not please Mama Stella could be hazardous to the herald's health.

The reporter addressed his mate. "There's no law against finger pointing."

"The cops can't do anything… again?" Bella glared at the Sarge, fists clenched.

Gaffney took a step backwards. "We can keep an eye on him," he assured. "Roosky has seven days to register a new home address with his parole officer. When he does, I'll task Patrolman Sullivan with monitoring Oleg's activity."

"Taking Sullivan off park patrol?" The reporter inquired, brow raised.

"Not while I'm in charge," Sergeant Gaffney assured. "Seamus doesn't sleep." The Sarge caught himself. "I mean, doesn't sleep much. Keeping tabs on Roosky will give him something productive to do with his free time."

Mama Stella flashed a frustrated frown.

"Until the Russian commits a crime," the Sarge continued with a self-protective air of authority. "I have no choice but to let it be. "

"Tell Sullivan to walk his big black dog on Roosky's block," Bella growled. "No one pays attention to dogs or their owners. Unless one of them craps on your lawn."

Ten days of memories crammed into as many minutes had given the gang supernatural jet-lag. For the first time in Seamus's sleepless undead life he craved a power nap. The only obstacle preventing him from avenging wakeful equilibrium was space—or lack of it. Claudia sought a siesta on the broken bed. TJ and Dragon slumbered on the sofa, and even Sevlow dozed in the tattered swivel chair. Seamus's eyelids were falling hard. He did a down dog on the dirty throw rug and commenced forty winks.

Margo hung up the phone, sighed, and conjured a smile as she composed herself with a chore—unpacking the Jean & Poluka foods from their recycled brown boxes. "I bought all of your favorites," Margo stated with cheery *joie de vivre*. "Fresh bread, grilled basil chicken over roasted potatoes, garlic green beans, and a romaine salad with bacon Roquefort dressing." She placed two of the three rectangular cardboard containers into the microwave. "Three minutes on HIGH to reheat."

"Whom were you whispering to on the telephone?" Jacques shoved his newly muscular arms into trench coat sleeves that now barely fit. "I heard you mention me and I want to know the reason."

Margo ignored his query. "Wash your hands." She gathered china, crystal, and linens from the kitchenette cabinet. "Our first home cooked meal together in New City."

"It isn't our home," Jacques replied. "And you don't cook."

"Then let's pretend." Margo set the table.

Jacques glowered at his mother. "I want to go out."

"First, dine with me." The microwave dinged. Margo removed the steamy containers from the oven and spooned their contents into a crystal serving dishes. She portioned the salad into two bowls and then sliced the baguette and tucked it into a breadbasket. "Wish I had some fresh flowers for a centerpiece."

Jacques pulled off his ill-fitting coat and threw it onto the floor. "I'm not hungry!" He plopped himself into a dining chair. "I prefer to go to the park."

"If you eat, I'll join you for a park outing."

Jacques picked on a piece of bread without removing it from the basket. "You called Vincent. Am I correct?"

"I did." Margo helped herself to petite portion of poultry. "You are keen to remain in New City. Therefore, our stay at the Piazza may extend longer than expected." She placed a crisp white linen napkin on her lap. "Having Vincent around will make our temporary quarters feel more Seacliff Manor, and less hotel suite."

"Since when does it matter what I want to do, Mother?" Jacques remarked with middling disdain. "Despite my requests, we have not engaged in any joyful activities for ages. Everything we do revolves around your search for serum."

"It is my duty."

"This new reserve of innocent and pure werewolf bloods will sustain me for quite some time." He bent forward into Margo's personal space. "But I do not believe that is the reason you have agreed to postpone our return home and summoned our servant."

She did not meet his aggressive glare.

Jacques leaned back in his chair. "Mother has been quite the nervous little school girl since arriving in New City." He picked up his butter knife. "Did stabbing Sevlow send your heart a flutter?" He observed her reaction.

Margo silence divulged nothing.

"Or could my father be the catalyst behind your dashing about in the dark?" Jacques bent the silver blade. "Does he reside in New City too? Or perhaps you have lied to me all these years—perhaps your husband and *mon père* are one in the same?"

"Your father fascination has become tiresome. Must we have this conversation?"

"Tell me!" The man-child bolted upright from his chair. "Who is my father?"

"Jacques," Margo replied with calm repose. "Your food is getting cold." The Captain pointed to her son's chair. "Sit down and eat."

Jacques threw himself onto his seat with the unsettled bearing of a jellyfish.

"Feet flat on the floor, spine straight, napkin on your lap," Margo instructed. "Posture and manners matter. I did not raise you in a barn."

Jacques acquiesced. "Happy?"

"Yes," she continued. "I have told you many times what I wish to share about your father." Margo reached for the green beans.

"Humor me again, Mother."

As if rehearsed, Margo repeated her lines. "Your father is a brave and honorable man. I am indebted to him for my life and yours. As such, I will always be grateful."

"Your verb tense implies much mystery. He *is*... My father lives for centuries. Clearly, he must also be a like us, monstrous mutants with a colorful past. Yet my sire and I are not acquainted and I have been told virtually nothing about him." Jacques sloppily served himself a hearty portion of dinner. "Why did he abandon us? Did you renounce your love for him? You can be a cold one..."

"Love was never an issue between your father and me."

"How ambiguous, Mother."

"And I did not say he was a deserter," Margo corrected. "It was my choice to raise you as I saw fit." She stared at her son for a long moment. Her expression softened. "For better and for worse, I am your architect."

"You loathe me." There was melancholy in Jacques' tone.

"No." Margo shook her head. "I love you." She inhaled a balancing breath. "However, I sometimes loathe myself for being vulnerable, for waging war with the only father we need trouble ourselves with—Father Time. Because I recognize, in the end, he will be victorious, at your expense, and mine."

Neither of them spoke during the remainder of the meal.

Margo broke the tense silence when she rose to clear dishes. "I will accompany you to Midtown Gardens, if you still wish to go."

"I don't require any favors." Jacques' surly sardonic mood had returned. He headed for the door. "I'll call my father and ask him to accompany me to the park." Jacques picked the hotel phone receiver and pretended to check his pockets for a missing item. "Oh, right, forgot, I don't have daddy's number… or his name."

Margo dropped a plate into the kitchenette sink with emphasis.

The resulting CRASH caught Jacques' immediate attention.

"Let it be," Margo warned via deliberate whisper. "Please, let it be…"

Jacques retrieved his overcoat from the floor and stormed out of the suite.

Seamus returned from the recharge zone rested and revived.

Claudia sat up on the bed. "Oh, my goodness," she yawned. "What happened?"

"Ask Stephen Hawking." Dragon entered the room. "Black holes and quantum physics might explain our recent journey into Sevlow's history."

"Man, I needed that nap!" TJ followed behind Dragon, clothes rumbled, arms stretched. "Memory space-time-warps are killer."

"Quantum physics—just gave me an idea," Claudia replied. "Why don't you three enroll in college with me?"

"Who wakes up from an awesome adventure and thinks about school?" TJ rummaged through a messy dresser drawer. "A sane person thinks about food." He found an unopened box of cookies. "Score!"

"You're going away to college?" Seamus asked. "It's the first time you've mentioned school."

"I received early admissions to Columbus University," Claudia replied. "Don't worry. I'm not going *away* to school. C.U. is uptown—I'll be a commuter."

Seamus breathed a sigh of relief.

"Well, Seamus, Dragon, TJ?" Claudia fished for a volunteer. "Summer session begins in a few weeks. You don't have to matriculate."

"Starting soon, no matriculation necessary." TJ popped a cookie into his mouth." Not a very convincing sales slogan."

Claudia shook her head. "It wasn't a sales slogan"

"True that." TJ brushed a patch of crumbs from his shirt. "Anyone see Sevlow? He was here when we zoned."

"Unlike some people, Sevlow has a busy schedule." Claudia's attention fixed on TJ. "He'll return to the wolf den when he's ready to discuss what we saw."

Seamus hadn't thought about it before—Sevlow on a schedule. The Master behaved like a man with a plan, or at very least a man with orders. *Can Sevlow sense what has to be done?* Seamus wondered. *Or is there someone else passing along information and giving orders?*

"So, what types of classes are you three interested in taking?"

Claudia continued. "History? Philosophy? Law?"

"Nothing, none, *nada*," TJ replied. "Everything I need to know I learn from TV." He picked-up an old remote off the floor and pointed it at Claudia. "My television has more channels than Columbus University has buildings and more programs than C.U. has classes. No matriculation necessary."

"Besides, TJ and I don't have papers," Dragon reminded. "We've been undead and under the radar a for very long time."

"Forgot about that." Claudia thought for a moment. "It's impossible to enroll in school without papers. You two probably don't have a driver's license, birth certificate, social security card, or a passport."

"Correct. Mark 'E', none of the above," TJ said.

Claudia turned to Seamus. "But you have documents."

"The police department pays for continuing education." Seamus had considered a return to school. "I've been thinking about taking a class or two." He shrugged. "Not as though I sleep during the day."

"Oh goodie!" Claudia clapped. "This will be fun!"

"Oh goodie," TJ mocked. "We can buy matching lunch boxes!"

Sevlow entered the room. He was dressed in his priestly garb.

"Sir!" Claudia exclaimed. "Your memory was incredible! Very romantic!"

"I'm pleased you found it to be entertaining and informative," Sevlow said. "My intent was to provide another view of Margo."

"An amazing woman," Claudia gushed. "We learned so much, about her, about politics on the high seas, about the significance of names—the Cock of the Flock. Who knew it was Margo's moniker? I have so many questions!"

TJ nudged Seamus. "Look what you have to look forward to in college. *Oh, teacher, teacher, pick me! I have all the answers!*"

"I heard that, TJ" Claudia said. "I am not a brown nose."

"You said it, not me." TJ stepped behind Seamus.

Dragon addressed Sevlow. "Sir, what should we do? Margo is obviously no longer the woman you showed us in your memory—I mean, she stabbed you in the heart." He looked at his friends. "We could at very least find out where she is staying in New City, and keep an eye on her."

They nodded in agreement.

"I appreciate your concern," Sevlow replied. "And I have a request."

The pack was all ears.

"Margo's return to New City is a personal matter," the Master said. "Unless I request assistance, let it be."

"Of course," Claudia replied, speaking for the three brutes. "Of course we'll respect your privacy."

TJ, Dragon, and Seamus concurred with nods and grumbles.

"Thank you." Sevlow glanced at Seamus. "Sergeant Gaffney called about perhaps employing some of your werewolf talents during off hours. He wishes to discuss the matter with you before your shift."

Seamus checked his watch. "Park patrol, totally lost track of time!" He gave Claudia a quick peck on the cheek and sprinted out of the wolf den.

****

Seamus sat in his radio car, interior light on, munching donuts and leafing through a packet of police homework—photocopied ancient newspaper articles, fugitive files, and arrest reports. Sgt. Gaffney had been adamant that Seamus review the information—*Oleg Roosky has the potential to wreck havoc on New City!*

Seamus agreed with Sarge's words of warning. From a lawman's point-of-view, Oleg Roosky's priors were extensive and noteworthy. There weren't many crimes the rogue Russian hadn't attempted or mastered. Add to the rap sheet, Roosky's drive-by "shooting" that very afternoon. *Gotta determine why he's after Newlin.* Seamus's work plate was suddenly full. *There goes taking classes with Claudia this semester. Instead, I have to play Cold War spy.* In truth, Seamus preferred 007 to college freshman.

Seamus set the Roosky report on top of the empty Krinkle Kreme box and stared into the flickering streetlamp. He was soon and lulled into a secret agent fantasy, complete with *Mission Improbable* staccato-piano-merged-into-spirited-brass theme song: *Agent Sullivan in the midst of enemy grenade launch retaliation while dangling precariously from the rudder of a burning Apache helicopter...*

His mind movie reel was stalled by the sound of heated voices, one of them female French and familiar.

Seamus exited his patrol car and headed east, towards the disturbance.

"Your company was NOT requested!" shouted the man. "Return to the Piazza!"

Atop the ridge Seamus had an unobstructed view of the arguing couple. He focused his keen eyes on the woman. It was Margo, without her black cloak, but who was the middle-aged man? Seamus detected a distinct resemblance. *Margo's father? Older brother?* He recalled Sevlow's memory. *Margo became captain after her father's death. She was an only child.*

"Don't be angry with me." Margo jogged to keep up with Jacques's hurried gait. "Please, let's walk together and enjoy the night."

"Go away! Your pleading disgusts me."

Neither father nor brother, thought Seamus, but whoever it was had no reservations about disrespecting *le coq du troupeau*. Park patrol spy slipped behind a tree and continued to observe the noisy drama.

"Stop. We need to speak."

Jacques hastened his pace and plugged his ears. "La, la, la, I can't hear you."

"Enough of this boorish behavior!" Margo gave up her futile pursuit. "Vincent will be here tomorrow," she huffed. "He can deal with your childish antics." Margo threw her hands up in defeat and made a U-turn.

"Well, well…" Seamus said. "Vincent lives, and he's coming to New City."

Jacques looked over his shoulder. His game of cat and mouse came to an abrupt halt when he realized that the cat was going home, and the mouse would be alone. "Come back here!" he shouted. "Or I will stay out all night!"

"Suit yourself, Jacques," Margo replied. "But take heed—Midtown Gardens is crawling with werewolves and Sevlow's blood won't protect you from their fangs."

"MOTHER!" Jacques screamed.

Mother? Sevlow's blood? Seamus could not believe his supernatural ears. In the spirit of unattended construction sites and bicycle stunts, Seamus made a spontaneous decision to ignore the Master's "let it be" request. *Mission Improbable* secret agent Sullivan pulled a small shiny metal tube from his pocket and blew. It was time to call for reinforcements.

Chapter 9

NIGHT MOVES

The Peña's Tacoma penthouse kitchen was ablaze with late-night sounds and energetic activities. Spanish songs rocked the radio, boxed double-fudge cake mix remains clouded the white marble counter tops, and animated chitchat channeled between *los padres* and their undead dancing daughter.

"Listen, *Amor Para Mi*!" Claudia turned up the tune as she sashayed to the rhythm of horns and bongos. "Reminds me of your parties when Alex and I were kids." She recalled her recent journey into Sevlow's past with wistful envy. "Wish there was a way I could take a vacation into your memories of my childhood."

"*Vamos de vacaciones*," Salvador said above the din, as he floated on air with his wife, Paz. "*El sol, y brisas calentes.*"

"You two are going on a tropical vacation?" Claudia echoed in English, tapping a salsa step over to the oven to inspect the baking bundt. "I had no idea souls could travel on the other side, for pleasure, that is."

Paz nodded. "*¿Sí, por qué no?*"

Claudia shrugged her shoulders. "I don't know, why not." Her feet continued to keep time with the music as she rinsed a mixing bowl and eggbeaters and placed them in the dishwasher. "Just never thought about dead people vacationing."

"That is why it is called the afterlife," Salvador replied with a grin. "Life requires that we work—after life there is much time for play."

"Now that I'm a werewolf and you don't have to worry about

me and Alex." Claudia added dish soap to the machine. "After years of hovering, you two can finally relax and enjoy death."

Los padres gave each other one of those guilty-happy glances, like when junior heads off for a long weekend with grandma. Mom and dad *should* give the impression that they'll miss him, but he's in good hands, and they need some well-deserved carefree couple's time.

"Where do ghosts holiday?" In *Boo-tapest…* Get it?" Claudia laughed at her own silly joke. "Guess I've been hanging out with the brutes too long. Their humor is rubbing off on me." She pressed the dishwasher ON button. "Your travel destination?"

"Old Cuba." Salvador hugged his wife. "Señor Hemingway has invited us to join him on his boat, Pilar."

"¡*Mi autor predilecto*!" Paz gushed.

"One of my favorite authors, too," Claudia said. "How exciting!"

The oven timer dinged. Claudia removed a bunt pan and placed it a large wire cooling rack. She'd bring the dessert treat to Seamus after his shift. Claudia hung up her mitts. "How long will you be gone?"

"I'm not going anywhere." The reply came not from *los padres* but from Alex, who leaned against the kitchen doorframe, looking as worn-out and disheveled as his favorite blue and white checkered pajama bottoms, which he was wearing. "The Bombers will be in town all week." Alex yawned. "Six games in five days, including the Mayor's Trophy exhibition. I have got to get some sleep."

"Sorry!" Claudia felt a wrench of remorse. "I keep forgetting that it's the middle of the night." She dashed across kitchen and turned off the music. "I am having a post-full moon energy rush. I can't stop moving."

"Relax." Alex held up his hand. "I'm not angry, just tired, but I have to ask a favor." He rubbed his bloodshot eyes. "Do you mind taking your post-full moon night moves to the bullpen?"

"Wolf den." Claudia crinkled her nose. "That place is a filthy mess."

"Hire an undead maid. Redecorate. Whatever it takes. Whatever it costs. I don't care." Alex yawned again. "During the season I need undisturbed sleep."

Claudia was about to promise to be more considerate. Instead, she covered her ears doubled over in pain. Her eardrums felt as if an arrow had shot through them. "Oh my gosh!" she screamed.

Alex and *los padres* flew to her aid.

"Werewolf whistle!" Claudia cried.

A dozen hours had transformed Oleg's dim dusty butcher shop cellar hideout into an illuminated modern-day war room. Highlighted, annotated maps and charts of New City hung with purpose on large whiteboard easels. Two newly acquired computers with 32" LED screens glowed and purred as they retrieved archived *Chronicle* articles and OogleEarth satellite composites of potential target sites in and around New City. The rogue Russian sat in his monogrammed director's chair ping ponging between the duel monitors and scrolling through words and images.

An abandoned bread factory adjacent to Bomber Stadium became Oleg's particular point of interest. He double-clicked his wireless mouse and zoomed-in for a closer look. *Perfect proximity, veiled in plain view…*

A sleepy sidekick interrupted Roosky's contemplative

calculations.

"AHHHWWWOOOAAAA!" Wally's yawn yowl reverberated in the subterraneous concrete room like flatulence in a pair of tight pants.

A startled Oleg gripped the tech rodent and sent the satellite screen into a facsimile frenzy. The layering pages multiplied into computer eternity before freezing.

Wally attempted an assist and in the process slipped out of his slipper, became tangled in his nightshirt, lost his nightcap, and tripped across the surge-protector with plugged power chords, rendering himself prone and both computer screens black.

Roosky saw red. "You idiot!" he bellowed.

"Sorry, Boss," came the feeble reply. Wally sat up and rubbed his lower back. "I think I've crushed my coccyx."

"Darwin rejoices." Oleg stomped about, reattaching wires and cables.

"Don't you need any sleep?" Wally asked through another, less amplified, yawn. "It's been release from prison, harass a reporter, shop for electronics—go, go, go all day. You're the battery bunny." He stood up and brushed off his bedclothes. "I'm exhausted, but I'll stay awake if you need me."

"Not do favors." Roosky rebooted. The computers were humming again. Oleg returned to his seat and his cyber search. He opened a *Chronicle* article about the Mayor's upcoming Baseball Trophy match-up.

Wally peered over his boss's shoulder. "Bombers vs. Metros. Went last year. Had my picture taken with Fink's dog. Five dollars a pose, all proceeds went to the NCPCA."

"Goodie for you."

"Brought two ball caps, one for each team." Wally chuckled. "Changed'm out, depending on who was winning. We going to this year's game? I can get 2-for-1 seats through the Butcher's Union. Tickets come with discount coupons for any meat product served at the concessions: burgers, franks, barbeque chicken on a stick, deep fried turkey legs, empanadas, bratwurst, but not the crispy calamari rings. Seafood isn't considered meat by the union. Although, there was a time when—" His soliloquy was interrupted.

"Shut up. Go away to sleep," Oleg growled. "You stories give me big headache when I working. When I not working, little headache."

"Want me to get you an aspirin, Boss?"

Roosky didn't reply. He was once again transfixed on a bird's eye view of the Pasty Dough factory displayed upon his computer screen. Boarded windows and doors, zero graffiti, surrounding chain-link fence intact. "No vandals..." Oleg muttered.

"Maybe it's stale spaces causing the headaches. First, prison, and now spending so much time in a cellar. You should get some fresh air, take a walk in the park."

"Park stink like pigeons and dog crap." Oleg typed "Pasty Dough" into the *Chronicle* search engine on the adjacent computer screen. He scrolled through the headlines until he came to a ten-year-old article. Roosky right-clicked on the bold print.

Pasty Dough Factory Is Toast After Suspicious Fire

New City's historic Pasty Dough factory went up in flames on Sunday, around midnight. Firefighters suspect the inferno was not accidental. An empty gasoline can was found near

```
the    scene.    Longtime    night    watchman,    Carl
Chapatti,  died  in  the  blaze.  No  other  injuries
were   reported.   The   incident   is   still   under
investigation.
```

"I remember that fire," Wally remarked. "The city smelled of burned bread for a month. Bakery sales really took a hit."

Oleg appeared to be interested in Wally's recollection. "What else you know?"

"I know the Pasty Dough theme song." Wally launched into the tune. *"Pasty Dough, helps me grow, big and strong from head-to-toe, with eight key vitamins in bread as white as snow, this smart kid loves Pasty Dough!"*

Oleg groaned. "Know besides stupid ditty copied from *This Old Man.*"

"Building sat for a few years," Wally recalled. "Renovations started and stopped, and then the Bombers tried to buy the property, wanted to knock it down and put up another parking garage. Deal fell through because the factory owners have been in a heated battle with their insurance company since the fire. Word on the street is arsons were hired to torch the place. There's one other thing..." Wally tapped his chin and thought for a moment. "Oh, yeah, and the place is haunted by the night watchman."

"Put on real clothes," Oleg ordered. "You look like bedtime Scrooge McDuck."

The Polish butcher perked-up. "Working on some night moves?"

"Night moving, start moving!" Roosky hopped out of his chair. "Find toolbox, chain cutters, flashlights, and get car. Going to Pasty Dough factory for look round."

The pack sat on a hill above the great meadow in Midtown Gardens Park, eating chocolate bundt cake and watching Jacques scurry around in the moonlight like an aimless rat on caffeine, his unbuttoned trench coat a giant tail, swishing in the breeze.

"What's this guy's problem?" TJ mumbled, mouth full of dessert. "He ain't no kid, and he ain't right."

"Told you," Seamus said. "Jacques is afraid of his own shadow now, but he was pretty full of himself earlier." Seamus shook his head. "You should have heard him arguing with Captain Margo. They put the "D" in dysfunctional."

"Parents who are afraid to put their foot down have children who step on toes." Dragon pointed to his shoes. "The Captain needs to get herself a pair of steel-toe boots."

"So weird," Claudia remarked. "You think this balding middle-aged man is really Margo's son?" She observed Jacques beneath a lamppost. "There is definitely a family resemblance."

"Jacques called her *mother*." Seamus helped himself to another slice of cake. "She gave him Sevlow's blood. I think that's how he stays alive."

"I don't know what to think," Claudia pondered. "Maybe the blood is slowing Jacques's aging process. Except, Sevlow and Margo haven't been together in over two hundred years, and this is the first time she's come back to stab him in the heart."

"Jacques could be Sevlow's son," Dragon supposed with a shrug. "Might explain his decelerated aging with a once-every-two-hundred-year werewolf blood tune-up."

"This is what I think—" TJ belched. It echoed through the trees.

Jacques startled. He ducked behind a park bench and cocked his head, as if to discern where the sound came from.

"No way that guy is related to the Master." TJ pointed towards Jacques. "I don't know if werewolves make human babies, but I am sure they don't make chickens."

"Margo really should return to the park and escort Jacques back to the Piazza," Claudia said. "It's obvious he's afraid to walk anywhere alone in the dark."

Seamus donned a mischievous smile "Then let's make him run." He closed his eyes and imagined a lit match. In his mind's eye the fire brushed against Jacques's heel. At the moment of contact, the real Jacques yelled and began hopping up and down. Seamus laughed aloud. "Hot foot! I couldn't resist."

The floodgates opened. TJ and Dragon were party to the pranks. Rains raged, flames fried, and winds walloped Jacques's every move. There was nowhere to run, nowhere to hide, but the terrified man tried. He tripped across the meadow, cowered beneath a boulder, crawled crying through a tunnel, and finally dangled in defeat from a low-hanging tree branch, all the while calling for his mother and Vincent to save him from the *invisible monsters*.

"It's not funny anymore." Claudia built a protective wall of elemental earth around Jacques. "We shouldn't misuse our powers."

The brute trio enacted an immediate cease and desists.

Seamus had a passing pang of regret. He was thankful that Sevlow hadn't witnessed the sophomoric display of werewolf bullying. "Now what?"

"Bet Jacques goes home, tells his mommy, she calls Sevlow, and we all get in trouble." TJ predicted. "Oh, well, my gut still hurts from laughing so it was worth it."

Claudia addressed TJ and Dragon. "You guys never get in trouble."

"What about him?" TJ pointed at Seamus. "He started the weather bullying."

"The three of you!" Claudia scolded. "I've noticed that Sevlow allows you to learn your own life lessons, often the hard way, and live like slobs!"

Seamus shook his head. "I knew that one was coming."

"Three guesses and the first two don't count," TJ replied. "Princess Peña wants to redecorate the wolf den."

"Cleanliness is next to godliness." Dragon licked the cake plate.

Claudia wrinkled her nose in disgust. "The furniture is mismatched and broken, there's trash everywhere, and it smells worse than an unkempt kennel."

"We are hounds of the gods," TJ reminded. "Not housekeepers of the gods."

"Then let me clean and redecorate," Claudia pleaded. "I am sure you'd like to watch a huge screen TV while sitting on a big comfy leather sofa."

TJ raised an eyebrow. "Does the big leather sofa recline and have cup holders and a built-in channel changer?"

"Maybe." Claudia seemed to planning in her mind. "How about if the main room of the wolf den is transformed into a home theater and game room, complete with framed cinema posters, an arcade, candy concession, and an ice cream machine?"

"You got my vote!" TJ surveyed the other brutes "All in favor say *aye*."

A fourth *aye* joined the unanimous chorus.

"Sir?" Seamus noticed the Master standing beside them. "Didn't see you arrive." *How long had the Master been watching?*

"An impressive display of elements." The Master's expression neither revealed approval nor disapproval.

Seamus felt his face flush.

A miserable moan in the distance drew their attention. Jacques had given up the fight. His tangled coat was victorious—it held him a defeated tree-bound prisoner.

Sevlow addressed Seamus. "Officer Sullivan."

Officer Sullivan… For a brief moment Seamus's recalled his reckless adolescence at St. Guinefort's. Fr. Benedict never raised his voice when challenging one of Seamus's many antics. Instead, *Mr. Sullivan* was all the Father had to say to make Seamus hop to attention. Not much had changed over the years. "My job is to protect and serve!" Seamus adjusted his cap and utility belt. "Back to work." He jogged away from the pack towards the stranded trespasser. "I'll unhook Jacques and take him back to the Piazza."

Carl Chapatti checked his pocket timepiece. Five minutes until door security rounds, twenty minutes until the next series of window checks, and forty minutes until room-to-room inspection. White Light be darned, Carl still had an important job to do on Earth. Thanks to the night watchman's diligence and haunting skills, there had not been a safety violation or a break-in at the abandoned Pasty Dough factory for years. Actually, no major breach to speak of since that fateful night…

Carl still blamed himself for the explosion that ended his life and the operations of his beloved bread company. *If only I'd smelled the gasoline sooner. Darn my cold. Darn me for forgetting to bring an umbrella and galoshes to work the night before. Had I checked the weather report, I wouldn't have gotten drenched by icy rain on the way home from my shift and given myself a stuffy head and sniffles. Darn, darn, darn! Now the Bombers want to knock down the Pasty Dough factory and turn it into a parking garage. Over my dead body! Greedy rich Sternfenner!* Carl had always been a Metros fan, since the Daggers moved to Angel City.

The sound of tires on gravel interrupted Carl's routine lament and rant. The watchman listened. Two car doors slamming prompted some ghostly night moves, across the hall and through the exterior wall for a peek outside.

＊＊＊＊＊＊＊＊＊＊＊＊＊＊＊

"Maybe we should stay in the car." Wally remained close to the vehicle. "Or come back in daylight. The Bomber's sign is giving everything a creepy orange glow." An illuminated billboard on the side of the stadium advertised *GOOD SEATS STILL AVAILABLE FOR THE MAYOR'S TROPHY GAME.* "Vacant factories look better when the sun is shining. Let's come back tomorrow."

Carl hovered beside the jittery sidekick chauffeur. "These two are up to no good!" He floated through Wally to get a better look at Oleg.

"Ah!" Wally screamed. "I've been touched by the icy aura of a spirit!"

"Ghost is no such thing." Roosky popped the trunk and removed a toolbox. "Don't be scaredy goose." He handed Wally a lit flashlight and kept one for himself.

Wally shined his beam on the fence. "My *busia* talked to

ghosts."

"Every family have one lunatic grandparent." Oleg approached the access gate and severed the rusty padlock with his pliers. The old door swung open with a *creek*. Roosky stepped inside.

"Now wait a minute, buddy!" Carl shouted.

"You hear something?" Wally shadowed his boss. "It wasn't exactly a *boo*. It was more like a *buh*, or a *bah*."

"Bah humbug! I hear nothing but you too much talking." Oleg tromped through the spotlighted weed path that led to the factory's main entrance. The door was ajar. Roosky entered.

Wally and Carl followed.

A decade of dust, mold, and cobwebs covered the fire hose water-warped plaster remains of lobby. Once upon a time it had been in orange, yellow, and lime green zigzagged stripes to match the vibrantly visible Pasty Dough packaging, distinguishable from all other items in the grocery store bread aisle.

Wally wheezed and sneezed.

"*Gesundheit*," Carl said.

Wally wiped his nose on his sleeve. "Thanks."

"Shirt not willing participant," Oleg remarked, with a confused look of disgust. He shined his flashlight along the walls and down the corridor that ended at a double-door passage to what remained of the massive industrial kitchen. "But maybe ask pants escort you to next room."

Wally took the lead. He aimed his beam and pushed through the double doors into a gymnasium-sized room filled with rusted-pitted-charred kneaders, mixers, conveyors, cooling racks, and ovens. After a decade, the room still smelled eerily of burned bread. The sidekick spotlighted what looked like a giant metal shoebox with an opening at one end. "Wonder how many loaves were baked a day?"

"Ten-thousand loaves a day, six days a week," Carl replied, floating with pride from appliance to appliance. "Sixty-thousand loaves of delicious Pasty Dough white bread made here in this room, Monday through Saturday. On the seventh day, machines and employees rested. Everyone except me." His expression turned somber. "I died here on a Sunday." Carl sighed. "The factory did too…"

"What day is it?" Wally shook his head as if to dislodge a stray thought.

"It today." Oleg pulled a lever on the conveyor. It clicked and manually moved the melted belt forward. A light bulb going off in Roosky's head lit up his eyes. "No electricity necessary."

"You got an idea, Boss?" Wally did a happy hop. "What are you thinking?"

"Thinking comeback caper need be special." Oleg rubbed his chin.

"What about ComicSci?" the sidekick asked. "You've been planning that kidnapping caper for ages. Ever since you discovered the-reporter-who-shall-not-be-named was a Sci-Fi fanatic."

"Pasty Dough not banquet, it entrée."

Wally appeared confused.

Roosky illuminated. "We need some kind exciting splash to get wet feet after long absence from crime activity."

"So the Pasty Dough caper is practice? Wally concluded. "It should look like an accident? No Roosky signature?"

"Precisely." Oleg nodded. "Want Bombers suffer with mysterious mishap to cause much publicity. Only you, me, and walls know it not mistake what happen."

"They want to secretly terrorize the Bombers?" Carl's interest was piqued. "Why didn't I think of that?" The giddy ghost flew around in circles pondering a possible plan. "I could scare all the fans away… No, that wouldn't work…Too many… Maybe boo the bullpen… How about haunt the toilets?"

"What about the toilets?" Wally surprised himself with the blurted question.

"What about toilets?" Oleg asked. "You have smart idea?"

"Exploding commodes!" Carl yelled, concocting a plan on the fly. "The sewers between Pasty Dough and Bomber's Stadium connect and empty into the main city line." He flew beside Wally and spoke into his ear. "You seem to have a slight case of sixth-sense," the ghost said. "So hear this—there are more than a hundred tons of flour in the basement, all stacked in sacks. Enough white powder to clog the adjoining sewer pipe and turn the Mayor's Trophy Game seventh-inning stretch into a seventh-inning stench!" Carl motioned with his hand. "Come with me."

"I have an idea." Wally took Oleg by the arm and led him through the colossal kitchen towards the basement stairs. "What if we caused toilet flushes to move in reverse on the night of the Mayor's Trophy Game? Nothing's been touched in this place since the fire. There's tons of unused flour. We could use it to clog the sewers and send wee-wee water and feces flying during the seventh-inning stench!"

"Incredible smart idea!" Rooskie raved. "So happy I not fire you!"

Chapter 10

I'LL TAKE YOU THERE

Night faded fast as the new morning made an ardent approach. Birds roused in their roosts and squirrels scurried from their nests to greet the day. The dangler's view of nature's conversion, however, was obstructed by his inverted trench coat.

"Please, don't hurt me," Jacques pleaded upon hearing approaching steps.

"Don't worry. I'm a police officer." Seamus lifted Jacques from the tree limb and set him feet-first on the dewy grass. He got a good glimpse at Jacques. The mother-son resemblance was striking, but Seamus saw no sign of Sevlow's angular features in the fretting frowning face before him.

Jacques's cheeks were blood-rush red and his hair punk vertical following the extended period of upside-down hang time. "My utmost gratitude." He brushed-off his Burberry. "I feared the werewolves had come to devour me."

"Werewolves?" Seamus replied. "There's no such thing." He watched for Jacques's reaction and thanked his lucky stars that Lyman Newlin was safely across town in a hospital bed. The reporter would have had a question field day with Jacques.

"Yes, certainly there are," Jacques continued in earnest. "A pack of werewolves roam Midtown Gardens at night." He looked over his shoulder. "And not only when the moon is full."

"If there is such a thing as werewolves, maybe they don't like being talked about," Seamus cautioned. "Canines have excellent hearing." As if on cue, there was a howl in the distance. Seamus recognized it as TJ's.

"Draw your weapon!" Jacques dashed behind the officer. "Secure the entry gates!" he cried. "The lupus beasts are on the assault!"

"Midtown Gardens is closed and nothing's going to attack." Seamus suppressed a chuckle with a voice of authority. "Let's go."

"Must we?" Jacques's body trembled. His feet seemed cemented to the sidewalk.

Seamus's werewolf ears could hear man-child's heart racing with fear. The patrolman opted for a more soothing tone. "Hey, don't worry. I'll give you a lift out of the park. My shift's almost over."

The terrified intruder relaxed a bit and stepped out from behind Seamus. "That would be brilliant," he sighed. "I'm lacquered."

"Don't sound as if you're from around here." Seamus delicately fished for information. "Where you visiting from?"

"Truro, England. My home is called Seacliff Manor," Jacques replied without hesitation, like a chatty unaware child sharing family secrets with an inquisitive stranger. "Mother and I came to New City because I've been ill. She knew of someone who could supply a more potent serum to counter my condition."

Seamus chose not to probe the man-child any further. Jacques had already revealed plenty. "Interesting," was the officer's easy reply as he led Jacques to the car.

Jacques nodded and continued. "We are temporarily residing at a hotel. Our butler Vincent is in transit. Mother and I do not fare well together without his assistance."

Margo and Jacques's quarreling wasn't pretty, that's for sure. Seamus liked to imagine that he would have been a loving and protective son. *Another time…*

"How much further?" Jacques rubbed his legs as they hiked up a ridge.

"About a hundred yards." Seamus scoped the area. There was no sign of the pack. They were probably back at the wolf den by now, Claudia planning her redecorating extravaganza. Seamus teased her about it, but in truth he looked forward to having a comfortable place to hangout with his friends. Not that Seamus planned to give up private time at his island bungalow. Maybe he'd ask Claudia to redecorate that as well. Summer was around the corner. The beach and water outside of his front door were devoid of crowds and full of promise—surfing, sailing, and maybe some starlight romance… Officer Sullivan unlocked the vehicle. "Hop in."

"You have a distinct musky body odor." Jacques slid into the radio car. "Which reminds me of my butler, Vincent."

"That so?" Seamus closed the rear passenger door and ruminated a reply. *Of course we both smell like wet dogs—we're both made werewolves.*

Jacques rolled down the rear passenger window. "Is it possible for you to drive me all the way to the Piazza Hotel?"

"Sure." Seamus took his seat behind the steering wheel. "I'll take you there."

Lyman's eyes opened in a room that was not his own. He had to remember for a moment where he was, *stiff pillow, attached wires, beeping machines… I'm in New City General Hospital.* With any luck, Oleg Roosky wouldn't pursue him here. Maybe it was time to think about retirement? He could write a novel or travel abroad, and maybe settle down with a good woman. A wheezy snort diverted Lyman's attention away from his contemplation and focused it on his overnight hospital room guest.

Mama Stella was asleep, bundled in her black velour jogging suit, curled up in the brown vinyl chair and coordinating ottoman she'd disinfected with hand sanitizer and draped in sheets the evening before. With each noisy breath Bella's pudgy feet jerked and her saggy jowls billowed like the boom and mainsail of a sloop. All the while her tussled hair clung to the static-y polyester bolster as if it were sun-dried seaweed strewn upon the little boat's deck.

The reporter's heart fluttered. He'd fallen overboard in love. The object of his desires opened her eyes. "Good morning," Lyman murmured. "Hope you slept well."

Bella replied with a stretch and a yawn.

"If you want to snuggle in beside me we can watch the sunrise together." Lyman squeezed over and patted the open bed space. "Come on," he cajoled. "The nurse won't be in for another hour. Elderly fat men with chest pain scares aren't at the top of their rounds priority list."

Mama Stella. hesitated.

"It's safe. We're adults. Promise, my bedpan is empty."

Bella chuckled. She took hold of the bedrail and hoisted herself onto the mattress beside him, wedging into his embrace and placing her head on his chest.

Lyman kissed her cheek. "You make me happy."

"I'm still mourning Mickey." Bella's tone was somber, but peaceful. "But for the first time in years I got dreams and desires." She squeezed his hand. "Thank you."

"Thank *you*," came the heartfelt reply. "Out of respect for

Mickey, I won't ask you to make any commitments until you're ready." Lyman wished he could pop the question at that very moment. "Hypothetically, let's just say we did marry someday, where would you like to go for our honeymoon?"

Bella didn't dither with her response. "*Tuoro sul Trasimeno*, my parents' birthplace in Italy. I keep an updated passport, in case I get a chance to visit before I die."

"Well then, wedding or no wedding, wish granted. I'll take you there." Lyman sealed the deal with a kiss.

Claudia commenced demo, design, and decorating before the brutes could change their minds about sprucing up the disastrous wolf den. An artist in motion, she drew sketches and jotted notes while measuring, examining, and contemplating the size and layout of the oversized ramshackle room. *Stone floor and walls. I could go ultra modern with chrome and black leather, or medieval-themed with tapestries and over-sized wood framed sofas.* She made another entry in her notebook.

There was a cacophony of bangs, crashes, and bumps in the background. TJ and Dragon were lugging the last load of broken furniture, trash bins, and rolled ratty rugs up the seventy secret stairs, through the hidden hall, and out the back door to the dirty dumpster behind the Cock of the Flock Tavern.

Only the decorating diva appeared to be enjoying the renovation process.

"Seamus should be helping." TJ carried a broken bicycle in one hand and an overstuffed garbage bag in the other.

"You look like the anti-Santa," Dragon remarked, as he

dismantled the splintered headboard from Mighty Mouse's former room.

"Remember, it's all for one and one for all—not just two hounds of the gods working like dogs." TJ flung the green plastic sack over his shoulder.

"Really?" Claudia pointed a finger at the brutes. "Don't forget, you two have lived here for ages."

"She's right," Dragon agreed. "This is our mess."

"Seamus still needs to come over after his park patrol shift to help sweep, mop, and paint the den he didn't wreck," TJ said. "Fair is fair."

"Why didn't I think of that sooner?" Claudia reviewed her annotations.

"Because Seamus is your boyfriend and you play favorites."

"No, TJ," Claudia dismissed his remark with a hand wave. "I didn't consider truck rental. How are we going to haul the fix up materials and furniture? DIY Expo delivers, but we can't have strangers tromping through our den."

"I'll take you there in the school bus." Sevlow entered from the hall. He was dressed in blue jean overalls, work boots, and a flannel shirt. "It's sizable enough to hold an assortment of furnishings and supplies."

"Well, well…" TJ grinned. "Might have mistaken you for Bill the Builder."

"Sir, the only things you're missing are the monogrammed tool belt and yellow hard hat," Dragon added. "Otherwise, you're an undead ringer."

Claudia observed that the Master seemed to be enjoying the

lighthearted ribbing. "Thanks for coming to help," she said. "Glad you approve of the wolf den redo."

Sevlow eyed the sketchbook in Claudia's hand. "Your enthusiasm is refreshing. I have neglected The Cock of the Flock for far too long. Having a woman in residence restores a balance and vibrancy that have been lacking for two centuries."

Since Margo left... thought Claudia. *But why would she leave someone like you?*

"DIY Expo?" Sevlow removed a bus key from his pocket. "I'll take you there."

Seamus pulled his radio car into the empty valet service lane in front of the Piazza Hotel. Two idle Moonrocks latte-sipping uniformed parking attendants sprung to action, opening the driver and passenger doors with pleasant dutiful haste.

Jacques and Seamus stepped out into the vibrant morning.

"Good morning, officer," the taller of the twosome said. "Is there a problem?"

"Yes, there is," Jacques replied, appearing, once again, to be teeming with tetchy self-importance. "I have spent a most miserable night in Midtown Gardens Park, being terrorized by renegade werewolves. I would like to see my mother or my butler, at once." He dismissed the employees with a wave. "Return to your valet station and dial the house phone. The surname is Heroux. We are residing in the penthouse suite." Jacques clapped his hands. "Summon them, immediately."

The attendants stood speechless. They looked the officer for guidance.

Beyond Jacques's view Seamus performed "crazy drunk" policeman charades for the valets. He touched his temple twice, and then sipped from an imaginary bottle.

The duo replied with comprehending nods before launching into purposeful motion. The tall valet jogged back to the parking station and commenced dialing the hotel phone, while the shorter attendant saw to Jacques.

"Sorry about your unpleasant evening," he seized Jacques by the arm and attempted to lead him out of the car lane.

"Release me!" Jacques declared. "I am neither an invalid nor a child!"

"There, there," the attendant soothed. "It's a high curb. Don't want you to trip and fall on Piazza property after the difficult night you've had. Step up…"

Jacques went rigid, is eyes bugged, and his face flushed. The man-child appeared ready for a torrential tantrum.

Seamus wasn't sure whether or not to rain on Jacque's pediatric parade. His gut told him it was best not to intervene. He watched the tempest in silence.

"Your daughter's been worried," relayed the tall valet, hanging up the telephone receiver. "She's waiting for you upstairs."

"I am not her father. I am her son!" Jacques yelled, stomping his foot and stumbling over a blip in the asphalt.

"If you'd like me to accompany you to your suite," the parking attendant offered, while preventing Jacques from taking a complete tumble onto the red sidewalk carpet. "I'll take you there."

Jacques released himself from his guide's hold with an angry yank. "It is your unwarranted aid that impeded my stride."

This time your coat will do you in, thought Seamus, anticipating the next foible.

As if choreographed on cue, Jacques spun on his heels, set his open Burberry in swirling motion, caught his unfastened belt buckle on a velvet partition rope, and in one fell swoop triggered a raucous domino collapse of the attached metal stanchions.

A small crowd of spectators began to gather.

The perpetrator stood shamefaced amid the tangle. "Yes, perhaps I would appreciate an escort up to my suite."

Seamus decided it was a good time to depart. "No crime has been committed." He slid behind the wheel of his radio car and started the engine. "You have everything under control. Pointless to alarm hotel guests with a police vehicle parked out front." Seamus was on the avenue before they could reply. In his rearview mirror he saw Margo arriving on the scene. She did not look pleased. "For everyone's sake," Seamus commented aloud. "I hope Vincent's trans-continental flight isn't delayed."

Chapter 11

LET'S GET IT ON

A black XAM credit card, one Gadgets R-Us buying spree, three trips to DIY Expo, five sets of supernatural toiling hands, and seventeen hours of elbow grease after operation clean sweep and redecorating commencement, the wolf den, including Mighty Mouse's former room, were transformed into *his and her* cribs, each worthy of a TVM special episode.

"The eagle has landed!" TJ parked his mass on the over-sized black leather reclining u-shaped sectional sofa, grabbed a ZBox controller, and lounged into horizontal gaming position. "And the landing pad is perfect, if I may say so myself."

Seamus admired the plush hi-tech surroundings that included a 80" flat screen television with surround sound, fully stocked theater concession stand, slushy-maker, and a collection of games to rival any video arcade. "Besides our own hard work, we have Claudia and Alex to thank for the wolf den transformation." Seamus gave his girlfriend an appreciative hug. "None of this would have been possible without them."

"Can't put a price on friendship," Dragon replied. "But this cost a small fortune."

There was a chorus of thanks.

"You're very welcome." Claudia beamed. "Alex would say the same." She glanced at her watch. "If he were here, and not home getting ready for a quiet post-game night of sleep. For which I know he is very grateful. Especially since tomorrow evening is the Mayor's exhibition.

Go Bombers! Forgot to mention earlier that my brother invited us to sit in the player's guest box." She looked at Seamus. "Sgt. Gaffney, too."

"Regrettably, I must pass," Sevlow said. "Mayor Fink has extended an invitation as well, which I have already accepted. We will most likely be seated in a neutral zone."

"At least we'll be at the game together," Claudia replied. "How about we meet in the player's lounge during the seventh-inning stretch?"

"Speaking of games and stretching." TJ pointed to the ZBox. "Reach over there and grab a controller. I challenge you all to a maiden round of *Cops and Aliens*."

Seamus was the first to oblige. "I'm on duty tonight so I'm going to have to beat you quick."

TJ flicked the power switch. "Let's get it on!"

Twenty-two hours after concocting the seventh-inning stench offense, the Slavic twosome was toiling, putting their plan into action while Carl the hovering poltergeist cohort offered subliminal directives and cheerleader praises.

The manual bread conveyor had been disassembled and moved to the basement where it was reassembled and repurposed as a flour-to-sewer pipe transport device. A generator powered spotlight illuminated the Wally-guided hoist that lifted hundred pound sacks onto the conveyor as Oleg moved the load down the line into the sewage conduit, one lever crank at a time.

"C'mon, let's get it on a little faster." Carl wished he could help. "Twenty bags per ton, and ten thousand more tons to go before tomorrow night's baseball game!" Carl calculated as he applauded the dauntless efforts. "Won't need a final score to know which New City team will be #1 and #2. Because #1 and #2 will be the winners of this toilet flushing fiasco!" The giggling ghost slapped his knee. "Get it? #1 and #2?"

Vincent watched his wards from the kitchenette as he washed the remaining dinner plates and set them on a towel to dry. Jacques sat on the suite sofa surfing television channels with the mute button engaged. Margo reclined on the chaise reading a novel. Lights were dim and soothing classical music resonated from the hotel suite stereo. The Penthouse was again tranquil and tidy. The ancient werewolf servant had a knack for creating harmony in the high-strung Heroux household.

"I wish to witness a live baseball competition," Jacques announced, pausing at a commercial for the Mayor's Trophy exhibition. He pointed to the screen. "There's a significant rival match tomorrow between the Bombers and Metros. May we attend?"

"A tedious sport: bend, stretch, scratch, spit, squint—what is the point?" Margo didn't shift her eyes from her book page. "At any rate, there's a baseball contest on the telly every hour of the day. Why would you wish to attend one in person and sit on a rigid plastic seat among screaming strangers when you are able to watch an assortment of teams pose and posture right here in the comfort of our salon?"

Jacques's body went rigid and his cheeks turned scarlet. "Mother!"

Vincent gave Jacques a compassionate nod.

The red recessed from the man boy's complexion. Jacques made a second, less heated, retort. "Mother, I did not seek your haughty misinformed opinion of the American pastime. I merely asked if we could partake in a match."

"Should you prefer a quiet evening, Madam," Vincent added. "I will accompany Jacques to the sporting event alone."

Margo's nostrils flared and her brow furled. She turned a page in her novel.

"That face, Mother," Jacques moaned. "It speaks volumes."

"Do not know what you are referring to," Margo remarked, still not looking up.

"Then perhaps let's get it on film." Jacques formed a rectangular box with his fingers and pretended to snap a photo. He examined the imaginary product. "Your vexed expression reveals that you have no desire to join Vincent and me."

"Not so," she defended. "I was considering the possibility."

"Considering the possibility," Jacques repeated. "Only because a compulsion to be the captain of every endeavor fuels your actions, and your restrictions."

Vincent suppressed a supportive smile. He too was eager to experience a pleasant evening out. Margo's lioness concerns and hunting habits had stifled their mobility, activity, and frivolity for many moons.

"Very well." Margo closed her book and set it on the adjacent coffee table. "It has been decided. We three will attend tomorrow's New City baseball trophy tournament." *Le coq du troupeau* rose from her chaise and sauntered like a plumed princess into the bedroom. She addressed her butler before closing the door. "Vincent, phone the hotel concierge and secure the best seating possible. I prefer a private box."

"Yes, Madam," came the werewolf's dutiful and delighted reply.

The midnight oil burned while WAGO's After Dark Café cooled the airwaves. Clarabella Stella sat behind her Songster model 709 Zig Zag oak cabinet sewing machine that occupied a living room place of honor. Mama Stella channeled her former sweatshop seamstress self as she pumped the pedal, gathered her darn magic, and constructed from memory the ComicSci costumes Lyman requested. For a few more hours she would be twelve again, creating *haute couture* for House of Noir.

The humming pulsing rat-tat-tat of stitching needle on fabric lulled sofa-prone Lyman into a sound snooze. Bella left her perch momentarily to cover him with a knitted throw and place a kiss on his forehead. She noticed an unsealed envelope addressed to her, protruding from his pocket. Mama Stella couldn't resist snooping. Inside there were two tickets, box seat passes to the Mayor's Trophy game and a handwritten note that read:

> *My Dearest Bella,*
> *Roses are red*
> *Violets are blue*
> *I would be honored*
> *To attend the ballgame with you*
> *Love,*
> *Lyman*

Bella's heart fluttered. She put the items back where she found them.

Initially Mama Stella thought that theirs would be a passing partnership, two old souls briefly brought together by tragedy. Why should it be any different? Bella's three previous relationships with men—father, husband, and son—had not been well tailored. In fact, her hem hung low and her personal life frayed at the seams more often than not. But darn it, she always managed to mend. Mama Stella was a patchwork of pluck.

Bella's father had been a stern hardworking man with scant time for parental playfulness or affections. A youthful marriage was sixteen-year-old Clarabella Dona Del Lago's pass to freedom and bliss, or so she thought. When the bloom wore off the rose, Bella realized she could never truly trust her late husband or their beloved son, who arrived after many years of heartbreaking infertility. As much as she preferred to deny the fact, both Michael and Mickey were sewn from the same flawed pattern. That realization was pinking sheers on toile, which as time wore on, made Bella a little more than jagged around the edges. But then came the reporter... In a few profound weeks he'd stitched her hopes and dreams into a cozy quilt. Lyman Newlin, so far, had proven himself to be a cut above. *Maybe I shouldn't hold back. Maybe we are meant to be together, just like Captain Milkyway and Princess Stardust.* Mama Stella tried to hold that romantic thought as she threaded her bobbin. The mood, however, was interrupted.

Lyman's snoring had escalated, from a purr to a roar.

Mama Stella reached around and upped the volume on her radio. Marvin Gaye took center stage. Bella found herself back in an amorous frame of mind, singing along and contemplating the invitation...

I've been really tryin', baby
Tryin' to hold back this feeling for so long
And if you feel like I feel, baby
Then, c'mon, oh, c'mon
Let's get it on...

Chapter 12

AIN'T SEEN NOTHING YET

The pack plus one were seated in box 101 behind the home team
first base dugout dressed in Bomber colors and caps. Sergeant Gaffney,
however, took the pack's modest fan attire to the next level. He sported
a day-glow Bomber cowboy hat (Yee-ha Salsa Day give away), and
autographed #29 Alejandro Peña jersey tucked into coordinating white
polyester pinstriped elastic ankle sweat pants that clung where they
should have hung.

Seamus hoped the Sarge would be chosen *Fan of the Inning*. A
dubious honor that awarded the recipient a face plastering on the
scoreboard big screen, a victory dance with Atom the Bomber mascot,
and commemorative foam rubber fan finger, just enough embarrassment
to provide Seamus with affable ribbing fodder for weeks to come.

"All please rise," Al Melon announced, distinctive voice of the
New City Bomber's since the spring of Lyman Newlin's Bar Mitzvah.
His words echoed off the stadium walls like long balls ricocheting back
into play. Fifty thousand fans and a field of participants stood at
attention. "And now country music sensation, Laurel Leah, to sing our
National Anthem."

Seamus removed his ball cap.

Claudia straightened hers.

Dragon saluted.

Sarge placed a container of concession stand munchies beside
his seat.

"Never heard of Laurel Leah," TJ remarked, hand on heart. "But if her voice is as pretty as her face, I won't soon forget either."

"Surely you've heard her song, *Tear Drops on My Mandolin*," Claudia whispered. "It was #1 Country cross-over hit last year."

The brutes plus one appeared perplexed.

"Top 40 clueless, but you know all of the *Cops & Aliens* characters." Claudia shook her head. "Maybe you'll recognize the voice."

"Oh say can you see, by the dawn's early light..."

"Nope," TJ whispered. "First time I've heard an angel sing. If you haven't noticed, I have a thing for angels."

Seamus wasn't interested in sounds. He preferred the sights. His eyes scoured the stands for familiar faces. There was Sevlow seated behind home plate VIP section with Mayor Fink, Liberace, and a gaggle of bodyguards in black shades. Seamus chuckled to himself. *One werewolf is protection enough.* The Master was sporting his priestly attire and an inscrutable grin. *Was he enjoying the moment? Had he spotted someone in the stands?* Seamus continued scanning the crowd.

"...gave proof through the night that our flag was still there..."

In the Press box along the right field line were Lyman Newlin and Bella Stella. He looked less moldy than Seamus remembered and she seemed sourly smitten—like Bella had been kissed after sucking a lemon. The werewolf continued his stadium scan. As far as his supernatural eye could see there was a human sea of blue or orange shirts. Nothing unusual. Still, supernatural senses told Seamus there was something brewing. He could smell it, but he just couldn't put his finger on it.

"O're the land of the free and the home of the brave..."

The stadium audience erupted in applause.

"No lip-syncing or flubbed lyrics," Dragon observed. "She's the real deal."

"Another good reason for me to fall in love with her." TJ watched with hungry hawk eyes as the singer walked across the field, past the Bomber's dugout, and through a gate that led into the stands. To his obvious delight, Laurel Leah, her manager, and a gal pal were being escorted towards box 101's unoccupied row of three. TJ jockeyed places with the Sarge, who was standing beside the trio of empty seats.

"Hey," the Sarge complained, mouth full of peanuts. "You made me miss His Honor throwing out the first pitch."

"Sorry, Sarge. Luckily, you didn't miss much," TJ said, tucking in his t-shirt.

"Mayor Fink should have warmed up with Liberace before the game." Dragon cringed. "He was way high and wide."

"TJ, I haven't seen this side of you before." Claudia gave the box a quick once-over, like a hostess readying for a visit from a special guest.

TJ reached forward and unhooked the chain-link barrier, letting in the threesome. His grin was worth a thousand words. "And you ain't seen nothing yet."

Bottom of the second inning, one out, one on, Bombers and Metros were tied 2-2, but Mayor Fink was still lamenting and reenacting his abysmal game-starting throw. "You ain't seen nothing yet," Fink said to no one in particular as he stood in the aisle beside his seat watching the pitcher with intent. A Metros player stepped into the batter's box. Fink contorted into a full wind-up, checked the imaginary runners on base, and tossed another invisible ball. "I'm sure that was a strike." Fink cocked his head and rolled his shoulders. "Letter-high, right down the middle."

Bodyguards remained seated and unfazed by the animated antics.

Liberace looked away with a whine. Faithful dog had gotten wise to his master's unfruitful game-of-fetch gyrations.

The werewolf in priestly garb was ignoring the gyrations too, for a different reason. He'd spied persons of interest in the cheap seats adjacent to the bullpen.

"Would anyone care for a refreshment?" Father Benedict stepped into the aisle behind the Mayor. "I'm going to stretch my legs."

Liberace's rigorous tail wagging indicated that he was interested in a treat.

"Mrs. Cooke fed you before the game," Fink reminded, addressing his wagging, panting dog.

"*Arf! Arf!*" came the reply.

"Very well, it is a special occasion" the Mayor acquiesced. "Liberace will have a medium-rare hamburger, no cheese, bun, or condiments. I'll wait for the seventh inning stretch. There will be food and drink for us in the VIP lounge." His Honor seated himself once again. "Father, perhaps one of my men should accompany you. These subway rivalry crowds have been known to get rowdy. Last year a group of derelicts with a—" Before Fink could complete his sentence or assign a bodyguard to his padre guest, Sevlow had vanished from sight.

The third inning of the Subway Series opened with a leadoff homer by the Metros' veteran pitcher who hadn't knocked one out of the park since his AAA days.

Bombers were behind by one on their home turf. An updated score appeared on the stadium board. Boos arose from the hosting blues.

Margo, Vincent, and Jacques were seated in a cheering sea of orange. The three seemed more than a little out of place, dressed in their Victorian era garb.

Bleacher section fans in orange embarked on an enthusiastic congratulatory version of the Metro Shuffle—hooting, hollering, and high-stepping slide to the left, slide to the right, big stomp left, big stomp right, clap, clap, clap.

Margo and Vincent remained seated for the dance. Jacques, however, joined in the dance celebration, to his mother's obvious chagrin.

"Hey, Night at the Museum, what's your problem?" yelled an orange-faced fanatic in the bleachers beside the trio. "You're hot but your outfit's not!"

Margo clutched her black cloak.

"Yeah, you and your two grandpas. It ain't Sherlock Holmes Day at the ballpark," continued the orange-faced man, to the amusement of his equally colorful and inebriated buddies. He took a gulp of his frothy beverage and belched his next taunting sentence. "Get a Metros jersey!"

"How repulsive!" Margo shielded her nose and mouth in disgust.

"You ain't seen nothing yet, lady!" The heckler bent over and forced flatulence.

"We are leaving!" Margo hopped to her feet. "I cannot tolerate wallowing in this foul sea of riffraff a moment longer.

"Listen—she even talks old fashioned!"

"The concierge owes us an apology and a refund." Margo stepped into the aisle and addressed her butler who was seated between his mistress and her son. "Vincent, hurry ahead and summon a taxi. I wish to return to the Piazza, at once." She motioned for Jacques to follow her.

Jacques tuned his attention to the game.

"Let's go," Margo ordered, with emphatic calm.

"No." Jacques picked up his frozen frosty cup and took a long loud straw slurp.

Vincent remained seated, silent, and stoic. As if watching a familiar tennis match, his eyes flitted between the two volleying players.

"I'm staying and I prefer that Vincent remains here with me." Margo scowled.

"Fret not." Jacques' tone mocking. "Certainly *le capitaine* is more than capable of summoning her own cab."

"Down in front!" a wadded candy wrapper whizzed past Margo's head.

"You're not wearing the cloak of invisibility, lady!" someone else screamed.

A second item grazed her cheek.

"Hey, Caped Crusader—you're blocking our view of the game!" a third paper object brushed her shoulder.

Margo appeared as confused by the barrage as she was annoyed.

"Pardon me, madam," came a man's mild-mannered request. "Is there a vacant seat where I may watch the remainder of the inning?" A pale-haired priest walked up beside Margo. "I seem to have lost the way back to my section." The padre's ice-blue eyes fixed on the woman in black.

The color drained from Margo's complexion.

Vincent gasped, his body shook, as if an earthquake rolled through his soul.

"There's no need to worry." Jacques whispered to his butler. "Mother's not going to confess her sins to the padre."

"Tis the least of my fears,"Vincent stammered, sweat beading on his brow.

"Now we got a penguin blocking our view too!" the orange-faced fan shouted. He took a sip of his drink and then chucked the cup. It landed with a splash on the padre's back, dousing him and splattering Margo with cold beer.

"Bull's eye!" High-fives and laughter rippled through the peanut gallery gang.

"Margo, please sit," Sevlow instructed.

She obeyed, sliding onto the bench beside Vincent, who seemed less agitated and more intrigued by the pending reprisal.

The padre narrowed his eyes.

"Oh shit!" The orange-faced man grabbed onto his buddy beside him. "I just got hit by a freaking wave!"

"Me too!"

"I can't swim!"

The drunken quintet flailed and gasped. "Help!" they shouted. "We're drowning!"

"What are those fools yelling about?" Jacques knelt on his seat like an enchanted child at the circus, watching the clowns perform slapstick in the center ring. "What do they mean?" he asked Vincent. "I see no waves, no water."

The butler's grin betrayed his own fascinated delight.

Margo too seemed to be transfixed by the commotion. She adjusted her seat to get a better view of the exploits.

"It was the flow of ale and not tides that doused your senses!" Jacques shouted to the drunkards. He spotted an approaching team of neon yellow vests. "At last," he said with satisfaction. "The guards are arriving."

The padre remained at ease and focused.

"Sevlow is using the elements," Vincent murmured for only Margo to hear. "Brings back fond memories, indeed."

Public Relations were paramount to the Bombers. Stadium security rushed into the bleachers and removed the raucous spectators. But not before the field video screen displayed the animated activity for all to see.

****

"Just as I feared!" Mayor Fink observed the ejection-in-progress upon the stadium big screen. "Father Benedict should not have ventured without an armed escort." Fink wrung his hands and cast his eyes towards the Press box. "The last thing Sternfenner and I need is for Lyman Newlin to write a negative article about lax stadium security."

Liberace whimpered.

"You," His Honor addressed the bodyguard beside him. "Go get Fr. Benedict and bring him back here. Hurry!"

****

Laurel Leah had TJ's undivided attention.

"Of course there have been lots of other black country music artists besides me," Laurel Leah declared with a Georgia twang. "Now, tell me you never heard of Charley Pride, Darius Rucker, DeFord Bailey, Candi Stanton, and Rissi Palmer?" She tossed her curly coffee locks and waving her French manicured fingers at TJ in a flirty-girly sort of way. "To name just a few."

TJ held up his index finger and shrugged. "One-out-of-five ain't bad. I'd give myself a two except in my book, Hootie will always be a Blowfish."

"Look." Dragon tapped Seamus on the shoulder and pointed to the monitor above center field. "Sevlow's found some action."

"Appears so," Claudia replied. "Oh, my gosh! I recognize the man kneeling on the bleachers too. Which means…"

"Margo and Jacques are baseball fans," Seamus marveled. "Who'd of thought it?"

TJ's attention was usurped. "Pardon me," he said to Laura Leah, who'd launched into an account about her upcoming World tour. The big man's focus was back on the pack. "Well what do you know? Maybe we should take ourselves a little walk over to the cheap seats and lend him a paw."

"Security seems to have a handle on things. If Sevlow needed our help, we'd know about it. Let's just keep an eye on that section." Seamus shook his head. "I've had a weird feeling since we got here that something was up."

"Maybe you were tuning into the queen of mean?" TJ said.

"Yeah, maybe." Seamus wasn't convinced.

"Well, it was great chatting, TJ, and meeting y'all." Laurel Leah gathered her belongings. "I wish we could stay for a few more innings, but we have a plane to catch, midnight flight, next stop, world tour."

"I love to travel," Claudia remarked. "Where are you headed first?"

"Opening show Tokyo, last show London, thirty-one concerts in between."

"How exciting!" Claudia leaned past Seamus and reached out her hand. "Lovely to have met you too, Laurel. Good luck with the tour and safe travels."

Sergeant Gaffney, Seamus, and Dragon bid farewells.

Only one pack member remained uncharacteristically silent.

The singer waited...

"Bon voyage," Claudia poked TJ. "Say it."

"What?" TJ's expression screamed, *don't go yet!* "I mean, have a good trip."

"I have a FanBook page, if you'd like to keep in touch." Laurel took hold of TJ's mammoth palm and squeezed it. "I check posts often."

"Sure," TJ stammered. "I don't read books much, though. Mostly I watch TV."

"You're a funny guy," Laurel giggled. Her companions had already left the box. She took two steps towards them and stopped. Her gaze fixed once again on TJ. "Hey, would you mind missing a little of the game and walking us out to our limo?"

TJ didn't hesitate for a moment. "Sure thing!" He was over the row and out of the box like a hungry wolf on the hunt.

"No burping or wedgies for the last hour!" the Sarge remarked. "A change sure took place in TJ thanks to Miss Laurel Leah."

"Sometimes it's the small events that bring about life's biggest changes," Dragon said. "TJ didn't ask if he should stop by the snack bar and bring something back."

Gaffney took a last sip of soda and shook his empty popcorn cup. "You guys are always hungry for junk food."

"I would have asked him to buy me a cookie." Dragon watched as TJ led Laurel by the arm, through the crowded walkway, into the exit tunnel, and out of view.

"Come on." The Sarge draped his arm over Dragon's shoulder and gave him a paternal tug. "I'll buy you a cookie." Gaffney nodded towards Seamus and Claudia as he led Dragon out of the box. "Heck, I'll buy you all a cookie."

"Cookies here are eight bucks," Seamus said. "Gonna dip into your retirement?"

Claudia poked Seamus. "Don't tease him about being frugal. Anyway, it's nice that he's being sweet to Dragon since there's three to go…"

"What does that mean?" Seamus raised an eyebrow. "Three to go?"

"TJ's fallen for Laurel," Claudia explained. "We have each other, and for better or worse, Sevlow's still stuck on Margo. Why else would he seek her out during the game?"

"Ah, decorator turned matchmaker," Seamus said.

"Now, if only Alex, Dragon, and the Sarge could find nice girlfriends."

"When you're counting lovebirds, don't forget Lyman Newlin and Mrs. Stella," Seamus reminded. "Even if they are odd ducks."

"True." Claudia chuckled. "Proves everybody can find somebody to love."

****

Thanks to swift work by Bomber security, the right-field peanut gallery was once again safe from debris-tossing drunks and boorish hecklers. Rubbernecking pitchers and coaches returned to their bullpen tasks—tossing warm-up throws and sunflower seeds.

Sevlow seated himself beside Margo, who scooted closer to Vincent, who moved over, pushing Jacques to the very end of the short bleacher bench.

The quartet sat in silence, three of the four squirming like worms freshly plucked from the earth. Only Sevlow seemed content with the awkward seating situation.

"Exciting game," the padre said. "You cheering for a particular team, Madam?"

"I could not care less about this foolish match," came Margo's brusque retort. She attempted to shift Vincent further to the left. He did not budge.

"I can't imagine you were forced to attend." Sevlow brushed his leg against hers. "Therefore, you must have come on your own free will."

Vincent snickered.

"What's amusing?" Jacques's voice was muted. "Mother's unease, being chatted up by a man with whom she's not acquainted?"

"I believe her discomfort stems from familiarity," Vincent replied, in an equally hushed tone. He kept a curious eye on his mistress and master.

"True, Mother the pirate captain would have been familiar with strange men," Jacques remarked. "All the more reason to be uneasy, even if he is a man of the cloth." Jacques watched his mother and the padre sit in silence for a few minutes before losing interest and returning his attention to the game. That too was short lived.

Umpires called a timeout to remove debris from the field.

Jacques fidgeted. He pulled stray threads from his trousers, buttoned and then unbuttoned his jacket, slurped the last of his frozen frosty. Jacques tapped Vincent on the shoulder. "I'm thirsty. Do not accompany me to the concession. If Mother tries to follow, stop her," Jacques instructed, before noisily sneaking away in plain sight, like a naughty child begging to be caught.

Vincent and Margo seemed relieved to see him go.

"What are you doing here?" Margo snapped as soon as Jacques was out of sight. "Such nerve seeking me out at a ball match to make idle conversation—do you not recall I recently stabbed you in the heart!"

"What's a little blood between family?" Sevlow smiled. "We pledged our love for an eternity, my wife." He placed his hand upon hers.

Margo snatched it away. "Truly incorrigible!"

Sevlow leaned past Margo and addressed the butler. "Good to see you, Vincent."

"And a joy to see you again, Sir. It has been too long." Vincent beamed. "When Madam informed me we would be together in New

City, I…" Vincent's lip quivered and his voice cracked. He was overcome with emotion.

"I harbor no animosity or bitterness regarding your departure," Sevlow assured. "Duty beckoned. Margo's decision to leave New City required your assistance."

"You speak of me as if I am not present," Margo remarked. "How impolite."

"Thank you." Vincent took a deep breath and composed himself. "Forgive the sentiment. My wish to see you again is granted, Sir. 'Tis a special evening, indeed."

"A most unpleasant evening, if you ask me," the Captain grumbled.

"More unpleasant than the evening you were captured by Spaniards and forced to walk the plank?" Sevlow asked. He gave Vincent a quick wink.

Margo's face went flush. "I cannot believe you allowed me to step off the end, blindfolded no less."

"Vincent and I arrived as soon as supernaturally possible," Sevlow said.

"Ah, and the Master had you in his arms before your boots touched the water," recalled Vincent. "In a stiff breeze, without capsizing our rowboat." The trusty butler chuckled. "The look of paralyzing fear on the Spaniards' faces when man turned to white beast and leapt aboard the ship!" Vincent slapped his thigh and chuckled. "Sent every sailor scurrying below deck before a shot was fired!"

The Captain's momentary expression betrayed her reminiscent amusement.

"Those were the days, Sir," Vincent pined. "Those were the days…"

"Father Benedict," an approaching bodyguard called. The tall man in dark shades spoke into a walkie-talkie. "Found him... Yes, right away."

"Huh?" The butler turned his attention towards the voice.

"Mayor Fink requests my return." Sevlow stood. "Thank you for the hospitality." He bowed to the Captain. "Perhaps I may repay the kindness? Will you join me for dinner at The Cock of the Flock tomorrow evening?"

Margo appeared as shocked as Vincent was thrilled.

"Very well, then. 6:30? I'll pick you up at the Piazza. Your son is welcome to join us, of course." Before a reply could be uttered, Father X. Francis Benedict ascended three steps to the aisle where his bodyguard escort waited. He did not look back.

Bottom of the fourth, two on, two out, Duane Robinson on deck. Alejandro Peña steps back into the batter's box after a long foul ball, just missing this side of the fair pole. Smitty reading, into his windup and the strike one pitch: curveball, tapped foul, "O" and two. Peña walks away and shakes himself a little bit, swings the bat. And Smitty a new ball, takes a hitch at his belt and walks behind the mound. These two veterans are former teammates, played for the Pirates. Peña steps in front of the catcher. He's gripping the bat a little higher these days. The pitch was outside, Manson tried to pull it over the plate but Van Horne, an experienced umpire, wouldn't go for it. One and two the count to Peña. Smitty reading signs, into his windup, one-two pitch: fastball, (crack) solid hit! That ball is see-you-bye out of here! Clears

the bases, three-run homer for the highest-paid player in baseball.
That's gotta feel good. There are a lot of fans that questioned the deal
that brought the slugger to New City. Peña rounds third, heads to home,
and steps on the bag. Players spill out of the dugout to offer
congratulations. Crowd is cheering. Peña seems to be making converts
out of the naysayers, one hit at a time. And the Bombers lead it 5-3 in
this Mayor's Trophy Game…

Wally turned down the volume on the portable radio, removed a handkerchief from his pocket, and wiped a glob of sweaty flour from his brow. "Bottom of the fourth," his voice cracked, his arms trembled, and his back creaked from laborious exhaustion as he lifted another sack of bread mix onto the conveyor. "A hundred tons of flour in the sewer line. Three more bags to go, we're rounding third base and headed home."

"Yippee!" Carl shouted, dancing the Metro Shuffle. "Better than a grand slam!"

"For sure headed home when last bag down," Roosky groaned. He used both of his red-blistered hands to pull the lever. "Next caper not should require manual labor."

"You said it, boss." Wally loaded another bag onto the belt. "We'll finish here and be back at the shop, sitting on the sofa, watching the game before the seventh inning even starts." He reached for the last sack. "Finally… The end." He breathed a sigh of relief, rubbed his arms, and leaned against a stack of empty pallets.

"No rest for weary bad guys." Oleg yanked the crank for the last time. "Pack tool gear, get car," he ordered his sidekick. "Just thinking, possibility toilet explosion make bread factory pasty pooh too."

"That's true," Carl replied, switching mood modes, from cheerleader to worry wart. "The sewer pipe is two-sided. What if there's enough flushing force on the stadium end to push everything in this direction instead? Talk about backfire!" The perplexed poltergeist pondered for a moment. "Only one way to check on our progress for certain." He swooped into the connecting chasm. "Time to do my rounds!"

****

"Well, I'll be…" Carl marveled, floating through a sea of semi-solidified cement made from rising dough and debris. "A barrier of unbaked bread for as far as the eye can see." He followed the dense mixture to its inevitable end—the base of the sewer pipe beneath Bomber Stadium. Four innings of digested concession food and waste-waters had already begun putting pressure on the bottom while backing up at the top. "Still two and a half more innings to go!" Carl cried with gloating glee. "What's building up is definitely disgusting, but they ain't seen nothing yet!"

Man on first, two out, bottom of the fifth, the leftie Maxwell in relief for Smitty. This kid gave up a full scholarship to Stratford to sign with the Metros as a second round draft pick. Checks the runner on first, takes a sign from the catcher, and goes into the windup. Dropping slider. Ramirez taps a short broken bat grounder to the first baseman who steps on the bag to end the inning, but not before the Bombers add four more runs to the scoreboard. As we go into the sixth inning, it's Bombers ahead 9-3.

"How come they transmit a live game broadcast into the press box?" Mama Stella asked, her words filtered through an embroidered lace hankie shielding her nose and mouth. "We can see the field and read the scoreboard for ourselves."

"When you were a kid, didn't you used to bring a transistor radio to the ballpark?" Lyman replied with a question as he filled in his scorecard. For a brief moment the newspaperman was lost in thought, reminiscent about his happy childhood ballpark trips, his most favorite father-son summer Sunday afternoon outings. Lyman's mother would always have beef brisket and barley for dinner when they returned home. "Whether we were in our seats, standing at the concession stand, or visiting the men's room," Lyman recalled, as if announcing the play-by-play of his mind's eye. "My dad and I would have our Regency TR-1 tuned to the game, transmitting all the Bomber action."

"Speaking of men's room, it still smells like an unflushed toilet." Bella opened her purse, took out cologne and gave her handkerchief another sprits. "Fat guy eating the chili dog left half an hour ago, so it wasn't him, and it ain't me."

"It isn't me," Lyman assured. He checked around him to see if any of the other reporters were listening to their conversation. "I swear, I don't have gas."

"Of course it ain't you passing wind." Bella zipped her purse.

Lyman was relieved that he was not the prime suspect.

"Because you'd of laughed about it by now if it was," she added. "Mickey enjoyed blowing toots out as much as he enjoyed blowing things up," Bella said. "He thought it was hysterical."

Lyman chuckled.

"See. Even polite guys can't help themselves," Bella observed. "Like a funny joke, they gotta share the punch line."

"It's a male phenomenon," Lyman admitted. "Just the way we are wired."

"Some females have the trait too," Mama Stella snickered. "About an hour after I eat raw onions you'd better clear the room. Mickey got his tooting talent from me." She pretended to sit on a whoopee cushion and imitated the sound. "*Pftpftpftpft!*"

Lyman could hardly believe his eyes or ears. Finally, a woman who found farts funny. He broke into a fit of delighted laughter.

"Think that's hilarious?" Mama Stella howled. "Wait until the seventh-inning stretch when I eat a frankfurter with sauerkraut. You ain't seen nothing yet!"

One more good reason, the reporter resolved then and there, to find a way and marry Bella, sooner rather than later.

Man on first, two out, top of the sixth. Players and fans here at the ballpark tonight are fidgety; everyone seems to be reacting to the odd smell permeating the air. Rookie centerfielder Brooks heads to the plate. Gambaro is on deck to pinch-hit for the Metro's injured third baseman, Nestor. Brooks stands beside the batter's box and takes a few warm-up swings. Have word from the front office that stadium custodial engineers are working to eliminate the odor, which they believe is coming from a clogged city sewer main. Brooks walks back beside the plate. Hunter checks the runner on first, takes the sign from the catcher, goes into the wind-up and delivers. Brooks gets under the slider and hits a high fly ball to left-center field. Peña calls for it, and makes a routine catch for the third out, but not before the New City Metros add two more runs to the board. As we go into the bottom half of the sixth inning, the Bombers lead the Metros 9-5 in this year's Mayor's Trophy Game.

"Hey, Al. Can you take a look at something?" Gus, the assistant custodial engineer asked. He stood outside the door of his boss's stadium basement office. Both men wore Bomber blue cover-alls with their names monogrammed on the breast pocket.

"What's up?" Al set aside a pile of paperwork and turned down the volume on his desktop radio before accompanying Gus down the hall to the control room. "Drain-go not fixing the clog? I told the front office we had a handle on the problem."

"Getting some weird reads." Gus pointed to the methane monitor that was registering sky high in the red zone. "There's a lot of trapped gas down there."

"Probably a massive paper blockage. Two-thousand toilets in Bomber Stadium, not including urinals," Al remarked. "From the looks of that methane number, every commode has seen their fair share of use tonight, and we've got three innings to go."

"So what do we do?" Gus scratched his head.

The boss thought for a moment before answering. "Increase the water pressure," Al replied, not sounding completely certain of his solution. "Water should help push the clog through after the Drain-go dissolves the mass."

Gus nodded. "In the mean time, what about the smell? Fans are complaining about the stink, not the lack of flush."

"I'll text a message to the janitorial technicians." Al reached for his cell phone. "Let'm know I want a double dose of air freshener sprayed and mothball pouches hung in every bathroom. If the toilet stench can't be eliminated, we'll do our best to cover it."

Oleg turned off the spigot and reached for his towel that hung on a hook beside the ironed shower curtain. Despite a cool water dousing, Roosky's body still felt warm, battered, and bruised. His hands were calloused, bloodied, and raw; his arms ached, and his legs longed to lounge on a comfy couch.

"Hey, Boss! The seventh-inning is beginning," Wally shouted from the hallway. "Wow, that rhymed," the sidekick marveled.

Oleg grumbled. His bathrobe was not in its usual spot.

"Your robe is folded, in the linen closet, middle shelf next to the towels," Wally called through the bathroom door. "I washed it."

Roosky exchanged his wet towel for a pair of fuzzy slippers and a red terrycloth robe with *OR* monogrammed in black on the lapel. He exited the bathroom and shuffled towards the living room. The scent of braised and broiled meats met him halfway down the hall. Oleg's starved stomach growled and gurgled. H hoped for an ice cold Czar to wash the food down.

"Chilled vodka, a splash of beet juice, with a potato wedge, just the way you like it," Wally declared, sporting plaid pajamas and placing an adult beverage on the coffee table in front of his boss. "Boiled and squeezed the beets myself."

Roosky passed his proboscis over the glass before taking a sip. The fragrant fumes sent tingles from his nose to his toes, followed by a cool flood of warmth. Oleg closed his eyes and sighed, "It perfect."

"Thanks. Try the tenderloin on toast too." Wally sampled a slice. "Great with a dollop of horseradish."

Oleg helped himself to *hors d'oeuvres* as he canvassed the worn but tidy room. Not much had changed since he'd last relaxed on the same sofa, thirty years ago. The apartment behind Kowalczyk's Butcher

Shop consisted of a single living and dining area with an open galley kitchen. There were two small bedrooms aft and a hallway fore, leading to the store, with the only bathroom along that connecting corridor. The rug, sofa, tables, chairs, and lamps were dark and Colonial style, circa post-war baby boom, when Wally's aunt and uncle were newly weds starting their own business and buying department store furnishings on a thing called credit.

Wally turned up the TV volume. "Look, the Bombers are so far ahead people are getting an early start on the seventh-inning stretch."

Roosky watched with intent as fans streamed out of their seats towards the bathrooms and concessions. Like a hungry cat minding a mousetrap he'd built with his own two paws, Oleg wondered if the spring would actually be sprung or would the rodent live to run? He reached into his robe pocket to rub his lucky rubles. They weren't there. A pang of panic shot Roosky through the gut and launched him off the sofa. "Where put rubles?" he asked himself and Wally.

"You had them at the Pasty Dough factory today," the sidekick replied. "Check your gray jacket?"

"Jacket," Roosky repeated, relieved. "Remember having in pocket." He returned his *derrière* to the seated position. "Now, where I hang jacket?" he murmured.

****

Baseball is an art and science played on a diamond field. The instant a ball hits a bat there is forceful collision. If a ball is going 90 mph and the batter swings at 70 mph then the total relative velocity of the ball is 160 mph. As that ball gets closer to the bat it has a great deal of kinetic energy. It then switches into potential, and then back again, into kinetic. In other words, there's an explosion of energy the moment ball meets bat. Sort of like two thousand loaded toilets flushing, their forceful contents meeting up with a hundred thousand pounds of risen dough and debris, energized by increased water pressure and a potent accumulation of methane gas. If combined energy can send a baseball 408' over a center field wall, then an explosion of gas, water, clog, and sewage can turn a stadium into a giant cesspit. That's Physics.

****

BOOM! *Ladies and gentlemen, there's been an explosion here at Bomber Stadium. Not sure where it originated. Players are rushing from the field to the dugout. Fans are scattering. The smell we had earlier has returned with a vengeance.*

Oleg and Wally were frozen in their seats, grins plastered on their lips, eyes glued to the television, witnessing fear and confusion at the ballpark, the smelly mushy ripe fruits of their hard labor.

BOOM! *Another explosion, folks! Where's it coming from?* The television screen went brown. *Thought the first explosion was bad... but I guess we ain't seen nothing yet!*

"Crap!" Oleg shouted.

"Yes it is!" Wally replied, dancing with delight. "Tons and tons of crap!"

"Other crap," Oleg moaned. "Remember, I leave jacket with rubles at factory…"

Chapter 13

WIPE OUT

"What was that?" Claudia asked, grabbing Seamus's arm.

"Cannon fire in surround sound?" Seamus employed all of his supernatural senses to assess the situation. "Feel that motion? It's more than stampeding fans. There's about to be another explosion. Get down! Take cover!"

The pack plus one hit the deck and tucked into protective pose, heads between knees, backs against the folded box seats. Claudia flipped her sweatshirt hood over her hair. The brutes did the same. Not a moment too soon.

BOOM! A second explosion rocked the stadium with furious force, and this time there was more than smelly noise permeating the air. The first explosion made toilets overflow; the second blast had enough oomph to wipe out plumbing pipes and send sewer line caps around the field perimeter flying like saucers. What goes up must come down. A doughy excrement waste-water deluge ensued.

****

Wally's celebratory dance came to an abrupt halt. "Sure you left your jacket at the Pasty Dough factory?" The sidekick swallowed hard. "Rubles in the pocket?"

Oleg nodded. "Grab car keys, no time for wasting!" Roosky ordered, heading to the door, still sporting his bedtime attire, and wondering, after thirty years in the slammer, if his bad guy crime wave comeback was destined to be a wipe out...

****

Claudia's shriek coupled with the realization that he'd been splattered with feces made Seamus see red. His black werewolf coat began to sprout as his muscles contorted and skin expanded.

A familiar voice called from a distance inside of Seamus's head. "Don't turn," the Master instructed. "The abandoned bread factory triggered the explosion. Investigate. For now I must remain with Mayor Fink."

Seamus wondered if Margo's presence at the game had distracted Sevlow, preventing him from sensing that trouble was brewing before it arrived with a vengeance.

"True…" concurred the Master, his reply fading.

ARGH! Need to keep comments to myself, thought Seamus, chiding himself as he dodged a transformation. He threw off his hood. "Crap!"

"What was your first clue," TJ replied, removing his soiled sweatshirt and tossing it to the ground.

Claudia and Dragon follow suit.

"See, I knew this big cowboy hat would come in handy," the Sarge announced through a gag. "I think I'm going to be sick."

"No, please." Claudia pleaded, covering her mouth. "Vomit makes me vomit."

"Politicians and diapers have one thing in common," Dragon remarked. "They should both be changed regularly, for the same reason." He examined his soiled jeans. "Who knew we'd get caught in the middle of a change."

"Yeah, well, I almost changed too." Seamus noticed that he had transformation tears in his clothes. "While I was wrestling with a turn,

Sevlow sent word that we need to check out the abandoned bread factory."

"I can't go on a mission without a shower," Claudia moaned. "This is gross!"

"Sorry, but the princess won't be bathing in her *boudoir* anytime soon." TJ pointed to the frenzied fans flocking the exits. "We're trapped."

"We need access to another exit." Dragon motioned towards the field. "And here comes someone who'll help us."

"Claudia," Alex called from beside the dugout. Except for a few grass stains, his pinstripes were unsoiled. "You guys OK?"

"Depends on your definition of OK." Claudia was standing in a sea of brown bubbly sludge.

Seamus pushed open the box exit gate with his foot and waited for Claudia to go first. "Is there another way out of the stadium, through the clubhouse?"

"Sure, c'mon." Alex reached for his sister's hand as she stepped onto the fetid field. "Watch your footing. Don't wanna wipe out." He removed a sweat rag from his back pocket and gave it to Claudia. "I'll grab water bottles and more towels when we pass the locker room."

"Thanks." Claudia dabbed her face.

"Can't imagine how this happened," marveled Alex. "There's gotta be more than a couple of clogged toilets to blame."

"Sevlow thinks so, too." Seamus planted his foot on the field with caution—a slide into home base would without doubt make his stomach and body turn. "He asked us to check out the abandoned factory by the stadium."

"A planned explosion?" Alex inquired as he escorted the pack and Sergeant Gaffney down the dugout steps and into a crowded hall that led past the Bomber locker room and beyond to the team's private parking lot exit. Players and coaches were standing around, soiled and stunned, glued to television monitors, watching live-on-the-scene newscasters speculate about the cause of the blast. *Terrorist attack* was mentioned as often as *faulty plumbing*. Mayor Fink's face appeared on the screen.

"Wait, can I watch this?" Sergeant Gaffney asked, stopping in front of a TV.

"Of course," Alex replied. "Let me get you guys those towels and waters." He disappeared into the locker room.

"NCPD's best men are on it." Fink cradled Liberace for the camera's close-up. "If terrorists were responsible for this disgusting assault, they will be brought to justice. Reminds me of the sanitation debacle of '99. I was a councilman at the time. My district was directly affected by trash barges that were hijacked on their way to the dump..." The screen went blank.

Gaffney's cell phone rang. He hesitated before reaching into his poopie pocket.

Claudia passed him her hand towel.

The Sarge used the cloth like a glove. "Gaffney here," he answered in an official tone. "Yes, Mayor Fink... Nothing for certain, but I have a hunch... Officer Sullivan is with me... Checking it out as we speak... Saw him in the Press box... I understand... Right..." The Sarge hung up and addressed Seamus. "The Mayor said we'd better get to the bottom of this before a certain reporter starts sniffing around."

Alex returned from the locker room with Bomber totes containing water bottles, towels, and souvenir lights.

✶✶✶✶✶✶✶✶✶✶✶✶✶✶✶✶✶✶✶✶

The westbound Cross City Expressway resembled a shopping mall parking lot on Black Friday. Eastbound rubbernecking slowed the flow of traffic to a similar standstill. Panicked pre and post Bomber exit evacuation prevailed.

Ruble recovery was imperative. There was no time for idling. Oleg tightened his lap belt, closed his eyes, and held onto his seat as Wally jockeyed the zippy Super Bee around stalled spectators, onto the shoulder, between two motorcycles, under a flashing yield sign, through a momentary break, down a divide, onto the service road, and along a divoty driveway that flanked the posterior of the Pasty Dough bread factory. Wally's driving prowess would have made Mario proud.

Carl returned to the Pasty Dough factory from his toilet triumph at Bomber stadium, the ghost's deceased energy meter maxed. He floated in victory circles around the deserted digs, his charged enthusiasm sent objects sailing and made lamps flicker.

The pack plus Sergeant Gaffney approached the abandoned bread building, each sporting a luminous Bomber key ring light on a promotional lanyard (left over from *Pop Lite* caramel corn night at the stadium). It was obvious from the sights and sounds within that the glowing group was not alone.

"Strobes and banging," TJ said. "But without music, it's not a rave."

"Don't hear any voices either." Seamus opened the front door. "Lucky us, it's unlocked." He caught a whiff of the air inside. "Ew, old burned toast."

The celebratory commotion ceased.

"Guess they heard us," Dragon said. "Party's over."

The pack plus one entered the factory foyer, penlights pointed.

"I remember when this place went up in flames." The Sarge coughed as he swiped at cobwebs. "The dust and mold in here will have a field day with my allergies."

TJ surveyed the once colorful walls. "I remember their commercial, but I'll spare you the song. This lobby was painted to match a Pasty Dough bag."

"That's been recently walked through." Dragon aimed his light at the sooty ground. "Footprints, two sets of them." He shined the beam down the corridor that ended at double-doors. "Entering and exiting whatever's on the other side."

Seamus examined the tracks. "One set left by round-toe shoes with treads, and the second set made by flat-soled shoes with pointy-toes. If these prints belong to two people who came and went, then who's still here and how'd they get inside?"

"Only one way to find out, Sherlock." TJ strode down the hall and pushed through the double doors that led into a massive kitchen. "Party's over," he yelled. "Come out, come out where ever you are!"

Carl floated behind a refrigerator.

The Sarge flipped a switch on the wall. The room remained dark. "That's weird. We saw the lights flickering, but it seems the electricity is out."

Claudia pointed to a tangle of burned wires hanging from the charred crumbly ceiling. "And it's most likely been out since the fire." She surveyed the room. "That's why my sixth sense has been tingling since we arrived."

"The factory's haunted?" Sergeant Gaffney gulped. "You sure?"

"Who's the ghost?" Seamus asked. Or should I say who *was* the ghost?"

Claudia closed her eyes. "I get the feeling it's a man, attached to this place because of duty, not a typical factory worker, but someone who felt they had to protect."

"A policeman?" Dragon guessed.

Claudia shook her head. "Not exactly. He wore a white uniform, no badge." She touched her wrist. "Something to do with a watch."

"A security guard died in the blaze," the Sarge recalled.

"Night watchman!" TJ shouted, as if he were playing a password guessing game.

"And he's still here?" Gaffney looked concerned. "Good ghost or bad?"

Claudia hesitated. "I definitely get the feeling he's angry."

"You're darn right I'm angry!" Carl appeared in front of Claudia. "You and your friends have a lot of nerve trespassing on Pasty Dough property!"

"We are investigating, not trespassing," Claudia replied. She stood her ground as Carl struck a menacing pose. "And don't think for a minute I'm afraid of you, either."

"I know she's not talking to me," the Sarge whispered. "But I also hope she's not talking to a dearly departed spirit."

"His name is Carl," Claudia said. "He's the one who guarded the factory."

"How do you know my name and that I do?" the ghost asked, sounding impressed and surprised by her knowledge.

"Because *Carl* and *security* are written on your uniform." Claudia's tone softened. "You should have moved on by now. What are you waiting for?"

"Those darn Bombers!" Carl shouted. "When they go away, so will I!"

The lights in the kitchen flashed. Mixers spun, refrigerator doors slammed, rusty loaf pans clanged against one another in the metal sink, and chunks of plaster fell.

Seamus felt the hairs on his neck prickle. "What the—?"

TJ and Dragon struck defensive stances. The Sarge scooted behind them.

"Don't worry," Claudia assured. "Carl is just showing off. He has a lot of pent up rage towards the Bombers and it manifests itself kinetically."

"*Habla en* English," TJ said. "*No comprende* poltergeist science."

"It means Carl's emotional outbursts convert to stray charges of electricity that can trigger lights, turn on appliances, and move objects."

"And explode toilets?" Sergeant Gaffney questioned. "Is that possible?"

"Possible but not probable," Claudia replied. "There was a huge amount of force behind those explosions. More than one mad ghost could muster."

Seamus thought he heard pounding sounds coming from the far rear corner of the room. *Do ghosts have a rapid heartbeat?* He wondered if he was tuning into spirit energy too. "Ask Carl about those footprints we saw in the entryway." Seamus shined his light into a drain on the tile floor. Also, does he know whether or not the Pasty Dough sewer line connects across to plumbing at Bomber stadium?"

"The night watchman can hear everything your saying." Claudia kept an eye on Carl. "He flinched when you mentioned the sewer line."

"Did not," the poltergeist protested. "And I don't know anything about the two men who were here today, and yesterday." He caught himself. "Oops."

"There were two men at the factory," Claudia relayed. "Yesterday and today."

"My guess is they were the masterminds," the Sarge noted.

"Dumped dynamite in the drains?" Seamus asked. "There'll be traces of powder."

"Who needs dynamite?" Carl scoffed. "It was powder, all right, sifted flour with active yeast that clogged the pipes. Tall guy and his boss who talked funny came here looking for trouble," the specter revealed. "They couldn't see me but I planted an idea in tall guy's head to fill the sewer line with bread mix—tons and tons. Carl Chapatti was the brains behind the great explosion!" The ghost danced the Metro shuffle while boasting. "Because of me the Bombers are swimming in sewage! Their stadium's wiped out!"

"What's he saying," Seamus asked.

"Basically, Carl confirms that the explosion started here. "Blowing up the sewer was the ghost's subliminal idea, but two guys did the dirty work, one tall, one who Carl says talks funny, maybe an accent."

"Roosky," the Sarge surmised. "Sounds like his MO, but we need evidence. Can't tell the Mayor we got our 411 from a dead security guard."

There was a sweet dirt smell in the air, reminded Seamus of fresh beets. He scanned the room with his light. "Maybe the Russian forgot something."

"Rubles are Roosky's calling card," the Sarge reminded. "In his heyday he left one at every crime scene."

TJ surveyed the scorched scene. "It'll be more like finding a ruble in a haystack."

The pounding sound Seamus heard earlier became louder, more intense. "Anyone else hear that thumping noise?"

Claudia's pocket was simultaneously buzzing and vibrating. "My cell phone's ringing." She looked at the caller ID. "It's Alex. Better answer… Hey, how's it going over there? Team must be pretty shook up. Looking forward to your road trip… Yeah, big clean up… We're fine… Yes, we did… Tips from beyond the grave… Very funny."

Carl scowled at Claudia. "Who are you talking to?"

"Sorry to be short, but can I call you back later? … Me too. Thanks." Claudia hung up and addressed the glaring ghost. "That was my brother, Alex Peña."

"Bomber superstar, Alex Pena!" A twister in a rusty trailer park hath no fury like a baseball fanatic scorched. "I hate him!" Carl seethed and sizzled. The Pasty Dough kitchen rumbled, devices roared, debris soared, bulbs burst, and soot swirled while chunks of the charred ceiling fell like filthy snow in a wild wintry blizzard.

The pack deflected the raging onslaught as they raced for the exit.

Sergeant Gaffney took a metal mixing bowl to the back of the head and wiped out with a CLUNK as the double doors swung shut behind him.

Two thumping-heart thugs hiding behind the oven saw their chance to escape through the service entrance at the back of the building. Robe-and-slippers-clad-beet juice-smelling-shorter-of-the-two individuals clutched a gray mohair jacket between his mitts, a set of rubles secure in its pocket.

Chapter 14

GIRLS JUST WANT TO HAVE FUN

Vincent scuttled around the penthouse, tending to the numerous capricious needs of his spoiled charges. Like poor Cinderella on ball night, the old werewolf hoped and prayed all the while that his chores would be completed in time to join in the evening festivities at the Cock of the Flock.

"Vincent," Jacques moaned from his prone position on the portico chaise. "Bring me a blanket. The breeze dilutes the scent of *merde* from my polluted nostrils. Yet in exchange, an afternoon chill has settled upon my sordid skin."

Vincent retrieved a goose down duvet from the linen closet.

"Vincent," Margo called from behind her locked bedroom door. "Phone my regrets!" Closet door slamming followed the declaration. "I own nothing presentable!"

"If Richard III would give his kingdom for a horse," Vincent professed as he stood betwixt and between the frays. "Tonight I would trade my lot as well, but for a fairy godmother who might conjure Mary Poppins to mind the babes, and a pumpkin cab to transport me to my desired destination."

"Quit muttering and cover me," Jacques ordered. "Should I succumb to the shivers, beware, for I am not a pleasant patient."

Vincent concurred in silence as he hurried to drape the duvet atop the man boy.

"Tell Mother I am already feeling too ill to dine with the platinum-haired priest." Jacques pulled the wrap to his chin and forced a cough. "What type of meal could he offer us, anyway?" he mocked. "Bread and wine?"

"Vincent," Margo exclaimed. "I need you at once."

The butler shuttled back into the apartment where his mistress waited, wearing her dressing gown and holding the Piazza Hotel magazine, open to the fashion section.

"The drunkard was correct." Margo was on the verge of tears. "My clothes are dreadfully dated and drab."

"Madam," Vincent's voice shone sympathy.

"If I am to consider joining S…" Margo caught herself before uttering her husband's name. "Joining the padre for dinner this evening, I must have contemporary attire." She handed Vincent the publication. "These ensembles are in the lobby boutique. Bring the marked items to me for a fitting. When you're done, call the hotel hair salon. Have a stylist sent to the suite." Margo removed the jeweled clip from her hair and shook her golden locks free. "Two centuries of growth." A mane flowed to her waist. "I no longer wish to resemble Rapunzel," she confessed. "Her secluded life in the tower was anything but fun."

Claudia emerged from her wolf den *boudoir* clean and coiffed, her damp hair arranged in a casual but chic French braid that brushed the petal collar of her pastel print peasant blouse, which topped a pair of faded fitted jeans tucked into lace-up buckskin boots. Buccaneering was still influencing Claudia's attitude and style. She seated herself beside Seamus on the sofa and placed a kiss upon her sweetheart's cheek, in hopes of distracting him from his video game.

"If I kiss you back I'll lose my place and have to quit." Seamus's eyes were glued to the giant TV game screen, thumbs thumping on controller.

"That was my plan," she confessed. "Who's winning?"

"Cops," Seamus replied. "Darn! That was a close one!"

"Unless TJ finds a key to the portal and helps the intergalactic Cyclopes escape from jail," Dragon added, bobbing and weaving with the action.

"Hide and weep!" TJ's fingers furiously pressed arrow buttons. "Rocket key is in my pocket and aliens are about to beat cops, yet again."

"If you've done it, it's not bragging." Dragon twisted a plastic wheel that drove his cyber cop car through the realistic cartoon prison gates. "But it ain't over 'till it's over and I just blocked your portal passageway. Ha!"

Sirens roared and GAME OVER flashed across the television screen. TJ threw his mass back against the sofa cushion and moaned. Seamus and Dragon exchanged a high-five victory slap. Cops had rid the planet of alien assassins.

"Rematch!" TJ returned the game to start.

"Sure. Got time before I need to head over to the station house and research Roosky files for the Sarge." Seamus was still clutching his controller. "Won't take long to beat you twice in a row."

Claudia cleared her throat.

"Need a cold drink?" TJ pointed to the refrigerator. "Mind bringing me a cherry cola while your there? *Gracias.*"

"Didn't you and Dragon promise to get Sevlow's car out of storage and detail it?" Claudia glanced at her watch. "He's picking Margo up at 6:30."

"Not going to take us three hours to wash a car that's been kept garaged and covered," TJ replied. "Anyway, if Sevlow makes Captain Chicken Feather and her flock of flunkies wait, serves them right." TJ placed his game controller on the coffee table. "But then again, I don't think Sevlow's ride has seen the road since E.T. phoned home." He stood up and motioned to Dragon. "Come on. Guess we got work to do." They sauntered towards the door. "Where's Wally's Filling Station when you need it?"

TJ and Dragon departed, clicking the wolf den door shut behind them.

Claudia scooted closer to Seamus and draped her arms across his shoulders. "Looks like we're all alone."

He grinned. "How about I mess up your lipstick?" Seamus planted a long slow kiss. "Glad you chose an extra wide sofa." Seamus used his weight to make a fully reclined body sandwich play for second base.

Despite grinding pleasure, the responsible voice in Claudia's head overpowered her libido. "Wait." She blocked Seamus's second base slide inches short of safe. "Before we get too *comfortable*, don't you have to check on Sergeant Gaffney? I know there was no concussion shown on the scan, but that was a nasty head bump."

"When I went by the Sarge's apartment earlier he was alive and well, watching an old movie and eating popcorn." Seamus untied Claudia's blouse sash while pecking his way up her neck on the return to first base. "His widow landlady's been checking in on him. From the

looks of things, you can focus your matchmaking on Alex and Dragon.
"

"In that case…" Claudia untucked Seamus's polo shirt and slipped her hands underneath. His skin turned to gooseflesh. She nibbled while whispering in his ear. "I'm all yours until I head uptown."

"Uptown?" Seamus repeated. "Is that some romantic code phrase?"

"You're bad." Claudia giggled. "Art lecture uptown, at the university."

Smooching and pawing ceased. "Columbus University?" Seamus raised himself in the push-up position. "That's not the safest part of the city. Who you going with?"

"Me, myself, and I," Claudia tugged Seamus towards her.

"No, really?" Seamus pulled away. "Alone?"

Claudia sensed unease in his voice. She stroked his cheek. "Hey, don't worry. In case you've forgotten, I'm a werewolf too."

"No offense," Seamus backpedaled. "It's just, I love you. I worry."

"I love you, too." Claudia kissed him. "And I can take care of myself."

"You haven't been turned for very long and haven't had a kill yet," Seamus said between smooches. "Think it's probably a good idea if you go out with me, Sevlow, the pack, your brother, or the Sarge. At least for now."

"Seriously?" Claudia wasn't sure she like the direction of their conversation. "How long did you wing it as a werewolf?"

"That was different. I'm a guy."

"Sevlow treats me the same as the brutes. Why can't you?"

"Because you're my girlfriend, and besides, Sevlow treats you different too. Who has the private room and bath? Who got flowers on their first full moon?"

"Are you jealous?" Claudia faked a smile.

Seamus grinned back. "Well, maybe, a little. But that's not what this is about." He stroked her hair. "Hey, I rather you're not out alone at night. OK?"

"Before my scent caused stampedes at the stable, and I had to send Pirate back to our Florida farm, I rode through Midtown Gardens every morning, by myself." Claudia found herself on the defensive. "Had I been locked up in an ivory tower, we wouldn't have met, except in my dreams." She wiggled out from under Seamus and sat up. "There's no reason I can't go to a lecture, in a public place, without an escort."

"Yeah, there is." Seamus nodded his head. "Listen, Claudia, don't take my concern the wrong way. It's not as if I'm trying to control you."

"You said it, not me." Claudia straightened her blouse and retied her sash before putting a couch cushion of distance between her and Seamus. "I don't try to control you."

"No?" Seamus raised an eyebrow. "Think you're not controlling? The wolf den doesn't meet your fancy standards—you redecorate. TJ and Dragon act like big kids—you scold them. Sometimes you suck all the fun out of things."

"So, I'm a fun-sucker?" Claudia felt her face flush. "That is not fair!"

"If you thought video games were cool, we could have played another round of *Cops & Aliens* this afternoon. But no, everyone has to hurry off and get to work so you can go to a boring art lecture tonight, by yourself. Is that fair?"

To think I was contemplating a run around the bases! Claudia could feel her eyes well up with tears. She hopped off the sofa and headed into her room. "Fine!"

"Fine?" Seamus looked puzzled. "What does that mean?"

"Whatever!" Claudia's heart raced. Her skin prickled and her stomach churned. There was no way she wanted Seamus to see her cry or, worse, turn in anger.

"I'm sorry," Seamus called. "Didn't mean to hurt your feelings. I'd rather make out with you than play video games. OK?" There was no reply.

Claudia composed herself before grabbing her purse and jacket.

"Claudia, c'mon," Seamus pleaded. "Don't leave angry."

She left the wolf den without uttering another word to Seamus, but her head was full of pointed and pithy retorts and a made-up mind. *Tonight I am going to have fun.*

"What'd you find out about the Peña girl? She some sort of crime-fighting ghost talker, like the one on that scary TV show?" Wally stood in front of Oleg's desk in their headquarter hideaway, holding a meat cleaver and sporting a bloody white apron.

Oleg peered over the top of his computer monitor. "Out of butcher shop context, you more creepy than dead ghost."

"Funny, Boss." Wally wiped the knife on his pocket rag. "Finished sparing ribs and getting ready to close the store."

Roosky pressed *Ctrl P*. The desk printer clicked and hummed. "Thanks to her FanBook page and *Chronicle* newspaper, I find where

Claudia Peña live." Oleg removed a real estate article from the machine's catch tray. "Pack picnic basket for dinner. Get car. We going to stake out Bomber sister apartment building."

"Goodie!" Wally grinned. "Speaking of steak, I'll slice last night's left over filet and make us some sandwiches." He headed up the squeaky cellar steps. "Crime capers make me hungry." Wally licked his lips. "Speaking of capers, I'll whip up a quick aioli sauce to drizzle on some sourdough rolls, then add the meat, sprinkle capers, garnish with a few sprigs of fresh arugula, and we'll wash it down with a slightly chilled Australian Shiraz. For dessert..." The sidekick butcher was still menu planning as his voice faded from beyond the first floor door.

The bedroom clock read 6:35 PM. Margo checked the mirror one last time. Perhaps she should have worn the red pencil skirt and animal print blouse instead of the aubergine cocktail dress. *Am I trying too hard not to appear drab?*

"Madam," Vincent tapped on the door. "Father Benedict's car has arrived."

"One moment," Margo replied, still reflecting upon her reflection. The clothes caused a quandary; however, the Captain's hair gave her no reservations. Margo admired how her newly sculpted soft layers. They framed her face and brushed past her shoulders. A hairdo result exactly as the stylist had promised—wild yet sophisticated. *Would Sevlow approve?* Margo caught herself. *His preferences no longer matter...* She grabbed her wrap and clutch before making an entrance through the bedroom door.

Vincent gasped.

"Mother!" Jacques rushed from his chaise to get a better look. "She's emerged from the pages of a fashion magazine." He touched Margo's hair and then her dress, like a little boy trying to determine if what he saw was real.

"Beautiful." The butler blushed as soon as the word was spoken.

Margo found herself thrilled by the attention, nepotism notwithstanding.

"Lovely appearances matter not. Your heyday has long passed," the boy man remarked. His snide side restored in time to douse his mother's supermodel moment.

Margo chose not to swallow her son's biting bait. Instead, the Captain took a calming breath as she donned her wrap and addressed her escorts. "Shouldn't keep Fr. Benedict waiting too long. Bring an umbrella, Vincent. There is rain in the forecast."

"My mind has changed," Jacques declared. "Vincent and I will not be joining you and the padre for dinner."

Vincent's exuberance deflated like a bouncy balloon pricked by a spoiled child.

Margo felt both pity for her caretaker and relief for herself. She could not recall the last time she had dinner alone with Sevlow, or any man besides the two before her.

Jacques addressed the butler as he returned to his prone position on the porch. "Your disappointment is obvious, but my condition is too grave for me to be left alone this evening." He snuggled under the downy duvet. "I might become delirious, leave the Piazza, and meet my demise on the dangerous streets of New City."

Margo exited the suite. It did not matter where she was going as long as she was going alone. *There are times when a woman wants to have a little fun.*

＊＊＊＊＊＊＊＊＊＊＊＊＊＊＊＊＊＊＊＊

Margo stepped onto the curb, past the taller of the two valets who had assisted Jacques the morning he'd been chauffeured home by a police officer, after wandering around Midtown Gardens Park all night, imagining monsters. The valet did a double take, and much to Margo's satisfaction, beamed like a besotted teen.

"Ms. Heroux," the valet gushed. "Your friend is waiting, parked beside the fountain. Allow me to escort you."

Sevlow came into view before Margo had an opportunity to accept or decline the shepherding offer. He handed the valet a generous tip and took the Captain's arm. "Thank you, but I will see to my wife from here."

The estranged couple walked to the car in silence. Margo's eyes inspected the white exotic-looking roadster. *Excalibur.* For some odd reason the vintage vehicle reminded her of the white carriage and draft horse team she and Sevlow had kept stabled and pastured behind the tavern. Margo tried to recall the mare's name… She'd been quite fond of the gentle gray giant. Margo rode the mare many a Sunday through Gardens Park, as it was called once upon a time. *There's so much of my past I have chosen to forget.*

"Our stable is now a garage and our pasture was long ago covered in concrete and turned into a parking lot." Sevlow opened the car door for Margo. "Sampson and Delilah enjoyed a pampered life until a ripe old age." He hesitated. "The mare missed you."

"Was that necessary?" Margo chided as Sevlow entered the automobile from the driver's side. "To manufacture melancholy regarding beasts I have not contemplated in over two hundred years?" Secretly, she was comforted by the information. Her husband had an uncanny way of tuning into the minds of men and creatures alike. It was why, Margo supposed, she had become adept at building barriers.

"My apologies. I received a mental picture of the horses and a fond feeling, which I attributed to you." Sevlow started the car and eased into a traffic fray along the bustling avenue. Between gearshifts he settled his hand upon hers.

Margo enjoyed the feeling of skin on skin. She did not resist. "No priestly garb. I suppose you envisioned us dining alone this evening as well," the pretty passenger declared, in a more playful tone as she peered into the tiny backseat. "Which is fortunate, for Jacques and Vincent would have been crammed too close for comfort." She laughed. "Although werewolf telepathy is not necessary to imagine my son's response!"

"It has been difficult for you and Vincent, retarding Jacques's aging process, and keeping him alive." There was no judgment associated with Sevlow's statement.

Margo took offense, nevertheless. "I do not wish to discuss the mode and means by which I've cared for my son," she snapped. She imagined for an instant that they were idling at a traffic signal where she feigned a dramatic exit.

"Jacques has learned your ways."

The observation gave Margo a start, followed by amusement. She knew her husband had once again tuned into her mental movie. "*Touché*," the Captain replied.

Sevlow kissed Margo's hand, his gaze tinged with apparent amour.

Margo monitored her notions until Sevlow entered the alley behind the Cock of the Flock. She could not, however, contain her elated emotions as she observed through the car window at her former home. The sea had been her passion, but the tavern was her dream, and it was alive and well. As soon as the vehicle stopped, Margo hopped out for a better site inspection. Besides having altered the barn and pasture to accommodate engines rather than equines, nothing about the building had changed. The tavern's rugged stone façade, bright red oak and iron front door, and beveled lead glass windows were as unsullied as the day they'd been installed, even the colorful Heroux coat of arms hanging above the transom appeared new and unweathered. "Truly Magnificent!"

"As are you," Sevlow replied. He passed his wife her cover and clutch.

Margo allowed herself to take an extended look at Sevlow. *The first time in centuries.* Her husband was magnificent as well, his facial features fine and regal, yet handsomely masculine. Even through his crisp blue Oxford shirt and tawny tweed blazer Margo could "see" Sevlow's his strong and taut presence and muscular physique. Still, it was his musky scent that sent her senses over the edge. "Take me…" she stammered, before composing herself. "Inside the tavern." Margo recovered. "I am anxious to see if it too remains unspoiled."

"As you wish," Sevlow replied. There was a lit glimmer in his azure eyes. He opened the front door and waited like a gentleman for his wife to enter.

Margo stepped into the paneled foyer and was struck with delight as she observed the pub decor. From the patterned Oriental entry rug, to the carved teak bar, to the sturdy dining tables, tall tapestries, sea-themed art adorning the walls, and stained glass chandeliers, every piece of furniture was original, chosen by Margo over two hundred years prior. "I feel as if I have entered a time machine," Margo marveled. "How were the tavern and its contents so perfectly preserved?"

"Credit must be given to the deserved," Sevlow replied. He ushered his wife into the main room. "And the deserved are anxious to greet you."

As if on cue, two little people ambled out from behind the kitchen curtain, small in stature, but sturdy and able-bodied, with an earthy aura, reminiscent of animated lawn figures sculpted from sod and clay.

"Terra! Erde!" Margo cried. She ran to embrace the couple. "I never imagined you would be here, after all this time!"

"Madam," the pair whispered in unison, wiping fresh tears from their cheeks, as they group hugged Margo, around her waist.

The floodgates were about to give way. Margo tried hard to swallow her sweet sorrow. *I have saddened many who cared.* She removed a handkerchief from her clutch.

Terra and Erde stepped aside and examined their former mistress.

"Lovely and scrawny ever she was," Terra declared in her high-pitched ticking voice that had always reminded Margo of rocks knocking against one another.

"Same the Master partial to," Erde added in a deeper but equally stony tone. "Believe I, you want again to pirate." The little man spoke in a dialect of English that Margo had not before or since encountered.

"But I say missus, you leave for dead child," Terre said.

Erde gave his white beard a deep scratch. "Who right?"

Tactless candor and curiosity, were gnome personality traits that Margo found both humorous and infuriating, at the moment she was stuck in limbo, somewhere between findings, and at a loss for words.

Terra and Erde stood wide-eyed, like patient puppies, waiting for a reply.

"You are both correct in your assumptions." Sevlow took Margo by the arm and led her to the second floor stairway. "Madam and I will be dining in our apartment this evening. Please serve the meal whenever it's convenient."

Margo breathed a sigh of relief. *Rescued by Sevlow, again.*

"Good sandwich, huh Boss?" Wally asked. He wiped a spray of aioli soaked breadcrumbs from his trousers. "Feels like we're having a picnic in the park without all the bugs and dirt and pollen that makes me sneeze and itch."

Oleg nodded, mouth full.

"Think the Peña girl is going out again?" Wally asked. He checked his glow-in-the-dark Captain Milkyway vintage collectable wristwatch. "It's seven-thirty on the dot."

"We stakeout until food finish," Roosky sipped chilled Shiraz from a floral print paper cup.

"That doorman keeps looking over here," Wally noted. "Maybe we should move the car out of his view." He reached into the dessert container and helped himself to a creampuff just as Claudia exited the building. "Rare re ris!" he mumbled, gathering food containers, utensils, napkins, and putting leftovers in the cooler before starting the car.

The elderly uniformed Tacoma doorman hailed a yellow cab and Claudia headed uptown, a zippy red Super Bee on her tail.

Freddy the doorman shook his head. "They be something wrong," he said. "Them two been waiting for Ms. Peña all along." He removed a cell phone from his pocket and scrolled through contacts until he came to Alex Peña.

Bella stood at the kitchen sink washing pots and pans. There was chicken in the broiler and a dozen jars of her homemade secret recipe spaghetti sauce lined up along the counter, cooling. Butter was the magic ingredient. Sweet white onions and garlic sautéed in unsalted butter, instead of olive oil, gave Bella's sauces a slightly creamy consistency. Mickey loved his mama's sauces so much he'd drink them like soda pop. He wasn't her only fan. In the short time Bella had been feeding Lyman, he'd confessed to becoming addicted to her *delicious red nectar*, as he called it. Lyman even suggested that Bella go into business, launch her own line of Mama Stella's signatures sauces: Marinara, meat, and hearty garden vegetable. The reporter offered to secure financial backing. His idea intrigued her. In fact Bella fantasized about seeing glass containers, sporting her smiling image, on refrigerated shelves of every specialty deli and grocery store in New City. Bella reveled in the thought of being a successful senior citizen entrepreneur as she slid on mitts and checked her roaster. She removed the foil cover and ladled juices over the rosemary and garlic bird before returning it to the oven and twisting the stove dial to broil. *Three*

minutes more. Her finishing touches ensured that the meat stayed moist while the skin crisped. Time to boil water and pick out the pasta. Food preparation was therapeutic. It quelled Bella's crabbiness, which after twenty-four hours, had finally subsided. The toilet explosion, followed by a stinky subway ride in a poopie pantsuit, three showers, six shampoos, and a night of nausea and nightmares were to blame for the angry attitude. The disgusting fiasco hadn't been Lyman's fault, but Mama Stella had taken her frustrations out on him, just the same.

She'd make it up to him tonight.

Bella turned off the oven and turned on the stereo. WAGO's Evening Jazz Café with host, Miles Daily. Smokey melodies put her in a relaxed frame of mind as she headed into the bedroom, powdered herself with Chantal, and slipped into something more comfortable, her Princess Stardust costume.

Back in the kitchen, mood and food were in order. Mama Stella set the table with her best china and poured two glasses of Chianti. The bell rang. She glanced at the wall clock. Lyman was right on time. Bella made her way to the front door, wine goblets in hand. *Life is short. This old broad is ready for some fun.*

Seamus sat in the station house records room amid a mountain of Roosky files, feeling like a fathead failure. *Can't believe I was such a jerk to Claudia.* He looked at his watch, it was still a little while before his park patrol shift. *Wonder if the lecture is over?* The cell phone affixed to his uniform belt vibrated and dinged. A text. His heavy heart heaved. *Hope it's her.* The message was from Alex. Excitement converted into concern.

Jst piked up voicemail from Tacoma drman. @ 7:00 red car w/ 2 men followed C's cab. Her phone is off. Can u check it out? Call u after game. Thx.

A tornado couldn't have cleared the table of files faster than Seamus. Not a moment to waste. He hastily slid evidence box #R964 back onto the shelf. Photos fluttered out of a file folder. A burst of color caught Seamus's eye. He took a closer look. It was Roosky and his sidekick beside a red Dodge Super Bee. The photo was thirty years old. *Could Alex be referring to the same car?* Seamus pocketed the picture. *If Sevlow is still driving his Excalibur, Roosky's probably riding around the hood in red, too.*

Claudia walked out of the Aragon Hall lecture facility feeling invigorated, by both the crisp night air and her newfound knowledge of cathedral frescos, Papal commissions, and flying buttresses. She was also pleased by the fact that she hadn't thought about Seamus in over three hours. *But thinking about not thinking about Seamus is the same as thinking about him. Right?* She was sure Seamus had called. Like popcorn consumption during a mesmerizing movie, Claudia's reflex was to reach into her purse. She froze mid-cell phone grab. *No, not turning on my phone until tomorrow.* Claudia closed her purse and held her head high as she exited the campus.

The avenue was eerily deserted. Columbus Coffee had closed, benches along the pedestrian path were empty, and the prospect of flagging a cab looked pretty darn dim. Claudia contemplated her options: take the subway (after beelzebubbles and being hit by a train she preferred to avoid the underground), call for a ride (Seamus was off-limits for obvious reasons; Alex was playing out-of-town; Sevlow was hosting a dinner, and the brutes neither had cell phones nor driver's licenses); final option, Claudia could start walking until a taxi or the M101 bus crossed her path. In the three minutes she stood pondering her plight, only one vehicle passed, a vintage shiny red sedan. Claudia took it as a sign. Walking won, it beat waiting, even at night. *Why not? Werewolves aren't afraid of the dark.* Claudia her zipped her jacket, tucked her purse beneath her arm, and headed south on the avenue towards the Tacoma.

****

"What's she doing?" Wally trailed Claudia from a safe distance.

"Going home, what we should be doing." Roosky yawned. "Stakeout delicious." Oleg rubbed his bulging belly. "Kids today not so private. She write more on computer FanBook page than we learn steak-out here all night."

"True, but I meant don't you think it's too late for the Peña girl to be walking streets by herself." Wally dimmed the car lights. "Should I offer her a ride back to the Tacoma?"

"Sure thing, and while at it give girl signed confession and fingerprints" Oleg's words were flippant but his tone betrayed concern as he craned his neck and watched Claudia turn off the avenue and make her way along the desolate side street towards the north end of Midtown Garden's park. "Hope girl have ghost bodyguard we don't see."

"A rich ballplayer like Alex Peña should hire a chauffeur to drive his sister around." Wally waited a moment and then veered the Super Bee onto the same street. "There are a whole lotta criminals in this city."

****

"Can you spare a dime for an old alter boy?" the gnarled bloodied apparition leaning against the flickering light post begged, his cheerless weepy eyes bulging from bruised sockets, the twisted barbed choke wire remnant of a violent death still tightened around his oozy incised neck.

Claudia kept her head down and hoped the grotesque ghost wouldn't realize she could hear his pathetic plea. Deserted streets were littered with stranded souls, especially in seedy neighborhoods after dark. The departed, who'd lived squalid lives before experiencing brutal deaths, often stayed at the crime scene and avoided the light.

"You see me," the ghost said in a labored raspy voice. He appeared beside her.

Claudia did not reply. She flipped her collar and picked up the pace.

"Stop!" The specter's dismal demeanor transformed into intimidating rage. "I will hurt you!" he threatened. A trio of garbage cans soared into the street.

Claudia did not notice the red Dodge swerving around the bouncing bins. The menacing poltergeist had triggered her defenses and seized her undivided attention. "Don't you dare harass me." She stopped short in her tracks and stared him square in the face. Claudia learned from *los padres* that fear energizes sinister ghosts. She figured this mean spirit must have terrified more than his share of the living. "I am not scared of you," she declared with firm assurance. "Want to be an angry earthbound spirit? Go ahead, hate and haunt, but do it far away from me."

"Well you got a bad attitude!" The specter disappeared.

Claudia resumed her walk.

Wally turned down an alley, put the Dodge in park, and hopped out to inspect debris damage. He spotted a dirty dent on the front fender. "Darn!"

Oleg opened his window. "Go back in car!" he ordered. "Peña girl talking to some person invisible what make trash bins fly. Mean ghost or no, last night we blow up Bomber stadium, not need any creepy spooky trouble."

The sidekick obeyed. "You're right boss. Things are getting too weird. We should head out of here before something horrible happens and the cops are called." Wally put the vehicle into reverse, butted back onto the street, and made a K-turn. As he glanced into his rearview mirror the sidekick saw two shady figures walking Claudia's way. They were very much alive, and their swaggers indicated neither was out for a stroll.

Oleg noticed them too.

"Now what do we do, Boss?" the chauffeur asked, fleeing the scene at a snail's pace. "Spirits are one thing, but muggers are another. What if they hurt her, or worse?" Wally grabbed the empty wine bottle protruding from the picnic basket beside him. "We're bad guys, not horrible men."

"You right." Roosky removed a tire iron from under the seat and commenced watch, out the rear car window. "Keep driving, but make slow."

****

Claudia had encountered dark spirits before; however, tonight the vibe in the air was different, more threatening. Her werewolf senses kicked into red-alert. *Footsteps.* Claudia checked left and right. The street was deserted; neither living nor dead was making an appearance. *Smells like men's cologne and perspiration.* She upped her walk to a trot. *More than one set of footsteps.* Stomach-churning angst propelled Claudia forward. *Safety.* The northern tip of Midtown Gardens Park loomed a hundred yards ahead. *I'll call Seamus.* Without missing a step, Claudia dug through purse contents and took hold of her cell phone. *Maybe he's on duty early.* She approached a boarded building and alleyway. Trot became canter; seventy-five yards to the park gate. Claudia pushed the phone power button. A black and white fruity icon appeared. It blinked, and blinked, and blinked... *Hurry! Turn on!*

THUNK! SHHH!

Claudia didn't see the shin-high trip chord until after it sent her skidding across the coarse concrete sidewalk. Like a potato rubbed against prickly peeler, the skin on Claudia's fall-breaking palms, wrists, and newly exposed right knee were shredded. At some point during the tattering tumble her phone and purse went sailing.

Before Claudia could gather her wherewithal or belongings, two men, one of whom reeked of sweat and spicy aftershave, dragged her into the dark dirty alley.

****

Seamus dialed Claudia's cell for the third time in as many minutes. The first two times his call went directly into voicemail, this time, however, it rang.

"C'mon, pick up," Seamus pleaded. "Don't have to talk to me, just let me know you're OK." Voicemail answered. He hung up. *She still hates me.*

Uptown traffic on a weekday night was normally light, which is why NCDOT took advantage of the low-flow when scheduling routine road maintenance. Instead of sailing up Columbus Avenue, Seamus found himself idling behind an asphalt truck and a trio of pothole fillers who appeared to be working for an hourly wage. *Slow and steady pads the paycheck.* Seamus assessed his options: activate his siren, or take a detour down the side street. Although he preferred the former, he chose the latter. Right-left-left-right, four turns and three streets later Seamus was back on Columbus Avenue, past the dawdling crew and voyaging north towards the university. Patrol car GPS indicated that he was two miles and eight minutes away from campus. *Where was the lecture? Was it over? If so, maybe Claudia already took a cab home?* Seamus figured the possibility was slim that he'd find his girlfriend walking down the avenue, happy to see him. *Maybe I should just turn around, get to work a little early.* In the land of occasional foolish choices and sometimes-reckless ways, Seamus was also a lucky guy who took chances and ran with them. The little voice inside Seamus's head told him he should ignore probability and stay the course. His projected path would cross Claudia's before the night was through.

****

Bloodied, bruised, and staring up at two ominous assailants, Claudia's grey matter grasped her deadly dilemma. *An ambush... Need to run.* She attempted an escape. One of the men latched onto her hair and tossed her to the grimy ground like a rubbish rag doll. Claudia burst into a torrent of tears.

"Shut up," said the man who reeked of spicy cologne. He pulled a knife from his pocket, pressed it against Claudia's neck, and yanked her down onto her hands and knees like a submissive leashed hound. "Die now or later, it's your choice."

Claudia heard a snap unsnap and a zipper unzip. She smelled the sickening scent of stale urine as something warm, wet, and firm pressed against her closed mouth.

"I want'm pretty," a second voice declared, even more frightening than the first.

Claudia clenched her teeth and pursed her lips.

"Open up!"

She felt the knife's blade pierce the skin below her ear. Claudia did not open her mouth to scream as a second blade made contact with her trousers. In two searing slashes the night air breezed her bottom and a trio of blade nicks began to bleed. An icy cold hand maneuvered beneath her frayed panties. The man in front continued to push himself against her lips. Claudia felt akin to a piece of raw meat, sandwiched between two evils.

"Quit crying," the man behind her growled, as he coaxed his manhood into the playing position.

The first time Claudia died, she had no fear or recollection. The train hit her while she was semi-conscious and delirious. Seamus turned her before she had the opportunity to experience a brutal death or the pain and terror that preceded it.

Right now, however, Claudia was fully aware, and stricken with fear.

"I'm ready for you," boasted the voice from behind.

Claudia was about to be taken in ways she had never been before imagined. *These monsters are going to rape and then kill me.* The terrifying realization fast became a hurricane encountering a house of straw; her fear was blown away by fury. *NO!*

Claudia's skin shivered and stretched as bones contorted and thick brown fur sprouted on a body frame that grew larger by the split second.

"Hey, what's happening?"

Those were the last words Claudia remembered hearing the assailant utter before she lost human consciousness and her animal instincts took hold.

She was turned.

Werewolf incisors latched onto the first erect piece of flesh they encountered. In a single jerk of the jaw, the man standing before canine Claudia was a man no more. He fell to the ground in a writhing heap of helplessness. Swift and savage, the werewolf put him out of his malicious misery.

There was an echo of boots banging against concrete as the second man fled to the far end of the alleyway. Slow human speed and sagging pants hindered the attacker's escape over the chain link fence.

Two paws pulled him back down to the grimy ground and commenced digging into his belly flesh. Claudia was a frantic dog searching for its buried bone.

The would-be rapist's pleas for mercy ceased when deserved death arrived.

Yet silence eluded the alley.

"Leave the girl alone!" Wally's cry led the chivalrous charge.

Oleg and his sidekick entered the skirmish, wine bottle and tire iron raised.

They were ready, willing, and able for battle. That is until Roosky tripped and landed atop an eviscerated bloody body mass, and Wally came nose-to-nose with a massive snarling hound.

Exploding toilets had nothing on the sudden and simultaneous reaction that took place in their pants.

The curious werewolf assessed the amount of evil energy associated with the whining, whimpering, fear-frozen duo. Was she justified making a grand slam out of the double? The she-wolf used her prodding snout to sniff the men's souls. Neither man had a saintly aroma. However, Claudia could not overlook the fact that the two had been willing to risk their own lives to defend hers.

In the end, that single selfless deed secured their fortunate fate. The creature howled. There would be no more kills tonight. The satisfied werewolf sprinted out of the alley and towards the park. Claudia had had enough fun for one day.

****

Seamus headed north along the avenue. He slowed his patrol car at each corner and performed a quick visual inspection of the side streets surrounding Columbus University. No solo females or unusual activity. That is, until he spotted a classic muscle car parked on the sidewalk beside an alleyway. The vehicle doors were ajar and its hazard blinkers were flashing. Seamus investigated. *Red Dodge Super Bee.* Seamus removed the old Roosky photo from his pocket. His brain didn't have time to put two and two together before the equation was solved.

"Help! Officer!"

Two men ran from the alley towards him. Seamus knew immediately who they were: Oleg Roosky and his sidekick, Waldemar Kowalczyk.

"So happy you come give us ticket for bad parking!" Oleg exclaimed, an expression of terror etched across his face. "Horrible thing happens here!"

"Things you're g-g-gonna find hard to b-b-believe," Wally stammered, his whole body quivering like clothesline laundry on a windy day.

"Try me," Seamus replied, catching the whiff of a too familiar stench.

"There was ghost throwing garbage." Oleg corrected himself. "Maybe ghost. We don't see, but girl who talk to ghost shout at him."

Seamus spotted a dumped purse and cell phone near the curb. "Where is she?" he asked, trying not to sound too alarmed as he gathered Claudia's belongings and placed them in the patrol car.

"Don't know," Roosky replied. "Bad guys follow girl but when we try save her we encounter big, big dog, with snarling face, what killed bad guys, rip them in many bloody pieces! So scary, I shit my pants!"

Wally nodded. "I p-p-pooped my p-p-pants too."

"Girl nowhere to be found. Maybe she jump fence," Oleg added. "Dog run away too, then bodies go POOF!"

"P-p-poof, as in disappeared," Wally explained. "Not a t-t-trace left b-b-behind."

Oleg pointed to his unsoiled shirt. "Dead man guts gone! But true story, I swear!"

Seamus was relieved. Werewolf Claudia was alive and had made her first kills. *She's probably headed to Midtown Gardens Park.* As much as the policeman in Seamus knew it was his duty to take Roosky downtown for questioning, the boyfriend in him had an obligation to find his girlfriend. Claudia trumped Oleg. Seamus played the "skeptic" exit card. "Ghosts, growling dogs, vanishing bodies, and illegal parking." The patrolman pointed to the Shiraz bottle in Wally's hand. "Have you two been drinking?"

"Yes, but no intoxication," Roosky assured. He glanced at Seamus's name tag, then his face, and then his name tag once again. "Officer Sullivan, please, must believe..." He stopped mid-sentence. Oleg seemed to be recalling something that prompted him to give Seamus an absorbed and curious stare. "I see you before?"

Seamus took out his notepad. "Gonna need your names and a contact number."

"Bud Abbot and Lou Costello," Roosky replied. "Call at CUcumber I-8-1-2."

"Right..." Seamus closed the blank pad. *Time to get out of here.*

"Policeman, what first name?" the Russian inquired, eyebrow raised.

Seamus ignored the question and slid into his radio car. "Bud, Lou, it's your lucky night. I'm not gonna write you up for public drunkenness and illegal parking." Seamus closed the door and then cranked the engine as he rolled down the driver's side window. "Why don't you both go home and change your pants?" Seamus held his nose and pulled onto the street. "I'll call you if anyone else reports a litterbug ghost dog."

Once Seamus sped out of view, Oleg remembered that *something* aloud. "He at factory and in Lyman Newlin newspaper article, Officer Seamus Sullivan with big black crime fighting dog."

Margo contemplated an after dinner doze as she reclined on the apartment parlor sofa, head upon Sevlow's lap, eyes fixed on the flickering fireplace, and stomach satisfied. The meal had been delicious.

Besides fine red wine and pleasant conversation, the three-course feast consisted of fruit pies, warm fresh hearty breads, aged cheeses, and an assortment of roasted nuts and vegetables slow simmered into a succulent stew.

The earth elementals preferred to cook for guests *sans* meat, and they personally never ate flesh. Margo found that paradoxical since the little couple had no qualms about working for a carnivorous werewolf. On the day they arrived at the tavern the gnomes made it very clear to Margo that assisting Sevlow was a volunteer mission, one they could terminate at any time. Two hundred plus years later Terra and Erde remained employed. *That's loyalty.*

Despite the detours Margo had taken, she too still believed in loyalty. She believed in her *missions*. Margo was committed and faithful, first as ship's captain, then as the wife of a werewolf, tavern proprietor, and finally as the mother of a child man. Although her morals had changed, they had not been abandoned. Margo bore a bastard son, but she had never been with a man other than her husband. She killed, only so Jacques could live. Margo stayed true to the promise she made her second son, the moment she laid eyes on him. *No deaths do us part.* At the time she had no idea what life-altering changes her promise would demand.

But tonight Margo found respite. She was home again, if only temporarily.

Sevlow sipped brandy and stroked his wife's hair. "Do you ever wonder where we would be today had you stayed?" He broke the pleasant pensive silence. "Had you not gone mad after the loss and blamed me for your misery."

"Are *you* mad?" Margo jolted upright and nearly spilled her husband's *digestif*. "How dare you make such a calloused statement?" She felt two centuries of unspoken rage rise to the surface and spew forth with a vengeance. "Only an utter fool would be clueless as to why I left." Memories broke through the floodgates and began to play in Margo's head like a tragic reel-to-reel.

"We could have come to terms with our child's death, together." Sevlow's voice was paternal, his demeanor calm.

"Together?" Margo shouted. "You were off on a mission when I gave birth!"

"I did not know the child would arrive early," Sevlow apologized, stroking his wife. "But you were not alone."

"No, you left your expectant wife in the care of two odd little creatures and a werewolf butler!" Margo put sofa distance between herself and her husband. "How could you not have known?" she said finally, staring into the fireplace flames. "You know what animals are thinking, what weather will arrive; you read the souls of men before ending their lives, yet you did not know your own child would be born early or that I would require you afterwards?"

"I did not." Sevlow words were drenched in remorse. "Marrying you was a detour, not part of my given mission. In exchange for the gift of loving you, I gave up aspects of my knowledge. I must learn to be a husband, as if I were a mortal man."

"Then you did not know, had no inkling, I would give birth to a premature child, a son who would fight to live, fight so furiously that his little body began to change from human to beast?" Margo glared at Sevlow as she questioned.

Her husband's composed countenance began to crumble.

Two hundred years of bearing the brunt of that birth took hold. Margo knew she should have pity, but instead she wanted Sevlow to feel her anguish. Margo resumed her detailed recollection. "I remember the event as if it were yesterday. Terra aided when my water broke. The pain was none I ever experienced, swords being thrust into my loins." Margo instinctively placed her hands on her belly. "The boy child arrived quickly. All my discomfort disappeared the instant Terra handed me the washed and swaddled babe. He was tiny, two kilos, at most. Nevertheless, he was perfect, white hair and pink skin. Our son was *you*. I cried for joy that he had arrived, but wept that you were not there to witness the blessed arrival." Margo's recollection gained momentum. "My emotion soon turned to agony. The babe lost his ability to breath. His body convulsed. I screamed for assistance but there was nothing Terra, Erde, or Vincent could do to comfort me or help the child." Margo's voice became less emotional and more defiant with each reminiscent word. "The infant fought death. His fingers and toes turned first, into tiny claws. Azure blue eyes opened and mouth clenched, as both became convex and canine. Had I given birth to beast or human?"

"I am sorry." Tears streamed down Sevlow's cheeks.

"Our son lost the battle before he was either, while he was both," Margo continued. "I held in my arms a lifeless grotesque deformity of nature." The heartbreaking memory fueled her tale further. "Did the sight make me mad? Yes! I demanded that Vincent find you; bring you home. He departed through the secret cellar tunnels, searched the city and returned the next morning alone." Her voice became more distant. "The summer heat was brutal. Our child rapidly began to decay. I would not allow Erde to bury him. My mind was delirious with hunger and sorrow. I took our son and sought refuge on the island, hoping to find you where our life in New City began. On the third day, I could neither take the stench nor the situation any longer. I climbed the cliffs and threw our rotting unnamed son into the sea, gave him to the only place I trusted. I would have given my life to the waves too, had Vincent not appeared and forced me to the ground, saving me from myself!" Margo exhaled. A sigh of confessional relief released her centuries old sorrow. "You had still not returned from your mission. I could not go back to the tavern. I required a peaceful place to recover. I begged Vincent to take me to Seacliff Manor, to my grandmother. I believed you would come for me when you learned from Terra and Erde what had happened."

"I believed you would come home when you were ready," Sevlow replied, still wrought with emotion. "Of your own free will."

"It appears we were both mistaken in our beliefs." Margo retrieved her purse and cover. "Free will is a two-way street." Margo took a long last look at the apartment. For a few hours it had felt like home, but her real home was elsewhere, with Jacques. "Life is not so bad." She opened the door. "In the end, we may not have each other, but we both have the children we desired." She forced a stoic smile. "You have a young pack, and I have an old son."

Sevlow reached for his jacket and keys. "Wait."

"Thank you for dinner. I will not require a ride back to the Piazza." Margo stepped into the hall. "I prefer to summon a cab... It is my own free will."

****

If New City never slept, then tonight the Piazza was the crown jewel of the Golden Apple insomniacs. The hotel valet station was bustling as cars. Cabs arrived and departed in equal numbers, well-dressed visitors disembarked for late dinners or ballroom events, while other guests set forth for a night on the town.

As she exited the taxi, Margo felt her body buzz with a sudden surge of newfound energy. The Captain was neither eager for bed, nor keen to discuss her evening with Jacques and Vincent. The night was young.

Lively piano music coming from the Swashbuckler, a buccaneer-themed bar in the Piazza lobby, caught the Captain's attention. She decided to stop in for a nightcap.

Every table was in use. Margo walked down the long bar and spied an unoccupied seat second to the end. "Is this taken?" she asked the tuxedo-clad red-haired-bearded man on a stool near the wall, beside the empty. Margo sat before the ogling patron could reply.

"My lucky night," he said in a brogue Margo noted to be Scottish. "Seated near such a lovely lady." The man gazed at her ring. "Will the husband be joining you?"

"No," Margo replied. She tried her best to sound uninterested, which she was. Nevertheless, she found herself observing the man longer than intended. *I've seen that face and scar before.*

The Scotsman took Margo's extended eye contact as an invitation for continued conversation. "I detect an accent. You must be in New City on holiday, as well." He took a sip of his frothy pint. "Uncle's destination wedding in the Terrace Room." The red-haired man pointed to his bowtie. "Hence the monkey-suit."

"An impressive venue," Margo replied. "Must be an extravagant affair."

"I would rather be here than there." He shrugged. "The bride is not his first, and not a family favorite, but she will receive a title, all the same. Even a trollop becomes a Lady when she marries a Lord."

"What did you say?" The man's words jolted Margo's memory further. *So much is familiar. What memory has I suppressed?*

"Forgive my crude remark," the read-haired man apologized. "Wallace family humor, I'm afraid it doesn't translate well outside of the clan."

"Forgiven." Margo was still trying to place the man and the words. *Appears to be in his late 30's, early 40's. Where would we have met before?*

The bartender arrived. "What can I get for you, mam?"

Margo returned from her thought. "Undecided." She was not in the mood for brandy or wine. She scoped the room. Many women were drinking something pink with a twist of lemon, served in a martini glass. "What is that rosy concoction?"

"Cosmopolitan, a Swashbuckler house specialty," the bartender replied. "Even have our own FanBook page."

"Very well," Margo said. "A Cosmopolitan it is."

"Put it on my tab," the scar-faced man instructed. He held up his hand before Margo could protest. "After my boorish comment, I insist."

"Thank you." The Captain smiled. She was enjoying the attention.

The Scotsman pointed to a painting on the wall, a tall ship flying the Jolly Roger. "My great-great-great, and then some, grandfather was a nobleman pirate, Sir Andrew Wallace," he remarked with pride. "There is a portrait of him on loan at London's National Gallery. We bare a striking resemblance, right down to the scar." He turned his cheek towards Margo. "Bloody botched skin cancer cut. Mustique sunshine is a foe of milky skin and ginger hair." He took a sip of beer. "Usually I prefer to fib, say the mark was earned in a sword fight. But there's something about you, or the alcohol that is prompting me to tell the truth."

The waiter delivered Margo's drink and departed.

"Let us toast to honesty!"

"Honesty." Margo touched rims then sipped from the sugar-rimmed glass. "Sweet, smooth, delicious."

"Good to hear." The Scotsman took another swig and then got up from his seat. He reached above the ship painting and removed an ornamental display sword from the wall. "*En guard!*" The Scotsman exclaimed mid-pose. "I was fencing team captain at university, which gives my scar falsehood perfect credibility. Dueling is in my blood."

"Oh my!" Margo looked as though she'd seen a ghost.

"Are you all right?" The Scotsman leaned the sword against his stool. "Is it the drink? Shall I order you another?"

"No, 'tis fine," Margo muttered. The sudden realization of whom she was sitting beside became vividly clear. She had to prevent herself from blurting that she once knew Sir Andrew Wallace. Although she had forgotten his name until today, she'd been courted and betrayed by him, and witnessed his death. "Your ancestor, you *are* his twin."

"And namesake. So you've seen the portrait? As I said, by a very famous British painter, can't recall his name. Hangs in the museum's second floor foyer. I've stood beside it and caused gallery visitors to spook." Andrew picked up the sword again and examined it. "Family legend claims the pirate Wallace was killed by a white werewolf. Seems married randy Andy made a play for the beast's beloved, who was also a pirate." The red-haired man rubbed his chin. "Don't believe I've heard her name mentioned." He laughed. "No matter. Foolish old tales. There is no such thing as werewolves. Despite what townspeople..." He caught himself mid-sentence and redirected. "A rabid white dog most likely bit Lord Wallace as he climbed from a woman's window after having had his way with her. The Wallace's are all sword-loving rogues, but harmless." Andrew reached for Margo's hand. "Come, let me show you how to hold a weapon."

"No, thank you," Margo replied.

"The bartender is occupied. There's no one down at this end of the bar to object" He whirled the weapon. "And if they do, I am armed!"

Margo smiled at the display of bravado. "Well, then, why not?" Andrew placed the sword into her hands. The Captain examined it closely. "*Un épée de cour*," Margo recognized the style. "Also called rapier or *spada*. Immediate predecessor of the French *foil*, not unlike the English smallsword."

Father was once a student of Domenico Angelo. He taught me well. "My father studied fencing and dueling as well." Margo, gave an abbreviated version of her thought. "He shared with me some of his learning."

"I am impressed," Andrew marveled. "Beautiful and knowledgeable."

Margo blushed.

"If you were not a married woman, I would certainly make a play for your affections," Andrew confessed. "Eighteenth-century swordsmanship is my passion, and L'École des Armes by Domenico Angelo is my bible. Have you heard of the treatise?"

The Captain owned a personalized signed first edition in her library at Seacliff Manor. She had studied the treatise and could recite the lessons word-for-word, in French as well as in English. "No, I haven't," she lied.

"Ah, thank goodness." Andrew wiped his brow in *faux* relief. "Had you been familiar with the book, I would have lost my heart instantly. By chance, if you owned a copy, I would have fallen on one knee and begged for you to be a polygamist and marry me, or adopt me, whichever your preference."

"Are you always this amiable and animated?" Margo found herself thoroughly amused and entertained by his court jester antics.

"How kind of you to notice." Andrew gave an exaggerated bow. "I have also been called juvenile and manic. All a matter of perception." He moved behind Margo, adjusting her sword grip and positioning. "If I may continue on with our lesson." He guided her through the motions. "Step, step, front foot pivot, thrust, dueling is like dancing without uncomfortable Italian shoes and blaring music. Did you know in some countries it's illegal to have red hair and dance poorly in public?"

"No, I was unaware." Margo chuckled. She played along with the silly banter. "And why is that?"

"Triggers fits of laughter, which can be hazardous, as it impedes the operation of large machinery and the blowing of glass. Have you ever tried to blow and laugh at the same time? It is humanly impossible. I invite you to give it a go."

Margo's smile prevented her from accepting the challenge. "It seems that it is truly impossible is for you to remain focused on a task." She readied her sword and repeated the dueling moves without her *de facto* instructor's assistance.

"You are a natural! Excellent maiden attempt!" Andrew applauded. "What do you think of the blade?"

"My hand is small, as such I favor lightness and a larger hilt, akin to the German *Pappenheimer*, which were quite difficult to come-by in the Caribbean." Margo found herself reminiscing aloud. "I paid handsomely for mine."

The bartender made an appearance. Before he could object to the fencing lesson, Andrew placed a hundred dollar bill on the counter. "Give this young woman and I your complete divided attention and a second gratuity of equal or greater value will be awarded." The Scotsman removed another sword from the wall. "That is if I don't sever a finger and need to be rushed to hospital."

The barman took his tip and departed.

"Very well, where were we?" Andrew examined his weapon. "Ah, yes, your rapid progress and obvious appreciation for my humor warrants a promotion to the next level—mock dueling with an adversary. I will play the role of ominous opponent." Andrew flipped up his jacket collar, shut one eye, and combed his coarse carroty curls forward. "How is this for ominous?" he growled.

Margo chuckled. "You resemble an over-dressed murmet that's been harassed by a flock of mischievous ravens."

Andrew pretended to be pierced through the heart. "Your words wound me, madam!" He quickly recovered. "I gather you have spent time in Devon, for murmet is an southwestern England regional name for what we in the Scottish Highlands refer to as the tattie bogle, and what Americans call the scarecrow."

"You are quite the wealth of miscellaneous information, Sir Wallace." Margo resumed her fencing pose. "What do you do when you are not entertaining strange women in foreign taverns?"

"Ah, my day job?" Andrew forced a scowl. "When I am not making a fool of myself before an exquisitely gorgeous and obviously erudite lady in a New City pirate-themed pub, I give unscripted tours of the family estate, Wallace Loch Castle, Inverness, to wealthy camera-clad, souvenir-laden, ghost-hunting tourists. The work satisfies a personal need to perform as it supplements my inheritance, which is so paltry, the accountant claims I must chose between yacht and jet upgrade. Thanks to those PIIGS, both are not an option this year." Andrew removed a card from his billfold and handed it to Margo. "If you are ever in the area, look me up. It would be an honor and a delight to host for you a private tour."

"Thank you." Margo placed the card in her clutch. "Now, may we return to our swords?" She struck a commencement pose. "*Allez!*"

Weapon metal clinked and clanked as the dueling duo exchanged tit for tat along the pathway at the end of the bar.

Margo's high-heels and cocktail dress put her at a slight disadvantage, but her speed and nimble ability to dodge and weave evened the swordplay.

"What grace!" Andrew avoided Margo's thrust by means of a *flèche*."

"Rising to the level of my rival." Margo maneuvered past Sir Wallace.

"*Passe Arriere!* Well done!" Sir Wallace declared. I wager your biography would compare to the Scarlet Pimpernel. It is evident that

214

there is more to you, madam, than meets the eye." He hopped upon the bar." And from this vantage, what an eyeful!"

The dance floor action halted. A crowd began to congregate and cheer.

"Are you trying to distract me?" The Captain felt a rush of competitive energy surge through her veins.

"Absolutely," Andrew confessed, stepping from bar, to a tabletop, to the ground again without missing a blade stroke. "Whatever it takes to keep pace with you, and peer down your cleavage."

Margo had forgotten what it was to engage in combat, to have spectators witness her skill, and her triumph. She glanced at the wall clock; it approached midnight. Andrew was a formidable opponent, but Margo believed she was better. *Time to prove it.*

The feigned fight moved to the dance floor. The piano player pounded a rousing tune to accompany the action.

Andrew continued his fanciful footwork.

Margo shortened her steps and composed her sword.

Andrew lunged forward.

Le coq du troupeau made twisting contact with the base of Sir Wallace's sword. She rotated her blade around his, once, twice, three times, until his grip gave way and sent the rapier sailing upward. Margo caught it by the handle on the downward return, before steel touched polished pine floor. Margo curtsied and handed both weapons to her defeated opponent.

"You have bested me." The Lord fell to his knees before the victorious Lady.

Applause erupted.

"Arise." Margo's winded chest swelled with pride and ebbed with relief. She'd proven much to herself tonight, without setting out to do so. *Serendipity.*

Andrew stood. He kissed her hand. Together they bowed before the crowd. "I've worked up quite a thirst," he declared through a parched grin and infatuated eye. "When they have finished their accolades, please join me for another drink."

The clock struck midnight.

Margo hesitated... *But why?* She was not Cinderella and there was no reason for her to leave the ball. The victor nodded. "Yes, thank you. I would welcome another refreshment."

"Splendid!"

Like Cinderella, the smitten royal she'd danced with, neither knew her name nor her circumstances. Margo enjoyed the little game of mystery. *All part of a woman's fun...*

Chapter 15

HIGHER GROUND

The ruckus of flying sod, tumbling trees, and breaking bushes, coupled with intermitted growls, howls, and groans marred the park's sounds of silence.

Claudia sat barefooted on the grassy knoll dressed in a pair of borrowed sweats, watching Seamus the werewolf Seamus tear up the terrain. He'd been changed and enraged since learning the descriptive details of her encounter.

"Seamus," Claudia called. "It's going to be daylight soon. Can you calm down and turn back? Please. We need to talk."

Seamus stopped short in his tracks and commenced change. His once angry human demeanor now appeared angst.

I scared him... Claudia didn't have prior experience with romantic relationships, but on a few memorable occasions she'd witnessed Alex transform from swaggering ballplayer to panicking beau in the time it took for one of his girlfriends to utter the paralyzing axiom, *We need to talk*, usually before a break-up. This was the first time Claudia wielded the daze phrase, and she hadn't done so on purpose. Just the same, she was relieved to have Seamus's attention. Claudia pointed to his gym bag atop the radio car trunk. "Put on some clothes, first."

The naked patrolman obeyed, and then joined Claudia on the hillside. Seamus's worried demeanor hadn't improved. He kept his head down and his hands to himself.

The fledgling couple sat in stillness for a few long minutes. The calm prompted nature's noises to return to the park. An owl screeched as it passed above.

It wasn't Claudia's intention to prolong Seamus's agony, but it worked out that way as she considered the best manner in which to begin a second talk, regarding their afternoon fight and the traumatic events that followed. The first conversation had ignited her tears and his transformation. Serious topics notwithstanding, Claudia hoped for a more mellow chat this time around. She was feeling different about matters.

"This is killing me," Seamus moaned, leaning back against the grassy ridge. "Say whatever is on your mind already!"

"I'm sorry," in the end, was all Claudia could reply.

"I'm sorry, what?" Seamus implored, hands over his face. "Sorry you're breaking up with me, or you're sorry that I completely screwed things up today?"

"Neither." Claudia placed her head on Seamus's chest. "What happened tonight wasn't your fault, or mine, but it might have been prevented. I'm sorry that I didn't call you for a ride, or wait on campus for the bus." She gave Seamus a playful squeeze. "Or at very least ask Roosky for a lift home."

Seamus put his arms around Claudia and returned the hug. "So, you're not mad? Not ditching me?" His tone still tinged with uncertainty.

"No." She held back maudlin tears. "I never want to lose you."

"Losing you would be worse than death." Seamus stroked Claudia's hair. "I know we're dead, so there's no reason to promise we'll stay together until death do us part." He rolled onto his side and pulled Claudia into the spoon position and clasped his hands in front of her belly. "I don't regret losing the chance to be Kid Blackie, Middle Weight Champion of the World, and I don't question my werewolf life anymore. All my regrets disappeared the day we met."

Claudia snuggled closer. "I know you'll always fight for me."

"Tonight when you told me about those two guys, what they did, I couldn't help turning to let off a little steam." Seamus's his voice remained cool. "But at the same time I surprised myself, because I didn't have the urge to kill or do anything too reckless."

"The plants would disagree." Claudia chuckled. "Midtown Garden's landscape crew will not be happy when they come on duty this morning."

Seamus grinned. "One good thing about the Sarge being out of commission—I won't be called in on the carpet for the mess."

"That's definitely a plus." Claudia paused. "I'm different too." She continued in the vein of Seamus's previous pondering. "The more hours that pass, the less emotionally attached I am to what happened. "And as horrible as the assault was, it was all for the greater good, somehow."

"Really?" Seamus raised an eyebrow.

"Yes. Two dangerous humans are gone. Maybe, hopefully, they will make amends and not choose the Darkside." Claudia felt her spirit lighten as a new day appeared upon the horizon. "I know I said I was sorry for putting myself in harms way, but actually, I feel as though the attack was meant to be, it was my mission. My psyche has already let go of the disturbing aspects. It's healed, similar to the way my body mended after the train hit. I feel like I'm whole again, this time from the inside out."

"You've evolved to higher ground," Seamus replied. "That's what Sevlow calls the conscious peace, and kill detachment you've just described." Seamus shook his head. "Took me five years to get to the level I'm at: *shrub shredder*.

"Shrub shredder?" Claudia laughed. "You're more enlightened than that."

"That's debatable. Your light bulb went off after the maiden kill, which was a double." Seamus kissed Claudia's cheek. "Smart, tough, and gorgeous. Columbus University lucked out, and so did I." He took a tube from his pocket and handed it to her.
"But humor me, in case you decide to go out alone again at night."

"Werewolf whistle, thanks." Claudia slid it into her purse and wiggled around to face Seamus. I'm lucky too. I love you more than ever before."

"But not as much as tomorrow?" Seamus pulled Claudia to him. "Think I've heard that song before." He placed his mouth against hers, the reconciliation kiss.

Claudia replied *sans* hesitation. Seamus's breath was warm, the caress of his lips soft, and the brush of his chin gritty. He explored confidently with his probing tongue. Claudia opened her mouth with a gentle gasp. Higher ground had many rewards.

Bella peered through her kitchen window curtain and watched with delighted pride as Lyman got into his car and drove off to his important job at the *Chronicle*. There was a smile on the smitten reporter's face and a lunch box on his passenger seat filled with leftover dinner packed with love by Mama Stella, who also included a little surprise, a handwritten note with a verse she'd borrowed from a

"Thinking of You" grocery store greeting card: *I hope your day is as special as you are to me. OX Bella*

When Lyman's vehicle was no longer in view, Bella resumed her chores. She didn't mind washing, ironing, and making a trip to the market, because the day would once again end with her man coming home for dinner. *The way it should be.* Bella's waking thoughts were consumed with having the traditional wedded life she'd always dreamed about. Her only stumbling block was time. *Is it too soon after Mickey's death to think about marriage?* The reporter hadn't exactly asked Bella for her hand, but he'd hinted recently. Lyman also wished aloud on more than one occasion after their smooching had prompted him to do the gentleman thing, excuse himself and get some fresh air outside, rather than go too far with a lady who was not his wife.

Bella knew what her womanly desires were telling her to do, but she also knew the old Catholic schoolgirl needed guidance, pious higher ground advice from a trustworthy priest who knew Lyman. Only one person came to mind, Father X. Francis Benedict. Mama Stella made up her mind to pay him a visit at St. Guinefort's.

Margo's dream was delightful. BANG! She was standing on the deck of *Le Coq.* BANG! The sea was calm and the breeze warm. BANG! A man stood beside her. He had an important message. BANG! Margo couldn't see his face, the sun was too bright, but his pleasant voice was familiar. BANG! BANG! BANG! *What is that banging?* Her dream began to fade. She resisted. *Whose voice? What did he say?* The banging was too loud. Margo opened her eyes and covered her ears.

"Mother!" Jacques whaled from the other side of the bedroom door as he knocked with a vengeance. "Wake up, this instant!"

"Go away!" Margo buried her head beneath a mountain of plush pillows. *I must see his face, hear his voice again.* She closed her eyes and tried to restart the reverie.

"I will not go! It is nearly noon!" Jacques rattled the doorknob. "How dare you, stay out until sunrise, with a priest!" He resumed banging. "We need to speak, at once!"

Margo abandoned her reverie reconnaissance. It was a futile effort, anyway. "Vincent!" she called. "Vincent, make him stop!"

"Madam," a third, more composed voice entered the chorus. "I have offered to take Jacques to the park, and then to lunch. He refuses, insisting that you join us."

"May I not have a moment's rest?" Margo hopped out of bed, grabbed her robe and stepped into silk slippers. She hesitated before opening the only barrier between her and the harassment that waited on the other side.

"I hear you breathing, Mother!" Jacques pressed his ear against the door seam. "Come out this instant."

Margo wished the entry opened outward. Jacques could benefit from having a little sense knocked into him. The thought lightened her mood. She released the lock.

"Finally!" Jacques stormed into Margo's *boudoir* and canvassed the room; he was a detective on the hunt for clues. "Is there someone else in here, hiding?" The wannabe Sherlock peered beneath the bed and in the closet. When he found nothing and no one, he smelled Margo's worn outfit that was draped over a chair. "You were in a pub,"

Jacques deduced. "I recognize the aroma of stale beer and salted peanuts."

"Father Benedict and I spent time together in church, singing dirges in the dark."

"Do not mock." Jacques placed hand on hip. "At very least you owe me an honest explanation regarding your evening and why it extend into the morning hours."

"I owe you nothing." Margo made her way to the kitchenette where a fresh pot of coffee sat upon the counter. She poured herself a mug and added a splash of cream to her hot java. There was no better way to begin an American day. Nor better way to end it, either. Margo and Andrew had enjoyed a sunrise cup of coffee and a hearty feast of Moon-Over-Midtown Gardens-bacon and eggs at the all-night diner around the corner from the Piazza. They'd worked up a pirate-sized appetite dueling and dancing and discussing until dawn.

"What are you smiling about?" Jacques questioned with distain. "While you were off gallivanting, I was here, alone with Vincent, bored to tears." He pointed at the butler. "Imagine playing a dozen games of gin-rummy against him until midnight? I was too exhausted and fraught with worry regarding your whereabouts to win a single hand. Vincent took unfair advantage."

"Is there a reason you don't mention the illness that required Vincent's care and prevented your accepting the padre's invitation?" Margo knew full well her son's reply would be angry and defensive. She grabbed an apple from the fruit basket on the counter and headed back to her private sanctuary, steaming coffee in hand.

"How dare you insinuate that my malady was feigned!" Jacques followed his mother across the room as she retreated back to her boudoir. "I am not one to manifest ailments." He forced a cacophony of coughs and snorts. "See why I am unable to join Vincent for lunch in the park? How selfishly unsympathetic you are."

Jacques's whiny tales of woe were spoiling Margo's residual happy humor. Unloading two hundred years of pent-up resentment on Sevlow, the soothing balm of Andrew's comical antics, and a night of much-earned merriment had changed Margo's outlook on life, in ways she was only beginning to comprehend. "I am not in the mood for arguing." The Captain wished to end their futile banter and return to the solitude of her room. "Go to the park, or stay, eat lunch, or go hungry. The choice is yours, but I will not be at your beck and call today."

"You are a horrible mother!"Jacques slapped the mug from Margo's hand and sent its hot contents sailing. "Do not dismiss me like a child!"

Margo stood stunned.

"Jacques, please!" Vincent implored, running to Margo's rescue with a handful of dry dish rags. "There was no cause for you to be destructive or disrespectful."

The Captain examined the fresh stain of steamy coffee on her pink robe and the light brown puddle seeping into the carpet fibers. She felt the liquid burn her skin, but Margo no longer suffered wrath in her heart. *The darkness has dissipated.* Perchance it was the occasion for Jacques to finally be set free as well. *How do I liberate Jacques from his perpetual childhood and allow him to, once and for all, grow old with dignity?* Sevlow's blood had given him a new lease on life, one that would last many years, ending Margo's need to hunt on his behalf. *I must go somewhere secluded to think.* Her mind and body craved the sea, the cliffs, higher ground would provide a better vantage point, a place to ponder the future. *The island.* Margo had not been there since the death of her first son…

"Are you hurt, Madam?" Vincent asked, concern tinting his tone. He handed her a clean towel and commenced dabbing the carpet. "Shall I call housekeeping?"

"What about me?" Jacques addressed the butler with scorn. He pointed to a red mark on the side of his palm, the impact point of skin vs. ceramic. "Fetch me ice, now."

"You fetch the ice or cease complaining," Margo entered her room. "If you've sustained an injury it was of your own impetuous doing." She closed and locked the door before acting upon a confessional urge that had crashed upon her conscious, prompting Margo to drop the spontaneous paternal "F" bomb. "Jacques, it's time you became a man." She took a deep breath. "And you can begin adulthood by not treating your father and me like second-class bootlickers anymore."

Chapter 16

WHO ARE YOU

Oleg sat behind his computer screen, a pile of printed, annotated, and highlighted blurbs and editorials beside him on the desk. "Who you are, black dog?" Roosky inquired aloud as he perused a mythical creatures website. He focused on a sketch of an oversized ominous canine with glowing amber eyes.

"What did you find out?" Wally entered the basement headquarters carrying a tea tray full of treats. "Still think Officer Sullivan commands a hell hound?"

"Not sure," Roosky replied. "Only one policeman article make mention. Most hated enemy, Lyman Newlin, write story that Sullivan have sidekick black dog. All other newspapers say only he hero cop. But Internet full of other dog legend stories."

Wally set the platter down and served Oleg a warm homemade mincemeat scone and a steaming cup of chamomile tea. He glanced at the picture on the computer screen. "That looks a lot like the demon dog we saw."

Oleg double-clicked on the image and read the entry. "In the Highlands of Scotland it is a local legend that the Mawtha Doo—"

"Dog related to Scooby Doo?" Wally interrupted. "Never liked that Scrappy Doo. He talked too much."

"No, Mawtha Doo meaning black dog. Scooby and Scrappy not black and long hairy. Now quit talking." Oleg continued. "Mawtha Doo has haunted Wallace Loch Castle, Inverness, since the unholy Crusades. Townspeople believe that anyone who sees the canine beast will die soon after. The dog is mentioned by writer, Sir Walter Scott, in his poem, *The Lay of the Last Minstrel*." Roosky clicked the bright blue hyperlink. "Want me read poem?"

"I don't get poetry, but go ahead." Wally bit into a scone.

Oleg read:

For he was speechless, ghastly, wan
Like him of whom the Story ran
Who spoke the spectre hound in Man

The sidekick shook his head and commented with a mouth full. "No idea what that means. What's a wan?"

"Don't know." Oleg shrugged. "Maybe it like van."

"Ah," Wally said. "I remember, the Mystery Mobile."

"Old poem not use cartoon reference!" Roosky clicked closed the computer page. "It mean somebody see dog, somebody die."

"Then why is Officer Sullivan still alive?" Wally asked. "And why are we still alive after seeing the dog?" He sipped his tea. "It's those bad guys who are dead, which makes me believe the dog is scary, but good. Saved the Peña girl and spared our lives too. Maybe these big dogs work for police departments around the world, packs of clandestine crime-fighting canine weapons. Almost makes me want to be a full-time good guy!"

"You read too much comic books and Sunday funny papers." Roosky paused to ponder. "But maybe not so far fetch what you say. If true there ghosts, then could be some type secret dog superhero exist besides."

"Well, we are in luck!" Wally exclaimed. "ComicSci is this weekend. If there's a cartoon or real superhero dog, that's the place to find out all about it." The sidekick checked his watch. "Almost time to open-up shop." He collected the breakfast dishes. "We still planning to kidnap Newlin at the event, and hold him for ransom, right?"

"Plan not written in stone." Oleg gathered his dog data.

"Got another idea how we can make money? Those four ComicSci tickets were a thousand bucks," Wally reminded, his tone divulging distress. "Not trying to be the voice of financial gloom and doom here, but we are nearly broke." He picked up the tea tray. "Your trial and appeals cost a small fortune, every penny we'd saved from our old capers. Running a crime headquarters is expensive, not to mention setting money aside for the lawyer fund each month, in case one of us gets arrested again. The butcher shop isn't the moneymaker it once was. In fact, last few years, I barely break-even. You'd be surprised how many vegetarians live in New City these days." Wally gave Oleg a warm loving look. "But besides that, we're healthy and we're back together, right? That's what matters most." The sidekick headed upstairs. "I know you'll think of some way to earn us a big payday, boss. I have confidence in you…"

Oleg watched Wally leave. Coming face-to-face with the dog and death had altered something deep inside the rogue Russian. As scared as he was of being eaten, he was even more fearful that Wally, his loyal and dedicated sidekick, partner, friend, confidant, cook, chauffeur, accountant, would be killed. The real reason *why* he was so terrified of loosing Wally hit Roosky broadside like a wayward iceberg. "Who else be faithful, write letters, send favorite cookies in mail package every week, wait thirty years, then pick me up from jail? How I be so blind?" Oleg felt his cold Siberian heart begin to thaw. "Biggest payoff of lifetime right under nose…"

Jacques's tantrum screams could be heard from the penthouse to the Piazza lobby. The front desk had called to inquire about the disturbance.

Vincent did his best to calm and quiet the flailing man-child. The butler was still in shock himself, grappling with Margo's unexpected divulgence and the onslaught of sentiments and memories it brought crashing forward. "Please, stop, we can explain," he pleaded, as Jacques bounded through the terrace doors.

"I will leap to my death!" Jacques threatened. "No one cares about me!"

"Madam, your assistance is required!" Vincent cried. The emotional onslaught was taking its toll on the old werewolf. He could feel his skin prickle; his vision begin to blur and blacken. "Madam!"

"I am coming!" The captain came from her room. "Jacques, we both love you very much. Stop this madness!"

Jacques broke away from the morphing butler and climbed atop the terrace wall.

"Vincent, pull yourself together. Jacques is going to jump!" Margo pleaded. "Please, Jacques, let's the three of us discuss this like adults."

It was too late. Vincent turned. Two hundred years of catering to a spoiled son and a mysterious mistress had come to a head. The grey werewolf lunged for Jacques, catching him by the seat of the pants before the man-child could tumble to his death or make another well-rehearsed threat.

"Vincent! Don't hurt him!" Margo begged. "What are you doing?"

What I should have done two hundred years ago, acted like a father, thought the werewolf, dragging his horrified son into the suite and depositing him on the sofa. *Stay.* The grey werewolf sat before his charge. *This time you will listen to your mother.*

Neither Jacques nor Margo could hear Vincent's thoughts; however, they both appeared to understand his will.

"All right then, it is time you learned the truth." Margo cleared her throat. "My husband, Sevlow, and the priest you met at the baseball match are one and the same. I left him many years ago because we'd had a son together, a son who died soon after birth, before Sevlow had an opportunity to see his child. The grief drove me…"

Margo's voice trailed off in Vincent's mind. Her words became images of the past. The werewolf found himself observing the events that led to his fathering Jacques.

Margo's grief failed to subside upon returning to Seacliff Manor. In fact, her sense of loss increased ten-fold when Sevlow did not come to England. Margo's pining and bereavement went on for many months.

It was Grandmother who schemed the last effort remedy.

One spring morning Grandmother returned to the manor from the barn with a metal cylindrical tube protruding from her apron pocket. She approached Vincent, who was working in the garden. "I have tried parties and patience and expensive presents, but nothing cheers Margo," she declared in her usual no-nonsense clip.

"Madam?" The butler was caught off-guard by Grandmother's abrupt appearance and forceful declaration. "Is Margo in need of assistance?" He set down his trimming tools.

"You know very well she is," the old woman huffed. *"That is why you must promise to facilitate my request, for I realize what Margo must have in order to recover."*

"Yes, Madam, of course. I will do anything to help," Vincent promised.

Grandmother handed Vincent the tube.

"What is this?" The butler examined the item. *"A medical device?"*

"Good guess." Grandmother smiled. *"I purchased it from the animal surgeon who came to deliver the breech calf."*

"Milk dispenser?" Vincent pressed the metal plunger. *"To nourish the calf while its mother recovers from the cesarean?"*

"A bottle works better for feeding." Grandmother leaned towards Vincent and whispered. *"According to the animal surgeon, this instrument can be used to make a calf, when filled with the bull's seed."*

The butler's eyes grew wide and his face flushed. He attempted to pass the silver cylinder back to Grandmother. "Oh, indeed, well…" he stammered.

Grandmother refused to take it back. "Return the tube to me, full, by nightfall," she instructed. *"I will see to the rest."*

"Madam!" the butler gasped. *"Surely you don't expect—"*

"Yes, I do." Grandmother interrupted Vincent's objection. *"Margo is married to a werewolf and she is a former pirate. Even if she divorced Sevlow, do you think any reputable man would risk his pride to marry a woman who has lived such adventure? My granddaughter's only hope of happiness is having another child, a healthy child, and her only hope of having that healthy child is through a donor, one who can be trusted to keep a secret, to look after mother and child when I am*

gone, one who will live indefinitely, or at least as long as Margo wears that enchanted wolf ring and remains young." Grandmother looked Vincent in the eye. She meant business. "You fit the description and you have already promised to assist."

"Yes, I suppose that's true." The butler took a seat upon the garden bench. "May I have a moment to quell my humiliation and grasp this request?" After a short pause he shook his head. "Who am I to deserve the honor of bringing a child in to the world?"

Grandmother sat beside him. "Who are you?" Her demeanor became gentler. "Vincent, besides those qualities afore mentioned, you are a kind and honest man who has served our family faithfully for years, a man who has twice saved Margo's life. I would be honored to be your child's grandmother." She took his hand. "Be the bull."

****

"My existence commenced with a bovine science experiment!" Jacques covered his face with a sofa pillow. "No wonder I am abnormal!"

"Your unorthodox conception does not make you abnormal." Margo hugged her son. "You are a spoiled child, because your father and I treated you as such. We tried to keep you young."

"Go away!"

"That was wrong, our selfish error." Margo held tight. "Despite my many unspeakable transgressions, Sevlow's blood has provided a second chance, for all of us. We must take advantage of the gift, and live."

Jacques attempted to flee his mother's clutches.

The grey werewolf blocked his escape.

"It is unnerving to me when Vincent is turned!" The man-child returned to the sofa. "I feel like one of the Darling children being over-protected by a possessed Nana." He stuck his tongue out at the werewolf. "If you love me mother, you'll send this old beast to the dog house, so I may leave."

"Do not speak about your father that way."

"After your disclosure, Mother, how can I be sure who anyone is?" He pointed to Vincent. "Who are you, really? Besides werewolf and butler, I know nothing about you. Therefore I must ask myself, who am I? What I would give to be Peter Pan, the boy with no parents who's free to have his own exciting exploits."

"Come to think of it," Margo laughed. "Jacques, you are a Peter Pan man."

"Mock me if you must." He stood. "I wasn't going to leap from the terrace."

"I never know for sure with you, Jacques," Margo said.

"If I promise to be safe and behave, may I go out? Take a walk, alone, to process this unsettling paternity news."

Margo looked at the werewolf, seemingly for guidance. The grey hound nodded. "Well, I suppose you may. However, don't be gone too long, or call if you'll be delayed." Margo stopped. "I sound like an over-protective mother."

"Because you consider me an reckless child." Jacques retrieved his jacket from the closet, pulled an umbrella from the stand, and leafed through the morning newspaper that had been slid under the suite door. "Perhaps after today, that assumption will be altered." He tucked the classified section beneath his arm before departing. "In the future when I am asked, *who are you?* I will be able to answer with pride.

Chapter 17

MONEY

Seamus sat on the wolf den sofa scanning his iTab screen. According to the New City Clerk of Court there were two persons by the name of Waldemar Kowalczyk who lived within the five boroughs. Only one of them owned commercial property. Seamus clicked on the corresponding bright blue link.

As stated in the estate records, Waldemar Kowalczyk inherited the butcher business and building from his uncle twenty years earlier. At the time there was no mortgage on the property and taxes were up-to-date. Over the years Wally had taken out two mortgages, and from what Seamus could gather, his taxes were delinquent. The sidekick butcher was hurting for money and in danger of losing his livelihood.

"What'd you find?" TJ peered over Seamus's shoulder. "Anything that can help us figure out what little red Roosky has planned for an exploding encore?"

"Yes and no," Seamus replied. "Haven't figured out what he and Wally have brewing, but my guess is it involves a big payday. They're broke and owe the tax man."

"A bank robbery?" Dragon suggested. "Or maybe a jewel heist?"

"Too obvious." Seamus shook his head. "The Russian prides himself on out-of-the-ordinary crimes." Seamus ran a Web search for upcoming New City events.

"Look, there's a Chinese art exhibit coming to the Museum of World Art." Claudia pointed to the computer screen. "Maybe Roosky plans to steal a painting and sell it on the black market?"

"After those recent Chinese spy and copy-cat fighter jet fiascos?" Dragon cringed.

"Yeah, the Russians were ticked," Seamus remarked. "Roosky wants quick cash and some front-page fame, not another international incident."

"Or two billion Chinese nationalists who wanna kick his art thief butt," TJ added.

"Astute deductions." Sevlow was listening unobserved from the doorway of the wolf den. He removed an envelope from his pocket and joined the think tank gathering. "This may be the event you're seeking." He handed the envelope to Seamus. "Compliments of Mayor Fink, a gift for the Bomber debacle, as well as a request for additional security services. He was impressed with my students', the pack's, ability to construe the source of explosion so quickly."

Seamus removed four VIP tickets to ComicSci. "Wow!"

"Nice peace offering," TJ eyed the passes. "You have any idea how much money they're worth?" He did a head count. "But there are four tickets and five of us. Who gets left out?"

"No one," the Master replied. "The Mayor spoke with Sgt. Gaffney. He and Seamus have been assigned the special events detail, giving them complete site access."

"Good thing." TJ sighed. "I'd have called age before beauty and told Claudia to find herself another art school lecture to go to instead."

Seamus cringed. Claudia had asked him not to share the details of her evening.

"What's the matter, Claudia?" Dragon asked. "You look upset. TJ was only kidding. We wouldn't exclude you from a mission."

"I know," Claudia answered. "I'm fine, really." Her tone wasn't convincing.

Sevlow fixed his gaze on Claudia. His expression was an invitation for discussion.

Claudia blushed and looked away.

Seamus was sure that Sevlow had the ability to be omniscient. So he was positive the Master knew about the attack on Claudia and her two maiden kills. Before Seamus could regret having to keep a secret from his pack mates, Claudia spoke up. With detached detail she conveyed the events. It was as if she were reciting the play-by-play of an incident that had happened to someone else.

"Damn!" TJ was the first to respond. "You are one brave *chica*!"

Seamus put his arm around Claudia.

"I was more afraid than brave," she confessed.

"Bravery is being the only one who knows you're afraid," Dragon replied. "Sorry you had to go through the ordeal alone, but I am glad you're handling it OK."

"We are all relieved that you have been able to separate yourself from the horrible occurrence," Sevlow said. "Unfortunately, this will not be the first time violence precedes a kill. We have all been attacked in the line of duty."

The pack nodded in agreement.

"Mickey shot me," Seamus reminded.

"The clan locked me in a burning building," TJ reminisced. "I was half barbequed before I was turned."

Dragon ran a finger across his neck. "Decapitated by a madman with a machete."

"How horrible!" Claudia grabbed her throat and winced.

"I'm sure, Sir, you've dealt with attacks worse than ours," Seamus said.

"My share, indeed."

"Worse than being stabbed in the heart by your wife?" TJ inquired. Claudia shot him a *be quiet* stare.

"Speaking of Margo," Claudia continued. "If I may change the subject, how was your dinner with her last night?"

"Our evening began on a pleasant note..." The Master paused.

"Say no more. That woman's holding some sort of grudge and she won't relax until you pay the price." TJ shook his head. "Hope you got lots of money in the bank."

Claudia nudged TJ. "Enough. This is a delicate subject for Sevlow."

"I do not mind discussing my wife's actions and motivations," Sevlow replied. "TJ is correct. "Margo blames me for our son's death. I was on a mission when he was born, and he succumbed shortly after birth. It is the impetus for much of Margo's rancor."

"Son?" Seamus's wide-eyed reply betrayed his astonishment.

"Sir, you don't mean Jacques?" Dragon asked, looking as incredulous as his trio of friends. "Did your blood bring him back from the dead?"

"Please tell us that weird acorn did not fall from your tree," TJ begged, sticking his fingers in his ears. "If you say he's yours, I'm gonna pretend I didn't hear."

The Master appeared amused. "Jacques belongs to Margo and another sire, one who was born a mortal, which is why Margo manipulates nature, via nurture."

"Who's the guy?" Seamus wondered how Sevlow had reacted

when he learned his wife had been with another man.

"Jacques conception did not involve adultery," Sevlow replied. "Margo's grandmother sent me a letter shortly before she died explaining the circumstances. Let it suffice to say his conception began with a donor and a syringe. I was impressed by the old woman's resourcefulness, and Vincent's loyalty."

"Butler turkey-baster baby?" TJ grimaced. "Well that explains a lot."

"Margo keeps Jacques alive with werewolf blood?" Claudia asked.

"Yes," the Master replied. "She used Vincent as the supply source, though over the centuries Jacques built up a tolerance to turned blood. It became less effective."

"Your blood did the trick, alright. Jacques was running around the park the other night full of oomph," TJ recalled. "Like a kid on werewolf caffeine."

"Some people expend tremendous energy, merely to be normal," Dragon said.

"Margo took blood from pure-hearted victims because Jacques didn't fit the bill," Seamus deduced. "Werewolf blood alone wasn't enough to keep him young."

"Prevention is cure." Dragon clasped his hands in a Confucius manner. "For badness is but spoiled goodness."

"Yep," TJ concurred. "Badness is a butt that never got a good spanking." He rubbed his bottom. "Jacques should have grown up on the plantation with my aunties."

"So, basically, Margo over-indulged Jacques," Claudia said. "He never matured, and then she compromised her sense of right and wrong to keep him young and alive."

"With a bloody Methuselah concoction," TJ added. "Potent stuff."

"Your son," Claudia questioned. "Was he werewolf or mortal?"

Seamus could tell from her face that Claudia was very interested in the topic. He figured she wanted to know if their children would one day be werewolf or human.

"Mortals and pure werewolves produce werewolf offspring," Sevlow replied. "However, turned werewolves always give birth to human offspring."

"I was afraid of that." Claudia sighed. "Seamus and I may find ourselves in the same dilemma as Margo. No ageless parent would want their child to grow old and—"

"Yeah, well, since you aren't married, in the motherly way, or plagued by the biological time clock," TJ interrupted. "I say we put the baby talk on hold for now and decide what's going to be done about Roosky before he fathers another mess." TJ pointed to the wall clock. "Tick-tock, ComicSci opens tomorrow and we got to figure out what the bad guys are planning."

"You're right," Claudia deferred to Seamus. "Back to business."

"OK, we know Roosky and his sidekick are short on cash, but they came to Claudia's aide, so violence is probably not on the to-do list," Seamus reminded, relieved that the topic of conversation was no longer paternity eternal. He queried the pack. "Any ideas about how they're might score a payday?"

"ComicSci is more show than sell," Dragon said. "No high-end merchandise."

"In that case, robbing the exhibits won't get him much."

Seamus took notes on his iTab.

"Though I hear that the vendor give-away bags are pretty awesome." TJ rubbed his hands together. "I'm bringing an empty suitcase for the haul."

"There'll be celebrities at the event," Claudia remarked. "They may have worth."

"Posing as the paparazzi and selling photos to the tabloids?" TJ supposed. "Hmm, maybe Roosky plans to set up some sort of humiliating hoax and capitalize on it?"

"Or else he's plotting a kidnapping," Seamus said, scouring the names of A-listers posted on the ComicSci website.

Dragon read the celebrity attendee register over Seamus's shoulder. "In some countries kidnapping is a huge moneymaking business."

"Wealthy people don't want the world to know they've been victims so it's pay-up and keep quiet." Claudia pointed to a featured name on the ComicSci site. "Imagine if The Stone was unlucky enough to be kidnapped by old Roosky and his sidekick?"

"If his fans found out, Stone's action-hero days would be over!" TJ exclaimed. "He'd be on B-Street auditioning for roles with the govern-ator."

"Posing as a photographer in order to ensnare a rich and famous target is highly plausible," Sevlow remarked. "Excellent team detective work." He checked his watch. "Please excuse my departure. I have an appointment at St. Guinefort's."

"We can handle this, Sir." Seamus felt honored that the pack appeared to be on the right track. He wondered if TJ, Dragon, and Sevlow had strategy sessions about former missions, or was this a new trend? Mid-thought, Seamus's phone tweeted, indicating he had a new text. "It's from the Sarge." Seamus read the message. "He has the building blueprints and ComicSci schematic for us to review."

"Ask the Sarge to scan and send as an attachment." Claudia pointed to an armoire at the back of the room. It was outfitted with office equipment. "I'll print copies for us."

"The Sarge is Old School." TJ laughed. "Tell him to attach a document and he'll probably search his pockets for a paper clip."

"So true." Seamus nodded and smiled. "This is Sgt. Gaffney's first text and he's had a cell phone for years." Seamus removed a motorcycle key from his pants pocket. "I'd better head over to the station house and pick up the documents."

"We'll comb through the attendees and come up with possible victims." Claudia took the iTab from Seamus. "Last thing Mayor Fink needs is another high-profile event with a messy ending."

"A dip in tourism could be costly to the city," Dragon noted.

"That's right," TJ agreed. "In our guard dog business, crime is money."

Jacques slumped on the bus stop feeling dejected and bewildered, like an unemployed Martian lost in space. He'd scoured the classifieds and answered a dozen HELP WANTED ads; however, not one employer had expressed an interest in hiring him. In fact, none even offered an interview after reading Jacques's application. Instead, in each instance he was thanked for his time and shown to the door. "At this rate," Jacques lamented. "I will be dependent on Mother *ad infinitum*."

"Mind sharing your bench?" came an aft request, interrupting Jacques's pity party. "We're waiting for the bus too."

"I am not waiting for public transportation, I am merely resting and recovering from rejection." Jacques turned around to see two colorful clowns, one sky scrapper tall, the other fire hydrant short, and both sporting red rubber noses, rainbow wigs, and tie-dye overalls. "Is the circus in town?" the man-child asked, his tone turned cheerful. He scooted two places to the right.

The clowns sat beside him, the shorter of the two in between, his stubby legs dangling off the edge of the bench. "Much obliged." He reached to shake Jacques's hand. Before their palms touched, a bouquet of plastic daisies appeared, seemingly from thin-air. He handed the flowers to Jacques. "A gift from me to you."

"How did you do that?" Jacques marveled, accepting the gift. "Truly amazing!"

"Awe, that's nothing," the taller of the two entertainers replied, leaning across his friend and touching the tip of Jacques's nose.

Quarters began to pour from the man-child's nostrils.

The petite clown caught them in his top hat, which also appeared from nowhere. "Look, you're made of money!" he exclaimed.

Jacques was afraid to move. He heard the clink of metal, but felt nothing leave his body. Still, the shiny proof was before him. "How can this be?" he muttered.

"It's magic!" The tall clown snapped his fingers, turning off the coin spigot. "Thanks for the bus fare." He waved his hand over the hat three times and then removed two MetroCards. "Much easier than counting change." He handed a plastic pass to his diminutive friend. "The name's Alto, and this is my friend and partner, Itsy," the giraffe of a jester said. "Hope we lightened your mood."

"Yes, yes, you both have," Jacques prattled, hopping up from the bench, wishing he had some spellbinding act to impress them with in return. "Such incredible talents, it must be a simple feat for you to find fulfilling employment." Jacques removed the newspaper classifieds from his coat pocket. The tattered pages were adorned with crossed-out highlights, a record of his unfruitful quest. Jacques's somber mood returned. "I have never held a job, not in over two hundred years, and fear my pointless providence is cemented in stone." He returned his bottom to the bus bench with a weighty sigh.

"Two hundred years?" Itsy remarked. "You got an accent. Maybe they count by 4's where you from." He nudged Alto. "Get it? Like dog math sort of in reverse."

"So, you're looking for a job?" Alto inquired. "What type?"

"Oh, any sort, really," Jacques replied. "As long as I can be in charge, and not have to wake up too early in the morning, or lift heavy objects. Hmmm, nothing that involves bad smells or dirt either, and I prefer excitement to tedium—no toiling behind a desk all day beneath diffused florescent lighting." He thought a moment. "The job venue must not be static, and the pay should be such that I can continue to live in the manner to which I've become accustomed. Although, I will make do without a butler, for reasons I prefer not to discuss." Jacques frowned. "But alas, no such job exists, and if it did, I would not qualify for the position."

The clowns whispered to one another.

"Are you athletic?" Alto asked. "Can you skip? Hop? Tumble? Run?"

"Oh, yes. I am very energetic since receiving the serum. But even before that I would partake in long strolls through the garden with

Vincent," Jacques said. "And every morning I jump on my mother's bed until the pillows and covers have been bounced onto the floor. Does that count?"

"Sure, why not?" Itsy declared. "What about public experiences? Have you been around crowds, or lots of different types of people?"

"Sadly not." Jacques shook his head. "I've spent an inordinate amount of time with three people, my mother, who used to be a pirate, and my father, who is our butler and a werewolf. Before that, my grandmother was a force and fixture in our lives. She, to my great sorrow, passed when I was a young man, on the same day as Napoleon."

Itsy blinked. "Dynamite?"

"Bonaparte."

The clowns again conferenced in hushed tones.

Jacques wondered why his disclosures made people react oddly. It was as if truth and honesty were no longer welcome commodities on the social stock exchange.

"We are prepared to make you an offer," Alto announced. "$500 a month to start, plus room, board, costumes, laundry service, travel expenses, and three days of paid vacation after a year."

"A job?" Jacques was flabbergasted. "With whom?"

"With Sideshow Inc. The parent company of Silly Circus, Clown Caravan, and Quigley's Believe It Or Not." Itsy pulled a multi-page contract from his pocket. "No better entertainment outfit to work for. The company let's us use the van for close gigs and they even have a road trip travel train complete with game room, snack bar, theater, and jungle-gym gymnasium. The three of us would share a sleeping birth. Hope you don't mind close quarters?"

Jacques shook his head. "Mother insists I sleep alone, but I prefer not to, especially when there's a rainstorm."

Alto pointed to the building where Jacques had visited. "We came downtown to post a HELP WANTED ad at the employment Agency. Our new act lacks a middleman."

Itsy stepped beside Alto. "See?"

Jacques observed the height disparity. "I do!" He wedged between them and pointed. "Small, medium, large. Symmetry and balance."

"Exactly. All we need is your signature and the trio is complete." Itsy handed Jacques the contract and a pen; he signed without question. "Welcome aboard!"

"Clown Caravan was hired for a one-day gig at ComicSci." Alto took Jacques by the arm. "There's lots to learn by tomorrow, so you'd better come with us."

Jacques saw the bus approaching. He thought about his mother and Vincent. If he didn't phone them or return to the hotel soon they'd worry. Was he really ready to run off and join the circus? To be the middleman in a clown act, with two people he'd just met, whose faces were obscured behind layers of white makeup and red rubber appendages? Jacques wavered. Then he remembered the money... $500 a month seemed like a grand sum, enough to finally give him freedom and independence, the chance to begin anew.

The downtown NC27 opened its doors.

Jacques hopped aboard.

Bella's mood was as bright as the afternoon sky gleaming through her open car window. She pulled her vintage silver Pacer up to the curb beside St. Guinefort's Home for Orphaned and Troubled Boys. Bella shifted into park before checking her watch. She was early for the appointment with Fr. Benedict, or maybe she was late. Mama Stella couldn't quite understand the marble-mouthed woman who'd answered the telephone and scheduled their meeting. Tardy or prompt, she figured the padre would be in residence regardless of the time. Like a cuckoo in a clock, what else did he have to do?

The iron gates leading onto the school grounds were locked. Bella scanned the key panel for a buzzer or bell. There was none. *Maybe there's another way in*? She walked around the corner to the back of the property and found an open entry that led into an expansive patch of wildflowers surrounded by a perimeter of sassafras and willow trees in full spring bloom. Bella ignored the NO TRESPASSING sign. She closed the garden door behind her.

Hoards of first-generation Monarchs feasted upon the colorful flora. Bella had never before witnessed such a display of winged brilliance. At the far end of the garden were three young boys dressed in Navy and white uniforms with St. Guinefort's haloed dog crests embroidered on blazer breast pockets. Each child was holding a different research tool, one a net, the other a magnifying glass, and the third a notebook and pen. Bella slipped behind the trunk of a willow and observed as the students examined butterflies and recorded data. The adolescent trio spoke in pleasant tones as they assisted one another. *What smart and happy children.* Father Benedict's boy's home seemed such a peaceful oasis. Mama Stella couldn't help but wonder if Mickey would have turned out differently had he attended a private boarding school, somewhere in the quiet, calm countryside, away from the good-for-nothing hooligans he ran amuck with in the city. But that would have required money, more than the Stella family income could have afforded. *What about bartering?* Bella didn't give up easily, not even on an irrelevant "what if" fantasy. *What if I'd asked Fr. Benedict to admit Mickey as a day student? In exchange I'd have worked at the home, cooked meals, sewed uniforms and costumes. Surely the school had athletic teams, a drama club?* Her fingers began to toil at the joyful thought. Bella missed adolescent Mickey; she missed having a job; she missed Lyman when he was at the office. That's why she was here to see the padre. If Bella were permitted to marry the Jewish multi-divorced Lyman, then she would once again have a family, and she could accept her new husband's offer to finance a Mama Stella's pasta sauce business. She kept her fingers crossed.

The sharp point of a garden trowel pressed against her pantsuit-covered thigh returned Bella from her matrimonial reverie.

"What doing you hiding here?" demanded a little woman sporting a yellow polka-dot apron and matching rubber galoshes that turned up at the toes.

Bella took a step back and gawked. *She's a dressed up toadstool, and that cartoon voice!* It reminded Bella of gravel sloshing around the wet bottom of an empty fishbowl. Mama Stella was sure it was the same woman who'd answered her call and scheduled the padre's appointment.

"Speak I but you not answer." The tiny woman scowled.

"The front gate was locked." Bella defended her presence in the garden. "I'm meeting with Fr. Benedict."

"He not now here." The gatekeeper's demeanor softened a bit.

"When will he be back?"

"Follow me wait." The woman took Bella by the wrist and escorted her onto a mossy cobble path that led to the school. "Me, Terra." She pointed to herself and smiled.

As they walked together Bella couldn't help but notice the little lady's oddities in more detail. Her front teeth, top and bottom, were long and squared-off, much like a rabbit's. *She's about the size of a bunny, too*. Her height (or lack of) made Bella feel tall for the first time in her life. The woman's age was also difficult to guess. There was a serene resolve about Terra that only came with the passing of time. Yet her skin was wrinkle-free, denoting youth. The woman's smooth white hand reminded Bella of marble that had been carved into a tiny statue. The resilient stone chosen by sculptors because it withstood the years and elements, like Terra.

The diminutive duo arrived at the school, an 18th century gothic revival edifice.

Bella stopped in her tracks and marveled at the building's stunning romantic architecture: ornate scrollwork around the windows and doors, ominous gargoyles atop the drainpipes, stone sentry hounds flanking the front entrance, beveled lead glass windows, and a grey slate gabled roof. If she were still a little girl, dreaming of being a princess, this would be her home.

"Step watch it." Terra pointed to the first of three granite slabs that led up to the open oak and iron double doors.

Bella minded her feet as she ascended.

Once inside, the little hostess walked her charge through the lobby to a wooden bench outside the office of Fr. X. Francis Benedict. "Sit here you. Bring I tea."

Bella's bottom fit comfortably in the bench's indent; the century old worn remainder of the many schoolboys who'd sat squirming as they waited to see the Head Master. *Mickey could never sit still, either.* The image in Mama Stella mind, of wiggly anxious young boys, made her heart warm. She liked this place. Despite all the stone and stained glass, the school felt welcoming and cozy. It truly was a *home*.

The noon lunch bell sent a flood of about thirty boys into the main corridor. They appeared to range in age from pre-school to late teen, represented numerous races, and came in a variety of sizes and shapes. As such, some student uniforms fit better than others. A dark-haired disheveled corpulent lad clutching the front of his stretched shirt caught Bella's attention. She waved him over.

"Yes, mam?" asked the boy now standing before her.

Bella pointed to his shirt. "Have you lost a button?" She figured him to be about seven and wondered if he were an orphan or a troubled child.

The boy nodded. "It popped off." He handed her a sweaty white button that he'd been holding in his fat fist.

Bella reached into her purse and took out a travel sewing kit that contained a scissor, thimble, needles and an assortment of threads, spare buttons, zippers, and dress hooks. In a jiffy the boy's button was reattached, and two loose ones tightened. She then quickly darned a hole in the snot-smeared sleeve of his blue blazer, tied his open Oxford shoelaces, and straightened his clip-on tie.

"Thanks!" The beaming boy admired his newly mended reflection in the hall mirror. "Are you someone's grandma?" He threw his arms around the seamstress and gave her a hearty hug. "I'm Eugene. I wish you could be my granny."

Mama Stella wasn't prepared for the innocent display of affection. Her emotional floodgate gave way. She cried for the joy of having made a child happy. She wept knowing her dream to be a grandmother was dashed the day Mickey died. She bawled and blubbered because her soul ached to love a little boy again.

"Did I hurt you?" Eugene looked stunned by Bella's sudden sobbing.

"Mrs. Stella?" a man's concerned voice inquired. It was Fr. Benedict.

Mama Stella dug a handkerchief out of her pantsuit pocket. "I'm fine," she stammered, mopping crocodile tears while gathering her sewing supplies and placing the kit back into her purse. "Have to go," she sniffled. Bella couldn't discuss Lyman or marriage with the padre when she was feeling emotionally maternal. "I'll call and make another appointment." She set her sights on the front door, but not before catching a glimpse of the bewildered boy.

Eugene smiled and waved. "Goodbye."

The tears flowed again, but this time instead of reaching for her handkerchief, Bella took out her wallet and handed a medley of $1's, $5's, and $10's to Fr. Benedict. "This is for your boys," she cried. With that, Mama Stella ambled out of the building, vowing to herself that if she ever struck it rich in the pasta sauce business, St. Guinefort's Home for Orphaned and Troubled Boys would share her money.

Margo contemplated Jacques's call as she sat atop a rocky cliff and stared into the brilliant orange sun that was setting upon the vast blueness beyond Round Island. On one hand she was pleased that her son had taken the initiative to find employment, on the other hand,

Margo was terrified. What type of "secret job" would require Jacques to leave home immediately, without so much as packing a suitcase or saying *adieu* face-to-face? *Had he joined the military? Been duped into taking part in an illegal endeavor?* She found slight solace in the fact that Vincent was investigating. In the mean time, all she could do was wait, and worry.

A stone landed beside Margo. She picked it up and scanned the sky for a bird that may have made the drop. There was none. Moments later a second sailing stone skidded to a halt when it encountered Margo's *derrière*. "What is going on here?" She stood and brushed off her slacks. A pebble bounced past her boot. "Jacques, is that you?"

"No, it is I, Andrew," declared a ginger-haired man stepping out of the afternoon shadows. "But if you prefer to watch the sunset with Jacques I can try to locate him."

Margo was not completely surprised that Andrew had followed her from the hotel. She was pleased to have the company. "You threw the stones?"

Andrew nodded. "Afraid if I startled you with words or an approach you'd tumble from the edge the cliff." He bowed with flair. "Of course, I would have saved you."

"Really?" Margo teased. "Unless you fly better than you fence, a rescue effort from such a height would have been futile."

"Ah, true, true," Andrew replied with a twinkle in his eye, like a smitten teen accepting barbs from his beloved beauty queen. "Perhaps your husband, Jacques would have saved you? Any man who could win your heart must have mystical powers."

Margo smiled. *You are correct... and quite wrong.* "Jacques is not my husband, he is..." she faltered briefly. "He is my father, and although my adroit husband owns this island, he will not be making an appearance." Margo had noticed a posting near the abandoned tollbooths that contained Sevlow's anagram surname corporation. It read:

Private Property
Owned and Maintained By LeVows, Ltd.
No Trespassing

"We are alone. I am relieved." Andrew sighed. "Are you here to consider island renovation plans?" He pointed to the ocean view. "Breathtaking, and such close proximity to New City. Perfect for developing into a resort community for the seafaring shopper. I'd be willing to invest in a luxury skyscraper condominium complex, or two."

"I highly doubt my estranged husband has any intention of turning these cliffs and dunes into a tourist resort. Although he has always been quite fortunate with investments and money, acquiring wealth is not his life mission." Margo caught herself before she uttered that being a werewolf was Sevlow's purpose and passion. That, and the island held many memories he wished to preserve.

"Well, bully for him," Andrew replied, his tone genuine. "So why did you come here, alone, to the cliffs? Forgive me for having noticed, but you appeared distressed upon leaving the Piazza, which is the only reason I hailed a cab to followed your cab." Andrew touched her shoulder. "Rest assured, I am not a stalker."

"My father has taken a sudden job and he will not disclose the employer," Margo said, unsure why she was telling the truth... or *almost* truth. "The position requires him to travel extensively," she continued. "Since leaving my husband, Jacques has been my constant companion. I am not sure how to deal with the many changes his departure will bring, and I worry for his safety."

"If I am to understand correctly." Andrew rubbed his fuzzy chin. "Your father, whom you call by his given name, has a secret occupation that may be dangerous. This is the same father who taught you to wield a sword like a buccaneer?"

"Something like that." *What a tangled web we weave when first we venture to deceive.* Margo turned away, not wanting Andrew to detect the white lies.

"Oh, well, then." Andrew made an about-face. "Perhaps I should depart before your UKSF father and your Bruce Wayne husband drop from the sky and teach me a violent painful lesson, one I had hoped never to learn: Do not fancy a complicated beautiful woman. Either/or, but never a woman who is both." Andrew raised his arms and addressed the deserted dunes. "Hold your weapons. I surrender. As you can clearly see, good Sirs, I have done no harm to Margo."

"Oh, Andrew!" Margo laughed. "Must you always be a clown?"

"Why? Do you not like clowns?" He grimaced. "A gypsy woman once told me I was a court jester in another life. History often repeats itself."

If truth be told, Margo loved clowns and she enjoyed the company of the ginger-haired jester. She also required his assistance. "Let it suffice to say I am amused." Margo observed that the daylight was quickly fading and she had no lantern or means of summoning a cab. "Now if I may inquire, how did you plan to return to the Piazza?"

Andrew removed a cell phone and an envelope from his jacket pocket. "The cabbie who drove me here is waiting on stand-by at the old tollbooth. I would be happy to give you a lift back to the hotel and

I'd be honored if you accept an invitation to join me tomorrow at ComicSci." Andrew crossed his heart. "Strictly platonic."

"A date?" Margo raised an eyebrow. "What is ComicSci?"

"To a pop-culture fan, sci-fi aficionado, computer geek, adventurer like me," Andrew replied. "It is the Justice League, World's Fair, and Oscar night rolled into one."

"How did a tourist from Scotland come by such coveted passes?" Margo did her best to contain her excitement at the prospect of attending such an event.

"At the risk of sounding snooty," Andrew said. "All it required was money."

Chapter 18

BALL OF CONFUSION

Seamus sat beside Dragon in the ComicSci control room. Seven surveillance screens sourced by twenty convention hall cameras recorded the floor and a trio of public entrances being manned by Claudia, TJ, and the Sarge. Sevlow was also in position, dressed in his priestly garb perched atop the theater balcony. Once the doors opened and hordes of eager costumed attendees spilled in, the hall would be one big ball of confusion. Keen observation and swift communication were paramount. Seamus turned on his walkie-talkie and pressed the conference button. "This is Seamus, do you read?"

The team each touched their earpiece and gave a thumbs-up sign.

"Audio and visual are good to go on our end." Dragon fine-tuned the monitor tint. "Request individual voice feedback."

"Sound check. Station one…" Seamus called and the pack replied as Dragon adjusted volumes from his control panel.

A red light on the wall was activated.
"We have five minutes," Seamus relayed into his mike. "Almost show time."

✶✶✶✶✶✶✶✶✶✶✶✶✶✶✶✶✶✶✶✶

The colorful costumed Clown Caravan trio pulled a washer-sized four-wheeled props trunk that was being ridden by their speckled terrier, Freckles. They stopped at the convention center employee entrance registration table. "Welcome to ComicSci. You must be the clowns." The attendant scanned his information sheet. "Third act, main stage, dressing room B," he said while checking the act off his list.

Vincent appeared as soon as the trio plus pooch had entered. He was wearing black-rimmed glasses, a fake grey beard, and a pair of harlequin overalls. The butler-in-disguise flashed a counterfeit Sideshow Inc ID. "Forgot something in the van," Vincent remarked, pointing to the entertainer register. "I'm with them."

The attendant nodded. "Your buddies are headed to dressing room B. Follow the signs. It's behind center stage."

Once inside, Vincent ducked into the men's unoccupied lavatory, removed the overalls, and dumped them into the trash bin before checking his visage in the mirror. *Jacques does not recognize me*, thought the butler, pressing on the uplifted corner of his gluey beard. He'd been following his son, watching in the recesses as the troupe practiced, stalled, and bonded together as a team in record time. After a series of failed back-flip attempts Jacques threw his usual frustration temper tantrum and threatened to quit the trio. Unlike his doting mother, Tiny and Alto shrugged and pointed to the door. The rookie clown hesitated, took a deep breath, and then gave the maneuver another try. He was successful. His teammates applauded. It was a turning point. Vincent was impressed at the theatrical and maturation progress Jacques made in 24 hours. His son was at ease in front of the dress rehearsal commuter audience that Clown Caravan had entertained in Midtown Gardens Park subway station earlier that morning. Centuries of being the center of attention had prepared the man-child for natural showman. *Who would have expected such talent?* Vincent's undead heart swelled with paternal pride. *If only Margo were here to watch Jacques perform.* The butler washed his hands, departed the restroom, and strolled across the exhibit hall floor looking forward to act number three.

****

Oleg and Wally stood in an animated cluster of anxious costumed fans awaiting the start of ComicSci. Within their general admission line were no fewer than a dozen sci-fi enthusiasts sporting Hank Solo flight gear, six representations of Commander Dirk, five fuzzy green Goyas, four *Fright of the Living Dead* zombies, three Creepers from the Dank Lagoon, two spandex-clad Wander Women, and a lone Duke Skyblazer who was swinging a glow-in-the-dark foam rubber saber sword to the serenade sound of the *Star Lords* theme song that was blaring on his vintage boom box.

Wally fiddled with Oleg's cape. "These snaps aren't as secure as buttons."

"It no big deal," Oleg grumbled. "This bad guy not go fly through galaxy." He yanked the fabric from Wally's hand. "Leotard itch place I don't scratch in public and mask make face wet from nose vapor." Roosky lifted the plastic makeshift visor and used the cape to dab his cheeks. "How much longer to door open, Sunshine Head?" Oleg pointed at Wally's spiky cardboard coronet. "You look like Statue of Liberty what dipped cranium in tomato paste."

"The name's Red Giant, dastardly brilliant sidekick to Baron Blackhole." Wally struck an ominous pose. "Faithful to a fault, he was!"

Oleg rolled his eyes. "Well goodie for make believe comic book person."

"It's a shame you didn't have Captain Milkyway action figures or the *Space Avenger* Saturday morning television series in Russia." Wally checked his watch. "ComicSci should start any minute." The vermilion-faced sidekick removed a to-do list and a smoke bomb from his pocket. "Let's go over this again, Boss," he whispered. "When the time is right I'm gonna light this little ball and create confusion. When everyone's distracted we capture Newlin and his girlfriend, then you get him to withdraw all his newspaper retirement account money while I hold her prisoner. That way Lyman doesn't do anything funny until we get the cash, escape, and no one's the wiser because these costumes protect our identities."

"That the plan." Oleg nodded despite not being convinced it would work. Regardless, there was no turning back. He and Wally had too much invested in the get-rich-quick scheme to stop midstream. Roosky crossed his fingers.

A cavalry trumpet announced the commencement of ComicSci.

****

Margo stepped out of the taxi and marveled at the mass spectacle that was ComicSci. It had been ages since she'd seen such a colossal crowd gathered for an event. The 1889 Paris World's Fair came to mind. It had also been a spectacle. Besides the exhibits, there was the newly unveiled Eiffel Tower. Margo, Jacques, and Vincent were one of the first family of spectators chosen to ascend the enormous edifice. Jacques's age was stalled in his twenties back then, and he was quite handsome. Women took notice, including the female event *attaché* who picked him from the crowd of anxious tourists wishing to view the tower. Jacques and Margo pretended to be brother and sister, with Vincent as their father. *I have masqueraded most of my life,* thought Margo as she returned from her memory and scanned the costumed crowd. She felt out of place. Margo had asked the hotel boutique to send up an outfit suitable for an afternoon fair. Her high-waited black slacks, fitted knit silk tee, and white leather bolero jacket now seemed inappropriate attire. "Should we have dressed for a day of make-believe, instead?"

258

Andrew chuckled. "We are here as *voyeurs*, not participants," he whispered in Margo's ear as he guided her through the masses to the VIP entrance. "As very important persons we bypass all commoner confusion." Andrew handed the uniformed entrance employee two gold foil tickets. "Think Cinderella making her grand entrance at the ball."

****

Claudia stood to the side and observed ComicSci attendees being admitted via the VIP entrance. A stylish pair prompted her to do an about-face double take. The woman had to be Margo, Claudia was sure, yet the Captain looked strikingly different, in a modern fashionable sort of way. *And who's that man she is with? He looks very familiar too.* Although Claudia was certain Sevlow's wife and the red-haired man had nothing to do with Roosky, the sighting was more than noteworthy. The sentinel engaged her radio. "Station three to base. Do you read?"

"Loud and clear." Seamus viewed Claudia on the control room monitor. "What do you have?"

"Margo with an unknown escort." Claudia spoke in a hushed tone, not wanting to be overheard by the nearby couple.

Dragon got a screen lock. "That's her, or a 21st Century twin." He enlarged the picture. "And if I weren't witness to his death, I'd wager Margo was walking with red beard the *noblesse oblige* pirate or his reincarnation."

"You're right," Seamus marveled. "Wait until Sevlow sees them."

"He may already have." Dragon pointed to an uninhabited screen. "The Master's left his position." Button number four on the communication panel was unlit. "And shut off his radio."

"Sevlow's on it." Claudia caught a glimpse of the Master pretending to be engaged in an exhibit near the approaching pirates. "Let him handle this one."

"Agreed." Another monitor attracted Seamus's interest. "Well if it isn't Lyman Newlin and Mrs. Stella, dressed up like space royalty." He observed to the duo also making their way through the VIP entrance.

"Seems I was assigned the busiest door." Claudia suppressed a chuckle upon also spotting the costumed couple. "Probably no need to worry about these lovebirds unless one of us loses our temper and turns."

"We definitely don't want any front page pack news," Seamus remarked.

"Well look here." Something else on the video monitor caught Dragon's eye. "Saw this guy go into the men's room before the doors opened." He rewound the tape. "Went in wearing baggy clown overalls and exited without."

"I heard that," TJ chimed in on the line. "I see grey beard and remember the clown pants. He's headed towards the theater. I'm on his tail."

"Right, follow him." Seamus tuned his frequency. "Sarge, you read?"

"Affirmative." Gaffney crossed through the crowd. "If I move to this side of the doors I can keep an eye on TJ's entry and my own."

"Good. I'm going downstairs." Seamus grabbed his backpack containing first-aide supplies. "Hope we won't need these. Call me if you spot Roosky and sidekick."

But it was too late. Baron Blackhole and Big Red had already made their masqueraded way through the momentarily unguarded commoner entrance and were headed to the exhibit floor.

****

"There they are!" Lyman pulled Bella across the floor towards the *Space Avenger* cast who were seated in wheelchairs in front of a video screen that was showing clips of the old series. "I'm so excited to finally meet my heroes!" Lyman's face flushed, hands jittered, sweat bathed his brow, and his heart was a delirious drum, thumping over the delighted din of the ComicSci crowd.

"Calm down," Bella scolded. "Quit acting like a star-stuck little kid with flu symptoms." She pulled a stray thread from his costume. "Today you're Captain Milkyway, protector of the universe, and all things honorable. Now take a deep breath or you're gonna have another heart attack end up making a fool out of yourself in front of those old fogies."

"You're right," Lyman replied. "Maybe we should wander around the other exhibits first so I can compose myself."

Bella removed a folded program from her purse. "Why don't we check out a show first?" She read from the list of performers. "Main stage opens with Martian the MC and his comic repartee, he's followed by a pop singer whose name I can't pronounce because it has no vowels, and then a clown act." Mama Stella stopped there. "I like clowns. The first ten years of his life Mickey was a clown for Halloween. I sewed every costume."

"Beautiful and talented." Lyman kissed Bella's crown. A robot walked past them holding a funnel cake. "Yum!" The wannabe hero sniffed the air and rubbed his tubby tummy. "I'm in the mood for something sweet and delicious?" He spoke softly into Bella's ear. "But not as delicious as it will be to nibble on your neck later."

Mama Stella blushed. "Oh Lyman!"

Lost in their own little love space, Captain Milkyway and Princess Stardust failed to detect their nemesis's presence.

****

"It's them!" Wally screeched, poking Roosky's breastplate. "What do we do?"

"For start, be quiet." Oleg wiped a finger smudge from his abs-illusion armor. "It too early for caper. Pay big money for tickets. Plan is enjoy show for while but keep eye on most hated enemy. They easy to spot and not leaving soon." Roosky reviewed his ComicSci program. He pointed to a colorful promotional picture and handed the folded leaflet to Wally. "We watch third act."

"Clowns?" Wally reviewed the schedule, his red eyebrows displaying disbelief. "I didn't think you liked clowns."

"True, dislike painty face, creepy, scary, not funny idiots," Oleg shrugged. "Famous Russian clown, Popov, different story. He in best own league. But something tell me Clown Caravan worth watching. Maybe it little doggie."

****

As Andrew and Margo wandered the ComicSci floor, the Captain had the odd sensation that they were being watched. Surveillance cameras were positioned throughout the convention center. *A routine safety measure, the source of my suspicion?* Still, her skin prickled as it did the night Sevlow trailed her through Midtown Gardens Park. His daybreak kiss had ignited her soul and opened her eyes to romantic possibilities. *If not with Sevlow, than why not with another?*

The Captain had lied to Vincent, told him she preferred solitude, to cope with Jacques's abrupt departure. The butler had been his usual accommodating sympathetic self, offering to give Margo her privacy while he trailed their son. He'd departed the apartment before dawn. *Gasp!* Someone brushed against Margo. She reacted with a start. *Now I feel as though I am being accosted too.* Margo picked up her pedestrian pace as she scoured the bustling crowd to no avail. *It's a sea of masks, make-up, and costumes.*

"Is there something the matter?" Andrew broke into a trot to keep up with his date. "Are we being chased?" He looked over his shoulder. "Is there some other entity, besides your estranged husband and spy father, whom I should fear?"

"I don't know," Margo professed. "I feel as though we are not alone."

"We are not alone," Andrew said. "We are amid the ComicSci masses."

Margo halted. He was right. Her paranoia passed. "I am behaving foolishly."

"Not in the least. Crowds can be maddening." Andrew led Margo out of the fray and into a less congested corridor. "Rest assured, we do not have to stay if you are out of sorts. Give the word and I will return you to the Piazza." He gave her a doe-eyed stare. "There, or anywhere else in this entire world you prefer to be, as long as journey and destination include me."

Margo found herself smitten with Andrew Wallace's doting charm. She smiled. "Here with you is where I wish to be."

"Excellent," the pirate progeny replied. "I propose we abandon the hustle and bustle of the convention floor for a spell." He removed a

ComicSci program from his pocket. "May I suggest refreshments and a show?"

The idea agreed with Margo. "I would welcome warm tea, a sweet pastry, and a comfortable seat away from this swarm."

"Very well." Andrew ushered his date across the exhibit hall to the theater, where their VIP passes secured them two assigned balcony folding chairs. "The first act begins in fifteen minutes," he noted after Margo was seated. "Please excuse me while I make a hasty jaunt over to the snack concession for our tea and crumpets, which on this side of the pond will most likely be disguised as coffee and donuts." Andrew handed his companion the performance agenda. "I shall return before they send in the clowns."

****

The festive ComicSci isles were alive with the sounds of movie and television series theme songs and episode reenactments as sci-fi stars mingled with faithful fans and outer space wannabes. It was the perfect backdrop for the pack to observe the action and follow their marks without drawing any unwanted attention.

Sarge trolled the entrance foyer.

Sevlow followed Margo and Andrew to the theater.

TJ hung close to the spectacled bearded man, and detected the scent of wet dog.

Claudia's undead arteries ached as she watched Lyman and Bella share funnel cake and deep-fried pizza, washed down with a triple-thick Italian cheesecake milkshake, all part of their gastronomic food court romancing.

Seamus scouted the scene for anything suspicious that might lead him to Roosky, while Dragon watched the action via control room video.

At noon, Sevlow, TJ, and Claudia merged with their respective marks at the main stage where the crowd was standing room only. The lights dimmed.

****

Jacques peeked his rainbow wigged, white faced, and red nosed head through the blue velvet show curtain. The spotlights made it impossible for him to see the audience beyond the stage. However, it was evident from the hum and energy radiating within the dark theater that it was a packed house. His adrenaline pumped for joy. In the last twenty-four hours Jacques went from feeling like a lead balloon to being a rising star.

"Time to take our places," Itsy instructed. He tapped Jacques on the shoulder while Alto set needle on vinyl and Freckles sat patiently on her duck tape mark.

The trio scurried to take their positions as Julius Fucik's *Thunder and Blazes* crackled on an old Victrola. The curtain was about to part.

****

Seamus slid into the back aisle beside Claudia, who was six rows behind Lyman and Bella. "Looks like the usual suspects are here, minus Roosky," he said before stealing a kiss. "I'd rather be clowning around with you than watching the show."

"Me too." Claudia scooted in front of Seamus and wrapped his arms around her waist. "But we're at work. Music means the curtain's about to open."

From where he was standing Seamus could see Margo and her redheaded pirate pal seated in the VIP area on the second level. Sevlow had to be close by. If Claudia were with another man, Seamus knew he'd be turned by now; the convention center would be trashed, deserted, and the *Chronicle* evening edition would tell the tale of a mad dog responsible for the mayhem. Seamus wasn't certain if it was love, fear, or selfish pride that triggered his furry fury. Maybe it was all three. Whatever the reason, Seamus was glad he'd fallen for sane and secure Claudia instead of someone who enjoyed taunting her mate. For the red haired pirate's sake, Margo was lucky she was married the Master, and not Kid Blackie.

****

Vincent's palms perspired as the curtain rose. The moisture stemmed from restraint as well as nerves. For the first time in centuries, the butler could not assist his charge. Jacques's fate was in his own white-gloved hands. *Was the morning's dress rehearsal a fluke?* Vincent wondered if the man-child could master the entire routine on a real stage, before a paying audience, illuminated by intense footlights, following the step-by-step instructions he'd so recently been taught. Clowning was not a simple endeavor. To hold attention via well-timed noises: a clap, snap, bell or buzzer, walk in a comic manner, fall without getting hurt, handle props and animals with ease, exaggerate every action without turning one's back on the audience, turn nimbly and back up with confidence. Live comedy requires enough time between happenings for the audience to absorb the action and laugh. And last, but certainly not least, the most successful clowning always has a surprise finish. Vincent stood transfixed as Jacques and his pals did all that was required, and more.

The audience was on its feet, cheering and howling with laughter. The greater the applause, the better the team seemed to perform. Even the little dog appeared to rise to the occasion. Her tiny tail wiggling with delight as she danced on two-legs beside Jacques who spun hula-hoops on his arms and legs while dodging juggling pins being tossed by Itsy and Alto. It was brilliant.

A familiar voice shouted, "*Encore!*" as the act approached its crescendo.

It was Margo on the balcony. Vincent was certain. *Does she know it is her son who entertains center stage?* There she was, on her feet, smiling the way she used to, many moons ago. *But who is beside Margo?* The butler's keen werewolf vision honed in on his mistress's companion. He gasped. *The scar-faced pirate who ended my life. How can that be possible?* The undead butler felt his skin prickle; his vision began to blur. "This is Jacques's time to shine. I mustn't ruin the performance," he muttered, forcing his attention to the stage. "The show must go on." The twenty-minute act was approaching its back-flipping, slap-sticking finale. Still, Vincent could not stay focused, could not control the violent centuries old death memories flooding his brain. He was angry, sweating, losing consciousness. A large black man was rushing towards him...

****

Oleg held his breath every time Alto tossed Freckles into the air. "Poor doggie!" the Russian moaned. "Throw midget clown instead, see how it feel!" he cried.

"Boss," Wally shouted above the roar of the enthusiastic crowd. "They're here too." He pointed to Lyman and Bella who were seated nearby, at the end of the bleachers.

"No pointing, no screaming in public." Oleg, looked away from the stage in disgust. "Enough of cruelty to animal show. Perfect time for caper."

"You're right," Wally replied. "If I light the smoke bomb now everyone will think it's part of the clown act finale. We can grab Newlin and his girlfriend without making a display of ourselves." The sidekick nodded. "That's why you're the boss, Boss."

****

Lyman set the last of his deep-fried jellybeans down on the bleachers. He wasn't feeling too hot. No, on second thought, he was hot, burning up, and chilly at the same time. *Maybe all this excitement and fatty foods have given me the flu?* Lyman suddenly felt jabbing, piercing pains in his back, neck, and jaw. It was hard to breath. He was hit by a wave of dizziness, nausea, and fatigue. The reporter wished he could lie down. His body was becoming rigid goop...

****

Seamus turned his gaze away from the stage to check on Newlin and the rest of the gang. *Two costumed audience members sneaking up behind Lyman and Mama Stella.* It was as if Seamus had taken a step back from the Monet. The picture was finally in focus. "Roosky's after Newlin!" He scooted past Claudia and scrambled his way through the packed isle. From the corner of his eye, Seamus spotted a gray wolf— part wolf, about to be bear-hugged by TJ. Smoke began billowing up behind the reporter. *Where was the smoke coming from? Was it part of the clown show?* A scream. *Bella.* Seamus hurdled a row divider and caught the reporter after he tumbled from the bleachers, but before his head hit the concrete floor.

****

There was a painful pounding in and on his chest. Lyman opened his eyes. It was that policeman, Sullivan.

"Hang in there, Mr. Newlin," pleaded the officer, removing a small oxygen tank from his backpack. "Paramedics are coming."

"I'm having a heart attack…" Lyman couldn't tell if he'd thought the words or uttered them. There was smoke, people rushing around. So many sights, smells, sounds, everything in view was melding together, becoming one big ball of confusion. Lyman gasped. Bella's screams began to fade. The pressure in his chest diminished. The grey haze was now being replaced by white light. "Beautiful," he muttered. Lyman wasn't afraid. The reporter in him was curious. *Is there life after living?* A voice in the recesses of his muddled murky mind told him to let go. He obeyed.

Lyman was gone.

Chapter 19

STAIRWAY TO HEAVEN

Lyman Newlin awoke pain-free with a smile, to the sound of lapping waves rolling beneath a brilliant blue sky. He was dressed in casual cruising attire, reclining upon a deckchair, atop a gently rocking raft. Warm light bathed him in love as it muted his memory. The excruciating events that lead him here were fast fading to fuzzy. *I'm dead?* Lyman wondered. It didn't matter. If this was Heaven, he never wanted to leave.

A 38' Wheeler Playmate fishing boat carrying three men and a woman pulled up along side Lyman. The woman unfastened a rope ladder while the man steadied Lyman's raft. Except for their ages, the two bore a striking resemblance to Alejandro Peña and his sister Claudia. "*Señor* Newlin," the woman said "*Dé la bienvenida, pero es temprano.*"

Lyman did not recall knowing Spanish, yet he understood her words. "Welcome to you too," he replied. "What do you mean I am early?"

"Your pickup was not scheduled for some time," the man with a slight Spanish accent explained. He reached out his hand. "No matter. Please, come aboard."

As Lyman climbed the ladder, he noticed the boat's name painted on the aft panel. "Pilar?" the reporter marveled. "Is this *the* Pilar?"

"She is my Pilar," a second man replied. He was tanned and shirtless, standing beneath the cabin overhang. His timbre voice, salt and pepper beard, firm paunch, and prominent square jaw were clearly recognizable.

"Ernest Hemingway…" Lyman was awestruck. "Then I must be in Heaven."

The author laughed. "This is my Heaven. Yours hasn't been determined."

Lyman was confused. "Who chooses where I spend eternity?"

"Your free will decides, but not at present." Ernest pointed to a bench seat along the wall of the covered compartment. "Make yourself comfortable while Gregorio ferries Pilar to the drop-off point."

A thin weathered man stood at the wheel. He nodded and waved.

"Gregorio Fuentes," Lyman gushed. "Also an honor. I wrote your obituary for the *Chronicle* a few years ago. Lived to be104-years-old, inspiration for *The Old Man and the Sea,* to actually meet you, and Mr. Hemingway, I just can't believe…" The crusty old newspaperman found himself at a loss for words. If he were alive he'd have another heart attack from the thrill of meeting his literary idol and his idol's first mate muse.

"That thoughtful tribute is the reason you're on our list," Ernest declared. "From time-to-time we transport journalists, cross them over. My writing career began as a correspondent on the front lines. It's the least I can do for *mis compañeros.*"

"To someday leave the newsroom and write a novel was always a dream of mine," the reporter remarked. "Unlike you, I never made the time or found my own inspiration." Lyman suddenly realized that was his biggest life regret.

"NO! PLEASE! NO!"

A shrill screeching voice ricocheted through Lyman's head. He covered his ears and sat down on the bench. "What was that?"

"*Tu novia*," the woman replied. "*Está triste*."

"Yes, my girlfriend is very sad." Lyman sighed. "The grief Bella's experiencing is heartbreaking. First to lose her son, Mickey, then me." Lyman wished he could hold Bella in his arms and tell how much he loved her, one last time.

"Paz was right," Ernest declared. "You arrived early. Returning is still an option."

The reporter peered across the boat into the tender peaceful light. He felt like a moth, unable to resist the brightness that filled his soul with peace, love, and joy. "Please take me to the other side," Lyman asked. "Before I change my mind."

Gregorio engaged the engine.

****

As they cruised through Ernest Hemingway's Caribbean azure Heaven, Lyman had the opportunity to glimpse upon the horizon those things that had given the author happiness in life. There were summers in Wyoming and winters in Key West. Lyman sensed the laughter of children and grandchildren and the passionate embrace of lovers. He saw books and manuscripts and fellow novelist friends in Paris: Gertrude Stein, Ezra Pound, and James Joyce. Work mattered. People mattered. Love mattered most of all.

Lyman wondered what would comprise his Heaven. Parents and childhood, Mom's cooking and Sunday afternoon baseball games with his father would be there for sure. His ex-wives… not such a good idea. Children, grandchildren, Lyman lamented having none to call his own. But he had his career, especially the exciting Scorpio days. The reporter chuckled. They didn't make cops like Hank Scorpio or bad guys like Oleg Roosky anymore. Pity the Russian never received recognition for his creative crimes. In his hay day, Roosky was certainly a notorious and memorable character. Speaking of characters, there was Clarabella Stella, beautiful, fiery, loyal, love of his life. Lyman would have the blissful but brief memories of their time together for his Heaven. *Can those few short weeks sustain me for an eternity?* Lyman suddenly had the overwhelming impression that he hadn't lived or loved enough.

"We're here," Ernest announced, as Gregorio steered Pilar beside a golden stairway that appeared to spring forth from the sea. "Pleasure to meet you, Lyman." The author offered his hand. "Another envoy is waiting for you up there."

With that, Lyman found himself standing on the first rung of the stairway as Pilar motored away. He ascended three steps and froze. Although the loving light was warm and welcoming, Lyman wasn't ready for a paradise of unfulfilled dreams and incomplete memories. "Wait!" he called to the departing vessel. "I've changed my mind. I want to go back!" They did not hear him above the hum of the boat's motor. Lyman couldn't let his ride get away. He dived from the stairway and landed chest-first atop the placid water with an electrifying jolt, like he'd been zapped by a pair of defibrillator paddles, the AED cranked up to high.

"We've got a heartbeat!" the paramedic yelled.

Chapter 20

I SAW THE LIGHT

"Stand back," Seamus instructed, flashing his badge and motioning to the gawking crowd that had gathered around the prone reporter. "Give the guy some air."

"Lyman's alive!" Bella pulled herself away from Claudia's comfort embrace and rushed to her man's side.

"His heart's ticking, mam, but we gotta get to the hospital. Don't want to lose him again." The paramedics lifted Lyman unto a gurney. "Have some papers for you to fill out in the ambulance. Need to know what types of medications your husband's on."

Bella gave the paramedic a blank look.

"You're his wife, right?"

"She's not," Claudia answered. "But they are very close. I'm sure Mr. Newlin would appreciate having Mrs. Stella riding beside him to the hospital."

"Against the rules." The paramedic shook his head as he lifted his end of the gurney and began rolling it towards the exit. "Only family's permitted in the ambulance."

Seamus saw the light in Bella's eyes fade as her tears welled.

"What if Lyman dies on the way and I'm not his wife?" Mama Stella sobbed.

Seamus found himself pitying the poor old mama. If Claudia's life hung in the balance, marriage or no marriage, rule or no rule, nothing would be able to keep him away from her. Seamus hoped they'd never have to cross that mortal bridge. He touched Claudia's shoulder. "You'd better go with Mrs. Stella. Now that I know Lyman was Roosky's intended target, the rest of us can handle things here."

"Good idea. I'll call when we arrive at the hospital." Claudia caught up with Bella, who was trailing after the paramedics. "Come on," she took Mama Stella by the arm. "I'll find us a cab and we'll follow Mr. Newlin to New City General together."

"Hey, Officer Sullivan."

Seamus heard a familiar voice call his name. He looked away from Claudia to see Dragon walking towards him, escorting an unmasked Oleg Roosky and his sunburst sidekick, Waldemar Kowalczyk. Roosky was holding a little brown and white spotted dog in his arms.

"Look who I caught trying to slip out the theater exit." Dragon checked behind him. Another threesome was tailing them. "Besides lighting off a smoke bomb, and giving Lyman Newlin a heart attack, they've gone and angered the circus act."

"Those thugs stole Freckles!" Alto pointed at the pup. "Give her back!"

"Don't deserving dog!" Oleg responded to the clown with ire. "If not for paralyzing superhero kung-fu grip on deltoid, I punch you nose for torture to animals!"

Dragon released his cranky catch.

Seamus shook his head at the sight of the motley crew. "What do we have here?"

"Have you again," Oleg grumbled, rubbing his shoulder. "Seem like you only cop in whole New City."

"Officer, we didn't touch Lyman Newlin." Wally crossed his heart while professing. "The guy grabbed his chest and fell off the bleacher as I lit the smoke bomb."

"No confessions," the Russian scolded. "Anyway, clearly as day anyone see most hated enemy get heart attack from eating too much garbage food." Oleg held Freckles in one hand as he patted his unitard-clad belly. "Only lean meats, vegetables, and boiled potatoes in this body." He hugged Freckles and cooed. "For now on doggie get same diet. No more funny clown food."

"That's our dog and we want her back!" Itsy demanded. He poked Seamus in the thigh. "Arrest that canine thief!"

"I give you $100 for dog," Oleg offered. "Then it not stealing."

"She isn't for sale!" Alto exclaimed.

"$200." Roosky upped the ante. "Take it or leave it, final offer."

Wally gulped. "Boss, we ain't got any extra cash."

"$300, most final last offer!" Roosky roared. "Or I continue stealing doggie and you get nothing!"

Jacques pulled his teammates into a conference huddle. "That's a lot of money we could split three ways."

"Well, we did adopt her from the pound," Itsy reminded. "Maybe we can go back and get a talking bird instead. Don't have to walk a bird."

Jacques and Alto concurred.

"It's unanimously agreed." Itsy addressed Roosky. "Pay us three-hundred buckaroos and Freckles is yours."

"No surprise greedy clowns see light of green money at end of dog tunnel." Oleg held his open palm out to a frowning Wally who counted a wad of bills pulled from his tattered wallet. The amount came to $300, exactly. The sidekick passed the sum to Oleg, who in turn handed it to Jacques.

"Thanks!" The jubilant jesters scurried off and ducked behind the stage curtain, presumably to divvy their spoils.

"We're officially broke," Wally lamented. "Not even enough change left in my pocket to pay the toll home."

"Where you're going there won't be any need for money." Sarge joined the cluster. "Taking you two down to the station house for questioning."

"For what charge?" Oleg scoffed. "Smoking in public? Dog not on leash?"

"Destroying private property," the Sarge replied. "Let's go."

"You have no proof we blew up the plumbing at Bomber Stadium." Wally covered his mouth. "Oops…"

"Devoted idiot sidekick not know what he saying." Oleg scowled at his partner in crime before addressing the Sarge. "Make it quick interrogation. Want to get out of costume before I forced to scratch pubic in public." The Russian pointed to Dragon. "Come along for police car ride. Want to know how to making such good death grip. You two fingers same as muscles from ten men."

"I could use another set of eyes on these wily characters." Sergeant Gaffney motioned to Dragon before glancing at Seamus. "Meet me at the station house when you're done here." The Sarge and Dragon led the suspects out to the radio car.

Four down, three to go, thought Seamus, shooing the last of the theater gawkers. "Nothing more to see. Move along. Next show begins at one." He surveyed the emptying theater and wondered why TJ and Sevlow had been conspicuously absent from the Lyman-Roosky circus.

He checked Margo's VIP box. It was vacant. There was no sign of the bearded, half-changed gray wolf, either. Seamus turned on his radio receiver as he made his way back onto the convention center floor. "TJ, you read? Over."

"Don't read much but I watch TV," TJ replied. "Walking in from the loading dock with Vincent. Ole Jeeves needed a little fresh air to recover from a hairy incident. He saw rotten red the pirate with Margo. Brought back some furious memories."

"Not surprised," Seamus said. "A dagger to the carotid artery would be hard to forgive and forget." The plainclothes patrolman headed past exhibits towards the freight area. "That means Vincent hadn't seen the guy earlier. Gotta be a logical explanation for the weird resemblance."

"Speaking of weird," TJ chuckled. "You'll never believe who's a clown."

Seamus considered the query. If Vincent wasn't at ComicSci with Margo and her pirate pal, then he was there in disguise keeping an eye on his son. Seamus spotted the big man and the butler approaching. Vincent had removed the fake beard and glasses. Seamus turned off his headset. "Going to take a wild guess and say Jacques joined the circus, and Margo's none the wiser even after seeing Clown Caravan in action," he deduced upon meeting up with his pack mate and Vincent.

"Not bad, Columbo." TJ nodded. "Vincent, meet Officer Seamus Sullivan, Seamus this is Vincent Wells. He's one of us." The men shook hands.

"Truly a pleasure and an honor." Vincent beamed. "Certainly not surprised to learn Sevlow's tutelary instincts have enabled him to amass a such fine pack of young men, and a young woman, as well, I hear."

Seamus sensed a longing in Vincent's tone. He wondered if the butler had once-upon-a-time hunted evil with the Master, or was he always Margo's personal watchdog? Reminded Seamus he had to keep his hovering habit in check. "Claudia's special," he replied, "Anyone who can put up with us and baby-sit for Mama Stella has to be."

"I was a little distracted in the theater," TJ reminded. "How's the reporter?"

"Thought Lyman was a goner when he first went down. Hope he pulls through. I've gotten used to having the old guy on my tail." Seamus checked his watch and wondered if Claudia and Bella had arrived at New City General.

****

Seat belts notwithstanding, Claudia and Bella slid to and fro across the rear bench seat of the speeding, jockeying cab in hot pursuit of the speeding, jockeying ambulance, which had the traffic-altering benefit of a siren and flashing signal light.

"We're gonna be bruised bananas if he doesn't take it easy!" Bella bellowed. "Tell him in whatever language he speaks to slow down!"

"I don't speak Farsi or Urdu." Claudia clutched the grimy door handle. "Pointing at the ambulance was enough to set him in pursuit."

"Well then un-point before we get killed!" Bella pressed her silver space boot heels against the back of the empty passenger's seat, Princess Stardust costume bunching around her waist. "I don't give a crap if Abdul sees my girdle and loses all his virgins!"

"Excuse me, Mister," Claudia called, waving her right hand behind the driver as she continued to clutch the door handle with her left.

The Pakistani cabbie peered into his rearview mirror and smiled with pride at the panicked passengers. "I drive fast for you." His Indy skills were impressive, indeed, but unfortunately he'd taken his eyes off the road a second too long.

Claudia saw the light change from green to red… Life shifted into slow motion.

CRASH! The little yellow taxi never had a chance against the big green garbage truck. The driver's side of the cab was annihilated on impact.

****

Margo left Andrew listening with rapt intent to a panel of writers and actors discussing their new sci-fi television series called GONE, about a Greyhound bus full of eclectic anguished passengers that leaves Sin City for West Plymouth and runs out of gas during in a dust storm, somewhere in the Mojave dessert. The stranded clan treks to a mysterious uncharted town run by coyote and jackalope. Government experiment gone awry or are they *really* GONE? The Captain scoffed at the preposterous premise. She took the opportunity to excuse herself to the ladies room and thus lure her lone wolf pursuer to a location more suitable for private conversation.

Margo glowered at her husband as she exited the women's restroom. "No paranoia. My suspicions were correct." Sevlow was waiting on the benches near the public pay phones with a gaggle of other doting mates. "Has the top-dog succumb to cat and mouse games?"

"You look beautiful, my darling." Sevlow ogled his wife. "Finally, I have you alone, away from the pirate progeny." He reached forward to embrace her.

"How incorrigible!" Margo stepped out of his grasp. "You've ignored me for two hundred years. Why now must you insist upon making a nuisance of yourself?"

"Time has little meaning to me, ergo I was a fool to let you be." Sevlow made a second attempt to his wife. This time she did not resist. "Love is everlasting, Margo. Please grant me another chance to prove my worth as your husband."

The Captain tried her utmost to thwart his emotional grasp, to no avail. Her tears of anger and pent-up passion began to well. "Sure, disrupt my life and then mar my makeup." she half-joked; hoping soggy mascara had not given her runny raccoon eyes.

"With or without adornment, there is no woman who trumps your beauty."

Before Margo could withdraw from his embrace Sevlow advanced and took the kiss she secretly desired. His arms were around her, as secure and strong as the sea that had kept *Le Coq* afloat. Margo succumbed to a wave of vulnerability that left her flaccid and feeble. *How could I ever replace him with another?* Margo thought the words as the jovial din of Andrew's voice and his pleasant face faded into oblivion. Sevlow cradled Margo and kissed her again, gently upon contact, then building to an ardor that forced her to grab his frock for fear of completely losing herself to the act. His unrelenting mouth caused her inner seas to ebb and flow with mad desire. Before Margo could forbear any longer she was kissing him back. "I hate myself for loving you," she cried, wishing they were alone, longing to be consumed by his adoring strength.

"Jacques belongs with the clowns, Vincent with the pack, and you with me," Sevlow whispered, his lips still brushing hers.

The love spell was broken. Margo tore herself from Sevlow's arms. "What do you mean Jacques belongs with the clowns?" she demanded.

"I assumed that is why you were here," Sevlow replied. His brow displayed wonder of a man caught unawares. "To observe your son perform with the circus act."

Before there was an opportunity for Margo to gather her stunned notions and reply, a silent alarm was sounded. Sevlow's innocent demeanor morphed into one of abject concern. He kissed his wife quickly. "Something has happened to one of my pack. I must go." The Master was in the midst of a hasty departure before Margo had the wherewithal to shout out that once again she was required to play second fiddle to all things mission related.

Andrew approached Margo. He cleared his throat.

"You following me too?" Margo snapped seeing the pirate progeny standing sheepishly beside her.

"No, the TV chat ended. I merely sought to catch up with you." Andrew cast his eyes to the ground and hesitated.

What has Andrew seen or heard? The Captain speculated, but at that instant she could not care less.

"What shock to find my date kissing a handsome priest outside the lieu." Andrew pointed to a group of people who were obviously discussing Margo's recent behavior. "I was not the only spectator stunned by your very public display of forbidden affection."

"I will kiss whomever I damn well please, whenever I damn well please!" Margo declared, loud enough for the onlookers to hear.

"Well, I suppose you have every right," Andrew stammered. "Nevertheless, priests do take vows, and we are on a proper outing, having a lovely time. Not at the point of kissing, but getting along famously, or so I assumed." Andrew's face had turned as red as his hair. "May I ask if doing as you damn well please is a frequent or an occasional urge? I will not make a judgment based on your response, I merely—"

Margo terminated Andrew's mid-sentence ramblings with a firmly planted kiss. A kiss that contained the same passion as the one she'd recently shared with Sevlow, except it originated in a very different place. Where Sevlow's kiss was rooted in love and desire, Andrew received his from a site of furious defiance and personal pride. *I am through being a caretaker! It is time, once again, I come first and wait for no one!* The words echoed through the halls of Margo's defiant mind.

More basic animal emotions reverberated through Andrew's being, manifesting themselves as quavering flesh and bulging trousers.

Margo ended the PDA before she had unintentionally pleasured the poor man too far. "Take me back to the theater to see the clowns," she instructed as soon as their lips were unlocked.

Awed and stupefied, Andrew resembled a man who'd seen the light and desired more. He complied.

****

Claudia awoke to the aroma of gasoline, garbage, and the metallic scent of fresh blood. She was covered in it. A mangled section of the door had pierced her side upon impact, skewering her flesh and organs like a ghoulish shish kabob. The pain was excruciating. Claudia knew her gruesome wounds would heal and her horrendous hurt soon subside. *What about the others?* With painful effort she was able to turn her neck to see how Mrs. Stella had fared. It was then Claudia noticed that the cab driver's lifeless head hung by a thread upon the seat divide, compliments of a shard of window glass lodged deep in his throat.

Bella moaned.

A good sign. Claudia could see that Mrs. Stella's side of the vehicle was banged, probably during a spin, but it had received the least amount of damage. The fact that she had moments before the crash purposely lodged her feet behind the seat in front of her had been a saving grace. Bella's body was intact. The only visible blood on her seemed to come from Claudia and the nearly decapitated cabbie. "Are you alright?" Claudia rasped, her voice compromised by two punctured lungs.

"I am dead," a man's voice replied in Urdu, yet Claudia understood as if he'd spoken in English or Spanish.

"Yes," Claudia confirmed. "You died instantly."

"Did I hurt you?" The ghost cabbie hovered in what remained of the front seat. His eyes were wide and blank. He stared at his tattered remains. "I can remember nothing of the crash."

"That's best." Claudia knew he had to enter the light if he saw it, or run the risk of guilt and remorse holding his spirit earthbound. "Do you see the brightness?"

The cabbie gazed through the shattered windshield and smiled. "Yes, it is very beautiful. My brother is there." With that he was gone.

Claudia heard a siren in the distance. *The hospital is close by.* A crowd had gathered. She reexamined her wounds. Some were healing, but not fast enough. Claudia required time to mend, but not with witnesses and medical staff. *I need Seamus.*

Mama Stella moaned again.

Claudia tried to retrieve the werewolf whistle from her purse. Her mangled hands were not cooperating. "Mrs. Stella, can you hear me?"

Bella looked around, her eyes were glassy, dazed, and confused.

"Reach into my purse." Claudia nudged her bloody bag over to Bella. "Find the whistle—it's a skinny silver tube."

Like a programmed robot, Mama Stella rummaged around and located it.

"Blow," Claudia pleaded. "Put it to your lips and blow as hard as you can!"

Bella obeyed.

To a mortal there was but a breathy silence channeling through the cylinder.

To a werewolf it was a sound quite different...

****

"Argh!" Seamus threw his hands over his ears.

TJ and Vincent did the same.

"Who blew the whistle?" Seamus looked around for the source.

"It was Claudia." Sevlow appeared behind his men.

This time the werewolves did not hesitate before kicking into gear.

Seamus knew 12th Avenue was the quickest route to New City General. He was out the door and on the sidewalk sprinting even before the Master. *Claudia needs me.*

Two blocks from the convention center, traffic had come to a standstill. Seamus suspected he must be close to whatever had caused Claudia to sound the alarm. His running path was also congested with walkers, gawkers, and dawdling tourists. Seamus leapt atop an idling car and shifted into high gear across vehicle hoods and roofs. Honks and hollers be damned, there was nothing going to stop a werewolf on a mission. Seamus caught sight of the wreck on the corner of 55th Street. A team of good Samaritans was working to open the doors of a mangled taxi. He could hear their urgent dialogue.

"I see three people," the unscathed driver of the trash truck shouted. "The cabbie is definitely dead. There are two women in the back. One's in pretty bad shape."

From his path atop a bus Seamus spotted fire engines making their way bit by bit through the gridlock. He had to get to Claudia before the Jaws of Life could be employed. Tarzan in the concrete jungle, Seamus traversed traffic, scaled a telephone pole, and swung onto the scene. "Claudia!" he shouted, peeling back a small jagged portion of the passenger side door beside Bella.

"Seamus," she replied, her voice thin but clear.

"How you two holding up?" Seamus peered through the serrated opening. All he saw were bent wrinkled knees.

"Mrs. Stella seems to be in shock. I'm on the other side. Can't fully mend because there's a hunk of metal stuck in my stomach. I'm still too weak to pull it out by myself."

"Don't go pulling anything out, miss!" the truck driver cautioned. "An ambulance is on its way." He addressed Seamus. "You a doctor?"

"I'm a cop, her boyfriend," Seamus answered, assessing the damage. His plan was to tear open the taxi, remove Claudia's obstruction, and currier Bella to the hospital, but that would garner the patrolman some unwanted attention. He required a diversion.

"Oh man!" TJ exclaimed, arriving like a freight train at the station. "We gotta get Claudia and Mrs. Stella out of there but not including an audience or videotaping." More than a few spectators with smart phones were recording the wreck and its aftermath.

"You thinking what I'm thinking?" Seamus eyed his pack mate.

"I'm thinking it's about to get pretty hot and windy around here." TJ caught sight of Sevlow, Vincent, and Dragon. "Got some capable reinforcements coming."

"Ran from the station house as soon as I heard the whistle," Dragon said. "What do you need me to do?"

"First I need everyone besides us to take a step back." Seamus flashed his badge and motioned to the group that had gathered. "We're a trained emergency team. But we gotta have room to work."

The trash truck driver ran to his vehicle and returned with a spool of yellow CAUTION tape. "This do you any good?"

"Thanks." Dragon roped off a circle around the crash site.

Seamus peeked into the vehicle. "Sit tight, Claudia. We're going to make this rescue as quick as possible."

TJ whispered the plan to his later arrival pack mates.

"Good thinking," Sevlow declared. "Operating in tandem we can penetrate a larger area while Seamus releases Claudia and Mrs. Stella."

A blustery fire commenced.

Phones and cameras fell out of hands like scorching hot potatoes as gale force virtual reality winds sent the crowd scurrying for cover.

Seamus peeled the cab door off as if it was a piece of tin foil on a squished sandwich roll. The grizzly scene he saw inside nearly made him turn. "Claudia!"

"I'm fine, really," Claudia assured. "Except I want this metal shaft out of my stomach." She tugged on the projectile. "It must be lodged between ribs."

Seamus flipped the driver's dangling head into the front seat. "Seamus!"

"Can't concentrate with him staring at me." Seamus stuck his hand into Claudia's belly and felt around for the end of the rod. "Yep, stuck between your broken ribs." He pushed a finger against cracked bone.

Claudia winced.

"Sorry. Almost have it out." Seamus gritted his teeth and maneuvered the tip of the rod as he pulled the end through her middle.

Claudia's gut was skewer-free. She pushed her organs back into place.

"Shut your eyes. The restoration process goes faster if you imagine yourself whole again." Seamus straightened Claudia's broken leg. The limb made a loud CREAK and POP. "For better or for worse, your mind is a power tool." The patrolman glanced over at Mama Stella who was staring transfixed at her silver go-go boots that were still pressed against the broken front seat. "An outer space cork about to pop."

"You are bad." Claudia's eyes were still closed, her body almost mended. "Better to have Mrs. Stella in quiet shock than be stuck back here listening to her scream, or worse, have her watch my body regenerate."

"True," Seamus agreed. "That would be a hard one to explain away."

Claudia inspected her limbs and torso. "Not 100%, but good enough, considering I'm still covered in the driver's blood."

Seamus assisted Claudia through the improvised taxi door and grabbed her purse. "You've had your share of excitement for the week."

"Without a doubt." Claudia shook her head "Never an dull undead moment."

Seamus motioned to the pack. "We're good to go!"

The elements ceased. An ambulance turned the corner.

Seamus pulled Bella from the taxi. "Don't worry, Mrs. Stella. I've got you."

Sevlow took over for the patrolman. "Excellent work."

"Padre?" Bella mumbled. "You here to give me last rights?"

"That won't be necessary." Sevlow helped Mama Stella into the ambulance.

"Claudia, I have to head over to the station house. Sarge took Roosky in for questioning. Seamus tried not to seem as if he were giving Claudia an order. "Let Sevlow make sure Bella gets to the hospital. TJ and Dragon know the routine—head back to the wolf den before reporters arrive and everyone touched by the elements starts blabbing about the strange phenomena… Do me a favor, please, ask Vincent to take you home."

"Vincent?" Claudia repeated, her voice sounding more than mildly surprised. She turned around to see the butler approaching. "He's on our team now?"

"Whistle cut our chat short. Didn't get the whole story." Seamus shrugged and smiled. "I'm sure you will, though."

"She's healed and walking!" The trash truck driver fell to is knees upon seeing Claudia. "It's a miracle! That cop performed a miracle! Who are you? What's your name?"

"This is why I'm on park patrol. The sooner we get out of here, the better." Seamus gave Claudia a quick kiss before making tracks towards the station house.

****

Margo's search for the clown trio led her to the convention center employee parking lot where she observed the colorful performers packing their gear into a white logo panel van. Margo realized immediately that the middle-sized clown was indeed Jacques. Her heart swelled with maternal pride. A poignant quote came to mind: *There are two lasting bequests we can give our children. One is roots, the other is wings.* Jacques appeared to have earned his wings, finally.

"You aren't planning to kiss the clowns as well, are you?" Andrew asked, his tone mimicking that of a petulant adolescent.

"Oh, really!" Margo wished that her date had remained inside the convention center building, but Andrew would not hear of it. "The medium-height clown in the center is my family."

"There are clowns in the Wallace family, too," Andrew replied. "Fortunately they do not dress the part." He shuddered. "Those costumes are more frightening than amusing, in my opinion. If your priest *friend* were here I would certainly be obligated to confess that my attendance at the third show today was for your benefit only. I would have left after the singing act."

His sarcasm and tone raised Margo's hackles. *Men!* If she and Andrew had any chance of seeing one another again, she would have to nip his unacceptable behavior in the proverbial bud, as she should have done with Jacques and Sevlow eons ago. *I have certainly endured enough temper tantrums and secret missions to last a dozen lifetimes!* Margo took a calming breath. "I am the captain of my own ship," she replied. "I sail the course I choose, which can make for complications. If you are not man enough to weather some storms, then abandon ship now, before I converse with these clowns." Margo hadn't been sure up to this point if sure if she should attract Jacques's attention, or not. There could be a scene. "My family is not expecting this visit."

"Ouch. Did you have to sucker punch me with *manhood*?" Andrew unfolded his arms. "Well, I suppose I have been juvenile and snarky since the kiss… The priest's kiss, not mine. But you knew to which I was referring." He glanced at the trio and then at the door that led back into ComicSci. "My decision's been made." He took two steps in the direction of the convention center and stopped. "I am not abandoning ship, I am merely acquiescing while you carryout familial duties unhindered. It's what any manly first mate would do, under these present sailing conditions. Previous bad weather, and all."

"I promise to return to port before long." Margo walked towards the clowns, devising a game plan along the way…

****

Jacques, still in costume and makeup placed a trunk into the back of the van.

"That's the last of it," Itsy closed the door.

Alto leafed through their performance schedule. "Don't have to meet the circus in Bean Town until tomorrow. Means we can earn some more dough in the subway tonight."

"Excuse me." Margo approached the group. "Do you have a minute?"

"Well, hubba-hubba!" Itsy gushed. "For you missy, I got hours!"

Jacques looked as if he'd seen a ghost and swallowed a canary. He slipped behind Alto and peeked out as his mother.

Margo put forth her best nonchalant demeanor. "I saw your ComicSci show earlier. Congratulations on an absolutely delightful performance."

"Gee, thanks, lady," Alto replied, his obvious pride making him eight feet tall.

"The way you three interact, must have taken years of team work." Margo hoped the statement would get a reaction from Jacques.

"Sorta," Itsy said. "Me and Alto have been doing the clown and circus show together for going on six years, but J—"

"Jock, I mean, Jack, ah, ah, Joker," Jacques stepped out from behind Alto and fumbled names, donning a fake New City gangster accent. "Right, they cawl me Joker."

"I like it!" Alto nodded. "Been trying to—."

"To expand the act." Jacques interrupted. "Me, Itsy, and Alto met, we tawked, bah-da-bing, it was a done deal."

My son the actor. Margo didn't know whether to laugh or cry. *Who would have thought?* "Will you be appearing in town again, perhaps another venue?"

Alto checked the calendar. "Won't be back in New City until July, Midtown Garden's Summer Fest. It's a lot of fun—big name bands, all kinds of food, of course, clowns. Bring the whole family."

"I live in England and my father travels for work, but perhaps we'll visit New City again. He would love your act." Margo reached into her wallet and removed a $100 bill. "Please accept this gratuity, my appreciation for a show well done."

Itsy took the money without hesitation. "Thanks, lady!"

Jacques handed his mother a Clown Caravan business card. "In case you ever want clowns for a party, or need anything before you go home, you could cawl."

"Yes." Margo peered at the colorful card. "I will."

Jacques gave her a lingering look. It was both poignant and pleased.

Margo slid the paper into her purse and bid them safe travels before returning to port. She saw the light of the afternoon sun peek through puffy clouds above the convention center. It made her eyes tear. Her childhood voyage with Jacques, Joker, was ended and a fresh journey had begun. Perhaps it was time to begin anew with Sevlow, too.

****

Seamus sat across the station house conference table from Roosky and Freckles. Three hours of interrogation hadn't gotten the con to admit to any additional crimes. However, Oleg was delighted to talk in length about his former crime life escapades, which the policeman found very entertaining. Even the Sarge, standing behind the two-way glass partition with sunburst Wally, had succumbed to bouts of uproarious laughter at the Russian's retelling of his crazy capers.

"Then when museum close, I step off pedestal and rob jewels from Egyptian princess showcase tomb. Nobody guess all day that statue really bad guy painted grey, not moving." Oleg placed a fist on his chin. "Looking same as posing Thinker."

Seamus knew he shouldn't be encouraging the levity of unlawful activity, but he figured Roosky had already served his time for the crimes. It was like getting a lesson in Crook History 101. "No idea you were a criminal master of disguise. Didn't learn this stuff at the

Police Academy." The patrolman kicked back in his chair. "I'd have picked you for my final research project instead of Willie Sutton."

The Russian's bright mood turned red. "That because most hated enemy, Lyman Newlin, sabotage career of dastardly deeds for stupid good guy story. Selfish reporter!"

Seamus was perplexed. He knew Oleg hated Lyman, but the reason was still unclear. "What selfishness are you talking about?" The patrolman resumed his interview posture. "Mr. Newlin not writing about you was some sort of hardship? I thought criminals try to operate in the shadows, without publicity, so they don't get caught."

"Two-bit idiot punk what put no effort into crime want secret," Oleg explained, his verve on high. "Same as good actor, master craftsman—genius crook deserve adoring audience! Al Capone, Bonnie and Clyde, Billy Kidd all make book character and movie idol because have newspaper writer telling story of crimes when it happen!"

Seamus was beginning to understand. "You wanted Lyman to make you famous?"

"Yes! Finally, get through you rock head!" Roosky sighed. "Why you thinking I move to New City and not Miami where weather better? Back in day, no newspaperman more talented. If Lyman Newlin write story, everybody in whole world read, that amazing happening when no Internet for sharing!"

"But you still would have gone to jail?" Seamus was trying to comprehend the lure of infamy if it meant doing time behind bars.

"Prison part of story," Oleg clarified. "It give public time to appreciate great talent. By now there should be chapter of Roosky in history books, exciting novels with Roosky as bad boy hero, five Roosky movies because Hollywood afraid of new thing, love to tell same story over and over. If life happen as plan, today I be rich man doing talk show circuit and *Pop Idol Apprentice*, with personal booking, fan mail, and PR office for sidekick to working, what look at Midtown Gardens Park view, not rubbing two nickel together in butcher shop basement, worrying all time how to paying bills." Oleg hugged Freckles and slumped in his chair like a prizefighter who just lost his championship title to the underdog. "All because Lyman Newlin think tattletale cop Hank Scorpio more worthy of newspaper story than Oleg Roosky."

Seamus saw the light and it bolted him out of his chair.

"Officer Sullivan?" Sergeant Gaffney called through the observation room intercom. "What's wrong?"

"Sarge, I recommend we release Oleg Roosky, Waldemar Kowalczyk, and their dog Freckles without filing any charges."

The Sarge shook his head. "I know you have a soft spot for the Russian because he came to Claudia's aide, but that doesn't mean we shouldn't pursue the Bomber issue. It's going to take months and cost millions to put the stadium back in commission. Mayor Fink is still up in arms about the stink."

"Can we talk in private for a minute, Sarge?"

Gaffney gave Seamus a *this better be good* scowl. "Meet me in the hallway."

Seamus leaned across the table and whispered to Roosky. "If you want to trade in your life of crime for fame and fortune, then go back to the butcher shop and lay low until you hear from me. In the mean time, no bothering Newlin and no exploding toilets."

"Working give self pride. What if I say no deal?" Oleg glanced at a visibly nervous Wally in the window. His tone softened. "Why you offer charity for doing good deed? Anyway, one police can't follow bad guy every minute of day, and in experience it not so good idea to trust copper."

"Suit yourself." Seamus made his way to the door. "Eventually you'll have the urge to steal in order to survive, and I know a big black dog that never sleeps."

Oleg's complexion lost all its color.

Seamus met Sergeant Gaffney in the hall.

"What's this about, Sullivan?" The Sarge removed a roll of antacids from his pocket and popped one into his mouth. "I know you're protective of Claudia and the pack, but you still have an obligation to your badge. A crime was committed at Bomber Stadium, and someone's gotta pay."

"According to Alex, an insurance settlement and Sternfenner's advertising deal with Total Rooter means the stadium clean-up is gonna be a money-maker for the team." Seamus could tell the Sarge hadn't been persuaded. He continued. "You know as well as I do that Carl the angry PastyDough ghost used Roosky and Wally to execute the toilet explosion, just like those beelzebubbles used Mayor Fink and his house staff to nearly blow up the Washington Tunnel."

The Sarge ate another antacid.

"Roosky and his sidekick saw Claudia talk to a ghost, and they've come nose-to-nose with a werewolf. How's that going to play out in a courtroom? Add to those facts I just peeled the crunched door off a totaled taxi while the pack created an elemental wind-fire diversion, and a bunch of witnesses to weird weather also noticed that Claudia was bloody and half-dead one minute, and miraculously healed the next."

Gaffney finished the roll of upset stomach tablets.

"I have an idea that will cover our tracks and give Mayor Fink some positive New City publicity. Let me have a few days to work out the details." A fretting frown on Gaffney's face indicated that Seamus's appeal had succeeded. "You won't regret this, Sarge." The victorious patrolman made a hasty exit. " If you need me, I'll be at New City General Hospital."

****

Mama Stella awoke from a sedative-induced snooze in a bed that was not her own. The room shades were partially drawn and the light behind them but a scant grayish-pink. Bella wasn't sure if it was dusk or dawn, whether she was injured or not, or if the gory images cluttering her mind were factual or the imagined remains of a nightmare brought on by medication. Bella attempted to sit up and acclimate herself, but her achy limbs would not oblige.

Someone handed her the mechanical bed controller. "Perhaps this will enable you to be more comfortable." A platinum haired man in black stood beside her.

"Thank you." Bella was surprised and relieved to see Father Benedict's familiar face. She pressed the *up* arrow and raised her back into the sitting position. "Have you been here the whole time? Am I going to be OK? Did you see Lyman?"

"Yes, yes, and yes," Sevlow the padre answered. He unfolded a wheelchair that was leaning against the wall. "The doctor was in earlier. She said that aside from a few bumps and bruises, you were fortunate not to have sustained serious injuries in the crash. Your chart indicates a morning release. Sevlow wheeled the chair beside her bed. "The doctor also said it would be permissible for me to take you to see Mr. Newlin, if you are up for the ride." He held out his hand. "May I?"

Bella accepted his assistance. "How's the Peña girl?" she asked, moving her sore self into the chair. Pain prompted Bella to recall the bloody backseat taxi scene.

"Claudia was even more fortunate," Sevlow assured. He maneuvered the wheelchair through the hospital room door. "She walked away from the wreck unscathed. Tragedy, however, befell the driver. Perhaps you are recalling his fatal injuries."

Did I he just read my mind? Mama Stella blessed herself and tried to purge all thoughts, which reminded her of childhood, going to children's mass and wondering if God knew she'd kept her collection box nickel to buy candy with at school the next day.

The padre grinned.

****

BEEP, BLIP, DRIP. Heart monitoring contraptions did their jobs as Lyman lay motionless in bed, staring at the blank white wall, hoping it would serve as a spontaneous screen for the remarkable dream that was fast fading into the recesses of his grey matter. He tried his best to grab hold of snippets as they shot by in his mind's eye. *Hemingway, Pilar, blue waters, books, something about the Peña siblings.* The fleeting images were clear, but the reporter could not summon their complete significance. Lyman was, however, able to hang on to the feelings associated with his realistic reverie. An ardent love for Bella kept his heart pumping with joy, and his overwhelming urge to write a novel gave the reporter hope that his muse would soon appear.

Officer Sullivan knocked on Lyman's hospital room door. "Mr. Newlin?"

"Come in." The images vanished completely. Still, Lyman was pleased to be receiving his first guest since his brush with death. He'd hoped to awaken to the sight of Bella standing by his side, but a visit from the hero cop was a close second. "Sullivan, you're the reason my head remains in one piece." Lyman wanted to shake the officer's hand but wires and machines prevented it. He nodded instead. "Thanks."

"You're welcome, Mr. Newlin." Seamus pulled a chair up beside Lyman's bed. "I know you had a heart attack this afternoon and need rest, but there's something I gotta speak with you about, and for a couple of reasons it can't wait."

"Sure," Lyman replied. He tried not to think about what would be the officer's worst-case scenario. *Should I ask Seamus if Bella is all right?*

"I'm not good with long detailed conversations," Seamus continued. "So I'll get to the point—write a book about Oleg Roosky."

Like a theater performance commencing, the reporter's psyche curtains were lifted. Lyman recalled every moment of his other side travels. "I saw the light!" Lyman declared as he proceeded to tell the officer details of his near death experience.

Seamus listened without displaying the slightest bit of skepticism.

Lyman Newlin completed his fantastic account with a heartfelt promise. "I will write Oleg Roosky's biography, marry the love of my life, and help her start a business."

"Is that you, Lyman, talking about me?" Fr. Benedict wheeled Bella into her boyfriend's room.

Claudia entered behind them. She was holding two colorful spring flower bouquets, one for each of the patients.

Lyman did a double take. He hadn't expected to see Bella in a hospital gown and wheelchair. "What happened?"

"Taxi cab fender-bender," Bella lied. "Nothing you should be getting your heart racing about. She took one of the flower bunches from her female escort and placed it into the water pitcher beside Lyman's bed. "These are a gift from Claudia. She crashed in the cab too. She's not hurt, either. See?"

The reporter was interested to hear the details of the accident, but not right now. He had a more pressing request. "Bella, will you marry me?"

Mama Stella did not hesitate for a second. "Of course, I'll be your wife," she replied in an a-matter-of-fact tone, as if she'd been waiting for the question, and rehearsed the answer. Bella hoisted herself out of the wheelchair and kissed Lyman.

"How wonderful!" Claudia clapped. "What a happy surprise!"

"Padre, when I came to St. Guinefort's the other day it was because I wanted to ask your permission, if a Catholic widow could marry a Jewish divorcee without going to the Darkside. I'm OK with doing some purgatory time." Bella blessed herself. "But I don't want to be getting sent to the other place for an eternity."

"Love, and not creed, color, race, or walks down the aisle determines eternal light." Sevlow assured. "You have no punishment to fear for following your heart."

"Well, if we've got your blessing, Fr. Benedict." Bella placed her hand upon Lyman's. "Could you marry us right now? Too much has happened since this morning to risk putting our future on hold. I won't spend another day not being Lyman's wife."

"Seamus and I will be your witnesses." Claudia trimmed the stems of Bella's flowers and tied the band from her hair around the base to create a makeshift wedding bouquet. She scanned the room. "You need something old, something new, something borrowed, and something blue."

"Lyman and I are old, these flowers are new and my hospital gown is blue," Bella said. "Anyone got rings we can borrow until Lyman and I go shopping?"

Claudia removed a turquoise and silver band from her finger. She handed it to Lyman. "I'd be honored if you borrowed my ring for the ceremony."

Seamus unfastened a metal loop from his keychain. "No need to return this one."

"If I may, my gift to the happy couple is a place to fulfill your culinary dreams," Sevlow said. "Mrs. Stella, you will require a large kitchen to prepare your signature sauces. St. Guinefort's cafeteria is at your disposal. I am sure Terre and the boys would welcome a pasta night, if you wouldn't mind taking a turn as dinner chef.

"Mind?" Bella's face lit up. "I insist! Cooking and sewing are my specialties."

"Wonderful," the padre replied. "Mr. Newlin, there is an office on the second floor of the school building that is not in use. It has a tranquil view of the grounds. You and Mr. Roosky are welcome to it while your book is being written."

Huh? Maybe Fr. Benedict over heard him reveal the book plans to Seamus, but Lyman did not recall mentioning his very recent thoughts about looking for office space. *Must be the medication are making me forgetful.*

Maid-of-honor Claudia held the bouquet and took her place beside Bella, while best man Seamus stood next to Lyman. Sevlow officiated from the foot of the bed.

"Shall we?" the padre asked.

The quartet nodded.

"We are gathered here today to join together Lyman Newlin and Clarabella Stella in holy matrimony." Fr. Benedict began. "Which is an honorable and solemn estate and therefore is not to be entered into unadvisedly or lightly, but reverently and soberly. Into this estate these two persons present come now to be joined. ..."

No death do us part. Lyman was sure of it.

Chapter 21

TIME PASSAGES

PUBLISHING WEEKLY
Newspaperman Turned Biographer Scores Big

Hardcourt Braces purchased the rights to **I, Oleg Roosky** by retired *Chronicle* crime writer and newspaper legend, Lyman Newlin. The lofty seven-figure advance is the largest sum ever paid to a first-time biographer. Details of the book are under wraps, but the story promises to be one of illicit intrigue, highbrow humor, and erudite excitement. Mr. Newlin is hard at work completing the manuscript, which Hardcourt Braces has pushed to the top of their front list. Hardcourt Braces is promising an end-of-year pub date, in time for the holiday gift-giving season.

NEW CITY CHRONICAL
After Long Wait, Same-Sex Couples Marry in New City

Hundreds of gay and lesbian couples, from retirees in Perrytown to college students in the Heights, rushed to clerks' offices across New City to wed in the first hours of legal same-sex marriage on Saturday, turning a slumbering summer day into a poignant celebration. Mayor Ed Fink officiated over the first wedding ceremony between long-time couple, reformed criminal, Oleg Roosky and emporium proprietor, Waldemar Kowalczyk. The service was performed on the steps of Tracy Mansion. Esteemed writer, Lyman Newlin and his wife Clarabella, owner of Mama Stella's Sauces Ltd., witnessed the joyous event, where the grooms exchanged rings made from Russian rubles. Freckles

Roosky and Liberace Fink acted as flower dog and ring-barer. "It was an honor and a privilege to take part in New City history," Mayor Fink declared. *continued on page 9B*

continued on page 9B

GREENPORT GAZETTE
Town of Greenport Announces Grand Re-Opening Event

Kowalczyk's butcher shop, a fixture on Greenport Avenue for nearly fifty years, will re-open this July 4th with a party for its patrons. The shop will sport a new name, a new look, and an expanded product line. KB Emporium, as it's now called, will specialize in free-range, organic, and hormone-free meats grown on family farms in the Tri-State area. In addition, KB Emporium has struck a deal with Mama Stella's Sauces, Ltd., to not only provide ingredient meats, but also act as the exclusive distributor of these fresh gourmet pasta sauces, which are made daily in Mama Stella's kitchen, not a factory. A portion of all sauce sales goes to local charity, St. Guinefort's Home for Orphaned and Troubled Boys. So celebrate America's birthday with KB Emporium. Bring the family, meet Mama Stella, sample the delicious foods, and enjoy live entertainment featuring St. Guinefort's jazz ensemble. Free fireworks will begin at dark.

ENTERTAINMENT TODAY
Move Over Harry Hills, There's a New Wise Guy on the Block

Tincup Studios announced today that they have purchased movie rights to the soon-to-be-released biography **I, Oleg Roosky** by Lyman Newlin. It's the exciting action-packed story of reformed criminal kingpin and master of disguise, Oleg Roosky. Veteran actor and film producer, Bobby DeGyro will play the mature Roosky.

Although a number of actors have expressed an interest in the part, Walker Christopher is most likely to co-star as Waldemar "Wally" Kowalczyk, Oleg Roosky's faithful sidekick. These two talents haven't shared the screen since *The Deer Slayer*. Filming will begin next summer on location in New City.

NEW CITY CHRONICAL
Sports Extra: Bomber Stadium Back In Business After All-Star Break

This Thursday night the Bombers will play their first home field game since a plumbing mishap closed the stadium for repairs back in April. The Bombers have teamed with Total Rooter to help celebrate the occasion with a special give-away event. All fans attending Thursday's game will receive a pinstriped plastic plunger and a roll of Bomber logo two-ply toilet paper. Come cheer for the league-leading New City Bombers as they battle the Miami Sharks. Good seats still available. Game begins at 7:05.

NEW CITY WEATHER BUREAU
Unusual Weather Brings Lower Crime

For the last few months strange and unexplained weather occurrences in and around New City have baffled scientists, especially in light of the fact that these anomalies are seemingly responsible for a decrease in crime in corresponding areas. Weatherman Coleman Johns of NCWB is researching the link between crime and weather. "We contacted government and local enforcement to establish if they had been performing clandestine experiments that included the creation of virtual reality heat, wind, rain, and earth tremors. None of the agencies admitted to mind-altering meteorological testing. However, an unnamed source did divulge that on days when weird weather patterns were reported, crime was nonexistent in the effected areas."

NEW CITY CHRONICLE

Bombers Are American League East Champions

The New City Bombers second American League East title in three years was pretty much inevitable. Alex Peña's two-RBI single in the eighth inning last night gave the Bombers a 4–2 lead they wouldn't surrender. Though he found himself on the DL early in the season after a fall on the ice in Midtown Gardens during the freak spring blizzard, Peña has been solid and sound since. "Glad I could help out the team," Peña said after last night's win. "It's been a group effort all year long. We're anxious for the post-season to start. Every game brings us one step closer to our goal of winning the World Series." Next up for the Bombers: trying to secure home-field advantage throughout the American League playoffs — they have a five-game lead over both Motor City and Tejas — and getting their rotation lined up for the playoffs. Manager Willie Barton has confidence in his bullpen's ability to withstand a long series.

THE DISH, CABLE & TV GUIDE

Guess Who's Coming to the Conference Table?

Renowned reformed thief turned celebrity, Oleg Roosky, has signed on to season eleven of *Pop Idol Apprentice*. The Russian joins a crew of "blast from the past" contestants, including Roosky's contemporary from the other side of the law, Hank Scorpio. Also competing for the top spot are the refreshing Doublemint twins.

NEW CITY CHRONICAL
Alex Peña Named World Series MVP

In a dramatic Game 6 of the World Series, MVP Alex Peña drove in a Series record-tying seven runs to secure his team the championship. Every season, the New City Bombers spend millions to infuse the roster with talent, including the purchase of perhaps the greatest player of his generation, Alex Peña. Many criticized the expensive move. But true institutions, no matter the jeers and cheers, endure through the ages. Thanks to this year's sage acquisition, the Bombers emerged on top again Wednesday night, beating the defending champion Liberty Town Libbies, 9-2.

NEW CITY CHRONICAL
Weird Weather, Stray Dog, and Bomb Threat Mar Bomber's Ticker-Tape Parade

A crisp November day turned hot and shaky as weird weather and a bomb scare forced a delay in the Bomber's ticker-tape parade down Garden Avenue. Eyewitnesses reported feeling the street tremble, as an intense heat seemingly came out of nowhere, minutes before the parade started. "All of a sudden me and my kid wasn't able to hardly stand up, the ground was shaking so much," said Tony Bologna, who attended the parade with his son, Tony junior. "It got hot too, like the oven door was left open. I couldn't hold onto my camera. Everyone started screaming and running for cover. In the fuss I could of sworn I saw a huge dog come out from under the float that was carrying Mayor Fink and Bomber manager Willie Barton. The stray dog had what looked like a shoe, full of wires, in its jaws. I was going to chase after the hound but an Asian kid with a kung-fu grip held me back and then he disappeared into the crowd and I fell down." Sergeant Gaffney of the NCPD assured the public that the bomb scare was a false alarm. He and his men were able to get the spectators under control and the ticker-tape parade commenced a half-hour behind schedule. The New City Weather Bureau did not detect any seismic activity in the area. The weird weather is being blamed on a malfunctioning steam pipe in an abandoned subway tunnel beneath Garden Avenue. No injuries were reported.

SCOTLAND HIGHLANDS COURIER
Mawtha Doo, Truth or Legend?

Inverness residents living near Wallace Loch Castle have reported a strange black dog appearance in their neighbourhood. The sightings correlated with full moon activity and the vanishing of unsavory characters. "The beast is Mawtha Doo," insists flower shop owner Petula Macleod. The proprietor said she feared for her life when a man wielding a cleaver robbed her store in Lochness Road. "I was closing at around 9pm yesterday when a man wearing a blue boiler suit entered the store waving a butcher knife and demanding money from the till. I feared for my life," she added. "Once the robber had the money, he ran out of the shop, but an eagle-eyed pedestrian noticed what had happened and chased him down the street. I grabbed a broom and followed." It's then that Mrs. Macleod saw an enormous dog in the full moon light. "The hound caught up with the robber and dragged him into a corridor. When we arrived the robber was gone. The hound gave us a fleeting glance before scaling a twelve-foot stone wall, leaving behind the theft money." After contacting police, Mrs. Macleod called

Haunt Hunters, at Middleton University, London. "This is not the first report of a vigilante dog," said Niles Strong, professor of Paranormal Studies and co-founder of the organization. "We believe the beast is Mawtha Doo." Strong suspects that the ancient local legend has its facts skewed. "The dog is a protector, not a murderer," he noted. "There are no bodies to correspond with the sightings." Investigators infer that the beast frightens violent thugs, causing them to flee the area. "We are hoping to interview lawbreakers who've met the beast, but none have been forthcoming." Criminals who wish to discuss Mawtha Doo may contact the Haunt Hunters at: 0880 555 111. Calls will be kept confidential.

MUSIC BEAT MAGAZINE
Country Music sensation, Laurel Leah to Extend European Tour
Laurel Leah has added dates to her European tour. Additional shows include a New Year's concert for the Duke and Duchess of Drawbridge at their estate in Devon.

DAILY CHATTER
Hardcourt Braces Hosts Star-Studded Book Launch Party
Hardcourt Braces had much to celebrate last night at its launch party for **I, Oleg Roosky** by Lyman Newlin. The biography, which was released December 15th, has already sold out its first printing and catapulted to the top of the New City Chronicle bestseller list. The star-studded literary gala was attended by an eclectic list of celebrities, including *Pop Idol Apprentice* host Ronald Frump, World Series MVP Alex Peña, and of course, the notoriously amusing Oleg Roosky. Also making a brief party appearance was the octogenarian cast of the

vintage sci-fi television series, *Space Avengers*. Guests dined on fresh pasta and a variety of roasted meats as Clown Caravan entertained, and WAGO disc jockey Brucie the K spun Roosky crime-era tunes. An ambulance had to be summoned when a scantily clad female fan crashed the bash and attempted to dance with the author. Clarabella Newlin accidentally scalded the woman with hot marinara sauce.

Chapter 22

LEAVING ON A JET PLANE

Flour covered the grey marble-top kitchen worktable like fresh snow on a wintry sidewalk. Bella cut strips of dough from a cushion-sized clump and rolled them into fist-sized balls before placing the spongy sections one-by-one into a manual pasta maker operated by her cheerful chubby assistant.

"Can I crank it yet, Granny Bella?" Eugene asked, fiddling with the handle. "It's fun making pasta."

"OK, remember, turn slowly or the dough will rip. That's it… *Buono lavoro!*"

"Means I didn't make a mistake, right?" The boy beamed.

"Yes it does," Mama Stella squeezed Eugene's rosy cheek. "Granny's boy is learning to be Italian." She knew it wasn't fair to have a favorite student, but he reminded Bella so much of her beloved meatball, Mickey. "Coach Gaffney said I shouldn't let you snack between meals," she whispered before handing him a *pizzelle* from the cookie jar. "It's our little secret."

"I won't tell, Granny Bella," Eugene mimicked her low voice before making the anise wafer cookie disappear in two bites and a swallow. "Is Papa Lyman coming to dinner tonight?"

"Of course he is!" Lyman entered through the cafeteria kitchen door. His arms were laden with shopping bags containing gifts adorned in red and green paper. "But first Papa Lyman has to do some important work for Santa, while you run along and see Coach Gaffney in the gym." He pointed to the wall clock. "Time for boxing class."

"Awe right." Eugene removed his apron. "Thanks for letting me help."

"You're welcome, *cucciola mia*." A school full of surrogate grandchildren and a loving husband, life really was a dream come true. Bella kissed Eugene on the forehead and ushered him out the door. "See you at dinner, my pet. Don't forget to wash."

Lyman set the packages down on the floor and took off his snowy overcoat before giving Bella a peck on the cheek. "Couldn't resist making another trip to the mall. Think there's enough room for these under the tree?"

She browsed the bags and examined the boxes. "You're gonna put the elves out of business." It made Mama Stella proud that her husband was such a generous man.

Lyman removed a manila envelope from his pocket and handed it to Bella.

"That's not fair!" She tore the seal without hesitation. "We promised, no gifts."

"It's not exactly a gift. It's more of a—"

"Honeymoon!" Bella cried, guessing the significance of the colorful travel brochure. "*Tuoro sul Trasimeno*! You remembered! We're really going?"

"Of course, I remembered." Lyman chuckled. "We are really going, and sooner rather than later."

Bella hugged her husband and checked the itinerary for a departure date. "Huh? December 26th?" Objections flooded Bella's mind as her belly churned with instant angst. "I can't be leaving on a jet plane the day after tomorrow! That's too quick. We'll never be able to pack and get ready. Who's gonna make New Year's dinner for the boys?

And what about Wally? He needs me to work in the shop. Our food business is booming this time of year." She attempted to return the envelope to her husband. "Anyway, aren't you supposed to do a book signing somewhere?"

"Covered, arranged, postponed, and nonrefundable." Lyman rubbed her back. "Take a deep breath. There's no reason to worry. We'll only be gone a week." His voice was calm and soothing. "Terre will tend to the boys, as she has for who knows how long, and Oleg will help Wally run the emporium."

Bella felt her body begin to relax. "You sure?"

"I'm sure." Lyman whispered into her ear. "Remember the promise we made one another on our wedding day—never to let life get in the way of living and loving?"

Bella nodded. "Because tomorrow is promised to no one." The last few months had comprised a whirlwind of events that changed their lives in ways neither of them could have imagined. "We do deserve a little honeymoon getaway."

"Yes. We've worked hard, enough to earn seven days of rest and relaxation in a romantic lakeside Italian villa." Lyman peered off into the distance. "Let's make some memories we'll cherish for an eternity."

Claudia sat on the wolf den sofa beside Seamus as the brutes whooped and hollered and battled their buff bloodied bombardiers through the police precincts and distant galaxies of *Cops & Aliens*. Claudia's attention, however, was fixed on red-pen comments that filled the margins of her A+ Art History final exam. In the paper she'd discussed a swagger portrait by the famed eightieth century British artist, Jeremiah Reynolds. In the tradition of Van Syke, the painting depicts Lord Andrew Wallace preparing to mount his grey horse, the nobleman's ginger hair silhouetted against a vivid blue sky. Reynolds skillfully balances the portrayal of aristocracy with a ship's battle scene in the background. The vessel does not fly the Union Jack. Hence, Claudia surmised in her essay that Wallace was a buccaneer, a fact the painter knew and alluded to via subtle visual clues.

Claudia's professor wrote: *I have examined this painting many times, in texts and in person at London's National Gallery, yet until now my eye never noticed the evidence you present. A straw hat on the ground beside Lord Wallace's boot did not strike me as noteworthy until your essay pointed out it's Caribbean significance, and the shadow on the horse's coat, which I can see how might resemble the Jolly Roger, validates your astute and well-presented claim that this nobleman was more than a seafaring merchant.*

Seamus glanced over Claudia's shoulder. "Nice job! Bet the straight-A student could beat the heck out of us in *Cops & Aliens* if she put her brilliant mind to it."

"I'm more comfortable with textbooks than video games." Claudia grimaced. "All those left, right, up, down buttons, and the controller twisting-shaking, makes me dizzy."

"Then I'm guessing you didn't ask Santa for *Cops & Aliens II: Call of Duty Martian Invasion*," TJ remarked, his eyes glued to the TV screen. "Missed my rocket!"

"Thought we all agreed, no gifts," Claudia reminded. She slid her exam into a Columbus University folder and placed it inside her red leather backpack.

"Yeah, well, speak for yourself. Maybe we aren't putting packages under the tree for each other, but Dragon and I like getting presents and Santa's promised us a new game for helping him guard the sleigh and watch the reindeer while he makes deliveries." TJ put down his controller. "But it's not like the two of us would refuse to help Santa, even if we weren't getting anything."

"Because there's no gift better than the reward we give ourselves when we make a child smile," Dragon added.

"Very true, Dragon," Claudia said. "Holiday gifts and make-believe stories are for children, and speaking of children, don't forget, Mrs. Newlin invited us all to Christmas dinner at St. Guinefort's tonight."

"We can't join you guys for pasta-fest." TJ nudged Dragon. "Claudia's not understanding. Take over. You're better at explaining."

"How can I put this?" Dragon rubbed his chin.

Seamus addressed his pensive pack mate. "Getting to the point works for me."

"OK, then. TJ and I are honorary elves," Dragon said. "We provide security for Santa while he and the reindeer are in the New City area."

"Really, Dragon?" Claudia laughed. "Werewolf elves?" She decided to go along with the joke. "I suppose you two are excused if Christmas Eve falls on a full moon?"

"Yep, but that's way more rare than a blue moon," Dragon clarified. "Odds are a particular lunar phase will happen twice on the same calendar date in any 59-year period. But we'll have to wait a little longer than the norm for New City's next Christmas Eve full moon— 2102. The last one happened here in 1996 and before that in 1950, 1931, and 1882. There will actually be Christmas Eve full moons in the

Eastern Hemisphere before then, in 2026, 2045 and 2083. Those are based on Universal Time."

"You're serious." Claudia wondered why supernatural strange still surprised her, but it did.

Sevlow and Vincent entered the wolf den. The butler was carrying a tray of frosted sugar cookies and the Master an Airborne Prompt package.

"Fresh from the oven." Vincent passed the tray. The brutes ate heartily, mumbling appreciation between bites.

Claudia reached for a sweet treat, grateful that calories no longer counted.

"TJ inherited my Christmas Eve guard duties." Sevlow addressed Claudia. "Dragon joined him on the detail after he became a member of the pack. It's a delightful way to spend an enchanted evening. You and Seamus should join them in the future."

"I'll be sure to ask for the night off next year." Seamus snatched the last cookie away from TJ. "I usually choose to work holidays."

"Perhaps this year will be different." Sevlow opened the envelope. "Sergeant Gaffney was kind enough to volunteer to cover your New Year's Eve park patrol duty. Seems he had plans with his landlady over the holidays, and he is not a fan of flying." The master removed three blue booklets. "Margo is hosting a dinner party at Seacliff Manor. The pack's company is requested. If you wish to accept Margo's invitation, these will be required." He handed a passport to Seamus, TJ, and Dragon. "Claudia has a school break and valid travel credentials."

"I do." Claudia examined Seamus's document. The passport photo matched the one on his driver's license. "Is this counterfeit?"

"Living for centuries does present paper problems," Vincent replied. "Let it suffice to say that Margo has found ways around pesky legalities."

Dragon opened his passport. He showed it to TJ. "This picture is from the photo booth at St. Guinefort's fall carnival."

"Mine too," TJ observed. "How'd Margo get these?"

"She had a bit of assistance," Vincent confessed. "While tidying the wolf den I uncovered a stash of photos beneath the sofa cushions, which I placed in a desk drawer for safekeeping. When Margo called about a possible group visit and subsequent travel planning, I retrieved and sent the two snapshots that were least comical." The butler glanced at the Master. "With Sevlow's complete consent, of course."

"What's good enough for the Master is good enough for me!" TJ gave Dragon a big bear hug. "This'll be our first vacation. I call window seat and the top bunk!"

Claudia wasn't sure how to view the well-orchestrated offer. Margo's exodus gesture had been pleasant enough. Before leaving on a jet plane back to her mansion by the sea, she'd stopped by the wolf den to apologize for her actions and ask if the pack would consider beginning anew. Out of respect for Sevlow, they had agreed to move forward. The brutes were convinced Margo's plea was merely a calculated con, playacted by a manipulative villain. Claudia wasn't so sure the Captain was a lost cause. Still…

"New Year's Eve is right around the corner." Seamus checked the date on his watch. "I'm guessing we leave soon."

"Evening of the 26th," Vincent replied. "I fly tonight to prepare the house for visitor arrival. Your World Tran Airway's red-eye flight lands at Heathcliff, on the morning of the 27th. I will drive the motorcar to the airport and chauffeur you to Truro.

A holiday at an English seaside manor... From the preparation, to the passports, to the elated expressions on everyone's faces, the pack's get-away seemed to be a done deal. Claudia began envisaging what she should pack.

"Very well then," Vincent concluded. "I must ready for my departure."

"We should get going too." Dragon handed Claudia his and TJ's passports. "You're better at keeping track of things than we are."

"One more item." Sevlow paused before making an exit with Vincent. His demeanor was one of reserved amusement. "By coincidence, Mr. and Mrs. Newlin also bought first-class seats on our flight to Heathcliff, where they are scheduled to change planes in route to *Tuoro sul Trasimeno* for an Italian lakeside honeymoon."

Seamus cocked an eyebrow and struck a semi-smile. "We're flying to England and those crusty old lovebirds are beginning their trip to *Tuoro sul Trasimeno* on the same plane?" He shook his head. "Sir, we all know there's no such thing as a coincidence."

Bella sat in the second row of first class, finally silent and still as she peered through the plane's plastic-coated window into the starry sapphire sky.

Lyman had watched with quiet amusement his wife's take-off preparations that included the sprinkling of holy water on both their seats, the chanting of Latin prayers (interspersed with fear-induced Italian obscenities), all while clutching a large metal antique crucifix that had nearly been confiscated during the pre-boarding carry-on luggage check for being deemed by TSA as *too similar to a double-sided tomahawk*. If not for Fr. Benedict's intercession, the icon surely would have been seized or the security attendant beheaded. Lyman preferred not to speculate on the avoided outcome.

Bells chimed.

Bella grabbed her husband's arm. "What's happening?"

"An announcement." Lyman patted her hand. "No need to worry."

"Ladies and gentlemen, the Captain has turned off the Fasten Seat Belt sign," the flight attendant recited her script through the PA system. "You may now move around the cabin. However, we always recommend keeping your seat belt fastened while you're seated. You may now turn on your electronic devices such as calculators, music players and laptop computers." A second set of chimes noted the end of the brief transmission.

"Where's Claudia?" Bella leaned over Lyman. "Said she'd bring me one of her magazines when the sign went off."

Lyman offered Bella earphones and the media program. "In the mean time, did you know there are a hundred in-flight movies and TV shows to choose from?"

Sevlow was seated alone in the bulkhead row ahead of the Newlins. He turned around and passed Lyman a business journal. The pages were folded to display a short article. "An affirmative piece about Mama Stella's Sauces."

"Hello, everyone," Claudia arrived promptly, as promised. Her arms were laden with periodicals. "I know, I know… I have a thing for airport newsstands." She leafed through the sizable stack. "*Entertainment Today, Fine Cuisine, Glamorous, Home & Yard, Sports*

Digest, Cars & Driving, American News & World Reporting, Vanity Flair, and *Music Beat.*" Bella reached for the cooking magazine, Lyman for the sports. "Sir?"

"No, thank you," the Master declined. He pointed to his own stack of magazines and books on the empty seat beside him. "My library is well-stocked at the moment."

A senior uniformed flight attendant emerged from behind the red polyester cabin divide. "Miss, may I ask you to return to your seat?" Her smile was saccharine. "We are about to begin our beverage service and the aisle needs to be clear."

"Oh, sure." Claudia gathered her wares. "Let me know if you want another later," she said to Bella and then headed back to her seat, but not before stopping mid-way to check on TJ and Dragon who were in the midst of a linguistics lesson.

"It's pronounced *shed-ule,* not *sked-ule,*" TJ instructed. "Don't want to sound like clueless tourists when we get to England."

Dragon leafed through the pages of his *American vs. British English* pocket-sized pamphlet. "If someone offers me bangers or tells me to look beneath the bonnet, doesn't mean I'm getting fireworks and peeking under a baby's hat—it's sausages and a car hood. Braces are pants suspenders, not metal teeth strengtheners." He turned the page. "Very important—English chips are the same as American French fries and our potato chips are their crisps."

"And remember we three and Seamus *mates,* not friends." TJ patted himself on the back. "Who knew it was this easy to learn a foreign language?"

"*Pan comido,*" Claudia said.

"*Pan* means pan, like a metal container or a bucket and *comido* is…" TJ scratched his head. "Commode? So you're saying in England we gotta use a chamber pot?"

"*Pan comido* or *bread eaten* is a Spanish idiom. It means *easy as pie*." She chuckled. "But I like your very interesting translation better, Mr. Bi-lingual." The beverage cart was approaching. "Don't want to be scolded twice." Claudia made tracks to the last First-Class row where Seamus stood to permit her window seat return. "Ah, thanks." She kissed him. "Everyone's settled. Now we can relax."

"And rest up for our vacation." Seamus fastened his lap belt. "Just in case."

"You don't think this is going to be a care-free holiday?" Claudia opened her current issue of *Music Beat*. "No school, no work, no full moons for a whole week."

Seamus raised both eyebrows.

"Wow, a double-skeptic stare…"

He pointed to her magazine page. "Check out that headline and article, then tell me I shouldn't wonder if we aren't confusing a vacation with a mission."

"Country Music sensation, Laurel Leah, to Extends British Tour for a private concert in Devon." Claudia read aloud. "Is Margo's manor near Devon?"

"Devon borders Cornwall," Seamus replied. "Think New City to Guernsey City."

Claudia's brows were now raised. "Interesting…"

"The singer TJ has the hots for will be in town; the Newlins are on our plane, and I don't think Margo's invited us across the pond so

t a fancy dinner party and ask Sevlow to renew their

ows. A pirate doesn't change their spots."

You seem pleased at the prospect of another weird werewolf

are." Claudia was also sporting a sly smirk.

"I am looking forward to what's about to happen next... And not

in England." Seamus pulled an opaque drape that shielded their

w from the aisle. "Hope you didn't want anything off the beverage
art because the other side of this curtain has a sign that says:
PRIVACY DO NOT DISTURB."

"Seamus!"

"Gets better..." He cranked a lever on Claudia's chair. It fully
reclined. "These seats turn into beds." Seamus put his in the downright
position too.

Claudia's face displayed a mix of shock, panic, and intrigue.
"What are you doing? We're in public. I can't..."

"Can't what? Make noise?" Seamus grabbed something from his
carry-on duffel. "Because I guarantee it's about to get very loud in
here."

"Seriously, Seamus." Claudia reached for the curtain. "We
shouldn't—"

"Play with each other?"

"Seamus!"

He handed Claudia a box. "Open it."

Claudia's countenance still displayed a hint of trepidation as she
unwrapped the cardboard container "What's a GameGuy?"

Seamus removed a second player from his bag. "It's a learning
device. Over the next six hours I'm going to teach you how to kick butt
in *Cops & Aliens*."

Claudia threw her arms around Seamus's neck and squealec with delighted relief. "You're so bad!"

"Had you going there for a minute."

"Yes, you did."

"Hope you know that I respect you even more than I love you, and I'd never do anything to spoil what we have together, not in public or in private." Seamus planted a lingering kiss. "I'm not good with mushy words so I rehearsed that. Could you tell?"

"I love you, Seamus."

"I love you equal. Which means we can have some fun, right?" He flicked on their GameGuy power buttons. "Our boards are already synched."

The beverage cart and two flight attendants pulled up alongside the shrouded row.

"Watch me launch my rocket," came a man's voice from behind the curtain.

"You're so good at this!" a woman squealed. "Show me how to do that."

"You have your own button. Down there, see? Push and wiggle it back and forth. Not too hard."

"Do it for me. Remember, this my first time."

"Should we notify the Captain?" the novice of the two flight attendants asked.

"No," the Chief Purser shifted the beverage cart into reverse." She sauntered backwards towards the galley like someone who'd had her share of leave-it-on-a-jet-plane, mile-high game playing. "It's time to turn the cabin lights out…"